Penguin Books
The Fuse

Tom Keene has worked with Thames Television and West-
ward Television as both researcher and producer of various current affairs programmes. In this capacity he has
travelled extensively in Europe, the Middle East and the
United States. He now lives and writes full-time at his
home in Devon.

Tom Keene is also the author of *Earthrace* (Penguin 1983),
and co-author with Brian Haynes of *Spyship* (Penguin
1981) and *Skyshroud* (Penguin 1982).

Tom Keene

# THE FUSE

Penguin Books

Penguin Books Ltd, Harmondsworth, Middlesex, England
Viking Penguin Inc., 40 West 23rd Street, New York, New York 10010, U.S.A.
Penguin Books Australia Ltd, Ringwood, Victoria, Australia
Penguin Books Canada Ltd, 2801 John Street, Markham, Ontario, Canada L3R 1B4
Penguin Books (N.Z.) Ltd, 182–190 Wairau Road, Auckland 10, New Zealand

First published by Allen Lane 1984
Published in Penguin Books 1985

The newspaper article extract appearing on p. 316
is reproduced by kind permission of the *Guardian*
and Reuters Ltd

Made and printed in Great Britain by
Richard Clay (The Chaucer Press) Ltd, Bungay, Suffolk
Set in Plantin·Light

*This one is for Edward, my father.*
*With love.*

*My thanks to M.H. in Switzerland,*
*who led me to the skeleton the month he died.*


*Also to Ian Hamilton, a gifted friend.*

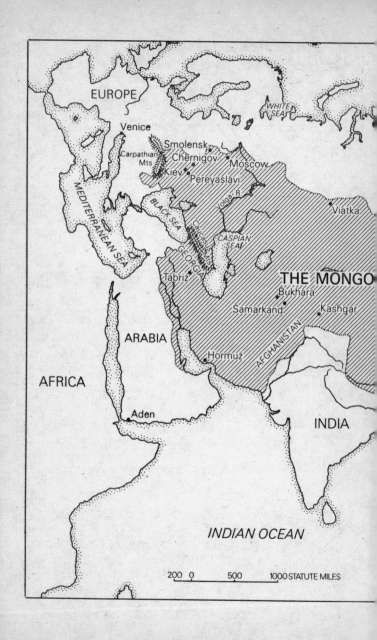

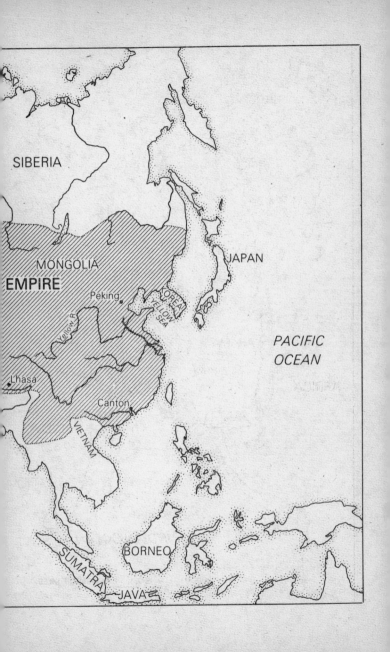

ARCTIC

BALTIC SEA

1  4  3  2

5

6

7

BLACK SEA

CASPIAN SEA

TURKEY

8

9

10  10

15

11  12

14

PERSIA

13

CHINA

AFGHANISTAN

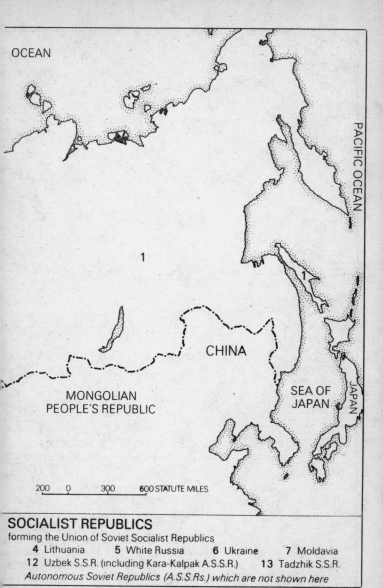

OCEAN

PACIFIC OCEAN

1

1

CHINA

MONGOLIAN
PEOPLE'S REPUBLIC

SEA OF
JAPAN

JAPAN

200  0    300    600 STATUTE MILES

## SOCIALIST REPUBLICS
forming the Union of Soviet Socialist Republics
**4** Lithuania   **5** White Russia   **6** Ukraine   **7** Moldavia
**12** Uzbek S.S.R. (including Kara-Kalpak A.S.S.R.)   **13** Tadzhik S.S.R.
*Autonomous Soviet Republics (A.S.S.Rs.) which are not shown here*

## Origins – AD 1227

He waited, motionless: a proud, dark-haired young warrior astride a short, shaggy hill pony. The sweat of hard riding had long dried and the pony's flanks were caked with the light grey dust of the Steppe.

That dust got everywhere. It matted his long, curly hair into thick dark ropes; it chafed beneath his saddle and made his mount restless; it sifted into the folds of his stained clothing and rubbed against naked skin.

Towards noon he stood in his stirrups and leant forward against the shoulders of his pony; dark, tawny eyes narrowing against the sun-glare as he caught the first drift of dust through the shimmering heat-haze as the funeral escort rode slowly over the horizon towards him.

He sat back against his saddle bundles and ran his tongue over wind-cracked lips, going over his duties again in his mind, anxious to forget nothing, conscious of the honour, the distinction that had fallen upon his father's household, upon him.

Now he steeled himself to what lay ahead and to what he must witness and remember, eased the leather sword-belt against his hips and took manly comfort from the heavy drag of the double-edged sword resting at his side. To others, that sword and the bow tied to his saddle had become a symbol of fear, of blazing homesteads and silent, galloping horsemen; of attack, pillage and terror. But to the dark-haired boy on the dusty pony it was a badge of manhood, of warrior caste – a talisman of tribal supremacy among the conquered, milk-white lands that stretched from the Yellow Sea to the Carpathian Mountains and north beyond the Vistula.

The riders came forward slowly, as though in no hurry to meet the fate that awaited them: four horsemen riding to the fingers of a spread hand, avoiding the dust of one another's trail as of old habit.

Time passed.

Now the young warrior could distinguish one rider from another: Balaan, General to the Escort of the mighty Kaidu himself, grandson of Genghis Khan; Sulthar, the Commander of the Sixth Tuman that had distinguished itself on that whirlwind ride to the banks of the Dniestr two summers gone; Vosbarnoy of the Watchguard and Drusus, the fiery Chieftain of the Khanate of the Golden Horde nine days' ride away to the north and east.

He watched them ride closer. Gone were the fine tunics, the rich embroideries of high rank won by valour in a dozen different battles. Each now wore the coarse, rough-cut tunic and leggings of the most humble horseman; each carried at his belt the simple sword of the novice untried in battle. Yet, as they rode closer, the young warrior saw that men such as these did not need the outward trappings of high position to retain the air of command that had swept them to camp-fire legend within their own lifetimes. They wore it still, like an invisible cloak.

General Balaan turned his mount in towards the rise of ground where the young warrior waited. When the first horse was still some distance away the boy called out in what he hoped was a firm, strong voice, 'Hold. Come no closer.'

General Balaan reined in his horse and raised a tired hand. His three companions halted also. 'I see you.'

'I see you also,' replied the boy. There was a long, dragging silence in the crackling heat as tired men sat in their saddles. There was the drone of flies, the soft plod of a hoof against hot sand, the tiny rattle of a dislodged pebble.

The boy studied the riders. They must have ridden far. Their faces were lined with strain and tiredness. The water-skins tied to their saddles flapped loose and empty. He glanced towards the glistening water-gourd that rested comfortably against his knee and leant forward. Balaan glared at him from beneath bushy, dust-caked eyebrows and the gesture died stillborn.

'We have no need of water,' announced Balaan.

The boy sat straighter in his saddle, the rebuke lying heavily across proud young shoulders. 'It is done?'

General Balaan nodded. 'It is done. The great Khan of Khans – the great Chieftain of all Mongol tribes – is buried.'

'And who witnessed this place where he sleeps?'

'We four only.'

'We four and no others,' echoed Sulthar, Vosbarnoy and Drusus each in his turn. There was another silence, broken only by Drusus's horse pawing the earth. Then the Generals and Chieftains wheeled their horses and rode slowly back down the slope. The young warrior watched, burning every moment, every word, into his memory. On his sword, he must not forget the smallest detail!

They chose a piece of flat, barren ground at the bottom of the slope. There the men dismounted, eased the girths from beneath their horses and took down their saddles. Then they slapped the flanks of their mounts and, freed from the weight of both saddle and rider, the horses galloped away.

All four men slowly stripped off their thick tunic-tops and cast them aside. The sun gleamed on broad brown chests and powerful shoulders, on muscled backs, upon the scars of old battles.

They drew their swords.

Vosbarnoy and Drusus, as though to some previous agreement, stepped a little apart from Balaan and Sulthar, thrust their swords deep into the sand and dropped to their knees. Balaan and Sulthar moved to their sides and raised their swords high above their heads for the killing stroke. The gleaming blades shone in the sunlight as they waited, poised.

Vosbarnoy reached down, grasped a handful of dry soil and held out his clenched fist level with his shoulder. He glanced up at Balaan, waiting silently above him. Their eyes met and understanding passed between them. 'When the last dust has gone, old friend,' urged Vosbarnoy quietly, 'that will be the time.' Balaan nodded, the tendons of his wrist standing out in sharp relief as he gripped the heavy sword.

Both victims lowered their heads and flicked their long hair forward as the sand began to trickle slowly from Vosbarnoy's clenched fist. The trickle strengthened as Vosbarnoy watched life itself slip through his own lean fingers. Finally, the trickle stopped. Time stood still for one frozen moment and then Vosbarnoy opened his empty hand.

The blades struck. Two heads sprang away into the dust, rolled over and were still. Two headless torsos toppled slowly forward, the blood soaking silently into the greedy earth.

Clenching strong white teeth until his jaw ached, the young warrior watched the executions below as his pony cropped passively at a clump of stunted vegetation. The flies droned.

Sulthar moved towards Balaan, his sword held down at his side. There was a moment's unspoken communion between the two friends and then Sulthar dropped to his knees and thrust his own bloodied sword into the sand.

For a second time Balaan raised his sword high above his head. The muscles of his broad shoulders rippled as the blade came scything down.

General Balaan looked down at the body of the man he had killed, the man he had known since boyhood, a man who had ridden at his side for fifteen, twenty campaigns of conquest and expansion so that now a man could ride towards the sun for one whole year and *still* be within the lands they had seized for the Mongol empire; a man with whom he had laughed and fought, shared hardship and danger, food and water, horses and women. Balaan lowered his sword and turned towards the young warrior.

The young warrior who waited, now, for him.

General Balaan looked up, massive chest heaving, as he caught and held the young warrior's eyes with his own. 'Remember,' counselled the General. 'Remember what you have seen. Bear us true witness. Swear it.'

The boy swallowed. 'I swear it,' he promised, digging his heels into the flanks of his pony and urging the animal down the soft slope. He reined to a halt a few paces from the General, kicked his feet out of the stirrup leathers and slid easily from the saddle.

The General stepped closer and rested a hand lightly upon his shoulder, as though thus he might pass strength and courage from one generation to another. 'You will be brave,' he ordered quietly. 'You will be brave and you will remember, so that others too may know the manner of our dying, and others too beyond them, in their turn.' General Balaan turned and pointed the tip of his sword towards his fallen comrades. 'Vosbarnoy, Drusus, Sulthar – these truly were men. Comrades. I loved them all, as brothers.' He turned abruptly. 'Come. It is time.' With a sudden, swift gesture General Balaan presented his sword, hilt first, across his own forearm towards the young warrior. These was a barely perceptible pause. 'Take it!' ordered Balaan fiercely.

The boy took the sword and the older man dropped swiftly to his knees. 'Quickly now. We are done with talking.'

The boy grasped the hilt of the heavy sword as the first tears, unchecked and unheeded, ran down his cheeks. 'I will remember, father, I swear it. I will remember – upon your sword,' whispered the young warrior chosen by destiny to begin a legend.

He wiped the tears away angrily and swung the heavy sword high above his head.

\*

16 March 1945 – and in Europe the Second World War was drawing to a close, although it didn't feel much like it at the time. The defiance of 1940 and the premature optimism of the D-Day landings in Normandy had evaporated in the failure of the airborne assault at Arnhem and the German breakthrough in the Ardennes in December 1944 – but the end *was* coming; the signs were there to be seen: 'Blackout' had been replaced by what was officially known as 'half-lighting' (and unofficially as 'dim-out') and though curtains still had to be tightly drawn at night, the black-out shutters had at last come down, headlamp masks had been abolished and drivers were permitted to light up their number plates again – one more milestone on the long road back to victory over powdered egg and clothing coupons, rationing and shortages.

All of which meant that, as the little convoy of vehicles drove slowly through the winding, bombed-out back streets of the blitzed East End of London, the R A S C drivers had more to go on than just the white cross-straps of the two dispatch-riders moving ahead of them through the misty gloom of evening, the sound of their Enfield motorcycles booming back at them off the tall buildings on either side of the narrow street.

Which, as Driver Bert Houseman had remarked only a little earlier, made a bleedin' change after five sodding years straining your eyes for white kerbs and running into lamp-posts.

The convoy consisted of a single one-ton lorry with canvas covering, a dark-green van for the R A S C Captain and his driver and a black Wolseley for the two civilians: sour-looking, untalk-ative types in dark suits and raincoats who said they were from the Ministry of Food. Driver Houseman hawked and spat out of the window. He didn't believe that, not for one moment. None of them did – not after they'd slipped in past all those guards with their Stens outside some museum or other an hour or so back and loaded what looked like a coffin into the back of the lorry. It was there now, a few feet behind his shoulder, lying there on the floor. It felt like a coffin an' all, he remembered. Driver Houseman shivered. 'This it, then?' he asked no one in particular, needing to hear the sound of his own voice as he drummed his fingers against the wheel and glanced up at the brooding pile of the warehouse that loomed over his cab. Hope that lot's stable, he thought uneasily: not one of them that suddenly come down with a rush months after a Jerry near-miss. He'd heard about them doing that. Never seen it, mind. Come on, come on, he muttered under his breath, let's not sod about . . .

Doors banged up and down the convoy and he could hear the muffled sound of voices. Christ, it was cold. Cold and raw and miserable. Damp, too. He could feel it seeping in off the river, gnawing away at his bones. He felt in the pocket of his battledress blouse for cigarettes and matches and lit up cautiously, ducking down in the cab and shielding the flame in the cup of his hand. One quick drag and –

'Driver Houseman!'

He groaned. Captain gaiters-bloody-Gaitskill, their very own seven-day wonder.

'Sir!' Now what?

'Down here, on the double! Bring the other men with you – and look sharp about it!'

'Sir!' Straight out of the manual, he was. Driver House-man took another careful drag of his cigarette, nipped the end between his fingers and stowed the cigarette back in the carton. He looked up. Ahead the two dispatch-riders were pulling their machines up onto their stands and marching back towards the black Wolseley, hob-nailed boots clattering on the cobbles, their bunched leather jerkins and gauntlets giving them an air of medieval toughness. Captain Gaitskill looked round, waiting for his men to muster around him. But for the war he would have been in a bank. Working behind the counter.

'Right then. Er . . . wait here,' he ordered, marching briskly round to the passenger door of the Wolseley. It opened as he approached and the younger of the two civilians stepped out. For some reason the Captain found himself standing at attention.

'All set, Captain?' inquired the civilian pleasantly, pulling on leather gloves and glancing round.

'Yes, sir. All set.'

The civilian frowned suddenly, looking beyond the Captain's shoulder. 'What are all those men doing there?' He gestured at the soldiers waiting just out of earshot behind their officer.

Captain Gaitskill turned, startled. 'I . . . er . . . that is, sir, I thought you would want –'

'Get them back in the vehicles, if you please. Have one man with the container in the back of the lorry, understand? He is to remain there until we move off.'

'I'm sorry, sir. I imagined you –'

'Do it now, there's a good fellow.'

'Sir.' He wheeled round. 'Right, you men,' he bawled, 'back in the trucks – Driver Houseman: into the back of your vehicle. You're to stay with that container until we move off, understand?'

'Understood. Sir.' Driver Houseman, the old soldier, managed to slip a note of weary contempt into the reply. Green, he was. Green as grass . . . He turned away.

'Driver Houseman.' The civilian, this time. A different kettle of fish altogether.

'Sir!'

'You have a rifle in your cab?'

'I have, yes, sir.'

'Live rounds?'

'Clip of five, sir.'

'Take it with you. No one is to approach that container until I return, do I make myself clear?'

'Sir.'

'Very well. Carry on.' As Driver Houseman hurried away the civilian returned to the Wolseley, opened the passenger door and leant inside. He exchanged a few words with someone unseen sitting back against the leather upholstery and then straightened up in the darkness.

He turned and crossed the road just as Driver Houseman knocked his Lee Enfield out of its clips behind his driver's seat, thumbed forward the safety catch and worked the bolt, chambering a round into the breech. He slipped back the safety catch, climbed down and slammed the cab door. He hurried round to the back of his lorry and climbed over the tailboard, the rifle swinging awkwardly from its webbing sling.

The civilian paused at the top of a steep flight of stone steps and then went nimbly down into the darkness towards the basement. There was no light showing but he knocked anyway, confidently, as though he was expected.

Driver Houseman felt his way gingerly forward in the darkness, his boots slipping on the ribbed metal floor of his lorry. Bending slightly, he groped forward with his hands and found the long wooden casket they had loaded into the vehicle earlier that evening. He sat down upon it, rifle held upright between his knees. They were potty, the lot of 'em: stark raving mad. What did they think he was guarding, the crown bleedin' jewels? He let out his breath in a careful sigh, propped his rifle against his knee and felt in his battledress pocket for his cigarettes. Sod this for a game of soldiers . . .

The civilian rang the doorbell.

The door opened and an old man in grey cardigan and collarless grubby white shirt was peering up into the darkness from behind a length of stout door-chain. Round metal spectacles that had only one arm framed a pale, frightened Jewish face capped with thin hair pushed untidily across a bald scalp. 'Mr Isaac Markstein?' asked the civilian quietly.

The old man paused, considering, his Adam's apple bobbing nervously. Then he nodded. 'I am Markstein,' he said carefully, as though some earlier admission of Semitic ancestry had already led his family into darkness.

'And I am Matthew,' replied the civilian evenly. 'You were told to expect me, I believe.' But still the door opened no further.

'You have papers – yes? Credentials?' The civilian nodded, reached into his pocket and handed an envelope across the door-chain. 'One moment.' The door closed. When it opened again the chain had gone. 'Please – come in,' said Markstein urgently, stepping back into the hallway and beckoning him. Markstein closed the door quickly, shot back the bolts and fumbled the chain across the door. He looked up with a sudden nervous little smile. 'Good . . . good. Please – this way.'

He led him down the narrow, dingy hallway and then stopped by another door across which hung a blanket that fell full-length to the floor. He pushed the blanket aside, reached round into the room and turned on the light.

They were in some sort of workshop. A long wooden bench ran the length of one wall, its scarred surface littered with tools and vices. There were jewellers' saws and an eyeglass; smooth-jawed, taper-nosed and round-nosed pliers in a little wooden rack; needle files and glass-paper, a brazing torch and little phials of chemicals in stoppered bottles. It smelt like a blacksmith's and looked like nothing Matthew had ever seen before. 'A drink perhaps, eh?' asked Markstein with continental hospitality, bustling to a cupboard at the back of his dark little workshop and muttering to himself as he sorted through his bottles like Merlin about to weave a spell.

Matthew shook his head as Markstein held a dusty tumbler up towards the unshaded light bulb. 'Thank you – no. And we're rather short of time, Mr Markstein. The vehicles are waiting outside.'

Markstein turned round, his face breaking into a sudden gap-toothed smile that gave a glimpse of the man he might once have been. He held up a finger. 'There's a war on, yes? Isn't that what the young people say?' Matthew nodded. 'But not for much longer, eh? Not for much longer. Soon the Allies will be victorious and we can go home.' He paused. 'Most of us, anyway.' He seemed to sink into some inner reverie his visitor could not share. Then he roused himself and held up the bottle of gin: 'You are quite sure . . .?'

'Quite sure. Could we move on, do you think? Time really is pressing,' said Matthew, thinking of the long drive to the Lockheed Hudson waiting on the runway at Tempsford airfield.

'Forgive me. Now then . . .' He looked around his cluttered workroom. 'Usually I keep my finished work there' – he pointed towards an ancient metal safe that took up most of one corner of the room – 'but this time?' He shook his head. 'This time, it would not fit! And I tell you this much: Isaac Markstein will be relieved to see the back of it – relieved, I tell you!' He fumbled under his shirt and pulled a length of dirty string from inside his shirt-front. A key was on the end of it. Markstein bent down over a long metal foot-locker pushed beneath his workbench and fitted the key to the lock. Then he lifted back the lid, reached inside and took out something that was about four feet long, six inches wide and wrapped in a piece of thick blanket.

He held it up carefully, as though the slightest careless movement could make it vanish, disappear forever. 'Here. You see?' he breathed. 'It is done. What Isaac Markstein says he will deliver – he delivers!' He looked up at his visitor, eyes shining with excitement, waiting for praise.

'Good. Excellent.'

'You would like to see it, eh?'

'Yes. Yes, of course.'

Markstein nodded. 'You will not be disappointed, I promise you,' he pledged softly. He laid the parcel carefully on his workbench and folded back the wrappings as carefully as a mother displaying her first-born to its father. 'There.'

Matthew bent forward.

Nestling on its bed of thick blanket lay a double-edged sword, its metal blade eaten and pitted with age, its hilt woven into an intricate hatchwork of gold and precious stones. It might have been a sword fit for a king – or a Mongol chieftain. A long time ago.

Markstein looked up into Matthew's face. 'It will do?' he asked slyly, seeing his answer in the other man's eyes.

'Yes,' nodded Matthew slowly. 'Yes, Mr Markstein. I rather think it will.'

In the back of the lorry, Driver Houseman was cold; cold and bored. He reached into his pocket for cigarettes and matches and then hesitated as a thought suddenly came to him. He got up, walked to the rear of the lorry and peered round the canvas side. There was no one in sight. Boots scraping along the metal floor, he moved swiftly back towards the casket and squatted down, fingers fumbling with his matches. Now he'd see what was so bloody important he had to sit over it with a loaded bloody rifle. He struck a match.

It was a long wooden box, fastened at regular intervals along one side by a series of simple catches.

Fingers raced along the casket as he flipped back the metal catches. Then the match burnt down to his fingers and he swore aloud at the pain in the sudden darkness. He struck another match and prised up the wooden lid.

There was padding on top. He pulled that away impatiently and then recoiled, his nose wrinkled up with disgust at the rank, sour smell of decay that rose towards him like a festering wraith.

He was looking down at a skull. At a human skeleton clothed in crumbling rags that had withered with age, yellowed and brittle as ancient parchment. Empty black eye-sockets stared into the flickering match-flame and Driver Houseman let out a sudden cry of terror as the match went out and the lorry was plunged again into darkness.

# : I :

## England: 1979

It was Boxing Day, the day after Christmas. Peace on earth, goodwill towards men.

And the Soviet Union had just invaded Afghanistan.

In the small village of Sidcott in Sussex, half-way between Lewes and Newhaven in south-east England, Walter Hallam sat alone in front of the electric fire, an atlas open on his knees as he leant forward intently, a cup of tea grown cold at his side as he watched the evening news on BBC television.

Walter Hallam was sixty-nine years old and had lived alone in Sidcott since the death of his wife some years earlier. He watched the BBC because to a man of his generation the BBC was the voice of authority. It had, after all, been that way in the war and old habits, even now, died hard. The newsreader was telling the British public that Soviet armed forces had crossed the border into Afghanistan and were even now streaming towards Kabul, the capital. When the newsreader's face was replaced by a map showing the axis of the Soviet advance, Walter Hallam traced their progress upon his atlas with a finger that was trembling with excitement . . .

The telephone began to ring.

So intent was Walter Hallam upon the news that it was fully twenty seconds before he laid the atlas aside, rose slowly to his feet and backed towards the phone, eyes still glued to the television. He lifted the receiver. 'Yes, speaking.' He listened for a moment and then began to nod. 'Yes . . . yes indeed. Good heavens . . . one . . . moment.' He laid down the receiver, turned off the television and picked up the phone once more. 'Hello? That's better . . . yes, yes – I was just watching it on television. Incredible – simply incredible! Why, it must be . . . let me see . . . thirty-five, thirty-six years now? Yes, of course I remember! What? What's that you say? No, no . . . all that's forgiven now. It's over and done with . . . Oh, pretty fit, you know. Mustn't grumble. Not at my age. Sixty-nine ... yes ... yes.' They talked on for several minutes, then – 'What shall we say, half an hour? No, no – wouldn't dream of it. I've been sitting down all day – the walk will do me good.' He laughed shortly. 'Golden Fleece, saloon bar, half past. I'll see you then, yes. Good bye for now.'

Walter Hallam replaced the receiver and sat back to stare unseeing at the far wall. 'Incredible ...' he muttered to himself once more, 'Simply ... incredible!' He pushed himself to his feet, turned off the fire and the lights in the sitting-room and went through into the narrow hallway where he put on his scarf and overcoat. Then he patted his pockets for the house key, picked up gloves and a pocket torch from the coat stand and banged the front door behind him. Thirty-six years. It hardly seemed possible. Not after all this time ...

It was cold and clear, the sky speckled with bright stars, as Walter Hallam closed the garden gate behind him. Breath pluming before him like a banner, he crossed the road and set off briskly up the lane towards the main road, the lit torch swinging from his left hand as he kept in against the bank so that he would face any oncoming traffic. But it was already after nine o'clock – nine o'clock on Boxing Day – and most motorists had already reached their destinations.

Most, but not all.

Four hundred yards away a man was standing outside an illuminated telephone kiosk. He appeared to be waiting for something as he stood beside the dark shape of a Volvo estate and banged gloved hands together against the cold. Then the phone began to ring. The man had the door open and had snatched up the receiver before the strident tone had shattered the silence for the second time.

'Hastings.'

'He should be on his way now.'

'Foot or vehicle?' They had covered both eventualities.

'Foot.'

'Any change?'

'No change.'

'Understood. Going now.' The man snapped the phone back on to its cradle and barged out of the phone box. He slid behind the wheel of the Volvo and switched on the engine. A careful glance in the rear-view mirror: nothing. The road was black and empty. He wound down the window and listened intently. Not a sound. He swung the car round in a gentle U-turn, glanced down at the map on the passenger seat beside him and pressed down on the accelerator.

Two minutes slipped by. Then he passed a lone figure walking briskly along the verge of the road towards him, a torch swinging up and down. The man in the Volvo slowed down and risked one long, raking stare at the figure caught in the beam of his headlights as he slid past. Then the Volvo pulled away, gathering speed. That was him, definitely: age, description, timing – it all fitted. He drove on a few hundred yards, turned the Volvo in a convenient T-junction and began driving slowly back the way he had come, gloved hands clenching the wheel as his eyes kept flicking up to the rear-view mirror and then forward again to catch the first faint glow of oncoming headlights. Of witnesses.

Nothing. He had the lane to himself.

Walter Hallam walked on, the sound of his own heels keeping him company as they clipped steadily along the edge of the road, the little hand-torch swinging up and down as dimly he became aware of the growl of an approaching car coming up behind him. The sound grew louder as the hedgerows turned milky-white and ghostlike in the glare of the headlights. But there was something about the noise that . . . Walter Hallam half turned, torch waving up and down with increasing urgency as the car slewed suddenly round the corner and accelerated towards him. Walter Hallam threw up a hand to ward off the dazzling glare of the headlights on full beam and then opened his mouth to scream as the car rushed down upon him with sudden, terrifying finality.

He was aware then only of a sudden terrible *thump* in his side and of being thrown, lifted ludicrously high into the air as the car scythed into soft, pitifully yielding flesh. Walter Hallam's last thought, in that shaven split-second before the darkness closed in around him forever, was that it was all so unnecessary, so *unfair*. He knew all about the dangers of walking down a dark lane at night: that was why he had been carrying the torch . . .

The driver jammed on his brakes and brought the Volvo to a halt twenty yards further down the road. He sat behind the wheel for a moment, breathing deeply. A glance in the mirror: the road was empty.

He opened the door and ran lightly down the silent road towards the body lying crumpled against the verge. He found the torch lying in the rain-gutter and stuffed it into his own pocket. Then he turned to the body, crouched down and examined it without remorse, searching not for signs of life but for evidence of death. The coat felt wet, sodden to the touch. He took out the torch and shone it quickly into the dead, staring face. Then he rose to his feet, ran back to the car, backed up, dragged the limp, broken body out into the centre of the lane and let it sprawl onto the ground. He stood back then, panting, waiting, listening.

Presently he saw the gleam of approaching lights, got a hand beneath the dead man's armpits and began dragging him towards the verge just as the oncoming vehicle turned the corner and went into a dry skid as the driver took in the terrible tableau in front of him.

The man who had driven the Volvo hauled the body to the side of the road and crouched down beside it, apparently aghast now at what had happened as he checked the broken body with simulated compassion. There was the sound of car doors slamming shut and of feet running across the road towards him. He looked up into a sudden torchlight, his face a nice blend of fear and supplication. 'Thank . . . thank God you've come,' he blurted out, the American accent immediately apparent. 'I . . . oh, Christ . . . I think I've killed him. He was there – right there!' He swung round and pointed wildly towards the centre of the lane. 'Just . . . just standing there!'

'Oh, God . . .' muttered the man with the torch as he caught sight of the dead, staring face. 'God, I . . . Jean – quickly, love: go and call an ambulance, will you? Quick as you can.'

Fifteen minutes later both the ambulance service and the police were in attendance and the dark, narrow little lane had been swamped in harsh white light by the incident lamps that ringed the scene and stared down implacably from their metal tripods. Walter Hallam lay in the road like so much discarded rubbish, one cheek laid open against the tarmac, one leg twisted awkwardly beneath his body, the blood thick and sticky where it had soaked through his overcoat. Thirty, forty minutes ago he had been alive. Now the only thing that moved was his grey hair, caught by an edge of breeze as the same stars looked down as though nothing had happened, nothing had changed.

The police sergeant crouched down carefully beside the corpse, his polished shoes and the neat creases in his dark-blue trousers in sharp contrast to the pathetic, sprawled untidiness of another elderly road-traffic fatality. He reached down, pulled back a heavy shoulder and felt inside the dead man's breast pocket. He took out an old leather wallet and flipped it open: one five-pound note, two singles, a pension book, a few stamps, an old photograph or two, a driving licence ... Poor old sod, thought the traffic sergeant with rough compassion, you can't have known much about it, anyway. If your time was up there were worse ways to go and fifteen years on the force had shown him most of them. He leant forward and closed the dead, staring eye that gazed with detached interest at the gravel beside his cheek. He looked up and shivered in the grim, bare winter night as a rook, disturbed by all the activity below, cawed somewhere in the woods beyond the lane as the two driver/attendants moved round to the back of the ambulance and began sliding the stretcher out of their vehicle with smooth, practised efficiency. The sergeant rose to his feet, took one of the folded red woollen blankets off the stretcher and shook it open. 'No need to ring any bells on this one, lads,' he advised quietly. 'He's had it.'

'Hit and run?'

The sergeant shrugged and jerked a thumb over his shoulder. 'Hit and stop, more like it.' Over by the verge his partner was sitting in the front passenger seat talking to the driver of a Volvo estate. 'American tourist comes round the corner and finds this old bloke just standing in the middle of the road. Slammed on the anchors and ran straight into him. Said the old guy just stood there, waiting for it to happen.'

'O K to move him then, Sarge?'

The policeman glanced down and nodded. 'Don't see why not. Incident officer's got all he needs and I've got this' – he tapped Walter Hallam's wallet against the palm of his hand. 'I'll do the necessary with the next of kin. Where are you taking him?'

'Lewes Victoria,' replied the ambulanceman with a grunt of effort as they rolled the body expertly onto the stretcher.

The sergeant nodded. 'Right, then. I'll let you get on with it.'

'Cheers then, Sarge. Oh –' The sergeant paused and glanced back – 'Happy Christmas.'

The policeman nodded sombrely. 'Aren't they always?' He gestured at the corpse lying on the stretcher. 'Aren't they bleeding always? This'll make someone's day, this will.'

# : 2 :

The tiny medieval hamlet of Stowcombe lies in west Devon between the village of Lewtrenchard and the river Lyd which runs from the western flank of Dartmoor towards Lifton. There the river joins the Tamar and Devon slips quietly into Cornwall. In summer, friendly tourists flock to this part of the south-west but in winter the tourists are gone. The quiet lanes and gentle, wooded valleys to the west of the moor fall silent and the residents emerge from behind their doors like cautious winter moles. When it is winter, Stowcombe lies quietly – and when it is winter, and dark, and still, you can hear a pin drop – or an owl hoot in a tree half a mile away.

A whitewashed farmhouse stood back from the crossroads, its neat windows spilling squares of warm yellow light across the cold winter lawns that ran down to the road. In recent years the farmhouse had been tastefully modernized, the adjoining stone-walled barn knocked through to become a timber-beamed lounge with massive stone fireplace. Inevitably, perhaps, it belonged to a partner in a local firm of estate agents and auctioneers and, as though to endorse the prosperity of its owner, the gravel drive-way was cluttered with the expensive cars of friends and neighbours. Indoors, a party was in full swing: Christmas, after all, was a time to smile over a glass at one's friends; congratulate oneself upon the achievements of another year; take stock.

It was a good party. The lounge was warm with the crackling log fire and the timber beams echoed to the ring of laughter and good cheer as the guests ate, drank and flirted harmlessly with one another's husbands and wives. Yet, despite such surroundings, Gordon Hallam was having a lousy party. It just wasn't working, not for him. Although it wasn't his house he knew most of the guests and had circulated agreeably enough in the hour or so since he and Rachel had walked down from their cottage at the end of the lane – yet still the depression persisted. Now Gordon made a determined effort to stop brooding about school and concentrate instead on another of Martin's golfing anecdotes.

The letter from the education authority had arrived with the last post on Christmas Eve. Ho bloody ho.

'How's your glass, Gordon?' asked Peter Salter, the owner of the house, standing at his elbow with a twelve-year-old bottle of scotch. 'Another wee dram, sor?' he mimicked, leaning closer and lowering his voice. 'You're very honoured, you know,' he confided, gesturing with the bottle. 'Only the select few . . .'

Gordon summoned a smile. 'In that case –' He held out his glass.

Peter poured with exact care and concentration and then raised his own glass in a toast, amber fluid mellow in the reflected firelight. He paused. 'Everything all right, Gordon?' he asked casually.

'Fine. Super party.'

But Peter shook his head and studied his friend more closely. Gordon was in his mid-thirties. A little under six feet tall, he was broader than Peter across the shoulders with a head of thick, glossy black hair.

'I didn't mean the party, old son. I meant you.'

Gordon stretched the smile a little wider. 'Me? Sure – why d'you ask?'

His host and nearest neighbour shrugged. 'Oh, nothing. Just thought you looked a bit low, that's all. You know – inward looking.'

'Nah, I'm fine,' lied Gordon cheerfully. 'Cheers, Peter, anyway. Happy Christmas.'

'Happy Christmas,' echoed Peter. 'Prosperous New Year.'

'I'll drink to that,' agreed Gordon as he looked over the rim of his glass towards his wife. Rachel stood beside the window, the centre of attraction amid a laughing cluster of men and women. As if on cue Rachel glanced up, caught Gordon's eye across the room and smiled a special, private smile. With a sudden flash of maudlin self-pity Gordon wondered what the hell she saw in him above all others – as a television continuity announcer she was already bringing home more money than he was. Or had been. When he had been in work. Gordon raised his glass towards her and managed to smile back.

Ten, perhaps fifteen minutes later Peter was at his elbow again. Only this time there was no twelve-year-old bottle of scotch and the smile had been replaced by an expression of haunted concern as he took Gordon's arm. 'Er . . . Gordon . . .'

'What's up, Peter? You look as if the roof just caved in.'

'Could you . . . could you come over here a minute, old son? There's . . . there's someone to see you . . .'

'Who?'

'Over here. In the . . . in the study.'

Gordon drained his glass, set it down on a small table and followed Peter through the throng of party-goers into the main hall. Peter was holding open the study door. 'In here please, Gordon.' Gordon gave Peter a puzzled glance and went through into the book-lined study as the door closed behind him with a soft click.

There were two people in the study. One was Rachel. The other was a police constable in uniform. He looked young, nervous and ill at ease, helmet tucked under his arm, the red mark of its liner still showing across the white of his forehead. As Gordon entered Rachel came to his side and grasped his arm.

'Er . . . good evening, sir. Sorry to disturb you . . .' began the policeman hesitantly.

'That's OK – what is it? What's the matter?'

'You are Mr Hallam?' Gordon nodded. 'Mr Gordon Walter Hallam?'

'That's right, yes.'

The policeman swallowed. He might have been nineteen, twenty at the most. 'I've . . . er . . . I've got a spot of bad news, I'm afraid, sir.' He paused. 'I tried the cottage first. Then I . . . then I saw all the lights on down here and thought I'd best try here too, just on the offchance . . .'

'What bad news? What's happened?'

The policeman clutched his helmet tightly under his arm. 'It's your father, I'm sorry to say, sir,' he began. And waited. That was the way to do it, the sergeant said. Plant the thought and then let them get there all by themselves. Kinder that way.

'Dad? What about him?'

The policeman shifted uncomfortably. 'He's . . . er . . . he's been killed.'

The words bounced off, didn't penetrate. 'Dad? Killed?' echoed Gordon stupidly, the drink draining from his head as if someone had just pulled a plug. 'Killed?' he repeated, trying the word out in his mouth. It seemed ugly, didn't fit. Like clinker.

'Yes, sir. Road traffic accident.'

'Road traffic accident? But . . . but he wasn't going anywhere! Not tonight! I . . . I spoke to him earlier this evening! Must have been . . . oh . . . seven? Seven thirty? Darling, when did I call Dad?' He turned suddenly towards Rachel as though her endorsement of his actions could make the words go away. 'I mean . . . are you . . . are you *sure*?'

The policeman nodded. 'I'm afraid so, yes, sir.' He glanced down at a little notebook. 'Walter Gordon Hallam, aged sixty-nine, of number 14, Sunley Rise, Sidcott.'

'Oh.'

'That is your father?'

Gordon nodded. 'Yes. That's him.' He sat down slowly.

'I . . . er . . . I understand he was involved in a collision with a motor vehicle,' supplied the police constable gently. 'As a pedestrian.'

Gordon looked up. 'You mean he was knocked down? By a car?'

'That is correct, yes, sir. In the lane near his home, so I am given to understand by my colleagues in Lewes. They rushed him to hospital, of course, but he was DOA . . . er . . . that is, dead on arrival. I'm sorry.'

'When did all this happen?' Someone else was asking the questions. This isn't really happening, thought Gordon. Not to me . . .

'Some time after eight this evening, sir. Near as they can place it.' Gordon nodded numbly, eyes seeing nothing as he thought of his father in the house in Sussex. 'If . . . if it's any consolation,' offered the young policeman hesitantly, 'death would have been instantaneous.'

Gordon looked up. 'How do they know?' he asked softly. There was a moment's awkward silence as the policeman covered his confusion by looking down at his notebook. 'I'm sorry,' said Gordon quietly after a moment, 'you're only doing your job.'

The young man looked up. 'Don't worry about that, sir.'

'Did it stop?' asked Rachel. 'The car, I mean?'

'The car? Oh, yes, madam. American tourist on his way to visit friends in Eastbourne, apparently.' Eastbourne, thought Gordon. He'd been there once, a long time ago. Day out with the whole family.

'There will have to be an inquest, of course, sir,' warned the PC, tearing off a slip of paper and handing it carefully to Gordon. 'There's the number of the Police at Lewes. They'll have all the details.'

'Thank you,' muttered Gordon. The policeman tugged down the hem of his tunic and fiddled with his chin-strap, anxious to be gone now that duty had been done. He hated Official Notifications, they all did. And this was only his second –

'Right then, sir – I'd best be getting back to the station – unless, that is, you have any other questions?'

Gordon shook his head. 'No, no. I don't think so. Thanks very much for coming round.' For some reason Gordon rose to his feet and they shook hands in another awkward silence, Gordon's mind suddenly blank. He had just been told that his father had been killed in an accident and he couldn't think of anything to say . . .

In London's Eaton Terrace a phone began to ring seven minutes later. Lord Porterfield placed his brandy glass to one side, reached across his cluttered desk and lifted the receiver. 'Yes?' He had been waiting for the call.

'This is Hastings.' Again, that American accent.

'Go on.'

'Walter Hallam had an accident. Confirmed dead on arrival at hospital. I've just left there.'

Lord Porterfield sighed. Perhaps with regret. 'Were there any . . . complications?'

'No, sir. He never regained consciousness.'

'Thank you. I shall be in touch with Mr Ottley shortly. Good night to you.'

'I know he would appreciate that. Good night, sir.'

At that moment a heavy, dark-green Rover saloon was pausing at the traffic lights at the bottom of London's Kew Bridge. The lights changed and the car pulled away smoothly down Mortlake Road.

Stephen Rowley decreased speed as the Rover slid under the railway bridge, indicated left and turned off the usually busy road that is sandwiched between Kew Gardens and the river Thames. There was little traffic now as he turned down Ruskin Avenue and eased the wide-bodied car between the rows of parked vehicles and the neat suburban bay windows framing small, illuminated Christmas trees that winked warmly from behind half-drawn curtains.

The Rover slid to a halt before a pair of high locked metal gates.

To those unfamiliar with the business of historical research, with the archives of public documentation, the very existence of Kew's vast Public Record Office tucked away behind such suburban surroundings comes as a considerable surprise, but it was not a surprise to Stephen Rowley. As an Assistant Secretary at the Foreign Office whose superior was responsible to the Secretary of State and the 'D' Committee for the declassification of secret Foreign Office papers, he was a frequent visitor.

Rowley sounded the horn sharply and glanced across at the gatehouse, gloved fingers drumming impatiently against the steering wheel as he waited. Trust the bloody Russians to walk into Afghanistan on Christmas Day and catch Britain, bulwark of democracy, dozing off over the mince pies and Christmas pudding. Come on, get a move on ... He sounded the horn again.

Two men emerged reluctantly from within, their breath pluming before them in the sharp, keen air as they crossed the pool of yellow light thrown by the open door: a portly, grey-haired security officer who fumbled now with the buttons of his tunic as he sorted through his keys and hurried towards the locked gates and a thin, donnish man with spectacles, in his mid-forties, wearing an open-necked checked shirt and heavy-knit cardigan, who walked briskly towards the waiting Rover, his lips compressed into a thin line of disapproval. He bent down, a hand resting on the car roof as the driver's window whirred down automatically. 'Mr Rowley? Foreign Office?'

Rowley nodded, catching the Christmas brandy on the man's

breath as he leaned forward. 'Sorry to drag you out like this,' offered Rowley pleasantly. 'Can't be helped, I'm afraid.'

The man glanced at his credentials, opened his mouth to say something and then thought better of it when he saw the security prefix. 'I see.' He looked up over the rim of stern, academic spectacles with eyes that had lost none of their earlier hostility. 'Elton, Mr Rowley. Kenneth Elton – Foreign Office Liaison. Let's get on, shall we?' The gate swung back and Elton leant down to point out a parking space next to the gate-house. 'If you pull in over there we –'

'I don't think we'll bother with any of that, Mr Elton, if you don't mind,' interrupted Rowley smoothly.

Elton bobbed suddenly closer. 'I'm sorry?'

'We would prefer it if you considered this visit . . . unofficial.' There was a deceptive softness to the visitor's voice that did not pass unnoticed. Rowley held out a hand for his wallet and a few awkward moments slipped by in silence as Elton wrestled with the conflicting interests of established procedure versus professional advancement. He had heard about people like Rowley, young men who could lift the telephone with one languid hand and smash careers into matchwood. Pensions too.

'Very well,' surrendered Elton sourly, closing the wallet and handing it back to its owner. Wallet and hand disappeared inside the car.

'Did that chap of yours make a note of my visit?' asked Rowley, waving vaguely towards the gate-keeper.

'Yes, of course – but he isn't *my* chap, as you put it,' corrected Elton testily. 'I told you: I'm Liaison, not Security or Administration. I don't always work here. And besides, they'd hardly consult me over a matter that –'

'Fine. Perhaps you could arrange for that entry to be deleted. Use your influence.' Rowley smiled.

'Influence? But you surely don't imagine –' There was a soft whine and the Rover's window rode upwards and shut off Elton's further protests with polite mechanical finality. Elton watched as the Rover swung down past the deserted car park towards the brick-fronted entrance on the right-hand side of the building. Then he hurried in its wake, watched with interest by the elderly security guard.

There were two more men on duty inside the main building on the ground floor, both wearing the grey rayon coats with the gold crowns at the lapels that signified they were working in a government building. When the Record Office was open to the public they were kept busy enough but now there was little to do but pass the time in desultory conversation and walk the silent, empty corridors.

Now, as Elton led Rowley up the short ramp towards the glass doors, they dropped their cigarettes surreptitiously into the pedestal ashtrays and assumed an air of cautious watchfulness.

Elton ushered Rowley through the doors ahead of him, nodded curtly at the two men on duty and led the way briskly across the concourse and up the wide, carpeted stairs that led to the public reading rooms and the reference sections on the first floor.

He halted at the top of the stairs and turned, his voice un-naturally loud in the still, deserted building. 'They didn't specify what it is you're after, Mr Rowley. They said only that I was to place myself at your disposal. However' – he shrugged with evident distaste – 'if I am to prevent your visit being a complete waste of time, I have to know what it is you're after. Everything is computerized here, as doubtless you are aware. Each piece of information, every document, has a group, class and item number unique unto itself.'

Rowley nodded, thinking.

Almost every British government document, every official paper, every Commons' reply and ministerial statement, finds its way eventually into the archives of the Public Record Office. Here it is catalogued and stored, its details encoded for identification and transferred onto computer tape.

A member of the public, armed only with a reader's ticket, is issued upon arrival with an electronic bleeper whose number corresponds with that of a chair at one of the many six-sided, green-topped tables that take up most of the reading room on the first floor. The investigator punches his seat and ticket number into one of the computer terminals and follows this with specific details of both the class and the item number traced through the extensive reference catalogues held next door in the central reference section. The document or file requested is then collected from the repository and stored behind a central counter in the reading room, much like hats and coats in a cloakroom.

When the piece is ready for collection a tiny, ruby-red light is activated on the visitor's electronic page. He then collects his fragment of recorded history and the business of retrieval is concluded. From start to finish not a word need have been spoken.

There is, however, a hefty proviso to this description of admirable public accessibility for, although all secret government papers and documents are supposed to be released for inspection after thirty years – the infamous 'thirty year rule' – there *are* exceptions. Into this category of excluded material fall documents – never specified, never listed – which, because of their extraordinary sensitivity, are withheld from public scrutiny by either the ministry concerned, the department of origin or, sometimes, the Public Record Office itself.

Thus historical Cabinet decisions with topical pertinence, private papers, orders and documents from both World Wars containing details of clandestine operations, even political blunders that might harm or embarrass one of a dozen different Whitehall ministries, may be held back from the glare of public scrutiny for fifty, seventy-five, even a hundred years.

After an initial review after five years, such files remain closed for the exact duration of the time specified on their covers. Only in very rare cases are closed papers temporarily released to a named biographer armed with a 'Privileged Access Certificate' issued by the Lord Chancellor's Office which permits rigidly defined access by this trusted individual to corroborate the accuracy of material gleaned from some other source.

Whitehall protects most jealously, therefore, the past reputations of her servants.

'I assume you have specific details?' prodded Elton.

Rowley nodded. 'World War Two. Mid '44, possibly early '45.'

Now it was Elton's turn to nod, his precise, ordered mind inspecting, selecting and discarding possibilities like one of the silent computer terminals under its plastic dust-cover in the deserted reference section.

'That's a start, anyway,' he commented dryly, taking a set of keys from his pocket and moving towards a pair of locked doors. 'We'd better have a run through the reference catalogues.'

'I am looking for a particular file from SOE,' said Rowley quietly.

Elton swung round, already angry. The man really *was* wasting their time. 'Special Operations Executive? But none of that is declassified yet,' he objected. 'Or at any rate, very little. It's all subject to Extended Closure.' It was obvious. Everyone knew that.

Rowley nodded patiently. 'That is perfectly true. Which means the file I am looking for is either with the Foreign Office – which it isn't; with the Ministry of Defence – which it isn't; or here – which I believe it is.' Rowley turned and aimed a careful finger at a door marked: Private. PRO Staff Only. 'In Section Seven.'

Elton looked startled. Section Seven was local code for the store of those Extended Closure documents which had found their way to the Public Record Office and which would remain classified until long after the turn of the century. No one outside was supposed to know of the repository's existence, far less its precise location and code-name.

'Section . . . Section Seven?' tried Elton weakly. Rowley nodded. Then Elton sighed, slipped a key off the chain at his waist and led Rowley towards the locked door.

There was a telephone on the wall near by. Elton lifted down the receiver, hesitated a moment longer and then dialled a number. 'This is Elton,' he announced shortly. 'I am about to enter Section Seven. You are to isolate circuit C9 until further notice, is that understood?' He nodded. 'Yes. Do it now, please.' He replaced the receiver and smiled at Rowley without warmth. 'One moment.'

There was a soft, audible click. Elton fitted his key into the lock, pushed the door open and ushered Rowley through. Almost immediately beyond was a flight of steep concrete steps. Elton locked the door carefully behind them. 'This way.'

At the top of the stairs they were confronted by a locked metal door set into a thick inner fence of stout wire mesh that stretched from floor to ceiling. Behind this inner perimeter Rowley saw row upon row of grey metal shelves, each piled with neatly docketed files of grey, buff or yellow folders that had faded with age. Cold white neon shone down from above and there was no sound except for the muted hum of air-conditioning in a sterile, little-visited room where the only smells were of dust and age, of dried ink and – curious throwback to another age – sealing wax. Secrets, thought Rowley suddenly, guilty secrets. All just waiting.

'And all these are Restricted Access?'

'Indeed. The earliest won't be released until the year 2010,' said Elton. He sounded glad about that, decided Rowley.

The inner door swung back and they went through to a metal desk at the head of the nearest row of shelves. On the desk was a single computer terminal. Elton pulled out a chair and sat down, pushed back the sleeves of his cardigan and bent forward, a concert pianist about to ripple through his masterpiece. He switched on the machine and looked up. 'Right, then: fire away.'

Rowley took a slip of paper from his wallet and glanced down. 'SOE/SO* 1944/45. Fieldfile Number 217/324.'

Elton's thin fingers flew over the keys and then he sat back as the computer digested his request. 'Code-name?' he asked over his shoulder as the brief details he had entered glowed back at him from the display screen.

'Apostle.'

Again Elton's fingers worked busily. As soon as he had typed out the code-name there came a low, urgent buzzing that was synchronized to a single acronym that flashed suddenly onto the screen: RESACC ... RESACC ... RESACC. Kenneth Elton appeared to find this amusing. He glanced round. 'Well now, Mr Rowley, it appears you've upset him. Even up here we have ... How shall I put this? *Degrees* of Restriction? Of Classification?'

'And Apostle?'

'One moment.' Again the fingers moved over the keys and presently Rowley had his answer in angry red letters: APOSTLE CLOSED UNTIL JULY 2045.

---

* SOE/SO: Special Operations Executive/Special Operations. SOE was set up in 1940 to create and foster the spirit of resistance in Nazi-occupied Europe – 'to set Europe ablaze' in Churchill's memorable phrase. By the summer of 1944 SOE had become an Anglo-American organization with the US Special Operations coming under the Office of Strategic Services commanded by General Donovan.

The full one hundred years, realized Rowley. Maximum burial.

'I need it now. Tonight,' said Rowley simply.

Elton sighed, turned off the terminal and rose reluctantly to his feet. 'You'd better follow me.'

They walked deep into the ordered maze of shelves until Elton paused and bent down. He searched briefly through a stack of piled folders and straightened up holding a bulky, dark-green folder fastened with string and sealed with red wax. Beneath the string was a series of ruled boxes, each with a long-forgotten signature in faded black ink. Across the top of the file were the letters S O E/S O and the file number: 217/324.

And below that the one word: APOSTLE.

# : 3 :

'. . . early reports indicate more than fifty thousand Soviet troops together with at least fifteen hundred tanks and armoured support vehicles have now crossed the Soviet border into Afghanistan. Herat and Kabul, the capital, are already in Soviet hands. There is fierce fighting around the Peoples' Palace at Daraluman with heavy losses on both sides. Soviet armoured units are reported to be driving east towards Jalalabad and the Khyber Pass . . .'

In the drawing-room of his Regency house in London's exclusive Eaton Terrace, Lord Porterfield pushed himself heavily to his feet, turned off the radio with an impatient flick of his wrist and returned to his desk.

Lord Porterfield was seventy-two years old. Heavy-jowled, with rounded shoulders beginning to stoop beneath the weight of the heavy, powerful body they supported, the face – and most particularly the eyes – still exuded power, determination, strength of purpose. He usually sat alone in this room and, despite the season, the high-ceilinged drawing-room showed no signs of festivity beyond the rows of expensive Christmas cards from foreign embassies and British government departments that stood in straight, regimented lines along the top of the bookcase.

There was a grand piano over by the tall windows. Its lid was lowered, the polished rosewood top bare except for two photographs in silver frames whose gleaming corners now caught the lamplight. In daylight, one would reveal a young, beautiful woman from an earlier, more graceful age; the other would show a proud, very young second lieutenant in the uniform of the Rifle Brigade. Wife and son, both now dead.

Lord Porterfield's desk was almost hidden beneath a sea of maps and atlases, all of which were open at Afghanistan and the lands directly to the north. There were other papers too, tucked in amongst the overlays and the detailed topographical projections; secret, classified government papers and appraisals that should never have moved beyond a small, closed circle of privileged readers and which should certainly never have appeared anywhere near the desk of a wealthy former civil servant who had retired four years previously.

Now he laid aside a Restricted projection from the Foreign Office Intelligence Unit and sat back from his desk, deep in thought.

Stephen Rowley had arrived at his home an hour earlier, driving up from the Public Record Office at Kew with the Apostle file on the passenger seat beside him. Lord Porterfield had not kept him long. After his departure he had settled down at his desk, snipped through the dry brown string and red wax seals that bound Apostle together and begun to read.

Lord Porterfield hunched forward over his heavy hands and stared for long moments at the notepad on the desk in front of him.

On it he had written three names in a neat column. In his personal view each name represented a dangerous link with the past and, just conceivably, with the future.

Mark. Luke. John.

After 'Mark' and 'John' he had drawn a question mark. Now, having read the Apostle file from cover to cover, Lord Porterfield was able to substitute two names: Bruno Tyschen and Peter Tillet.

There had already been a name beside 'Luke' – Walter Hallam. Lord Porterfield considered for a moment and then drew a careful line through Hallam's name and entered the date – 26/12/79.

He looked at the carriage clock on the mantelpiece. It was a few minutes after eleven. He tore off the top sheet of his notepad and slipped it into his notecase. Then he closed the Apostle file, locked it into a black briefcase and went through into the hall where he put on his overcoat and hat. Then he went down to the maroon Bentley parked in a residents' parking bay near by, placed the briefcase on the passenger seat beside him and pulled smoothly away from the kerb.

He drove east through light traffic towards Buckingham Palace Gardens, skirted the Royal Mews and drove slowly round the Queen Victoria Memorial. At the bottom of The Mall he swung right into Horse Guards Road and a minute later turned left off the road onto the groomed gravel of Horseguards Parade, coming to a gentle stop in front of a looped chain barrier.

A policeman stepped out of the shadows and came forward, his shoes crunching across the gravel. A window whined down as the policeman bent forward to look into the darkened Bentley, then a hand went to the rim of his helmet as he recognized the occupant. 'Good evening, sir. We were told to expect you. Just one moment, please.' He unlocked the chain, let it fall to the ground and beckoned the Bentley forward. Lord Porterfield drove on slowly and parked in the shadows thrown by the western walls of the Treasury buildings.

He got out and walked towards a locked metal wicket set into a wall of weathered brick, his briefcase at his side. Here he was stopped again and his credentials were examined with meticulous care before he was escorted along worn grey flagstones to another gate set in another high brick wall. He passed through this and stepped into a pleasing square of well-kept garden dominated by the brooding shape of tall, dark buildings on three sides.

Now Lord Porterfield walked on alone down the narrow garden path as a door opened at the rear of the house and yellow light spilled onto a terrace. A young aide in three-piece suit was waiting to greet him as he stepped from the terrace into the rear hall of Number 10 Downing Street.

'Good evening, my Lord,' the aide said quietly without offering to shake hands. 'May I take your hat and coat? The Prime Minister will see you immediately. In the study.' Lord Porterfield permitted the aide to take his hat and coat and smoothed a hand over his hair. 'If you would care to go —'

'Yes. I do know the way, thank you,' said Lord Porterfield quietly. He walked down the silent corridor past the Cabinet Room on his right. The door was ajar and he could see domestic staff busy straightening the red-backed chairs ranged around the long boat-shaped table. He walked on and up the gold-carpeted staircase past the double rows of framed pictures of former British prime ministers to the first floor.

The Prime Minister herself was waiting for him at the top of the stairs, immaculate in dark-blue suit and white silk blouse with every lacquered hair perfectly in place. She stretched out a hand in greeting.

'Phillip. How very good to see you again.'

Lord Porterfield managed a formal little bow of the head. 'Prime Minister.' He smiled. They were old friends.

On paper, at least, Lord Porterfield had retired from the civil service four years ago – but the inclusion of his name on the Civil Service Retirement List of 1976 had merely drawn a convenient line beneath public activities that spanned almost forty years.

Few of his former colleagues realized Lord Porterfield had used the Retirement List as a vehicle upon which he had been able to slip away from the wearisome spotlight of public accountability and merge into the shadows thrown by the shoulders of those elected to govern, or that it was this same political influence that gave him access to even the most secret Cabinet papers.

As the Prime Minister's most private confidant, Lord Porterfield moved in the shadows, unseen and unrecognized by a British public who chose to place their trust in the fostered illusion of comfortable, accountable democracy. And, while he guided and advised, steered the powerful and tugged gently upon invisible strings, the press virtually ignored him as a man whose star had waned with retirement. Which suited Lord Porterfield rather well.

'Please. Do come through.' The Prime Minister turned and led the way into her study. It was a large, comfortable room with green walls and three wide, tall windows facing west towards St James's Park. It was dominated by a wide circular table with, beyond that, the Prime Minister's leather-topped desk illuminated by a single porcelain lamp. She now seated herself elegantly in one of the chairs beside the circular table and gestured her visitor to another. 'So,' she began without preamble in the manner of a woman with no time to waste, 'have you read the file?'

'Indeed I have, Ma'am, yes. I have it here, should you wish to see it.' Lord Porterfield tapped his briefcase.

The Prime Minister shook her head. 'And – in your opinion, Phillip – does it pose the threat you feared?'

Lord Porterfield paused before replying, then – 'Yes, Ma'am. I believe that it does.'

The Prime Minister leant forward. If she was tired, wearied by a sixteen-hour day of intense political activity, she chose not to show it. Even to him.

'Why?' That disconcerting directness, head cocked to one side.

'Because the Soviet invasion of Afghanistan *must* destabilize the situation inside the Soviet Union – it can hardly fail to do anything less. When you turn your tanks against yesterday's friend and neighbour you invite dissent and hostility within your own country – perhaps even rebellion. Most of those people for thousands of miles on *both* sides of the Afghan border are Moslems. They see themselves as Moslems. As nationalists. Not Soviet citizens. In the present climate it would take very little to turn unrest into rebellion – and still less for that rebellion to spread. All it would need is a trigger – and Apostle could be that trigger.' He paused. 'Were that to happen, Moscow could well feel compelled towards further military adventurism – not simply for reasons of conquest but in an attempt to unify the Republics by setting them against a common external enemy – against NATO, against the West. With the Union under threat of internal disintegration, Moscow might feel they had little to lose.'

An old, familiar nightmare: Soviet tanks swarming westwards across free Europe.

'And Apostle has that . . . that power? To trigger revolution on that scale?'

'It could tip the balance, yes, Ma'am. The events of the last few days have placed those who know about Apostle in a unique position to profit from their knowledge, should they be tempted to . . . take it to the marketplace, as it were.'

'Can we not trust upon their . . . their integrity, their loyalty? Their sense of duty?'

'We may pin our hopes upon such qualities, yes, Ma'am. But our trust? I would advise against it. Too much is at stake.'

The Prime Minister sighed. 'But we know who these men are?'

Lord Porterfield nodded. 'I have their names now, yes, Ma'am. Their current addresses will take a little longer.'

'Then I would like to leave the matter in your hands, Phillip. There is no need for something like this to go through Cabinet.'

Lord Porterfield bowed his head gravely. 'That will be my honour, Prime Minister.'

Wednesday, 2 January 1980 – and in Sussex, the inquest into the death of Walter Hallam was over. An hour later Gordon Hallam came down the steps outside Lewes police station and the formalities surrounding his father's death were almost completed: he was now free to arrange the funeral and put his father's affairs in order.

Gordon climbed behind the wheel of his Volkswagen and began the short, winding drive along twisting Sussex lanes towards Sidcott. He had his father's front-door key in his pocket and a large buff police envelope containing his father's personal effects on the passenger seat beside him. Gordon found himself glancing at that envelope again and again as he drove along.

Although there was a radio fitted to the car, Gordon preferred the company of his own thoughts, much as he had on the journey up from Stowcombe the night before. As he had set out into the darkness across the moor towards Exeter and the A30 he had half expected to find himself breaking down, giving way to grief. He would have welcomed tears, he realized – welcomed them as a natural, healthy sign of bereavement – yet no tears came. Now, as Gordon sorted memory and emotion from a childhood reduced by distance to a series of faded family snapshots, he realized with a dawning sense of loss that, in the years since his mother had died, in the years when father and only child should have drawn together, they had grown apart. He saw now, too late, that he was about to attend to the affairs of a man, of a father, whom he had never really known.

Gordon slowed down, turned left between the pub and the garage and drove slowly along the lane, realizing with a sense of shame that it was almost nine months since he had last been to his father's house.

The house itself was three-bedroomed and semi-detached, the grounds scissored off on either side by thickets of privet. Gordon unlocked the front door and it swung back with a faint creak as Gordon found himself biting back an urge to call a greeting into the house as he saw the coat stand with all the familiar old garments, each now charged with a sudden poignancy.

He bent down to the doormat and picked up a handful of circulars. He pushed the door shut and went through into the sitting-room, half expecting to see his father rising to his feet, a cup of tea in his hand as he apologized for not being at the front door to greet him. The room was empty.

Gordon went upstairs and into each bedroom quickly in turn, getting it over with, this first taste of trespass as the silence pressed in around him. 'Hello?' he called suddenly, listening as his voice echoed against the watching walls.

He dropped down the stairs again, filled the kettle and put it on the stove. There was a radio beside the sink and he put that on too, filling the house quite deliberately with the little everyday sounds of normality. When the kettle had boiled he made himself a cup of black coffee and took it back with him into the sitting-room where he dialled Rachel's work number and asked for her extension.

'Hello?'

'Hi. It's me.'

'Gordon!' Relief and summer sunshine poured down the line. 'Hello, darling – where are you?'

'At Dad's. Got in about ten minutes ago, I suppose.'

'How did it go? The inquest, I mean?'

'O K, I suppose, as these things go. The Coroner brought in a verdict of accidental death.'

'Oh. That . . . that was what you more or less expected, wasn't it? Did you . . . you know . . . did you have to see him? For identification?'

'That had already been done, thank God. A neighbour did that the morning after Dad was killed. Bloke called Hopkirk. Lives just opposite.'

'What did he say – the Coroner, I mean?'

'Not a lot. Talked about people of advancing years getting confused and disoriented. Reckoned that's what happened to Dad. Wasn't the American's fault, anyway.'

'But Dad wasn't that old, Gordon! There was nothing doddery about him, for goodness' sake!'

'Yeah, well, that's what he said. At least the inquest's over and done with.'

'What are you going to do now?'

'I've arranged to see the solicitors, undertakers and estate agents later this afternoon. Till then I thought I'd make a start by going through Dad's papers, sorting out things in his desk . . .'

'Gordon? You sound sort of funny. Distant.'

Gordon laughed uneasily. 'It's a bit weird, you know? Being here without him, I mean.' He glanced round. 'Can't get over the feeling that I'm prying; that any moment he's going to come round the corner and say: Oi! What d'you think you're playing at . . .?'

When the call was over Gordon took his coffee over to his father's desk, sat down and began going through the drawers.

He had opened one of the longer drawers and was pushing his hands to the back when his fingers closed around a slim case. He lifted it out and sat back on his heels, intrigued. The case was about six inches long, four inches wide and covered in a tight skin of dark-blue satin. There was a tiny gold stud on the edge of the case and Gordon prised back the hinged lid.

He found himself looking at a medal.

It was a silver gilt cross, the upper arm of which was surmounted by a crown with a medallion in the centre bearing the conjoint busts of King George V and Queen Mary encircled by the words 'For God and Empire'. The cross was attached to a rose-pink ribbon two inches wide that carried down its centre and at each edge a single thin, pearl-grey stripe. On the back of the cross were engraved three initials and a date: WGH 1945.

Gordon sat back, the medal swinging freely from its length of ribbon, the gleam of silver catching the light from the desk lamp. A medal. His father had won a bloody medal! He had never known that, never been told. He searched back in his memory, trying to remember any mention of valour, of heroism, of wartime action. Nothing came. As far as he could remember his father had spent the entire war working in London. Something to do with the Ministry of Supply.

The words 'Reserved Occupation' swam into focus suddenly and Gordon shook his head, wishing he could remember more. Not that he had any interest in the war, it was all so long ago, but a medal . . .? He studied it closely. What the hell was it? With renewed interest Gordon pushed back his chair, lifted the entire drawer down onto the carpet and began to search more thoroughly.

Beneath a pair of old photograph albums Gordon found a large, thick white envelope bearing the crest of the Court of St James. It was addressed to his father at the house they had lived in near Oxted when he had been a small boy. Inside the envelope Gordon found a magazine creased and marked with age together with two sheets of thick, expensive velum. He turned to the magazine first.

It was a copy of the *London Gazette* dated 7 March 1947 and had been folded open to an inside page where one of the columns had been neatly asterisked. It was headed 'General List' and read simply:

'OBE (Mil.) Hallam, Walter Gordon. For personal services.'

Gordon slowly unfolded the first sheet of vellum. Beneath the royal crest in dark-red ink at the top left-hand corner was the one word: CONFIDENTIAL.

Gordon's eyes were drawn down the page to a series of beautifully printed paragraphs:

Sir, I have the honour to inform you

THE KING will hold an Investiture at Buckingham Palace on July 6th., 1948, at which your attendance is requested.

It is requested that you should be at the Palace not later than 10.15 o'clock a.m. DRESS: Service Dress, Morning Dress or Civil Defence Uniform.

This letter should be produced on entering the Palace, as no further card of admission will be issued.

Two tickets for relations or friends to witness the Investiture may be obtained on application to this office and you are requested to state your requirements on the form enclosed.

Please complete the enclosed form and return *immediately* to: The Secretary, Central Chancery of the Orders of Knighthood, St James's Palace, London SW1.

I am, Sir,
Your Obedient Servant,

The signature was illegible.

There was another document also. This one, Gordon discovered as he turned the heavy, formal pages, was the Warrant of Appointment:

GEORGE THE SIXTH, by the Grace of God of Great Britain, Ireland and the British Dominions beyond the seas, King, Defender of the Faith, Emperor of India and Sovereign of the Most Excellent Order of the British Empire, to our trusty and well beloved WALTER GORDON HALLAM Greetings!

Whereas We have thought fit to nominate and appoint you to be an Additional Officer of the Military Division of our said Most Excellent Order of the British Empire, We do by these presents grant Unto you the Dignity of an Additional Officer of Our Aforesaid Order together with all and singular privileges thereto belonging or appertaining.

Given at Our Court of St James under Our Sign Manual and the Seal of Our Said Order this sixth day of July in the twelfth year of Our Reign.

By The Sovereign's Command,
Mary R
Grand Master

Gordon sat back, thunderstruck, the sheets of vellum lying in front of him, the silver cross swinging from his fingers, as one huge question loomed unanswered before him: why had his father never told him about this? Why was it only now, when his father was dead, that he had learnt about the existence of the medal? And another thing – what was all this about the Military Division of the award? His father hadn't been a serviceman, for God's sake: he'd been working in a Reserved Occupation; in the Ministry of Supply.

Hadn't he?

Gordon dropped to his knees and began searching through the drawers once more, looking for answers, for more clues to a man, and a medal, that had suddenly become a mystery. He felt angry, too; almost cheated: why hadn't he been *told*?

He found nothing else in the drawers.

It wasn't until he sat back on the sofa, the medal on the table beside its satin-lined case, that he remembered the buff envelope he had brought back with him from the police station.

It wasn't until he had tipped its contents onto the table and sorted through the pathetic collection of personal effects – the wooden-handled penknife, the crumpled handkerchief, the silver propelling pencil and the handful of small change – that he opened the wallet.

And it wasn't until his fingers felt inside the last compartment of all that he discovered the photograph, so faded with age that black and white had turned to sepia.

It was an amateur snapshot. It showed three men in one-piece overalls standing in front of a low-bellied World War Two bomber. The men had their arms around one another's shoulders and were grinning confidently into the camera. Peering closer, Gordon saw that each man was strapped tightly into a parachute harness. Gordon turned the photograph over and read the faded inscription with diminishing belief: 'Self with Mark and John, March '45.'

One of the men, Gordon saw quite clearly, was his father. And he didn't need to be a military historian to realize it was unusual for a civilian clerk in a Reserved Occupation with the Ministry of Supply to be given a parachute.

Or, for that matter, an O B E. Military Division.

# : 4 :

## Uzbekistan, Soviet Central Asia

It had been a long, cold and uncomfortable journey down from
the hills with the three of them – Yuri, his mother and father –
all crowded together shoulder to shoulder in the cab of the ancient, battered green lorry they used on the collective when it
was time to gather in the cotton from their vast, irrigated fields.

Yuri's father swung the heavy wheel to avoid another pothole
in this frozen, deeply-rutted track that wound down from the
hills towards the town, visible now in the distance a couple of
kilometres away. Behind lay the snow-covered rolling Steppe
that marched away towards the lofty northern border with
Kazakhstan, another of the Soviet Union's fifteen Republics.

Yuri's father wound down the window, spat angrily into the
snow, wiped the back of his hand across a moustache no larger
than a hearth-brush and began stirring around with the long-
handled gear stick that disappeared through a draughty hole in
the floorboards. With much crashing and screeching of metal he
banged the lorry into a lower gear and they jolted downhill towards the town. From the station, Yuri and a hundred or so
other fit young men, all born in 1961, would be going on alone.

Little drifts of cotton continued to blow around the cab's icy
interior, legacies of those days in the fields. Some settled now on
Yuri's coat. His mother reached across and brushed impatiently
at her son's sleeve, dark eyes anxious and protective above the
yashmak that was customarily worn in public by all Sunni
Moslem women.

Yuri brushed her hand away as though he was waving off a
cloud of summer flies. 'It's all right, mother. Stop fussing, will
you? They don't care what we look like. It's our bodies they're
after, not the clothes on our backs. We get uniforms anyway,
right from the start.' He was looking forward to that, secretly.

His mother nodded glumly, tapping a finger against her forehead. 'Your bodies? Yes – but they are after your minds too,

Yuri Rashidov – your minds too; never forget that. They will want to make you into a Russian, eh? One of themselves.' She reached out and pinched his cheek roughly between finger and thumb. It was an old gesture of affection from his boyhood and Yuri bore it stoically. It would not, after all, be for very much longer . . .

Yuri's mother looked into the face of the boy she was about to lose for two years, saw the inner uncertainty behind the deep brown eyes and decided to soften the message. She reached out and pressed his arm impulsively. 'Put your mind to it,' she urged, more softly now. 'Listen to what they tell you, eh? Learn from them.' She smiled. 'Maybe they will make you an outstanding soldier. Then they will give you special leave.'

'Him? Special leave? Ha!' scoffed Yuri's father, hunching over the steering wheel. 'Outstanding soldier? They'll have him for breakfast, more like!' He snorted. 'He won't be getting any leave, woman! None of 'em will – not unless they change the way they look, the way they speak.' He glanced at his son out of the corner of his eye. 'You'll see,' he said gruffly. 'You'll see soon enough.' It was the nearest he could come to pity and thus, to a gesture of affection.

Although he was forty-eight years old, Yuri's father was still on the Reserve with another two years to go before he was finally released from further military obligation. He had been recalled for refresher training only once after his initial three years,* served in a Pioneer Battalion when he had been Yuri's age, yet he still remembered the tough, gruelling days of basic instruction: the physical hardship, the weapon training and live firing, the moments of rare excitement when the unit moved away from the static routine of barracks to flex its muscles on field manoeuvres with the rest of the Regiment.

He was a simple man who chose to forget, in the way of old soldiers the world over, the monotony, the boredom, the difficulties of mastering even a few words of Russian and the casual, mindless victimization that had come his way simply because he was an Uzbek, a 'blackass', not a Russian, and therefore different. Inferior.

---

* The 1967 Universal Military Service law reduced the duration of conscript service for most Soviet draftees from three years to two.

Yuri's mother reached out and touched the back of Yuri's head. A few days ago her fingers would have felt thick black hair; now there was only stubble through which the bone of his skull gleamed like dull ivory. 'Why did they have to shave you so close?' she demanded angrily. 'You look like a lamb after shearing.'

Yuri shrugged awkwardly. 'It's just their way, that's all.'

She sighed. Their way. It covered so much, justified so little.

The last few minutes ticked away as the lorry rattled past the first cluster of houses and workers' apartments that stuck up out of the snow on the town's straggling outskirts. There was silence in the cab as Yuri sat stiffly upright, frowning straight ahead through the dirty windscreen, a young man whose immature self-image did not include a portrait of himself as a shorn lamb. He was off to be a soldier, wasn't he? Older men returned from military service had warned him about the hardship, the victimization that lay ahead, but the stories had not worried him unduly. Besides, they were sure to be exaggerating. It was still, after all, an adventure. His very first.

Nine months ago, shortly after his seventeenth birthday, Yuri and a dozen other young men from the near-by countryside had reported to the *rayon*\* military commissariat to register for military service. There they had been stripped, subjected to a searching physical examination and assessed for duty. Then back to their farms and collectives set among the rolling orchards and cotton fields, the wheat fields and the vineyards to wait – until a few weeks ago when they had been called forward for yet another medical examination and told to report today to the railhead that was the *Oblast*, the regional assembly point for conscripts.

There was another sudden lurch and a terrible clashing of gears that set their teeth on edge, then they were on smooth asphalt and Yuri's father reduced speed as they drove down the frozen, snow-banked road between rows of drab, identical, two-storey concrete buildings that marked the start of the industrial area.

A hundred metres further on and shops began to appear, sprinkled in haphazardly among the low, slab-sided buildings, and immediately Yuri's mother started craning her head this

---

\* *Rayon*: government unit roughly equivalent to a rural ward.

way and that as she scanned the shop signs. A practical woman who had wept brief, emotional tears for her two older sons when they had gone off to serve in their time, she nevertheless had every intention of exploiting their government travel concession to the full: just as soon as the bands had stopped playing, the last patriotic address had ended and the train had left the station, she was going shopping – shopping for saucepans. She had brought along a bolt of their finest cotton as barter and so had few worries about returning home empty-handed.

The road was becoming more crowded now as they approached the town centre. By Western standards, the streets were not busy but there were lorries and bicycles and a few old-fashioned, closed-in private cars belonging to local officials. Cattle plodded along at the edge of the road and chickens squawked and flustered under the wheels of swaying, top-heavy buses bringing their precariously balanced loads in from the outlying countryside. Here and there they passed other small family groups, each with a shaven-headed young man at its centre clutching a suitcase as he too made his way towards the railway terminal.

Yuri's father turned left and then braked the lorry to a sudden shuddering, squealing halt that stalled the engine and threw them all forward against the windscreen. 'For the love of –' began Yuri's mother, rubbing a bruised elbow painfully.

'Don't blame me, woman – look at the stupid idiot!' gestured Yuri's father angrily, banging his fist against the steering wheel. A bus and another lorry were stopped directly across the road, blocking their path. They waited. Nothing seemed to be happening. Yuri's father waited a moment longer, then wound down the window violently and started shouting: 'Hey! What's the matter? Keep moving up there! Why are you stopping?' A blast of bitter, freezing air came swirling around his muffled, waiting passengers as a soldier in long greatcoat, fur cap and polished black jackboots came suddenly around the side of the stationary lorry. There was a pistol strapped to his waist in a gleaming brown leather holster.

The soldier looked up with bored distaste at the shouting driver, the tip of his nose white with cold. 'What's so special about you, comrade?' he demanded shortly. His moustache quivering, Yuri's father gestured angrily at the stationary vehicles. 'Are you blind? See for yourself – go on, look at them! This is a road, not a . . . public car park! Besides, we're in a hurry.'

The soldier remained unimpressed. He had his orders and they were quite categoric. 'What's the rush?'

'My boy here' – he jerked an oil-stained thumb towards Yuri sitting silently beside him – 'he's away to do his two years. We'll be late for the ceremonies if those oafs don't shift along.' The soldier regarded him impassively. Ahead, through the windscreen, Yuri saw that passengers were now getting out of the two vehicles and were being herded down a side street by a soldier with officers' shoulder-boards who brushed their questions impatiently aside.

'This road is closed.'

'Closed? But it goes right to the station. Last time we –'

'I don't care about last time, comrade,' interrupted the soldier tiredly. 'I don't even care about next time. I only care about now, see? And the road is closed. Orders.'

'How are we –?'

'Permits. Authorization of Travel documents – and you' – he swung round and pointed a gloved finger at Yuri – 'Draft Registration papers.' Yuri's father began muttering under his breath as he burrowed beneath layers of winter clothing before finally tugging loose a creased dark-brown envelope. He took out a sheaf of papers and smoothed them out roughly. Yuri gave his father his draft book and both sets of papers were held out of the window at arm's length. The soldier plucked them from his fingers and studied them closely. Finally he handed them back, apparently satisfied.

'Leave the lorry here. You must walk to the station. Another route has been authorized.' He gestured towards the side street thronged with other pedestrians who were moving away from the soldiers with only an occasional, uncomprehending glance back over their shoulders at the abandoned vehicles.

'I can't just leave it here,' protested Yuri's father, thinking of the valuable petrol that could be siphoned off while he was watching the ceremonies and listening to the same interminable, boring speeches.

'Just do it!' snapped the soldier.

Yuri's father exchanged baffled glances with his wife and admitted defeat. He shrugged. 'Come on.' He knocked open the door with his shoulder and climbed down. Yuri reached behind him for the single suitcase he was permitted to take to barracks and then he too climbed down to join his parents. They stood together on the cold, frozen ground, unsure what would happen next.

'Over there,' gestured the soldier, waving them towards the others. As they moved towards the side road a whistle blast came from somewhere up ahead. They turned. Another army officer in winter greatcoat was waving the soldier hurriedly towards him. As they watched, three more men in uniform came out of another side street dragging knife-rest road barriers across the street. The officer shouted something to the soldier who had inspected their papers. He cursed under his breath and began running heavily up the icy road towards the other soldiers, the tails of his greatcoat flapping against his heavy boots.

'What d'you think all that's about?' asked Yuri.

His mother shrugged. 'Who knows? Who cares? Come on –' They turned and followed the others.

The diversion led away from the town's main square through a series of narrow side streets that brought them round to the station in a wide curve. Town dwellers familiar with the methodology of town planners might perhaps have noticed that the route they were obliged to take always kept at least two blocks of tall buildings between the pedestrians and the central square with its statutory memorial to the Great Patriotic War, but to families in from the country just for the day, such a curious coincidence passed unnoticed. Now, as Yuri and his parents turned into a final side street that led directly to the station, Yuri stopped suddenly and cocked his head to one side. 'Listen!' he ordered excitedly. 'Listen!'

They listened.

Faintly at first but growing steadily louder came the sound of a military band. Yuri grinned widely and shifted his heavy suitcase from one hand to another. That was *his* band. That sombre, patriotic crashing of cymbals, the thumping of drums – they were playing for him!

'Come on now, quickly!' he urged. They pressed on down towards the end of the street but here they had to wait, taking their turn in a log-jam of people who waited while uniformed soldiers examined the special passes issued by the military commissariat that permitted the holders through to the station forecourt and the ceremony that was about to start.

Craning between the shoulders of the waiting crowd, Yuri caught sight of the military band playing in the centre of the yard, the weak winter sun catching on the gleam of polished brass instruments and upon the gold buttons of their warm, high-collared coats. There seemed to be flowers and garlands everywhere, noticed Yuri, glancing round quickly, his eyes drinking it all in excitedly: flowers hanging in baskets slung from the lamp-posts, flowers surrounding the base of the ornamental fountain, flowers clustered beneath the giant banners and printed Party slogans that swung and shivered in the cold, biting wind . . .

Behind the band, flanking the concrete steps that led up to the station, neatly-dressed members of the Young Pioneers, smart in their creased black trousers and red neckerchiefs, stood stiffly at attention, their gloved hands gripped firmly around the polished poles of the flags that snapped and fluttered above their heads. Yuri felt a sudden glow of excitement: if *this* was what it was going to be like, he wouldn't mind at all . . . A young girl with a mass of rich dark curls caught his eye and he smiled broadly as she looked away in confusion. Not one little bit . . .

'Papers.'

He became aware that they were shuffling towards the head of the queue – and that his father was fumbling uneasily in his pockets, searching for something.

'Papers. You-your papers.' Soon it would be their turn.

'Papa? What is it?'

'The passes,' muttered his father without looking up as he patted his pockets. 'I can't find the passes.'

'What?' demanded his mother incredulously. 'But you had them! You had them a moment ago – in the lorry! You showed them to that soldier! He gave them back to you – I saw him!'

Her husband continued to pat his pockets helplessly. 'Well, I haven't got them now. I must have dropped them –'

'Dropped them? We come all this way and you . . . you *drop* them? How in the name of –'

'Here – woman: what would you do? Strip me naked in front of all these people? Tear my clothes from my back?' demanded her husband angrily. 'Go on – search me yourself. Find them!' He held his arms wide away from his body as the heads began to turn and Yuri curled up inside with embarrassment. Of all the –

'You're sure they're not in your pocket?' insisted Yuri urgently.

His father nodded impatiently. 'Yes, yes – I'm sure. How many more times? They're not here. Perhaps back at the lorry, I don't know . . .'

'I'll go and see.'

'Yuri – you can't –' began his mother. But she was too late. Before they could stop him, Yuri had put down his suitcase, pushed his way through the waiting knot of people and was running back along the narrow side streets. It would only take a moment, he reasoned. He ran on alone down streets suddenly empty as the music from the military band receded behind him.

At the end of the street which led into the main road Yuri stopped, warm now beneath his winter clothes. He was panting lightly as he stepped out onto the road. It was silent. Silent and deserted. There were the lorry and the bus that had been stopped so suddenly in their path – and he saw now, with a start of surprise, that the road behind his father's lorry had been closed off too: an army truck was pulled across the mouth of the road and, from where he was standing, Yuri could see the back of a soldier's cap and the tip of the rifle slung over his shoulder as he patrolled slowly up and down.

Glancing round, Yuri saw no sign of the soldier who had ordered them down from the lorry and no sign of the officer who had blown his whistle – just the knife-rest trestles, still in position blocking off the end of the road twenty metres further on.

And overall, it came to him now, there hung an ominous, waiting silence.

Moving lightly on his feet, Yuri hurried across to the lorry, eased open the door and looked inside. His eyes searched quickly. Ah. The passes were there, on the floor where his father had dropped them. He leant over, scooped them up and thrust them deep into his own pocket. Then Yuri slipped down from the cab and shut the door. He closed it gently, prompted to do so by some inner, subconscious instinct he did not fully understand. He was just about to hurry back to his parents when he heard a sound that, quite literally, stopped him in his tracks.

It was the sound of low chanting. It came from around the corner at the top of the road, out of sight beyond the knife-rest barriers. The sound seemed to be getting louder, although it was still too indistinct for him to be able to make out the words.

He glanced over his shoulder. The soldier with the rifle was still twenty metres away, facing in the opposite direction and plodding stolidly up and down. No one else was in sight. He glanced up at the windows near by and they were empty. Almost before he knew what he was doing, Yuri was running up the road towards the knife-rest barriers. He squeezed through the gap beside the wall and looked around the corner.

There were people coming down the road towards him – twenty, thirty, perhaps even forty civilians of all ages: men and women – a few small children too, all walking slowly towards him, chanting and carrying furled banners. The untidy procession appeared to be led by an elderly, bald-headed man with round metal-framed spectacles.

As Yuri watched, the elderly man turned to those behind him and held up both hands. The procession shuffled to a halt and fell silent. There was a brief delay while home-made banners were unfurled and a hurried consultation ensued. Then – a little uncertainly, it seemed to Yuri – the procession started forward and the chanting began once more, faintly at first and then with growing confidence as the protesters drew strength from one another.

Their banners had been daubed hastily with bright red paint that had started to run before it was dry, so that in places the letters themselves looked as if they were bleeding. 'MOSLEMS! RESIST RUSSIAN AGGRESSION!' pleaded one. 'HELP YOUR AFGHAN BROTHERS!' proclaimed another, while a third read: 'TARTARS! UZBEKS! WATCH AFGHANISTAN! REMEMBER THE CRIMEA!, and a fourth 'OUR FORCE IS OUR FAITH.'

Yuri stood there, amazed. He had never seen anything like it. The procession came nearer. Behind the leader the men and women spread out across the width of the road. One or two small children tottered uncertainly beside their parents, grubby hands clutching at a mother's skirts.

They had been walking forward for less than a minute when a squad of armed soldiers ran suddenly out of a side street fifty metres ahead and deployed across the road, blocking their path. There were perhaps twenty soldiers, each wearing belted greatcoat and fur cap above polished jackboots. They carried automatic rifles across their chests. Now, at a signal from the officer at the centre, the men slung their automatics back over their shoulders and drew long wooden batons from beneath their greatcoats.

The procession faltered and stopped. The chanting died away. Yuri watched, mesmerized, as the old man at the head of the protesters turned and urged his followers forward. Again there was a hurried, murmured consultation as heads turned fearfully towards the soldiers. One of the banners wavered and was then lowered as a mother grasped the hand of her small child and pushed her way to the back of the march to hurry away up the street, glancing back anxiously over her shoulder as she dragged her wailing child away from danger.

The soldiers had not moved. They stood there, watching silently, waiting for orders, the officer slightly in front of his men with legs braced apart, baton stick held across his thighs. Yuri watched as he lifted a little silver whistle to his lips. It glittered briefly in the weak sunlight as he gave one short, sharp blast and the line of soldiers began to move slowly forward. They came on, step by solid step, as the gap between army and civilians closed remorselessly.

The back of the protest march began to peel away, slowly at first and then with gathering momentum as the soldiers' advance continued. One banner after another wobbled and then came down as people lost their nerve and backed away from confrontation. Within moments uncertainty had become fear, fear had turned into panic and panic into rout as those at the front pushed and shoved to get out of the way as the troops advanced upon them. In a matter of moments, it seemed to the watching Yuri, only the old man and a young woman were left, holding a single defiant banner between them as they stood their ground.

'IN THE NAME OF ISLAM,' it read, 'RUSSIAN AGGRESSION MUST CEASE!'

The officer gave another short blast on his whistle and a group of soldiers at either end of the line broke into a run and, with batons raised, charged forward past the two stationary protesters to harry the last of the fleeing stragglers as they streamed up the road to safety.

Now the officer began to walk slowly forward as Yuri counted breathlessly, heart hammering against his ribs: eighteen soldiers. Eighteen soldiers with batons and automatic rifles against one old man and a young girl.

The officer came forward until he was no more than a metre away from the couple standing in the roadway, their banner stretched between them. Yuri could see them talking angrily for a moment, the girl gesturing emphatically, the old man nodding, his spectacles flashing earnestly in the sunlight. The officer then turned and beckoned towards a group of three waiting soldiers. They ran forward obediently. He pointed at the girl and they moved towards her with not a word spoken between them. While one soldier grabbed the girl from behind the others ripped the banner from her hands and tossed it contemptuously onto the ground. As the old man struggled feebly to help her he was sent reeling with an offhand shove in the chest. The girl was lifted off her feet and bodily carried away out of sight down the side street.

As her cries faded away, Yuri looked back at the old man standing defiantly alone, surrounded by a litter of broken, discarded banners. The Russian officer gave another curt order and two of his men began gathering up the evidence of demonstration, of dissent. The banners disappeared down the same side street and Yuri heard the clang of a metal tail-gate.

There was a moment of complete silence. Then the officer stepped up to the old man, smacking the end of his baton thoughtfully against the gloved palm of his left hand. He turned on his polished heel, glanced casually up and down the quiet road – and then he struck.

Without the slightest warning he suddenly brought his baton sweeping round in a vicious, scything arc against the side of the old man's head. The spectacles flew off and the old man crumpled to his knees with a terrible groan of pain. The officer swiftly reversed the baton and rammed its blunt rounded end into the man's stomach. As he doubled forward the officer stepped back and swung a polished boot with all his strength into the man's face. He went down, sprawling unconscious in a crumpled heap of fluttering rags onto the hard, frozen road.

The officer moved carefully around the still body, studying his work dispassionately as his men stood back. Yuri then watched, horrified, as he used those beautifully polished black boots to kick the old man to death.

It did not take very long.

When it was done the officer bent down beside the bloodied corpse and wiped his boots clean with the hem of the dead man's coat. He rose to his feet, adjusted the set of his cap, glanced round, saw what he was looking for and walked slowly over to the old man's metal spectacles lying in the gutter. He picked them up and carried them over to the corpse at arm's length. He dropped them beside the dead, staring eyes and trod on them carefully with the heel of one boot, grinding them into the roadway like a spent cigarette.

Yuri crouched lower, shaking violently and panting with the horror of what he had just witnessed. Suddenly he gagged, clutching at the wooden trestle for support, and then blundered away from the soldiers to vomit helplessly into the road, an outstretched hand propping him against the wall as the waves of nausea and disgust rolled over him. He retched and retched until there was nothing left inside his stomach, nothing inside his head except the vision that would stay with him forever: a vision of an old man being kicked to death by a nameless, faceless Russian officer with a silver whistle who then carefully cleaned the toes of his boots with the cloth of the dead man's coat.

Yuri turned and blundered back down the side road towards his parents. Presently, he began to run. He ran faster and faster, chased and harried by devils clawing at his shoulders. Was that why the road had been closed, the route changed at the very last minute? To keep the demonstrators away from the crowds? He raced downhill and flew round a corner. If the road had not been closed, Yuri saw suddenly as the station came into view, then the demonstrators' path would have carried them right into the station forecourt itself. Among the flowers, the bands and the banners, the Party officials and the bureaucrats in their shiny suits and carefully calibrated orders of seniority gathering now to witness the induction ceremony and make their timeless, self-important little speeches about patriotic duty and self-sacrifice.

Yuri swung wildly round the last corner and forced himself to break into a walk. His parents were waiting, standing beside the solitary soldier on the gate. All the other spectators had passed through ahead of them.

'Yuri! At long last! Where have you been? We've been waiting –' began his mother impatiently.

'I'm . . . I'm sorry.' He swallowed hastily. 'I . . . here –' He reached suddenly into his pocket for the passes. 'I . . . I found them. In the lorry. On the . . . on the floor. Just like you said.' His mother and father were looking at him oddly. 'What is it? What are you staring at me like that for?' he challenged.

'Yuri? What's the matter?'

He tried to look blank. 'The . . . the matter? Nothing's the matter. I . . .' He followed his mother's gaze and saw she was looking down at his shoes. They were spattered with vomit. 'I . . .' He looked up, awkward and embarrassed. 'I got sick,' he explained sheepishly, wiping a hand across his sweating face. 'It's . . . it's nothing. Just excitement. Here –' He thrust the passes into his father's hand.

The soldier glanced at them briefly and then tore them in half. 'Family through there' – he gestured to the left. 'Conscripts – report to the Sergeant through there' – he jerked a thumb towards some unseen NCO on the right beyond the barrier.

The family separated. Yuri hurried over to a tall, uniformed soldier holding a clipboard. Hard, small eyes like polished pebbles regarded him bleakly from beneath the visor of his peaked cap and Yuri was reminded again of his dishevelled appearance. He stood before the physical embodiment of Soviet strength and waited until the NCO deigned to notice him.

'Yes?' Finally.

'Soldier Rashidov, Comrade Sergeant. Reporting as ordered,' panted Yuri.

The NCO ran a finger down a long list and made a small tick. 'You are late, Rashidov. A bad start. It will be noted. Now – get

65 :

over and join the others' – he jerked his head towards a low building beside the station – 'in there.'

'Yes, Comrade Sergeant. At once.' Yuri turned away.

'And Rashidov –'

'Comrade Sergeant?'

The NCO waved the pencil disdainfully at Yuri's shoes. 'Wipe that puke off your shoes. This is a parade, not a throwing-up contest.'

'At once, Comrade Sergeant.' Yuri stood on one leg and wiped the toe of one shoe up and down the back of the other trouser-leg.

The NCO watched this antic contemptuously. 'Go on, little soldier. Get out of my sight.' Yuri turned and hurried away, gratefully. It was not a propitious beginning to two years of military service.

Inside the building he found the rest of his intake, all with their shaved heads, all with that same dumb look of apprehension as they waited for someone to reach down and immerse them in the machine. Yuri gave his name to another NCO, his suitcase was almost torn from his hand and in a confusingly short time he found himself thrust into the middle rank of waiting recruits. There were five ranks, graded off according to height with the shortest bald-head in the middle. Heavy wooden doors were drawn almost closed across the far end of the building and, through a crack, Yuri could see that when the doors were opened the recruits would be able to march out dramatically into the courtyard directly towards the waiting band, the dais of officials and the tiers of flower-bedecked benches of proud, waiting parents.

Yuri found himself standing next to a tall, gangling young man with jug ears whose bare wrists poked out of sleeves that were too short for his arms. They nodded at one another warily. 'Rashidov – Yuri Rashidov,' whispered Yuri out of the corner of his mouth, a toe-cap rubbing furiously up and down the back of a trouser-leg.

'Samlar – Nikolai Samlar. At least, I was until they did this to me.' He gestured wryly at his bald head and grinned, revealing large, even white teeth.

'You Russian?' asked Yuri directly, for it was as well to know and both men had been speaking Jagatai Turkish, the language of convenience in Uzbekistan.

'Do I *look* like a fucking Russian?' countered Nikolai. Yuri registered the slight Asiatic slant to the eyes, the high cheekbones and shook his head. He too grinned as the beginnings of friendship sprang between them as both men reached for an ally on the adventure that was about to grip their lives.

'Can't say that you do, no.'

'I'm a Tartar. You?'

'Uzbek.' They shook hands quickly.

'What happened?' demanded Nikolai, gesturing at Yuri's boots.

'I threw up,' admitted Yuri in a whisper. 'You would have too. I had to go back to where my old man had parked the truck. When I got there some of your –'

'QUIET!' roared a voice at the front of the square of waiting recruits. The word boomed and echoed around the huge, bare building as yet another uniformed NCO strutted with deliberate, measured tread along the front rank and glared sternly into each frozen young face as he passed. 'Right, pay attention . . .' He paused until there was absolute silence. 'Better . . . In a moment you will all march – and I said MARCH – out of this place to be greeted by the applause and good wishes of your countrymen. Do you understand?' There were a few nods as Yuri frowned, concentrating hard. The NCO had addressed them in Russian, the language of 'The Centre', of officialdom, of the Soviet Army. Although he had been forced to learn Russian at school it was still a second, rusty language that could never become anything else, never become the language of home, no matter how hard They tried to make it so. He glanced sideways at Nikolai. He too was having the same problem.

'DO YOU UNDERSTAND?' roared the NCO.

'Yes, Comrade Sergeant,' mumbled a few voices.

'AGAIN! ALL OF YOU!'

'YES, COMRADE SERGEANT!' they roared.

The NCO hawked disparagingly. 'Applause? I suppose they will clap – God knows what they think you have done to deserve it – you have certainly *not* become soldiers.' He gazed round silently at the sea of puzzled, waiting, anxious faces. 'Not yet, anyway. Some of you will never aspire to such heights. A few of you . . .' He shrugged. 'One or two, perhaps. We shall see. For the moment – STAND STILL, THAT MAN! – it is enough only that you are here: the rough clay dropped upon the potter's wheel.'

There was an uneasy snigger of laughter from someone in the second rank. The NCO swung round, glaring, and the noise was instantly silenced behind a mask of blank anonymity as no one else joined in. 'I and my comrades – we are the potters,' continued the NCO, pausing and then adding softly, ominously, 'And *that*, *salagi*,\* is your misfortune, I promise you. Now, wait for the command.'

They waited in absolute silence, two soldiers in uniform standing at the high wooden doors ready to roll them back at the given moment. The band crashed on for a moment longer and then stopped. There was a sudden hum of static and then an unseen voice began talking, his words fading in and out weirdly as the antiquated public address system distorted the twice-yearly message of cant and patriotic cliché:

'A solemn moment in the historic destiny of our Soviet peoples . . . a guard against aggression from Imperialist enemies united in their determination to bring about the downfall of our mighty nation . . . descendants of those heroes of the Soviet Union who, with bricks and stones and with their own bare hands, defeated the German invader at Volgograd and Odessa . . .' The senior NCO began to think ahead now as he recognized the words. Year in, year out, they never varied.

'Cadre . . . Cadre . . . shun!' roared the NCO. Two hundred conscripts came to attention, left leg slapping in straight-kneed against right foot.

'– we send them out from their homes and loved ones, confident in our hearts that in them we may entrust with absolute certainty the safety, the security and the future of our great nation, brother-hood in arms . . .' He was winding up now. The NCO nodded curtly at the two soldiers who heaved strongly on the heavy wooden doors. They rolled back with an impressive rumble.

'Cadre! Quick . . . March!' bawled the NCO. The front rank stepped off smartly and began to march towards the sea of waving,

---

\* *Salagi*: raw recruits. *Salaga* is a fish found in the Neva river.

clapping spectators and the stout little men in their pork-pie hats and Party badges and military decorations who clapped politely from the red-carpeted dais as the band struck up another stirring, patriotic march.

But as eighteen-year-old Yuri Rashidov marched from the gloom of the shed into the bright, brittle winter sunshine, his thoughts were not of bands and banners, of flags, of uniforms or patriotic pride, but of an old man and a pair of broken metal spectacles.

The first reports of the demonstration reached Moscow two hours later.

They were transmitted – in code – to the cypher and communications centre at 2, Dzerzhinsky Square, the grey stone, nine-storey building two blocks away from the Kremlin. That building – together with a new, purpose-built complex on the outskirts of the city – is headquarters to 'The Centre', to Komitet Gosudarstvdnnoi Bezopasnosti – the KGB.

The KGB serves not the State but the Communist Party of the Soviet Union and is divided into four Chief Directorates. One of these is responsible for operations against the Soviet population at home. Set up in 1969 to counter the growing dissident movement inside the USSR, it is this Directorate that is primarily responsible for such examples of psychiatric abuse as periodically inflame the selective conscience of the West.

First Secretary of this Directorate is Anatol Blukov. Now his assistant, Aliev, stood back and waited apprehensively as Blukov closed the report and glanced up.

'It ... it appears almost insignificant,' hazarded Aliev tentatively. Blukov slammed an angry hand down on the report and Aliev winced.

'*Almost* insignificant?'

Aliev shifted uncomfortably. 'By which I mean, Comrade Secretary, that it appears to have been ... contained. Isolated.'

Blukov nodded slowly, although not in agreement. 'Tell me, Aliev, how many "insignificant" demonstrations are recorded in that book of yours for, say, five years ago?'

Aliev flicked readily to a particular page in his red bound folder. Nowadays Aliev and his dossier on minority unrest were seldom parted. Blukov suspected he even slept with it in his arms.

'Er . . . forty-two, Comrade Secretary.'

Again Blukov nodded. 'Forty-two. And four years ago?'

'Sixty-seven, Comrade Secretary.'

'Go on.'

'The . . . er . . . the following year, eighty-one. Then ninety-eight.'

'And last year?' queried Blukov sweetly. Aliev told him: one hundred and nine.

'One hundred and nine,' echoed Blukov. 'I see.' He picked up the report, weighed it speculatively and then dropped it gently on his desk. 'No, comrade, I do not believe this demonstration to be . . . insignificant. They are none of them . . . insignificant.' He paused. 'Do you know what will happen if this trend cannot be reversed?'

Aliev's Adam's apple bobbed nervously. 'I . . . er.'

'You will be replaced, comrade.'

'Me, Comrade Secretary?'

'You, Aliev. And me. And this. All of it.' He waved a languid hand at their sombre, intimidating surroundings. 'Or do you believe that we, the Russians who presently hold control, are truly capable of dousing such a fire once it gains hold?'

Aliev looked about him helplessly. 'Comrade Secretary, we are told that it is –'

'I asked you what you believe, not what you have been told. Answer me!'

Aliev swallowed. 'No, Comrade Secretary. I do not believe it.'

'Neither do I, comrade. Neither do I. We might as well try nailing down quicksilver.'

# : 5 :

It was night. Night in the northern mountains of Afghanistan.

There was no moon and although the snow had stopped falling it was still bitterly cold at this altitude with a temperature of minus nine degrees Centigrade and a biting wind that slashed like angry razors through even the thickest layers of clothing.

Dressed in the traditional turban of the Afghan Pathan tribesman, the man moved alone, climbing in swift, easy strides over the frozen scree towards the cave hidden on the far side of the ridge. He had been moving steadily up the mountainside for the last two hours on thick, tireless legs that had carried him away from the last tiny village that clung precariously to the rugged, barren hills above Falzabad on the river Kokcha near Afghanistan's north-eastern frontier with the Soviet Union.

He had spent six hours in that village – talking, watching and listening. Mostly, however, he had been listening. Now he was going home. Back into the mountains.

He had stopped only once. And that had not been for rest.

Fifty minutes ago he had heard the sudden clatter of a Soviet helicopter gunship nearby and had melted motionless into the frozen hillside as the machine swept down between the mountain peaks and then sheared away to the west with a random spray of unsighted machine-gun fire that sent splinters of age-old rock whining away into the valley below.

The man had waited, pressed against the rock face, until even the echo of the machine's passing had rolled away down the silent, darkened hillside. Then and only then had he resumed his silent climbing.

Now he crossed the ridge-line, descended a few metres on the far side and stopped suddenly. Bending low, he moved rapidly twenty metres along the slope, dropped to his stomach and wormed his way back to the skyline. Moving infinitely slowly he eased his head between two boulders and looked down. There was no movement, no sound above the low growl of the wind as it twisted between the mountains – yet still he waited. He waited fifteen, twenty minutes; he waited long after fingers had grown numb and he could no longer feel the sharp, angular rocks that dug into his lean stomach as steady, unblinking eyes tracked over the slopes below searching for the first glint of movement or the tiny rattle of a dislodged pebble that would tell him he was being followed.

Finally, he was satisfied. He eased himself gently back over the skyline, rose to his feet and moved obliquely across the reverse slope towards the cave.

He paused again ten metres from the mouth of the cave that was hidden in the darkness behind a shoulder of rock. He drew his knife from the folds of his clothing and tapped its curved blade lightly against a stone. The sound carried only a few metres. 'Ratbag,' he called out softly into the darkness.

He spoke in English, his native tongue.

'OK, Ratbag. In you come.' The reply was also spoken quietly in English, though this time with an unmistakably Scottish accent.

Ratbag moved around the rock and slipped gratefully past the shoulder of the crouching, motionless sentry: a dark, hunched shape hardly seen among the rocks that loomed around him. This man too wore the dress of an Afghan tribesman and, in keeping with that deception, the rifle that he lowered from his shoulder was a British Short Magazine Lee Enfield .303.

The new arrival crouched down beside the sentry. 'Nothing to worry about,' he breathed. 'Quiet as the proverbial.' He paused. 'Hear that chopper go over?'

The other man nodded imperceptibly in the darkness. 'Yeah. What was it?'

'HIND Mi-24. Recognize that sound anywhere.'

'What was he firing at?'

'Fuck all. Just clearing his guns.'

'Hope the bastard has to clean 'em, an' all.'

'Too right.' Ratbag tapped the sentry lightly on the shoulder and moved silently past him towards their hide.

The cave was no more than a deep, winding cleft between two

steep walls of rock that ran back side by side another twelve metres into the depths of the mountain. The fissure twisted back upon itself a few paces away from the entrance to form a natural corner that cut down the worst of the wind, the snow and the freezing rain. Ratbag moved slowly down the narrow gap, a hand stretched out in front of him. In a moment he felt the first rough blanket that acted as a light-trap. He pushed this gently aside. A few more paces, another light-trap. He parted this too and stepped into the bowl of the cave that had been their temporary base for the past three days.

All such bases were always temporary. Tomorrow, once again, they would painstakingly remove all traces of their stay and set off east across the mountains. Their very survival depended upon constant mobility, constant vigilance.

There were two other men inside this inner sanctum, their shapes dark and sinister in the dim red glow of a single hand torch. One was off watch, curled up on the rocky floor in a waterproof olive drab sleeping-bag with only a head of curly dark hair sticking out of the top. A Sterling submachine-gun lay at arm's reach beside him, a magazine fitted and silencer attached.

The other man – the leader of the team – was crouched beside a lightweight radio transmitter/receiver, an earphone cupped against one ear as nimble fingers tapped in the computer-coded transmission frequencies that would enable them to 'hop' their outbound signal over all but the most sophisticated attempts at electronic jamming.

These four men, all aged between twenty-six and thirty-eight, were members of the British Army. Highly-skilled, highly-trained, they made up a single operational patrol from one of four regular Sabre Squadrons attached to 22 Special Air Service Regiment whose headquarters are at Bradbury Lines, Hereford, on the Welsh border with England. Travelling by foot over the border from Peshawar in Pakistan and carrying all their equipment with them, the SAS deep-penetration team was one of three that had made its way into Afghanistan during and immediately after the Soviet invasion of that country.

Primarily, their task was reconnaissance: to avoid detection, observe and report back. But, in addition to monitoring the true extent of the Soviet invasion, the SAS teams were also ordered to carry out clandestine combat evaluation of Soviet tactics, weapons and morale. One team had already crossed back safely over the Pakistan border taking with it a two-foot-square section of Titanium armour-plate together with the new optical battle sight from a Soviet T-72 tank. The sight had been stripped overnight from one of the earliest casualties of the invasion and whipped away into the mountains before the first Soviet recovery team, sensing ambush behind every bend in the road, had churned nervously over the horizon.

So absorbed was the radio operator in what he was doing, such was his confidence in the watchful sentry outside, that he merely glanced casually over his shoulder as Ratbag came into the cave. He nodded a greeting. 'Any problems?' he asked quietly. He wasn't expecting any. Ratbag had been down into the valleys twice in the last six days.

Ratbag shook his head, shivering violently now from the cold. Although the cave offered shelter after his hard climb it did not offer warmth: warmth came from heat and heat came from fire – and fire, from whatever source, could betray their presence. The best they could manage was an infrequent brew-up on one of the hexamene tommy-cookers. Wordlessly, the radio operator handed Ratbag his own thick black plastic mug of steaming sweet tea. Ratbag took it with frozen hands and slurped down the hot liquid gratefully. Then he thrust the mug towards the radio operator. 'Ta, boss. When are you sending?'

The radio operator peeled back a dirty sleeve and looked at his watch. 'Four hours' time.'

Ratbag nodded, crouched down and unfolded a map. It bore no markings; there were no ringed objectives, no straight lines that could tell hostile eyes where they were going or where they had come from. The map was always folded along its original creases and grid references were memorized, never written down – that too had once been a part of their training on the cold, rain-lashed Brecon Beacons selection course for entry into the SAS. Ninety-five per cent of all entrants failed the course. Now Ratbag tapped a twisting, winding ribbon of road with a dirty finger and the radio operator bent closer.

'I lay up here for the first six hours, three hundred metres from the road,' Ratbag explained quietly. 'Vehicles on the road the whole time heading south towards Kabul – here.' The finger moved across the map. 'Mostly soft-skinned vehicles, always in convoy and always with a couple of T-62s on transporters front and back to keep 'em all happy. Distance between vehicles was four metres or less, so they're not exactly worried about local air superiority or artillery fire lobbing in from the Afghan army.'

'What about APCs?'*

'A few. Mostly it was canvas-topped three-tonners with troops in the back. About thirty men to each vehicle.' Ratbag paused, remembering. Once again, nothing had been committed to paper. 'A civvy lorry ran off the road and the driver tried getting the army to help. Truck stopped right enough but no one could make out what the old guy was on about.'

'So they've been shipped in from outside, that what you're saying?'

Ratbag nodded. 'That's the way I read it, yeah.' He tapped his own stained and bearded cheek. 'Different bone structure. Ukrainians, Balts maybe.'

'What category?' asked the officer. Ratbag paused again, remembering the huddle of cold, miserable faces hunched into the back of the trucks, their weapons jammed upright between their knees.

'Second category,' he decided. 'No more than that. Replacements for Spearhead units once everything's buttoned down. Road-block types.'

'Weapons?'

'AK 47s. A few old SKS carbines.'

'What about the village?'

Ratbag paused, nodding thoughtfully. 'Yeah – the village. Picked up an interesting rumour there, boss. Word is there's been some sort of demonstration: banners, protest march – the whole works.'

'Banners and demos? Sounds a bit sophisticated,' said the officer doubtfully. 'Down this part of the world they still pour molten lead down your cock if you screw the neighbour's wife.'

'Not here, boss – over there.' He jerked a thumb outside.

* APC: Armoured Personnel Carrier.

'Across the border: Uzbekistan, inside the old Soviet mother-land. Some Moslem organized a demonstration about the invasion and the loss of the Tartar homelands in the Crimea. Got his face kicked in for his trouble and the whole thing was hushed up by the army; brushed under the carpet. It's generated a lot of hate.'

'What sort of hate?' asked the officer quietly, looking always for possibilities, for the soft, vulnerable underbelly.

Ratbag shrugged and scratched at his beard. 'Again, it's just talk, but some of the old boys up in the hills are already muttering about a possible *Jihad* – a holy war. The bloke who snuffed it was some kind of Imam, a holy leader. Knocking him off was like kicking sand in the face of the whole bleedin' Moslem world – and they're Moslems here too, don't forget. Quite a few of them are Uzbeks as well . . .'

There was silence as the officer thought for a moment. Then he took another glance at his watch and came swiftly to a decision: 'OK, Ratbag – I'll code that up with the rest. Someone in London might be interested.' He took a signal pad out of a pack and rummaged around in his clothes for a stump of pencil. 'Right, then – let's start breaking it down: how many T-62s did you see . . .?'

It took the young SAS officer forty-five minutes of careful, detailed cross-examination to debrief Ratbag before he was reasonably satisfied that he had extracted all he could from the man's stealthy reconnaissance. By then he had filled half a page of the signal pad with a short, cryptic military shorthand that must now be broken down still further to reduce to an absolute, brutal minimum the duration of his transmission to London: the longer he transmitted, the greater the chance of their position being plotted by triangulation and the greater, therefore, the risk of detection.

He now wrote the twenty-six letters of the alphabet in a single long column. Next he wrote the number nine – he had been born on the ninth day of the month – beside the letter A, the number ten beside the letter B and so on until he reached the letter R, which became twenty-six. He then began again, so that Z became the eighth number of this new alphabet. The code was taking shape.

He now swiftly turned words into numbers.

Next, he lifted the heavy skirts of his mountain clothes and tore a strip of adhesive tape away from the outside of his thigh. On the inside of the tape, wrapped in a tiny square of plastic, was the one-time code book. No larger than a book of stamps and about the same thickness, each page of highly inflammable cellulose nitrate film was divided into six vertical columns of ten five-figure blocks of numerals.

These numbers had been chosen at random and each book of numbers had only one duplicate.

Working methodically to a pre-arranged pattern, the officer now listed all the sets of numbers from the page of the code book he was using into a single column and added to these the numerical value he had just written beside each letter that was to be transmitted. It was this final total that would shortly be transmitted back to London.

Using his own copy of the same code, his control officer in Signals' Intelligence in London would compare the original book prefix against that which had been received from the operational transmitter. He would then subtract the difference and convert that back into a letter.

When the SAS officer had finished encoding the plain text of his message he would destroy his copy of the page in the code book. Control would do the same when he had decoded the signal and the code would cease to exist.

It was slow and it was complicated. But it was also safe and unbreakable. And that, ultimately, was all that mattered.

Two hours later the task was finished and the SAS officer began transmitting in rapid morse from a keyboard strapped to his knee.

His radio signal had a range of just over one thousand miles. It was first picked up by the waiting, bristling array of aerials on the wheelhouse roof of a rust-covered, deep-water trawler fishing innocently in international waters in the Gulf of Oman. From there it was transmitted back to Britain where it was plucked out of the sky by the BBC's Receiving Station at Crowsley Park, turned into a meaningless jumble of holes on a half-inch roll of punch-tape and then fed directly to the headquarters of the BBC's Monitoring Service at Caversham Park above the Thames near Reading.

*

A little over three hours later there was a discreet tap on the door of George Vickers' office overlooking Downing Street. Vickers was a Deputy Secretary at the Foreign Office. Tall, conscientious, in his mid-sixties and coming up for retirement, George Vickers was also worked off his feet.

Somewhere amid the diplomatic urgency and near-chaos, the flurry of phone calls, ministerial briefings, transatlantic cables and embassy dispatches that had followed in the wake of the Soviet invasion, Vickers' body had forgotten that it needed a minimum of six hours sleep each night. The pressure had built remorselessly until now it seemed that the Foreign Office Emergency Unit had developed a destructive momentum of its own. Half an hour ago Vickers had at last managed to slip away from the Unit to hack into the backlog of more pedestrian traffic that had built up on his own desk during the emergency. And now there was this knock on his door.

'Come in,' called out Vickers without glancing up from his papers.

The door opened and a young man came briskly into the office, his every move exuding an air of quiet, purposeful efficiency.

It was Stephen Rowley.

'Ah, Stephen –' Vickers reached across his desk for a green file and held it up. 'This came in prefixed "Most Immediate" from the chaps in Defence. Have a glance at it and see it goes over to the Emergency Unit right away, will you?'

'Certainly, sir.' Rowley took the file, scrawled his own initials across the 'Eyes To View' panel and flicked the folder open.

The rumour of nationalist unrest inside the Soviet Union, of demonstration and suppression in far-off Uzbekistan, ran to nine cautious, speculative lines in the Foreign Office daily internal Intelligence summary. Rowley glanced up, his inner secret thoughts hidden behind a pleasant smile. Lord Porterfield would want to see this as soon as possible.

'Right then, sir.' He turned on his heel and the door closed silently behind him.

# : 6 :

'Order! . . . Order!' called the bewigged Speaker seated behind the Dispatch Box in the House of Commons as the crowded Opposition benches to his right erupted once more into shouts and hoots of derision.

'Mr Speaker –' The Rt Hon. Ashley Parsons MP, Secretary of State, whirled towards the Speaker's chair, one hand held out as though for support. 'If the Honourable Gentleman would have the common courtesy to permit a Minister of the Crown to finish what he –' a fresh bout of jeering drowned his words – 'he would readily see that Her Majesty's Government has not the slightest intention of abandoning its obligations to the international community. Far from it. The Soviet invasion of –'

'Get on with it, Minister!' roared a Labour back-bencher from the north of England with a reputation for blunt speaking. 'By the time you get to the point they'll be in the Persian Gulf!' This was greeted by another roar of laughter as even the Prime Minister began to shift restlessly in her seat.

Lord Porterfield watched from the gallery with a growing sense of dismay as he leant forward against the polished handrail with knuckles that were white with outrage. Years ago he had sat here in this same seat and listened to Gaitskell, Macmillan, even Churchill, as they reached out and stilled the chamber with the power of their oratory, the strength of their characters and the force of their convictions. And today? Today a senior Minister of the Crown had his words drowned by laughter.

'Lord Porterfield?' A respectful voice at his elbow interrupted his moody thoughts and he twisted round to find one of the uniformed serjeants-at-arms bent attentively at his side.

'Yes? What is it?'

'Gentleman waiting outside to speak to you, my Lord,' said the official, raising his voice slightly above the rising clamour on the floor below. 'A Mr Rowley – from the Foreign Office.'

Lord Porterfield nodded and rose to his feet, not unwilling to be drawn away from the mauling. He followed the serjeant up the polished stairs and out through the ancient, glass-panelled doors into the corridor beyond. 'This way, my Lord.'

He found Stephen Rowley waiting for him at the bottom of the staircase leading to the Members' chambers.

'Stephen, m'boy! Delighted to see you,' greeted Lord Porterfield warmly as he took Rowley's arm and steered him round so they could walk together down the deserted, marble-floored corridor.

'I hope I haven't picked an awkward moment,' began Rowley. Lord Porterfield shook his head as they went on slowly together, their heels ringing in unison on polished marble.

'Not at all.' Lord Porterfield waved a dismissive hand towards the House. 'Not a damn' thing of any consequence, I assure you.' He grimaced and lowered himself slowly into an alcove seat. 'Now then – what's all this about?' Rowley sat down beside him, took a folded sheet of paper out of his breast pocket and glanced casually up and down the corridor.

'You asked me to keep you informed if there were any developments that might have any bearing upon Soviet internal stability,' reminded Rowley.

Lord Porterfield grunted. 'I remember.'

'This came in at lunchtime from the Ministry of Defence.' Rowley handed him the sheet of paper and Lord Porterfield read the message carefully. He looked up.

'Vickers has seen this, I take it?'

'Yes, sir. He has.'

'What was his reaction?'

'Well, sir.' Rowley paused, reflecting carefully before committing himself to a reply that might compromise his own reputation. Officially, at least, he still worked for George Vickers and the Foreign Office, not Lord Porterfield. 'I rather gathered he had other things on his mind.'

'Such as?'

'Brussels, I should imagine: the Council of Ministers, the Olympic boycott.' Lord Porterfield nodded and there was a brief silence. 'So – this is all we have,' mused Lord Porterfield at length, tapping a finger against his notecase. 'One unconfirmed report about a possible nationalist demonstration in Uzbekistan. Nothing more about the rumoured death of this Islamic leader? No idea who he might have been?'

'I'm afraid not, no, sir.'

'Pity. I see. Thank you, Stephen.' Rowley nodded agreeably and rose to leave. As he buttoned his jacket – 'Oh, Stephen, just a couple of other things before you go.'

'Sir?'

'I'd like you to have a discreet dig around Reference Section if you will: update this Tartar–Uzbek business, put it in current context. I'd like it by the morning. Think you could manage that?'

'Certainly, sir,' decided Rowley with a bright smile. It would mean cancelling dinner and whatever might follow with that new clerical assistant in Cyphers but Stephen Rowley had never had any trouble selecting priorities. Not when his own advancement was at stake. Now he decided he might even risk a joke: 'Usual terms and conditions, sir?'

'Terms and conditions? What terms and conditions?' demanded Lord Porterfield suspiciously, looking up with eyes that were suddenly dark and cold and empty so that for one chilling moment Rowley thought he might have overstepped the bounds of permissible familiarity. And wrecked everything.

'It's . . . it's to go through the Department, I meant, sir: through George Vickers' Department.'

Lord Porterfield inclined his head gravely. 'I see what you mean, Stephen.' When he looked up his eyes were friendly once more. 'But of course,' he chided gently, 'I am retired, am I not? A spent force. Of course it must go through Vickers' Department.' He paused. 'Perhaps you would meet me for breakfast at the Hotel Bristol, Berkeley Square? Shall we say eight o'clock?'

'Er . . . yes, yes of course, sir.' Bloody hell. He'd be up most of the night. 'Eight o'clock.'

'Good man. And Stephen . . .'

Rowley turned. 'Sir?'

'What about those two names I gave you – Tillet and Tyschen?'

Rowley shook his head. 'Nothing as yet, I'm afraid, sir. CRO is clearing a lot of the undergrowth but it'll still take a couple of days. Tillet's a popular name.'

Lord Porterfield grunted. 'What about Tyschen? There can't be too many Tyschens knocking about the British Isles.'

'Nothing, I'm afraid, sir. Not so much as a whiff.' He hesitated. 'He . . . he could perhaps have died, sir . . .'

Lord Porterfield shook his head emphatically. 'Don't you believe it, Stephen. They're still alive somewhere, the pair of 'em. You're to keep looking, understand? Keep looking.'

Gordon Hallam was awake before dawn the next morning. It was the day of the funeral. He lay in bed for some time, hands linked behind his head as he gazed up at the ceiling of his father's spare bedroom in Sussex and listened to the rain as it lashed against the closed windows.

Gordon had slept badly, twisting and turning in the crumpled sheets as his mind roamed restlessly in that worried, twilight limbo between sleep and true wakefulness, worrying over the order of service and about the sombre domestic details that accompanied this last act of filial duty. He had been thinking, too, about the medal: the O B E. Since its discovery the mystery surrounding its promulgation had come to symbolize in his own mind a wider ignorance that embraced most of his father's life: you know nothing about me, the medal seemed to accuse – thus you know nothing about your father. Nothing!

There was a sudden sound downstairs as Gordon heard the rattle of the letter-box and the clip of the postman's shoes as he went away back down the path. Gordon turned on the bedside light, threw back the covers and swung his feet to the floor. He went downstairs, walked to the end of the hallway and bent down. He picked up a couple of circulars and a colourful postcard from Switzerland, reminding himself as he did so that the postman was someone else who would have to be told, notified about the death of the occupant at number 14. Gordon went through into the kitchen, plugged in the kettle and glanced idly at the back of the postcard.

It was from somewhere called Zug, postmarked 2 January and read simply: 'What price Apostle now? Trust all is well with you. Your old friend and comrade, Mark.'

Gordon tossed the postcard down on the kitchen worktop and yawned . . .

'More bacon, sir?' asked the elderly waiter attentively, his back bent into a permanent stoop. Stephen Rowley nodded. 'Yes, please.' When the waiter had moved away Stephen Rowley glanced up from his plate of bacon and eggs, kidneys, sauté potatoes, mushrooms and sausages to see Lord Porterfield nodding approvingly.

'Never does to skip breakfast, Stephen. Miss any other meal you like but never breakfast. Court martial offence in the services, did you know that?'

Rowley shook his head. 'No, sir. I didn't know that.'

They made little patterns of small-talk around the grapefruit segments and the fragrant waftings of freshly-brewed coffee. Only when the plates had been removed, the linen brushed free of crumbs and their coffee cups replenished did Porterfield move obliquely towards the true reason for this meeting.

'You will remember, Stephen, that I asked you to retrieve a certain file for me from the Public Record Office?'

Rowley nodded, coffee cup half-way to his lips. 'The Apostle file. Yes, sir. I remember it quite clearly.'

Lord Porterfield nodded. 'Indeed.' Although the nearest table was three paces away and their voices were hidden beneath the genteel clatter of cutlery and the casual turning of the morning's newspapers, Lord Porterfield still chose to lower his voice. 'I would be grateful if you would do something for me. Regarding the same business.'

'Without telling George Vickers, I take it?'

Lord Porterfield nodded. 'Without telling George Vickers.' He picked up a silver teaspoon and studied it intently. 'The whole Apostle business is still . . . live. Dangerous. It requires very special handling. One of those . . . involved during the war died in an accident just recently.' He placed the teaspoon carefully beside his saucer and glanced up. 'He is being buried today, as a matter of fact. Down in Sussex.' Rowley took another sip of coffee and wondered where the hell Lord Porterfield was leading him. 'Naturally, now that he is dead, his relatives will be sorting through his papers, going through his diaries. That sort of thing.'

'And you think he might have left notes, mentioned Apostle in some way?'

Lord Porterfield nodded carefully. 'It is a possibility, certainly. Which could prove . . . embarrassing. If there were questions.'

'And the man's wife – what about her? Wouldn't she know anything about it?'

'She died some years ago. He has been living alone since that time.' He slid a folded slip of paper across the table. 'At this address.' Rowley took the piece of paper and glanced at the address as Lord Porterfield went on, 'Ordinarily, of course, I would simply place this in the hands of Five – perhaps even the police. But this calls for a little extra . . . ah . . . discretion. I should much prefer it if we were to handle it ourselves.'

'You would like me to go down to Sussex, I take it?'

'I would consider it a personal favour. No one else would be involved, d'you see?'

'But you said just now the house would be empty –'

Lord Porterfield nodded patiently. 'Precisely so.' There was a little silence as understanding passed between them. 'If that presents you with any . . . problems, Stephen, perhaps it would be as well if you told me now.'

Rowley shook his head. 'No, sir. That doesn't present any problems. None at all.'

Lord Porterfield smiled. 'Good. Excellent.'

Stephen Rowley felt in his inside coat pocket and drew out a sealed, bulky envelope. 'The information you asked for, sir.' He held it out but the older man shook his head and sat back in his seat.

'Impressions first, Stephen. Let me know what you make of it. I can read the details for myself later.'

Rowley slid a thumb under the back flap and tore it open. He extracted half a dozen sheets of paper, smoothed them out and looked up. 'That demonstration in Uzbekistan, sir: I looked first of all for similar recorded disturbances, demonstrations inside the Soviet Union. Since the Opera House fire in Tbilisi, Georgia, in 1973, we have recorded a further sixty-seven separate incidents, nineteen of which resulted in loss of life. And the nearer we come to the present day, the more frequent those incidents become.' He glanced up from his notes. 'There may well have been more, of course. These are only the ones our embassy and trade people got to hear about.' He paused. 'None of those incidents received more than a paragraph or two in the papers over here. I've got the cuttings if you want them.' He turned over a page carefully. 'Of the fifteen Federated Republics brought into the Soviet fold out of the "Prison of the Peoples" as Lenin liked to call the empire of the Tsars, Georgia appears to have been the most . . . ah . . . insubordinate, although Armenia, Lithuania and lately even the Ukraine have been getting . . . restless.'

'But not Uzbekistan, is that what you're telling me?'

Rowley nodded. 'Not Uzbekistan. Until now – hardly a ripple, although all the "elements of combustion", if I might call them that, appear to be present. It's conceivable, I suppose, that what that SAS team stumbled upon was the beginnings of some sort of wider, concerted campaign of protest: the lighting of the fuse, as it were.'

'What makes you think that?'

'Well, sir –' Rowley leant forward. 'It's another Moslem country, just like Afghanistan – that's the first thing. It's got a largely rural population sixty-five per cent of whom are Uzbeks, twelve per cent are Russian and about five per cent are Tartar, exiled to Uzbekistan from the Crimea by Joe Stalin back in 1946. They're still trying to get home to the Crimea – that's what those banners were about.'

'*Exiled*, you say?'

'Yes, sir,' replied Rowley readily, warming to his subject. 'The Crimea Tartar homelands were occcupied by the Nazis until April 1944, after which Stalin declared the Tartars a "collaborator nation" and exiled the entire population to central Asia, the Urals and Siberia. The next year a decree announced the Crimean Republic had ceased to exist. It had been eliminated. Thousands of Russian and Ukrainian colonists arrived to settle the country in the Tartars' place – Tartars who had been there, farmed the land, fought for it, died for it, since the time of Genghis Khan.

'Six other nations were also branded with the same slur of treason, of collective national guilt. They too lived in exile until 1956 when Khruschev made reparations, listed the policy of forcible exile among Stalin's crimes and permitted all the exiled peoples to return to their homelands, the past forgiven and forgotten.' Rowley paused and then added softly, 'Only someone forgot to put the Crimean Tartars on the list: they're still waiting to go home. And they're getting impatient: deputations to Moscow, petitions signed by virtually the entire Tartar population – they all get nowhere. So – if the Tartars in Uzbekistan aren't exactly first in line to sing the praises of Mother Russia, you can understand their point of view.' He sat back. 'That's the first consideration, sir: the homeland issue. There are others, but perhaps you would prefer it if –'

'Please – continue. I find this most informative,' urged Lord Porterfield from across the breakfast table as Rowley turned another page.

'Secondly – religion: religion coupled to birthrate. Most Uzbeks – and Tartars, and Afghans, come to that – are Sunni Moslems. Followers of "The Path", of tradition. And just recently the Moslem birthrate has shot up from twenty-four to thirty-five millions at a time when, for the first time since the creation of the Soviet Union, the number of *Russians* has begun to decline.'

Lord Porterfield stirred in his chair. 'But it will be twenty, thirty years before such a trend begins to have any significant effect upon –'

'Sir, with respect, every Soviet policy from the Revolution onwards has been marked by a . . . by an underestimation of the nationalities problem. It has always been seen as a legacy from the past, rather than a problem that is growing. Now. Today.' He paused again, searching for the right tools to hammer home the message. 'We're talking about control, sir, control from the centre. From Moscow. To begin with, certainly, Moscow was the natural hub of empire: it had the population, the intellectual superiority, the communications, the means of production. But not any more. Modernization has changed all that: modernization, population growth, national awareness, religious revival. The minorities are growing stronger, sir. They're gaining confidence, becoming more and more restless.' He held up both hands, one on either side of his body like a pair of scales. 'The Moscow balancing act, sir: it's not going to be there forever.'

# : 7 :

The canvas-covered lorry paused beneath the cluster of bright arc lights at the main gate. The barriers swung up, the lorry lurched forward and then braked to a sudden halt.

Inside the cold, dark interior the recruits glanced at one another and exchanged nervous grins, sensing in that final, convulsive shudder that they had reached the Regimental Depot that was home to the 117th Motor Rifle Battalion and thus home now to them too. For the next two years.

'Out!' ordered a harsh new voice. 'Out! Come on! Let's have a look at you!' A heavy fist banged against the metal side of the lorry, the tailboard went down with a sudden crash and Yuri, Nikolai and the other recruits climbed down stiffly to glance around with a mixture of awe and apprehension at their surroundings.

The lorry that had brought them these last few kilometres from the station had come to a halt on the edge of the biggest parade ground Yuri or any of the others had ever seen. It stretched away vastly into the dusk and turned the low, wooden, single-storey barracks that flanked it on three sides into insignificant matchwood toys. 'Bloody hell,' muttered Nikolai, looking round as the other recruits tumbled down around him in a welter of kitbags and cardboard suitcases. 'We're going to love it here, I can see that already. Love it to bloody pieces.' He looked down at Yuri and grinned.

It was three days since their train had pulled out of the station with much blowing of whistles and fanfares from the military band as wives, mothers and girlfriends, veterans and Party officials waved their young men off to two years' compulsory military service.

That honeymoon lasted exactly six minutes. Then the train pulled in to a drab siding on the industrial outskirts of the town and the men were ordered out onto the platform.

And this time there wasn't a garland, band or pretty girl in sight.

They were herded together, pushed roughly into line like so many cattle and marched away to a nondescript draughty barracks where they spent the next two days being processed, kitted out and posted on to a score of different units scattered across the length and breadth of the Soviet Union: the lights would go on in the middle of the night, an NCO would bawl out a list of names and half a dozen recruits would gather up their kit, stumble sleepily to the door and vanish into the night. Such diaspora is deliberate Soviet policy for, among much else, the Soviet Army acts as a shock absorber for dissent between the dangerous, volatile ages of eighteen and twenty. Within a matter of hours two hundred young Moslems from Uzbekistan would find themselves dispersed among units that were both dominated and commanded by Russians.

Thus it was that Nikolai Samlar, Yuri Rashidov and a dozen others found themselves stumbling down the same icy road, their kitbags balanced precariously on their shoulders, heavy suitcases biting into numb hands as they hurried back to the station.

They were on that train for twenty-seven hours during which time they stopped eight times to pick up more recruits – a journey of such cramped, bone-aching misery as they crawled westwards across the snowbound countryside that the garlands and the speeches, the fanfares and the brass bands seemed little more than a figment of imagination from another world impossibly far away. Disjointed sleep had been the only refuge.

Now Yuri turned as, across the parade ground, a platoon of helmeted, uniformed soldiers doubled steadily towards them, each man in step with his comrades, an AK 47 assault rifle held rigidly across his chest. As they doubled past, the squad leader barked an order and twenty heads whipped across on 'Eyes left' and twenty throats roared out the traditional, derisive greeting shouted down the years from trained soldiers to recruits.

'What was that?' demanded Yuri anxiously as the squad doubled past. The soldiers had shouted in Russian and Yuri had only caught half of it. Nikolai turned from watching them disappear around the side of one of the barrack huts and clapped his new-found friend gently on the shoulder.

'They said we'll be sorry.'

'Right – pay attention,' barked a voice from the edge of the parade ground. The recruits fell silent, straightening up and giving their undivided attention to a short, stocky NCO with a hard, lean face who glared at them now from beneath the polished visor of his cap. 'Behind me there' – he gestured briefly over his shoulder – 'is hut 544. As from this moment, until you take the Military Oath upon completion of the Course of the New Soldier and are assigned to your operational companies, that is *your* hut, understand? Hut 544. When I give the command you are to pick up all this ... this mess' – he gestured disparagingly at the mountain of kit spilling onto the parade ground – 'get over there and sort yourselves out. One bunk to each man' – a finger stabbed out towards a pair of dark-haired Estonians standing together by the lorry – 'and no sharing! If we find any of you bumming up together you'll be wishing you'd had it cut off at birth, understand?' The two Estonians grinned nervously and moved apart. 'Right. Move!'

They moved. Twenty-four recruits sprang at the mountain of suitcases and kitbags and straggled across the parade ground towards hut 544.

Forty years earlier the barracks had been built on the outskirts of the Ukrainian mining town of Sambor to provide accommodation for four hundred members of Hitler's SS. Then the camp had been overrun, the war had ended and the barracks had been taken over by successive units of the Red Army. The partitions and lockers had been torn down and the furniture removed so that now one hundred men slept in quarters designed to hold thirty. Beside each bunk with its brick-hard mattress was a low wooden stool. On each stool, neatly folded, would lie the soldier's working uniform. There was a shower block where the men bathed by squads once a week and a locked arms' cache for rifles at the end of the corridor.

Each hut had four windows – four small windows a boy couldn't crawl through set high up on the wall to provide fresh air and ventilation for one hundred healthy young men. The smell at night as men slept side by side with less than a metre between one bed and the next was unpleasant enough, they would discover, even in winter. In summer, with the tiny windows wedged open and the temperature somewhere up in the eighties, the stench of stale sweat and closely-packed, unwashed bodies would rise to levels of such gagging vileness that sleep would be impossible for all but the senior NCO who slept alone in a tiny wooden-walled cubicle at the end of each hut.

The recruits clattered up the wooden steps, pushed open the door and looked with dismay at their quarters. The best positions – those beneath the windows or by the doors – had been taken already by some earlier intake. Then the men at the back pressed forward and the recruits spilled into the long hut, racing one another for the best of those places that were left. Nikolai Samlar grabbed one half-way down on the left, Yuri settled for one opposite.

'Er . . . excuse me . . .' Yuri turned to see a thin awkward looking boy of his own age standing hesitantly in the aisle, kitbag and suitcase trailing on the floor behind him. 'Is that . . . is that one taken?' He indicated the bed on Yuri's left.

'Doesn't look like it – help yourself,' said Yuri off-handedly. Already in the few short days they had been together he had privately marked the boy down as a weakling, a suspect link in whatever bonds of friendship he might form with those who had been drafted with him.

'Thank you. Thank you very much.' Yuri shrugged and began tugging at the knot fastening the neck of his kitbag. When he glanced around again it was to see Private Tinrass place a photograph in a cardboard frame almost tenderly on the stool beside his bed: a middle-aged man and woman in formal best staring severely into the camera. It was a photograph that spoke of poverty and pride, destitution and religious tradition. Tinrass glanced round, saw Yuri watching and gestured at the photograph apologetically. 'My . . . my parents,' he admitted, straightening up and thrusting his hand forward. 'My name is Tinrass, Georgi Tinrass. From Bukhara. And you?'

'Rashidov. Yuri Rashidov,' said Yuri, shaking hands reluctantly.

Tinrass smiled again nervously. 'I hope we –'

'QUIET! STAND STILL!' The voice lashed out across the long rows of beds and every other voice fell instantly silent. 'BY YOUR BEDS – NOW!' The recruits leapt to do as they were ordered and stood at rigid attention as they waited for this new threat to identify itself. There was complete silence. Then the silence was broken by the measured thud of steel-shod boots coming down the aisle between the rows of young faces so that each recruit in turn had a brief glimpse of the face beneath the obligatory stiff-peaked cap with its five-pointed red star: a face that was thin and hard and without weakness of any kind.

'Listen to me – AS YOU WERE! – I said listen, didn't I? Not look – face your front! My name is Sergeant Barak. I am your squad leader. That means, *salagi*, that for the rest of your time here, I am the most important person IN YOUR LIFE!' He paused and then added softly, 'You will forget that at your peril, I promise you.' He picked up a pair of civilian shoes, held them at arm's length and then dropped them contemptuously on the floor. 'Stores,' he said simply. 'Now – pay attention. As from this moment several things will change. One: whenever I come into this hut, the first man to see me will call the rest of the squad to attention – I don't care if you're having a shit, I don't care if it's four o'clock in the fucking morning – you will come to attention! Clear?' There was silence. 'CLEAR?'

'Yes, Sergeant,' came the reply in half a dozen different dialects and languages.

Sergeant Barak glared around the hut. 'Two: as from now you will speak only Russian in the performance of your military duties. Whenever I ask a question, you will reply: "Yes, Comrade Sergeant!" In Russian. Is that clear?'

'Yes, Comrade Sergeant!' they chorused dutifully.

Sergeant Barak walked slowly down the centre of the silent hut, stopped in front of Private Tinrass's bed and picked up a short length of carpet. 'Stores,' he announced briefly, letting it fall haphazardly onto the floor and moving on.

Across the aisle Nikolai watched this humiliation with mounting anger. Go on, he urged Tinrass silently, stand up to the bastard . . .

'But . . .' began Tinrass.

Sergeant Barak stopped theatrically in mid-stride and turned. 'What?' he snapped.

Tinrass swallowed nervously. 'I . . . I am a Moslem, Comrade Sergeant – a Sunni Moslem. That is my . . . my *jay-nimaz* . . .'

Sergeant Barak affected to consider this possibility, then – 'I don't care if you're Mohammad himself, Private Tinrass. That thing goes into stores.' He turned to face the other recruits. 'And the same goes for the rest of your floor-kissers.' He turned on his heel and was thus staring straight across the aisle as Nikolai Samlar came to attention.

'Comrade Sergeant!'

'What is it?'

'Begging the Sergeant's pardon, but I was told that we would be permitted to observe religious traditions while we were in the army.'

'Religious traditions? What religious traditions?'

'The . . . the praying, certainly. *Jay-nimaz* are very important to us, Comrade Sergeant. An article of our faith . . .'

'So you're another one, are you?' demanded Sergeant Barak, face now inches away from that of Nikolai.

'Comrade Sergeant?'

'Another Moslem. Another fucking Moslem.'

Nikolai drew himself up a little taller so that he was actually looking down at the Sergeant. 'I am a Believer, yes, Comrade Sergeant. I was only pointing out what is permitted under the Statutes –'

'Statutes? What do you know about fucking Statutes?' demanded Sergeant Barak, his eyes narrowing with suspicion and the first dawning awareness that this one could be different. This one could be dangerous . . .

'I know only that we are permitted our prayers. And our *jay-nimaz*.' There was an electric silence.

'Name?' demanded Barak finally.

'Samlar, N., 95986455, Comrade Sergeant!' snapped Nikolai.

Sergeant Barak nodded pensively. 'I shall remember, Samlar, believe it. I shall remember your name.'


In Sussex, icy rain sliced down from a leaden sky.

It stung the pinched, averted faces of the pallbearers as they carried their swaying burden out of the little Norman church, the coffin gleaming wetly on their shoulders as they turned slowly down the gravel path towards the freshly-dug grave beside the western wall of the churchyard. Old men soon to make their own final journey upon someone else's shoulders, the pallbearers faltered and for one ghastly moment Gordon thought his father's coffin was going to slide off their shoulders, burst open at their feet. Then they paused, steadied their burden and set off again in the wake of the priest whose white surplice floated ahead of them through the winter graveyard, a splash of piety among the blacks and greys of mourning as the cortège moved between the rows of lichen-covered headstones and marble crosses.

There were few mourners: Gordon and Rachel, Gordon uncomfortable and awkward in suit, collar and tie, sharing the same umbrella as they followed directly behind the coffin. Behind them, Gordon's aunt, his father's only sister, who had made the long train journey down from Newcastle out of a sense of guilt tinged with duty as she paid her last respects to a brother she had not seen or spoken to for more than three years. Behind her, Mr and Mrs Hopkirk, Walter Hallam's neighbours. And that was all.

They arrived at the graveside, a dark, yawning hole in the wet earth, the mound of dug soil covered by a garish sheet of green plastic grass as the elderly priest wiped the rain off his spectacles and opened his prayer book at a well-worn page. Then he lifted his head and glanced up at the dark clouds.

'Man that is born of woman hath but a short time to live,' he intoned automatically as the pallbearers slipped their canvas lowering straps into place with practised ease, took the strain and swung the coffin out over the hole. 'He cometh up and is cut down like a flower; he fleeth as it were a shadow and never continueth in one stay. In the midst of life we are in death . . .'

The road was empty. Stephen Rowley had parked the Rover in the lane and walked the two hundred yards to the house. Now he glanced from side to side and pushed open the garden gate. He went up the path and rang the front door bell, a few words of apology already rehearsed in his mind. They were not needed, for there was no reply. He rang again and waited, just to be sure. Then he moved round to the side window, leant across the flower-bed and pressed a gloved hand against the glass. He was looking through into the sitting-room. Sofa and chairs had been pushed back against one wall and he could see a table set with plates of food that had been draped with clean tea towels. Bottles and glasses stood on a tray near by. But there was no one in sight. Feet swishing wetly through the long grass, Rowley moved towards the rear of the property, the houses on either side hidden behind a line of thick hedge. Down the path towards the back door. It was unlocked.

Rowley hesitated, conscious perhaps for the first time that he was about to step over the dividing line between curiosity and trespass. He looked at his watch. The funeral service had been scheduled to start at eleven o'clock – he had found that out by a telephone call to the verger on the way down from London. It was now eleven fifteen. The food and drink suggested the mourners were going to return here after the service – but who had gone to such trouble, laid out the food, bought the drinks? Lord Porterfield had not warned him to expect this.

So what? he asked himself suddenly. What are you going to do about it? Go back empty-handed with nothing accomplished? Tell him you hadn't the nerve? Rowley was not accustomed to failure. He glanced over his shoulder, turned the handle and slipped inside. The door closed quietly behind him.

Informant, trespasser, burglar: for Lord Porterfield, Stephen Rowley had become all three. He turned and walked quietly through into the hallway, conscious of the sound of his own nervous breathing. Ten minutes, that was all, he promised himself. Just ten minutes inside. He came to the end of the narrow hallway and began to climb the stairs . . .

'. . . blessed are the dead which lie in the Lord. Even so, saith the Spirit, for they rest from their labours.' The priest glanced up from his prayer book. 'Lord, have mercy upon us.'

'Christ, have mercy upon us,' came the reply, the thin voices lost against a sudden gust of rain-laden wind.

There was a half-packed holdall lying open on the bed. Rowley stood over it for a moment, looking down at the untidy jumble of clothes and toilet things that lay inside the lid. He held up a red sweat shirt: these were things that belonged to a younger man; they might almost have belonged to himself. He picked up a small leather photograph wallet and turned it over. A man and a woman stood together outside a stone-walled cottage somewhere, the woman smiling up at the camera with an arm around the man's waist. They looked happy, comfortable together. Peering closer, Rowley could just make out the gleam of a wedding ring on the woman's finger. He slipped the photograph back in the holdall and eased a paperback out of one of the pockets. He flicked through the pages and looked at the flyleaf: Gordon W. Hallam.

Rowley tapped the book thoughtfully against the palm of his hand and replaced it carefully where he had found it. Then he crossed to the chest and pulled open one of the drawers. It was empty. So too was the wardrobe: the dead man's clothes had been removed. He turned and went downstairs. Five minutes gone, five left. He went into the sitting-room and made straight for the desk. Folding back the top he began sifting carefully through the papers and documents, searching for references to Apostle. But there was nothing of any consequence: a few family photograph albums, bills and household papers. The man had been decorated, though. Rowley found the papers of promulgation in a thick envelope one drawer up from the bottom of the desk. He made a brief note of the details but found nothing else of interest: no memoirs, no angry letters, no diaries about wartime adventure, nothing about Apostle. Lord Porterfield would be relieved.

Now Rowley looked at his watch. Right. That was it. Time to be gone. He rearranged the papers carefully and looked around the room, forcing himself not to hurry, to take his time, make sure nothing was overlooked.

Satisfied at last, he went into the empty hall and back into the kitchen.

It was then that he saw the postcard from Zug lying pinned beneath the sugar caddy. He turned it over idly and the sound of his own heart was suddenly very loud in his ears. It was addressed to Walter Hallam and read: 'What price Apostle now? Trust all is well with you. Your old friend and comrade, Mark.'

After a moment's hesitation Rowley slipped the postcard into a pocket and let himself quietly out by the back door.

★

'Another scotch, Mr Hopkirk?' offered Gordon politely, playing dutiful host in his father's house after the funeral.

Hopkirk shook his head. 'Thank you, no, Mr Hallam. We must be getting along in a moment, mustn't we, dear?'

'Oh yes. Yes, I'm afraid so,' agreed Mrs Hopkirk stoutly, standing loyally behind her husband as she treated Gordon to a tight little smile.

'Of course. I understand.' They want to get away, thought Gordon; can't wait. He didn't blame them, for they made a subdued, awkward little group: Gordon and Rachel, the Hopkirks and Walter Hallam's sister, all drawn together by the one man who could not be with them as they picked away at the plates of sandwiches and took cautious little sips of scotch and sherry.

Gordon poured himself another hefty drink and knocked back half the spirit at one gulp, welcoming the sudden fire as the alcohol burnt its way down to his guts and soaked up the damp chill depression of the graveyard. He suddenly caught a mental snapshot of bored labourers shovelling the wet earth onto his father's coffin. Thump, thump, thump as they buried him underground. Gordon shut his eyes and then turned suddenly towards Hopkirk.

'Tell me, how well did you know my father?'

Hopkirk looked a little startled. 'Well now; I'd like to think I knew him very well. We chatted together over a fair number of years as I think I may have mentioned to you at the . . . er . . . at the . . . er . . . inquest. Naturally, we used to have the odd drink together, that sort of thing. Not on a regular basis, you understand, just every once in a while, when the mood suited. Used to pop off down to the pub there.' He gestured vaguely towards the main road. 'I don't know . . . I suppose, living alone, he sometimes just wanted to get out, have a bit of a chat. When he did, well' – he shrugged – 'I was only too happy to oblige, frankly. Splendid fellow, your father. Absolutely first class.'

'Thank you. You served in the war, I take it?'

'What? Yes, yes I did, as a matter of fact.' He drew himself up a little straighter so that Gordon could almost see the swagger stick tucked under the armpit. 'Royal Armoured Corps, First Armoured Div. Kidney Ridge and all that nonsense.'

'Freddie was a Desert Rat,' supplied Mrs Hopkirk proudly.

Gordon nodded. Then he held up his father's medal on its strip of pink ribbon with the grey stripe running down the centre. 'I found this in the desk over there,' he said, spinning the medal round so that Hopkirk could see his father's initials engraved on the back. 'Did he ever mention it to you?'

Hopkirk took the medal and examined it carefully. 'Haven't seen one of these in years,' he murmured.

'It's the Order of –'

'Oh, I know what it is, all right,' interrupted Hopkirk, nodding vigorously. 'It's the OBE, Military Division – see this here?' He pointed at the grey stripe in the centre and at the edges. 'That's a mite unusual, I must say.'

'Is it? I didn't know that.'

Hopkirk smiled apologetically. 'Medals used to be a bit of a hobby of mine. And you say you found this here? In your father's desk?'

Gordon nodded. 'That's right, yes. Along with all the other bits and pieces: the certificate and so forth.'

Hopkirk shook his head, obviously puzzled. 'Can't understand it. Unless I'm making an absolute ass of myself, Mr Hallam, this was the sort of medal they gave to those undercover chappies. You know: for services rendered.'

'And my father never mentioned it? Chatted about the war?'

Hopkirk shook his head. 'Sorry, old man. Not a dicky bird.'

# : 8 :

'– Could you look this way, Minister? That's it – super.' The face of the Prime Minister's most trusted Cabinet member turned obligingly as the motor-driven cameras whirred away busily in the afternoon sunshine: 'This way, sir. Fine.' Click. Click.

It was the Right Honourable Ashley Parsons MP's sixtieth birthday. Fleet Street had descended upon his country house on the outskirts of Leatherhead to catch the Minister in a moment of carefully-staged informality. It would make a reassuring picture for the nation: Secretary of State in thick-knit sweater; Guernsey man surrounded by devoted family against a backdrop of rolling lawns and an imposing, seven-bedroomed Surrey mansion.

Ashley Parsons turned and his face broke into a showman's smile of greeting as he raised a hand towards his attractive wife. 'Here she comes, gentlemen – my administering angel!' The photographers turned as, all smiles, Alison Parsons came down the flagged pathway towards them, a silver tray bearing champagne and glasses balanced in her hands Five years ago she would have postponed the celebrations until the photographers had gone. Today, there was a glass for every single pressman as well. She too had learned the subtle ground-rules that must accompany serious political ambition.

Intent only upon their free drinks, not one of the photographers so much as glanced towards the house. Even if they had, it is unlikely they would have noticed the solitary figure standing beside the drawing-room curtains watching them silently as he waited for the owner of the house.

Presently a telephone began to ring and a moment later a young housemaid entered the drawing-room with a deferential knock. 'Excuse me, my Lord, there's a telephone call for you.'

Lord Porterfield followed the maid into the spacious hall and lifted the receiver. 'Yes?'

'Stephen Rowley here, sir. I'm in a public call box outside the office.'

Lord Porterfield glanced at the face of the grandfather clock beside him. It was shortly after 2 p.m. 'Give me the number,' he instructed shortly. 'I'll call you straight back.' He did so.

'Sorry about that, sir. I thought it best if I used an outside line.'

'You've been down to Sussex, I take it?'

'Yes, sir. Got back half an hour ago.'

'Everything go off all right?'

'I think so, yes, sir. I did find one reference to the business we discussed. There was a postcard from someone called Mark.'

'What?' snapped Lord Porterfield. 'What was that?'

'A postcard. I've got it here.'

'Read it to me.'

'It's from a place called Zug, in Switzerland. It was posted –'

'Read it to me!'

'Sir. It reads: "What price Apostle now? Trust all is well with you. Your old friend and comrade, Mark." '

'Good God,' breathed Lord Porterfield.

'Sir?'

'Nothing . . . nothing at all. Was there anything else?'

'It looked as though his son had been sorting through his things already, so I may have been too late.'

'His *son*, you say?' Lord Porterfield's grip on the telephone tightened.

'Yes, sir. Gordon Hallam. I found his things in a spare room.'

'And would he have seen this . . . this postcard?'

'Must have done. It was in the kitchen.' There was a brief silence.

'I see.'

'One piece of good news, sir: C R O say they've tracked down your man Tillet.'

'Have they, by God! Where did they find him?'

'North Shields. He's now living at number 17, Banner Crescent.'

'Good. Excellent, Stephen.'

'Oh. One final thing, sir. You remember that report I showed you? The one about internal unrest within Uzbekistan and that anti-Russian demonstration?'

'What about it?'

'Near as I can gather Vickers intends to release it to the Press Department late this afternoon. Got quite a bee in his bonnet about publicizing the growing disarray within the Soviet Union.'

Lord Porterfield groaned. 'All right, Stephen, leave that one with me. I'm coming back to town in an hour or so. After that you can reach me at the usual number in Suffolk. Oh – and Stephen?'

'Sir?'

'Very well done.'

'Thank you, sir.'

Lord Porterfield rang off and returned to the drawing-room where he watched Ashley Parsons and his wife say good-bye to the photographers. As the last car pulled away Ashley Parsons came up the stone steps, tipped the remains of his champagne into a flower-bed and let himself into the drawing-room by the french windows. Then he turned, saw Lord Porterfield waiting for him and crossed the room, hand outstretched. 'Phillip! I didn't see you arrive – what a pleasant surprise!' They shook hands and exchanged greetings. Then the MP pulled a face and gestured over his shoulder. 'God, how I hate those things. Make you feel like a performing seal.'

Lord Porterfield permitted himself a smile. 'You should learn to stand back, Ashley. Keep to the shadows.'

'Like you, you mean? No, no, Phillip – someone's got to stand out in front, provide the point of focus. Besides, I've got a constituency to consider! Now then, what can I get you? There should be some champagne . . .'

Lord Porterfield shook his head. 'Nothing, thank you. I wonder – could we talk in the study?'

Ashley Parsons glanced at him speculatively. 'Yes. Yes, of course. By all means.'

Lord Porterfield picked up his briefcase and followed the Secretary of State across the hall and into a comfortable, book-lined study. A small table was set beside the desk and upon this, stacked like so many telephone directories, were half a dozen of the red dispatch boxes delivered each day to government ministers and which contain their most urgent and confidential papers.

Ashley Parsons gestured Lord Porterfield to an armchair and stood for a moment gazing with distaste at the boxes that still awaited his attention. 'When I first took over the ministry there were three of these each weekend – four at the absolute outside. Now it's six if I'm lucky, eight as a rule. All to be read, digested and minuted.' He smiled wryly. 'To travel, as they say, is better than to arrive. So – Phillip: what brings you down from London?'

Lord Porterfield sat back, both hands resting lightly on the arms of his chair. 'I have just come from a meeting with the Prime Minister,' he said quietly. ' "Boadicea" is to go ahead.' Lord Porterfield paused, waiting for that to sink in as Ashley Parsons sat down. The Prime Minister had chosen the code-name herself.

'Definitely?'

'Definitely. William Ottley is flying in tonight to discuss deployment and security. The Prime Minister has asked me to brief him.'

'How soon – deployment, I mean?'

Lord Porterfield shrugged. 'I don't know. Weeks rather than months, certainly. There is to be another meeting tomorrow. You, me, the PM, this Mr Ottley, Rear Admiral Weeks, General Inkermann –'

'But not the full Cabinet?' interjected Parsons softly.

Lord Porterfield shook his head. 'No. Not the full Cabinet. The PM feels there is little point.' He bent down, opened his briefcase and withdrew a ring-bound folder in a slim yellow cover. 'There is no need for them to know. Consequently they will not be told.'

Ashley Parsons dragged a hand through his hair. 'But if they find out that –'

Lord Porterfield looked up sharply. 'They will not find out. Why should they? Unless,' he added softly, 'you or I were to tell them. And that would be unthinkable.'

Parsons shifted uncomfortably. 'Yes. Quite. Did the . . . did the PM say *why* she was moving Boadicea forward?'

'Part of the reason lies here,' answered Lord Porterfield quietly, tapping a hand against the folder. 'This is a National Opinion Survey commissioned by one of your Cabinet colleagues. It landed on the PM's desk late last night. You will be seeing your copy – officially, that is – sometime tomorrow.' He paused: 'In this, respondents were asked to list half a dozen concerns in order of importance: unemployment, inflation, defence and so on. The results were predictable, almost comforting: unemployment came top of the list.' Lord Porterfield looked up. 'That's what they found when they stopped people in the street.

'Taken at face value, this survey tells the government what it needs to hear: that despite all the talk about nuclear disarmament, CND and Britain out of NATO, attitudes aren't changing to any marked degree.' Lord Porterfield turned over several pages with slow, deliberate care. 'Then some bright young statistician came up with a novel suggestion: why didn't we run the poll again, ask the same questions – only this time run it blind: send it out for anonymous, pre-paid return to an identically weighted sample of respondents. Just to be certain.'

'And what did *that* reveal?'

'As you will hear at full Cabinet, the response was quite devastating. Defence issues – specifically, the fear of nuclear war – went to the top of the list with sixty-nine per cent of respondents. And forty-seven per cent were in favour of unilateral disarmament. *Forty-seven per cent!*'

'Good heavens. But –'

'– And this survey was conducted *after* the Soviet invasion of Afghanistan. After, Ashley; not before.' He tapped the report. 'Every indication is that those percentages, high as they are, can only increase as the anti-war, anti-nuclear lobby becomes more organized and gathers momentum. The Prime Minister believes it is time steps were taken to ensure a more realistic, a more . . . useful perception of threat prevails. Our American allies too are worried. They want proof that Britain's commitment to mutual support is unshakable. The decision to bring Boadicea forward is the Prime Minister's unequivocal response to that need.'

Gordon and Rachel Hallam were sitting cross-legged on the floor of the sitting-room in Sussex. It was early evening, dark outside, and the curtains were drawn. Earlier that afternoon

Rachel had been on the telephone to Plymouth, squeezing another day's absence out of a harassed schedules' officer. Meanwhile, they were sorting through Walter Hallam's papers.

On the carpet beside them were the half-empty plates of sandwiches and the opened packets of crisps left over after the funeral reception. Now Gordon hunched forward, eyes fixed on his father's medal swinging from his fingers by its length of ribbon. 'First there's this, right? Then that photograph. But what I don't understand is what a civil servant in a Reserved Occupation –'

'– Is doing with an OBE, Military Division, and wearing a parachute,' finished Rachel with a sigh. 'Not again, love, please? You've gone over it again and again and again.'

Gordon watched the medal swinging from his fingers. 'It's as if there's some other man, you know? Some other Walter Hallam, just hiding there in the shadows. It's as if –'

'Gordon? Please?' Gordon sighed, picked up the plate of stale ham sandwiches and proffered it to his wife. The gesture had long lost its novelty. Rachel pulled a face and fended it off with a raised hand.

'Absolutely not. If I just *look* at one more of those Hallam Ham Specials I shall explode. Everywhere. But go on – you made them: fill your boots.' Rachel picked up the address book she had been leafing through and turned another page.

'I like ham,' replied Gordon defensively. 'Anyway, I thought they might be hungry.'

Rachel glanced up. 'Some of your father's friends had some pretty weird names, didn't they? Here's another one: Mark Apostle. You'd think his parents would avoid that sort of word association, wouldn't you? Like someone with Mouse for a surname calling a son Michael.'

'What's that?' Gordon glanced up, his mouth full of sandwich.

'Here – see?' Rachel held out the address book. 'Mark Apostle. Zug 854399, Walderberg Strasse, Zug, Switzerla –'

Gordon's hand shot out. 'Let me see that.' He snatched the address book from Rachel's grasp.

'There's no need to –'

'Wait a minute, wait a minute. Just . . . wait a minute.' Gordon scrambled to his feet and pulled out his wallet from his hip pocket. He flipped it open and took out the sepia photograph he had found among his father's personal effects on the day of the inquest. He turned it over. 'You see?' He smacked the back of the photograph triumphantly. 'Listen to this: "Self with Mark and John, March '45." You see?'

Rachel looked up, puzzled. 'No, I don't. See what?'

'It's there! In black and white! The names – Mark and John!' He picked up his father's address book and studied it closely. 'It's not "Mark Apostle" like, say, Gordon Hallam – it's Mark, full stop; Apostle! They're two separate names!' Gordon turned and erupted into the kitchen.

Rachel twisted round. 'Gordon? You going to tell me what this is all about or are you going tó keep it to yourself?' She listened to the sounds coming from the kitchen as Gordon rummaged around. There was a pause, then –

'Rachel?' The voice was puzzled now, uncertain. 'What have you done with that postcard?'

'What postcard?'

'Addressed to Dad. It was jusť here. By the sugar caddy.'

'Haven't touched it – why?'

'It's gone. Only that mentioned something about Apostle too, I'm sure it did.'

'Gone? It can't have done. Anyway, I haven't touched it. Didn't even know it was there.'

'Then where the hell is it? It can't just have disappeared.'

'Maybe you threw it out.'

'I didn't. Anyway, I'd remember.' Rachel shrugged as Gordon turned out the contents of the kitchen pedal bin. 'No, it's not here.'

'Gordon . . .' Rachel hesitated. 'That Apostle thing you mentioned just now – the code-name or whatever it was.'

Gordon stood in the doorway. 'What about it?'

'It's probably nothing but . . . can I see the photograph again?' Gordon handed it over and Rachel studied the three men in overalls and parachutes standing in front of a twin-engined bomber. 'We've been looking at this the wrong way,' she decided finally.

'Wrong way? What d'you mean?'

'Don't you see? We've been looking at someone called Mark,

someone called John *and someone called Walter Hallam.* Only don't you see? To them, wouldn't he have been –'

'Matthew or Luke,' supplied Gordon, getting there at last.

'Yes, that's what I mean,' agreed Rachel quietly. 'Matthew or Luke.'

# : 9 :

The east wind moaned low across the flat, desolate Suffolk airfield sending thick banks of pewter-coloured cloud scudding across the face of the moon. Once, many years ago, American B-17 bombers of the 1st Bomb Wing, US Eighth Air Force, had lumbered across these same scarred runways to strain into the sky and carry their loads deep into the heart of Hitler's Festung Europa. That war was long over, yet the Americans remained, their B-17s replaced now by A-10 Thunderbolts and F1-11 Fighter-Bombers of the 81st Tactical Fighter Wing whose aircraft gave teeth to the 'special relationship' between Great Britain and the United States.

Tucked away from prying eyes more than a mile and a half from the hangers and armouries, the offices and stores and the round-the-clock activity of a front-line Air Force base, four vehicles stood waiting silently in the dripping darkness, their lights extinguished: an Air Force jeep, two USAF motorcycle outriders – and a dark maroon Bentley.

Inside the Bentley the leather cushions creaked as Lord Porterfield leaned forward, pressed a switch and the rear window slid down smoothly. There was a sudden swirl of raw, cold air as the escort officer loomed suddenly out of the darkness, the rain gleaming on his white helmet. 'Message from Air Traffic Control, sir,' he almost shouted above the din of the rain as it ran off the rim of his helmet and dripped onto his cape in glittering streams. 'They have the aircraft on scope now. Should be turning onto finals in a coupla minutes.' The American pointed a gloved hand away to the east as the runway lights sprang into life. 'If you'd have your driver wait for my signal, then follow the jeep, sir?'

Minutes passed. Then Porterfield saw the flashing red belly light of an aircraft sink slowly down towards the perimeter fencing at the far end of the runway. A moment more and there was a sudden coughing roar as the two motorcycles were kicked into life. Headlights were turned on and the little convoy swung out onto the runway, picked up speed and set off after the taxiing aircraft, their tyres hissing wetly on the runway.

The officer led them round in a sweeping arc that brought the jeep to a halt twenty yards from the stationary aircraft. It was an executive jet with civilian markings.

A man in his trim mid-fifties with short grey hair, wearing a fawn raincoat, came swiftly down the steps to shake hands with the saluting officer. He was carrying a leather briefcase. There was a moment's conversation and then both men turned and hurried towards the Bentley, heads bowed against the wind and the rain, the stranger's raincoat slapping against his legs.

Lord Porterfield held out his hand as the man he had driven down from London to see stooped and climbed in beside him, bringing with him into the snug interior the smell of rain and chill winter. They shook hands awkwardly in the confined space.

'Welcome to England, Mr Ottley.'

The C I A's Deputy Director nodded. 'Thank you. Good to be here.' They broke the ice with the usual small talk. Then Ottley sat back, blowing out his cheeks. 'I'll say one thing – you sure know how to set the cat among the pigeons back at Langley.'

'What do you mean?' asked Lord Porterfield as the convoy began to move off the concrete apron into sudden darkness as the runway lights were extinguished.

'Come on now! Getting our London Bureau out on your streets? Sanitization on that guy ... what was his name – Hallam?'

Lord Porterfield grimaced. 'What perfectly appalling words you people choose.'

Ottley shrugged. 'Dress it up any way you like, it still comes out the same. All I know is, from Washington it looks like you pulled strings to get our people take care of a problem that was wholly British. There's no liaison, no discussion – first thing we know some guy's been hit and we're left holding the hammer. The Director wants to know why you couldn't use your own people.' He paused. 'Guess you and I are going to be working pretty close together on this Boadicea business, right? Might be an idea if we cleared the air first.'

Lord Porterfield sighed. 'Executive action in this country – "sanitization", Mr Ottley – must be sanctioned by "C", the head of SIS. He in turn must receive the approval of certain sections of the British Cabinet. In view of Apostle's current . . . sensitivity it was decided simply to short-circuit established procedures.'

'What you're saying is that after Blunt you don't know who the hell you can trust, is that it?'

Lord Porterfield inclined his head. 'That's a little harsh. In any event, Mr Ottley, Walter Hallam's death directly affected American interests.'

'How? Bradley says this thing goes back thirty, forty years – is that so?'

'It goes back rather further than that, Mr Ottley, I promise you. It goes back to the thirteenth century, as a matter of fact. Just one moment.'

The convoy was now approaching one of the airfield crash exits and the jeep and motorcycles in front had come to a halt. Lord Porterfield watched in silence as the steel gates were unlocked and they were waved through. Then the Bentley gathered speed as they swept past the captain's rigid salute and turned right onto the empty lane beyond the base perimeter.

'I would like to show you something, Mr Ottley. It has a certain . . . relevance. I think you will find it interesting.'

The chauffeur took the Bentley along the dark lanes for several minutes and then stopped at a crossroads. He turned left at the signpost 'USAFB FRENCHAM COMMON – 1¼' as his two passengers sat together in silence. That silence was broken a little later by a soft click as Lord Porterfield reached up and extinguished the light. The Bentley sped on, its two passengers cloaked in darkness.

Presently the Bentley crested a rise and again Lord Porterfield leaned forward and tapped on the window. 'This will do, Carson. Pull in and turn off the lights.'

The heavy limousine sighed to a halt, its wheels crunching on the gravel verge. From where they were sitting Porterfield and Ottley could see the main gate to the base about sixty yards ahead and slightly below their own position: they could see the brightly-lit guardhouse with the armed sentries parading slowly up and down behind the gleaming chain link fence and they could clearly read the illuminated sign: FRENCHAM COMMON AIR BASE UNITED STATES AIR FORCE. OUR STRENGTH IS YOUR SHIELD.

And they could also see, beyond that sign, a cluster of brightly coloured tents pitched around two battered VW campers whose sides were daubed with brightly painted CND slogans. Beside the sad little huddle of pitched tents was the remains of a log fire that had been doused by the rain, its smoke rising dismally into the windy night. As they watched, a young woman with long hair and ankle-length skirt wriggled out of one of the tents, wrapped a shawl around her shoulders and hurried away into some bushes beside a cluster of banners that had been planted in the ground, their home-made shafts garlanded with flowers that once had been fresh. The slogans they carried flapped and swung in the wind but Ottley saw that one of them read: 'Our Children Cannot Survive Nuclear War. No Cruise.'

'I've read about these peace freaks,' muttered Ottley. 'Reports are all over my desk. They're camping here, right?'

'Yes, they're camping. It is January, the temperature is somewhere near freezing, they have no running water, no proper toilets, it has been raining without pause for the last four hours – and yet they are still here. Camping, as you say.'

'Can't you shift them on, for Chrissakes? Invent a pretext?'

Lord Porterfield shrugged. 'It isn't quite as easy as that, Mr Ottley. They haven't broken any law; they aren't on the base itself, they're on common land. They give no trouble, there have been no arrests. They smile a great deal and they talk to anyone who will listen. Many are teachers, housewives, mothers of small children. They have become, in a few short months . . .' he hesitated, searching for the *mot juste*, '. . . a force to be reckoned with.'

'But there's –'

'Please. Let me finish. A month ago, I am told, those women out there discovered it was the Base Commander's birthday. What do you think they did?'

Ottley shrugged, his eyes on the cluster of brightly coloured tents, his mind running towards violence, demonstrations and shouted abuse. 'Threw bricks? Burnt his effigy at the stake?'

Lord Porterfield shook his head slowly. 'They baked him a birthday cake. No cheap tricks, no slogans, they just . . . baked him a cake. Then they stopped his car with a human chain across the road and as the guard came doubling down the road with rifles raised and bayonets fixed, they sang Happy Birthday.' Lord Porterfield waited as Ottley turned to stare at the cluster of sodden tents. As he turned back slowly – 'They are dangerous, Mr Ottley. Very, very dangerous,' he warned softly. 'To your country – and to mine. To Western freedom. I am told that already half a dozen US servicemen inside Frencham Common have been reassigned elsewhere. At their own request. Even they, you see, have begun to have doubts, second thoughts.'

Lord Porterfield leant forward. 'Thank you, Carson. On to Huntingdon, if you please.' The headlights sprang on and the Bentley began to gather speed as Lord Porterfield added, 'And each week, each month, their numbers are growing. What you see down there' – he pointed at the tents – 'is just the tip. The tip of the iceberg.'

In a mews flat behind Chelsea's fashionable Cheyne Walk in London, Foreign Office civil servant George Vickers poured himself a large scotch and soda and took a deep swallow, conscious of the sticky feel of his collar and the prickling, smarting tiredness behind his eyes. He coughed as the fiery spirit burnt its way down to an empty stomach.

'George? That you, darling?'

He smiled, despite his tiredness. 'Who else are you expecting, Bunny? Just coming.' Bunny. What an absurd name. But he had been calling her that ever since they had met in Gibraltar when he was a junior second secretary and she had been the dazzling and much sought-after youngest daughter of Rear Admiral Francis Cotton, CD, DSC. Now, as she called to him from the bedroom, he could still hear the warmth, the eagerness and affection that had been the hallmark of their marriage for almost thirty years.

He went slowly through into the master bedroom, turning off the lights as he went. As he had thought, Bunny was sitting up in bed, reading by the soft light thrown by the tasseled bedside lamp. As he came into the bedroom she marked her place with a silk book mark, laid her novel carefully aside and held out her arms. He stooped and kissed her gently on both cheeks as she hugged him to her. 'Mmmm, I've missed you.'

'Me too. It's been a long day.' She watched critically as he took off his jacket, hung it up in the wardrobe and fiddled with his starched collar. He was one of a dwindling number of 'old school' civil servants who still used separate collars.

'You look tired,' observed his wife quietly.

George Vickers ran a hand through his thinning hair and sighed. 'I feel tired, frankly. Seems to be just one crisis after another just now.' They had talked increasingly about the days of retirement they would soon share. Buy a boat. A place in the country. Be together.

'How are things?'

'Afghanistan? Pretty bleak,' he confided. 'Everyone's still running around like headless chickens waiting to see how the Americans react, what they do.' He sighed.

'But that isn't what's bothering you,' prompted Bunny shrewdly.

George Vickers glanced up, surprised. He shook his head. 'No,' he said finally, 'no, it's not.' He unfastened his belt and continued undressing. 'Remember a chap called Porterfield? Lord Phillip Porterfield? Big, substantial, elder statesman type who retired three or four years back?'

'Yes, of course. We met him at the Harrisons',' replied Bunny after a moment's thought. 'Rather daunting, with the most commanding eyes I think I've ever seen.'

'That's the man.' George Vickers sat down on the end of the bed and began peeling off his socks. 'Damned if the chap doesn't turn up at my office mid-afternoon, asking me to withhold all further stories about anti-Soviet demonstrations inside the Soviet Union from our chaps in the Press Department. Said it would be . . . "politic". That was his word – "politic"!'

'Why?'

George Vickers shrugged. 'Damned if I know.'

'So?'

'So – I agreed –' George Vickers lifted his hands helplessly into the air. 'That's the damned silly thing: I agreed! I've been kicking myself ever since! The man's a menace,' he muttered angrily, folding his trousers over a hanger and turning to the wardrobe. 'He put me in a damned awkward position, asking me to do that as a . . . as a personal favour. I mean' – he swung back from the wardrobe and saw that his wife had settled back against the pillows, hands linked behind her head, grey eyes lined by age twinkling now with amusement – 'who else do we know who could get away with that? Just riding rough-shod over laid-down, established departmental procedures?'

'Saunders?' offered Bunny.

George Vickers shook his head emphatically. 'Saunders? Ian Saunders? They're not in the same league, Bunny. Dammit, the man's supposed to have retired four years ago . . .'

'Complain, then. Make a formal complaint to D6 or whoever it is.'

'Not a chance,' said George Vickers gloomily.

'Why not? That's what they're there for, surely?'

'Because . . .' He sighed, sat down and took one of his wife's hands in his. 'Because that's not the way it works. Not in practice. The man still has contacts; friends in high places.'

'But he's *retired*, George. You said so yourself.'

Again that sigh. George Vickers put on his pyjamas and climbed into bed beside his wife. Ten minutes later, as they turned off the bedside light – 'He's up to something. I just know it . . .' muttered George Vickers restlessly.

'Go on, darling, go to sleep,' mumbled Bunny drowsily. 'Put him out of your mind.'

But he couldn't.


Lord Porterfield and William Ottley sat together in deep leather armchairs on either side of the inglenook fireplace that graced Lord Porterfield's study in his sixteenth-century mansion set in fourteen acres of private parkland to the east of Huntingdon. Now Lord Porterfield gazed sightlessly into the flames as dark shadows leapt and flickered up the walls behind him, a glass of brandy at his elbow. '– And that, I may say,' he continued quietly, 'is merely the cheapest of the options open to my country. Whatever we choose will be . . . expensive.' *My country*, thought Ottley. He makes it sound like a personal possession.

'Britain's nuclear modernization depends upon two things:

firstly – upon trust. Trust in those at the very top.' He glanced dolefully at the American. 'You will forgive me when I say that the . . . er . . . antics of your presidents in recent years have sent shivers down the spines of all your NATO partners.' He paused. 'Trust – a precious commodity: the belief that, when crisis looms, there is a cool, steady finger on the trigger.' He smiled for what seemed like the first time. 'We British rather like that, stuck out here on our little island.'

Ottley nodded, his face impassive. 'And second?'

'Ah! That is much easier to define,' brightened Porterfield. 'It is this: perception – perception of threat.'

'Soviet threat?'

'Precisely. Show the population that their lives are *directly* threatened and they will tolerate any defence expenditure the government tells them is necessary, to safeguard the future for their homes and families. Every time the television shows that huge red stain that is the Soviet Union looming towards western Europe, that sense of fear increases.' He paused. 'Conversely it would be . . . dangerous if that fear were permitted to diminish – if people began to look at the metal fatigue, if you like, behind the Iron Curtain.'

'You want to clarify that a little?'

'It's perfectly simple: if the public thought that the Soviet Union was edging towards internal collapse then, to a section of that public, defence spending on the scale now envisaged would be quite pointless. Why cripple ourselves buying new weapons, runs the argument, when within our own lifetimes the Soviet Union – the threat – will collapse inwards upon itself?'

'With respect, Lord Porterfield, that's a load of bull. Pie in the sky.'

Lord Porterfield nodded. 'Indeed it is. But a growing section of the electorate would disagree.'

'Let me get this right: you're saying people's fears of the Soviet Union should be *exploited*? As a defined policy of government?'

Lord Porterfield nodded. 'That is precisely what I am advocating, yes. It is time steps were taken to ensure a more useful perception of threat prevails upon public consciousness. It follows, obviously, that anything which dilutes the strength of that perception is to be . . . discouraged.' He paused.

'And Apostle?' interrupted Ottley.

'– falls into that category,' affirmed Lord Porterfield, rising to his feet, crossing to his desk and bending to unlock a drawer. He took out a bulky green file and held it up so that Ottley could make out its shape against the shadows thrown by the fire's flickering flames. 'This is Apostle. A wartime mission mounted in the closing months of the war in Europe by your own O S S and our S O E, the assumption, naturally, was that it was directly related to the war effort.' Lord Porterfield returned to his seat, sat down and shook his head, the file lying in his lap. 'It wasn't. The Germans were on their last legs by then, anyway. Apostle was targeted towards the East, towards the Soviet Union.'

The older man paused, gauging the right way to break into his story.

'Go on,' pressed William Ottley, his eyes on the thick file on Porterfield's lap.

'What do you know about Genghis Khan?' he asked suddenly, quizzically.

The question took Ottley by surprise and he looked blank for a moment. Then he stirred and leaned forward. 'Not a whole lot, I guess. He was some kind of Mongol chieftain, right? A butcher. Grabbed a whole lot of Asia, killed a lot of folks and founded an empire on their bones . . .' He shrugged. 'That's about it.'

'There's rather more to him than that,' said Lord Porterfield quietly. 'His real name was Temuchin. He was born in the twelfth century.

'The Mongol tribesmen were cattle- and horse-breeders, warriors of Central Asia whose sworn enemies were the Tartars. Temuchin's father was murdered by the Tartars and Temuchin succeeded him as tribal ruler at the age of thirteen, leading his men on a campaign of carnage and revenge unparalleled even in those bloody times.

'In the next twenty-five years Temuchin first subdued and then united all the Steppe tribes, and the *Kuriltai* – the Council of Mongol chiefs – proclaimed him Genghis – the Most Great Khan. Others saw him rather differently: as the "Mighty Killer", the "Perfect Warrior". What he wanted he took – and what he took he paid for with the edge of the sword as the Mongol empire expanded west, north and south from the Yellow Sea to the brink of Europe itself.*

'Thirty thousand Mongol horsemen crossed the Caucasus into Georgia and pressed still westwards defeating every superior army that was thrown hastily in their path – killing, burning, looting, asking for no quarter and sparing neither man, woman nor child. "They gloried in the slaughter of men," wrote Chronicler Vincent of Beauvais. "Blood to them was spilt as freely as water."

'Their European adversaries saw the Mongol hordes as both superhuman and inhuman – "The brood of the Anti-Christ" – sent to punish the many sins of a Christian Europe obsessed with papal squabbles and disputes over the Holy Land.

'By 1228 Genghis Khan's horsemen had seized what we know today as the Soviet Union. They stood poised to sweep into northern Italy, into Germany, into Austria itself. They were running out of lands to conquer. Europe was in the grip of panic, its people fleeing westwards towards the illusion of safety, away from the brood of the Anti-Christ.

'And then, quite suddenly, the Mongols halted.

'An imperial messenger arrived from Genghis Khan's camp thousands of miles away to the east. The Khan of Khans had been thrown from his horse and mortally wounded.

'The news came at the zenith of Mongol fortunes as they stood poised on the brink of total conquest. There was a fateful, fatal pause – and then the Mongol armies withdrew as their leaders hurried eastwards to make their bids for the mantle of their dead chieftain.

'Europe could breathe again, for she had been spared. A different battle was about to engulf the Mongol chieftains: the battle for succession.

'In the years that followed the death of Genghis Khan, the empire that once had stretched without interruption from China to Vienna, from India to Siberia, the conquered lands that had been colonized, settled and ultimately tended by the peasant descendants of Genghis Khan, began to disintegrate.'

Lord Porterfield stirred and stared into the dying embers of

* See map.

the fire, a hand cupped beneath his heavy chin. 'That process of disintegration took two hundred and fifty years as first the Crimean Tartars and then the Princes of Muscovy – the ancestors of present-day Russia – began to challenge the concept of fealty to a distant Mongol Khan. As power slipped from the Mongols, as they ceased to control events and became instead controlled by others, so the legends grew in strength and importance to a proud but now conquered people.' Lord Porterfield looked up. 'One legend in particular became the linchpin of all their hopes, their dreams of future revival.' He opened the Apostle file for the first time and glanced down as though to refresh his memory.

'When Genghis Khan died he was buried with his golden-hilted sword in an unmarked grave in the desert somewhere between what is now Samarkand and Bukhara in Uzbekistan inside the Soviet Union. Then, of course, it was all part of the Mongol empire.

'To ensure the secrecy of that grave's location, every living thing along the funeral route was destroyed. Even the four Generals who had buried their chieftain were executed in a series of ritual self-sacrifices that ensured the absolute secrecy of that grave's location. The last to die – General Balaan – chose to do so at the hand of his own son.

'As the Mongol empire decayed, so the legend was born: when the grave of Genghis Khan is discovered, that will be the signal for the Mongol peoples to rise again to a position of greatness and self-determination; to throw off the yoke of oppression.' Bill Ottley smothered a smile and Lord Porterfield held up a hand in warning.

'You may smile, but I assure you it is a legend the people believe in – now more than ever. The world has forgotten about the Mongols – the years have hidden them beneath a dozen different names. Today they are Tartars, Ukrainians, Kirghiz, Tadzhiks, Uzbeks – a score of different nationalities all locked within that aberration of modern history we call the Soviet Union.' He wagged a finger slowly. 'But they are still, beneath it all, descendants of Genghis Khan.'

'And they're waiting? For that legend to come true?' asked William Ottley incredulously. 'You can't be serious!'

'I was never more serious in my life,' replied Lord Porterfield.

'But what about Apostle. How does *that* tie in to this . . . this legend?'

Lord Porterfield told him.

When he had finished – 'That is why it was . . . necessary for Walter Hallam to die. You do see that, Mr Ottley, don't you?'

There was a pause and then the American nodded slowly. 'Yes. I see that now.'

'Good.' Lord Porterfield handed Ottley a narrow slip of paper. 'Because I fear two more men must also be . . . removed. Here are their names.' Ottley unfolded the slip of paper: Peter Tillet, 17 Banner Crescent, North Shields; Gordon Hallam, c/o 14 Sunley Rise, Sidcott, Sussex.

Ottley glanced up. 'Hallam? You've got the same name here.'

Lord Porterfield nodded. 'Walter Hallam's son. He appears to have stumbled across the name, across Apostle. There is a possibility he may decide to start digging around, asking questions. I would prefer there to be no loose ends.'

'You're sure? What I mean is, I guess it sounds a little extreme . . .'

'Quite sure, Mr Ottley, thank you,' replied Lord Porterfield with glacial politeness. 'Perhaps you could arrange a discreet accident?'

Ottley shrugged. 'Sure. No problem.'


While two men plotted his death, Gordon Hallam lay in bed with his wife. They were sharing the single bed in the spare room and the bedroom itself was in darkness. Rachel snuggled down against the warmth of her husband, her arms around his neck. 'Come back with me tomorrow, darling,' she urged. 'I don't really want to drive all that way on my own.'

Gordon felt himself wavering. 'I'd like to,' he said, meaning it.

'Well, then?'

He shrugged in the darkness and linked his hands behind his head. 'I can't.'

Rachel stirred beside him. 'Why, for God's sake?'

'I have to go to the Imperial War Museum in the morning –'

'You don't have to. You don't *have* to go anywhere!'

'O K – agreed: I don't have to. I want to go to the War Museum in the morning, O K?'

Rachel pushed herself up onto an elbow. 'But why, Gordon? It's . . . it's illogical! You could telephone . . . write . . . call from home. Couldn't you?'

'No, I couldn't,' countered Gordon stubbornly.

'Why couldn't you?'

'I just . . . couldn't, that's all. It wouldn't be the same.'

The bedside light snapped on and Rachel bent forward, hugging her knees, and studied him over her shoulder. 'It's . . . it's getting like an obsession, you know that, don't you?' she said quietly, seeing it for the first time.

Gordon shrugged. 'OK, it's an obsession. Gordon Hallam's losing his marbles.'

'No, you're not,' said Rachel seriously. 'But what I do think is that you're using the medal, Dad's photograph, all that, as a . . . as a distraction.'

There was a sudden stillness.

'You think I'm copping out, is that what you're trying to say? That I should be beavering away looking for another job and scanning the *Guardian Education Supplement* –'

'I just think you need to put things back in perspective, that's all. There are plenty of other jobs, other teaching posts. Just because –'

'And Dad's photograph? His medal? You think I should just chuck them in a drawer and forget about them – is that it?'

'He didn't *want* you to know about it, can't you see that, Gordon? If he never mentioned it to you in . . . in thirty years, why would he want you digging up the past now? It doesn't matter anymore,' she pleaded. 'It's over – done with. Finished! Whatever it was, whatever Dad did – it happened forty years ago! Before you were even born! It's got nothing to do with us, with what's happening now! It doesn't *matter* anymore!'

'It matters to me, right?' ground out Gordon. 'It bloody well matters to me!'

High in the mountains beyond Aibaq, half a dozen miles inside the Soviet–Uzbek border with Afghanistan, eight fiercely-bearded villagers sat cross-legged around the glowing embers of their fire, the smoke swirling around the hunched figures and eddying between the folds of their thick winter clothing.

It was dark inside the mud-walled hut and the only light came from the dull glow of the fire. Every so often one of the men would lean forward and poke his fingers into the steaming mound of meat and rice on the beaten copper pan that rested in the fire's ashes before sucking his fingers noisily and merging back into the shadows. There were no women in the hut, nor any children, and the men sat together in a loose circle, their rifles – that most prized possession – held upright beside them as they listened to the stories of outrage and atrocity that seeped up daily now from the valleys. And, as they listened, their eyes became dark pools of anger and hatred.

One of the men leant forward, picked a glistening sheep's eyeball from the copper pan and held it out towards the bearded stranger who had emerged out of the darkness to ask them about the infidels in the valleys near by. It meant nothing to men such as these that they lived inside the Soviet border and that therefore the tanks, the helicopter gunships and the armoured columns hacking into Afghanistan were 'theirs'.

It was enough simply that brothers were being attacked and killed. Brother Moslems.

The SAS trooper nicknamed Ratbag took the sheep's eyeball and popped the delicacy into his mouth, conscious of the honour, conscious too of the watching eyes that missed nothing. He chewed, swallowed, licked his fingers and then repeated his question. 'How many?' he asked softly. 'How many of the infidels were killed?' A shrug, a murmured consultation and then four fingers went up. The hand opened and closed four times.

Ratbag nodded. 'Sixteen.'

'Yes. Sixteen. With many lorries. Many trucks.' One of the men hawked and spat into the fire. They talked on and Ratbag listened, head cowelled in the hood of his *jabul*, lazy eyes missing nothing as the rambling stories flowed on in the disjointed patois of the true mountain dweller: an ambush in this valley; soldiers killed in that town. Here, two entire companies of Soviet troops had deserted to the rebels taking their weapons with them; there, three children had lost their hands playing with the pretty green butterflies that fell from the sky and exploded when they picked them up; there, the local commissioner had been dragged from his car and stoned to death by women for collaborating with the

Russians. Reprisals? A shrug and a nod: of course there had been reprisals.

Ratbag listened carefully, noting the names, the places and the estimates of enemy strength as he gathered the facts he would take back with him to the cave and the other members of the SAS penetration team before first light.

It was almost two hours later when the old man on the far side of the fire began to rock gently backwards and forwards, his eyes closed, his hands clasped tightly together in his lap. The other men around the fire fell silent as the old man now began muttering inaudibly to himself, his eyes still closed.

'What is it?' muttered Ratbag. 'What's the matter with him?'

The man beside him shrugged. 'It is Radij. The gifted one, we call him. He can see things. Things that are yet to happen. In the future.'

The soothsayer's movement became more pronounced and then ceased as suddenly as it had begun. The old man seemed to wake up. His eyes cleared, as if from a dream.

'The Time. It is coming,' he announced simply. The men around the fire turned to one another excitedly, then began to shower the mystic with a babble of questions. Radij held up both hands in protest. When the hut had fallen silent – 'That is all I know, all I am told,' he said simply. 'It will be soon.'

There was a moment's silence. Then one of the younger men began to sing quietly beneath his breath. A moment more and one by one the others joined in, the sound rising and swelling with each new voice.

They sang a ballad of hope. An age-old song of unity, conquest and victory that had been handed down through the generations from father to son. The ballad told of the discovery of a chieftain's grave. And of the rebellion, conquest and final victory that must follow that discovery.

Ratbag noted every word.

# : 10 :

'Mr Hallam?' Gordon turned from his inspection of an oil painting on the wall of the Ministry of Defence's Air Historical Branch in High Holborn. It depicted a Coastal Command Sunderland depth-charging a surfaced U-boat.

'Yep, that's me.'

'Would you come this way, please? Mr Reader will be with you in just one moment.' Gordon followed the bespectacled clerical officer across a narrow corridor and into a small, square office whose grey walls were lined with a series of narrow filing cabinets. The clerical officer withdrew and Gordon was left alone.

He had caught an early train up from Sussex and had been outside the Imperial War Museum in Lambeth when the doors had opened, armed with his father's medal and a long list of questions.

He had spent forty minutes with the museum's senior numismatist who had told him, firstly, that the OBE was not a gallantry medal; secondly, that it ranked between the CBE and the MBE and, thirdly, that the papers related to the original recommendation of the award were almost certainly locked away in the vaults of the Honours and Awards Committee. And were not available for inspection. Not even to next-of-kin.

It was at that point, almost in desperation, that Gordon had shown her the wartime photograph of his father and the two other men standing in front of the bomber. And it was Miss Fox, the Imperial War Museum's numismatist, who had tapped a fingernail against the fuselage, pointed out the barely discernible aircraft registration letters – GXN – and told him about the Air Historical people. 'They'll be able to help you. They keep a record of every single aircraft that ever entered RAF service. From the day it left the factory to the day it was written off charge.'

And here he was. Waiting for Mr Reader.

The door opened and a pleasant-faced man in his mid-fifties wearing a baggy tweed jacket came into the room. A livid white scar ran from above his hairline down to the corner of his mouth and, perhaps to draw the eye away from this disfigurement, he sported a thick moustache. Aircrew put out to pasture, thought Gordon instinctively, pushing to his feet.

'You must be Mr Hallam? Peter Reader – sorry to have kept you,' he began breezily. They shook hands and Reader sat down abruptly on the other side of the table. 'Now then – where's this photograph of yours?'

Gordon had phoned ahead from the Imperial War Museum. He pushed the photograph across the table with the tip of his finger. 'Here.'

'Right then – let's have a decko.' He turned the picture round and glanced down. 'Hudson,' he said emphatically after only the briefest of pauses. 'Lockheed Hudson.'

'You're sure?'

Reader treated Gordon to a very odd look indeed. 'Yes, Mr Hallam, I'm sure. Why – d'you have reason to doubt it?'

'No, no. I just wondered, that's all.'

'Well, you can wonder no more, laddie: Lockheed Hudson. Twin-engined light bomber, beyond the shadow of a doubt. Built in Burbank, California and used over here by Coastal up until . . . oh, must have been the tail end of '42.'

'Coastal?'

'Coastal Command. For a couple of years, at any rate. Then they moved on to something with a bit more range, better endurance – Liberators, Sunderlands and so forth. The old Hudson was shunted around a bit after that if I remember rightly: Air–Sea Rescue work down in the Med., that sort of thing.'

'They were used for Special Operations as well, weren't they?' asked Gordon.

Reader bent over the photograph again, as though somehow it might suddenly have turned into a Lysander. It hadn't. 'Daresay they were, yes. Lots of kites were called upon to do a great many things the Almighty never intended by the time that little lot was over.'

Gordon leant forward. 'What about that one?' he asked quietly. 'That particular aircraft?'

'Haven't a clue, old love,' said Reader cheerfully. 'Might have been, I suppose . . .'

Gordon pointed at the photograph. 'D'you think you could tell me what happened? To the plane, I mean? Where it was stationed – see? There's the registration letters, you can just make them out: GXN . . .'

'Yes . . .' mused Reader. 'Yes . . . that shouldn't present too many problems.' He rose to his feet, went over to a set of files standing chest-high against the far wall and pulled open the top drawer. 'Now then – let's see . . .'

As Peter Reader began searching for one particular Lockheed Hudson in the Branch files, Rachel Hallam was packing upstairs in the spare bedroom in Sussex. The telephone began to ring and she hurried downstairs and lifted the receiver. Perhaps it was the estate agent about putting Dad's house on the market. 'Hello?'

'Is Mr Hallam there? Mr Gordon Hallam?'

'No, I'm afraid he isn't.'

'D'you know where he is?'

'Well, yes. He's . . . he's gone to London for the day, as a matter of fact. To the Imperial War Museum.'

'When will he be back?'

'I don't . . . who is this calling, please?'

'When will he be back?'

'I said: who is this calling, please?'

'Just a friend.'

'If you'd like to leave your name I can –'

'No, no. That won't be necessary. I'll be in touch again soon.'

'Well, if –'

Click.

Rachel replaced the receiver slowly and frowned.

As far as she knew Gordon didn't have any American friends. And the voice had been American. Definitely.

'Yes! Here we are,' exclaimed Peter Reader, extracting an index card and holding it aloft triumphantly. 'Golf X-Ray November! You're in luck, Mr Hallam: Hudson, Lockheed, GXN: file card number 2564. Now then – what exactly is it you wish to know?'

'Just . . . tell me about the aircraft. What it was used for,' said Gordon with a helpless shrug of his shoulders as he reached inside his jacket for notebook and pencil.

Reader nodded agreeably and sat down opposite. 'Right then, here goes: place of manufacture – yes, I thought so: Burbank, California, 1939.' He looked up. 'Must have been one of the very first. Arrived Liverpool docks, January 1940.' He glanced down again at the little card. 'Then straight on to Maintenance Unit 17 until March of that year. Then down to St Mawgan in Cornwall with 291 Squadron – that must have been with Coastal Command – until the end of that month. Then back to MU 5 near Taunton for undercarriage repairs. Reassigned to 544 (New Zealand) Squadron, RAF Aldergrove until April '43 – that would have been Coastal too, at a guess – covering the approaches to Londonderry. Then in April '43, let's see . . .' He turned over the little card. 'That's strange . . .'

'What is?' asked Gordon immediately.

Reader shrugged. 'It's probably nothing, but . . .'

'Please – I'd like to know.'

'Well . . .' said Reader doubtfully. 'According to this, Hudson GXN was then detached, sent into workshop for modification and chucked back into service with 161 Squadron.' He frowned, as though the words didn't ring true.

'And that's significant?'

Reader shrugged. 'I'm not sure. Probably some mistake. It's just that I don't recall 161 Squadron being part of the Coastal Command set-up. Pretty sure it wasn't with the Air–Sea Rescue boys either . . . Hang on a minute, I'll just go and do a spot of checking. Shan't be a tick.'

He was back less than two minutes later.

'I was right,' he said quietly, intrigued now by another man's mystery. '161 wasn't with either Coastal Command or Air–Sea Rescue. It was based at Tempsford.'

'Tempsford? Where was that?'

'Bedfordshire, just outside London. Started life as an emergency airstrip and then became home base to what became known as the two "Moon" Squadrons, 138 – and 161.' He tapped the photograph. 'Old GXN here.'

'What the hell was a "Moon" Squadron?'

'Ah! I can tell you that right away: they were the bods who carried agents and supplies across the Channel into enemy-occupied Europe. Most of the weapons and so forth dropped to the various resistance circuits passed through Tempsford at one time or another. They got the name "Moon" because that's when they operated – in moonlight.' Reader turned the photograph over, glanced at the inscription on the back and shook his head doubtfully. 'Though that would be a bit late for Europe, I'd have thought – March '45. It was all over by then, bar the shouting. Most of the resistance groups would have been overrun by the Allies months before that.'

Gordon began to feel it all slipping away once more. 'OK,' he said tiredly. 'Where would I find out about that? These "Moon" Squadrons – 161 and . . . the other one?'

'138,' supplied Reader helpfully. Then he shook his head. 'You won't. Not here. Not anywhere. You'd be banging your head up against a brick wall. All that behind-the-lines stuff is still locked away. Classified. It would come under SOE and SIS, you see, Mr Hallam – perhaps even PWE.' Gordon did not see. He didn't see at all. Reader looked up and saw the glazed look of incomprehension. 'Special Operations Executive?' he tried gently. 'Secret Intelligence Service? No? Political Warfare Executive?'

Gordon shook his head wearily. 'No. Sorry. Not a clue.' He felt beaten, lost in an alien world of military abbreviations and cryptic initials, a world he did not and never would remotely understand. All he wanted to do was find out why his father had been wearing a parachute; why he had won the OBE.

And never told his son.

Gordon put his notebook away, slipped his pencil back into his breast pocket and reached across for the photograph. 'Many thanks,' he said quietly. 'I'm sorry I troubled you.'

'No trouble, old boy,' replied Reader brightly. 'That's what we're here for. If people like you don't come banging on our door once in a while we'd all be out of business, wouldn't we?' he beamed.

Gordon nodded. 'I suppose so, yes.' He rose to his feet feeling suddenly tired.

'Here – hang on a minute: don't you want to know what's on the rest of the card now I've dug the thing out?'

Gordon paused, a hand on the door. 'Yes. Yes, of course. I'm sorry. What does it say?'

Reader glanced down and shrugged apologetically. 'Not a great deal, actually. GXN came to a bit of a sticky end, by all accounts.'

'When was that?'

'Just before the end of the war: March 21st, 1945. It's listed here as category "E".' He looked up, waiting.

'What the hell's category "E"?' asked Gordon wearily, suddenly sated now with the whole pointless business of investigation. It was over, for God's sake – finished. It had all been over a long, long time ago – and it was time he got back to reality: to Sussex and the journey back to Devon; to school and other realities . . .

'Category "E"? Oh, sorry – thought you knew: "E" means destroyed. Written off. Total loss.' He glanced down at the card. 'In Albania, of all God-forsaken places. Took off on something called . . .' He peered closer. 'Well . . .' he began apologetically, 'it *looks* like "Apostle". Ran into some mountains on the way home. Crew killed, the lot of 'em. Perhaps if you –'

'What was that?' demanded Gordon, tiredness pushed roughly aside. He had almost missed it.

'"Apostle" – that's what it looks like, anyway. Here – see for yourself.'

Gordon saw. The word had been written many years ago in longhand, scrawled at the foot of the index card by some unknown hand, but it was unmistakable: Apostle. So too was the location: Albania.

Albania?

Gordon took a deep breath. 'Now then,' he said, marshalling his thoughts with renewed effort. 'Apostle. That would be some sort of code-name, right?'

Reader nodded: 'Almost certainly. Every wartime mission had a code-name of one kind or another.'

'Quite,' agreed Gordon shortly, anxious now not to get sidetracked. 'So who would I need to go and see about this one? About Apostle?'

Reader thought for a moment. 'The Public Record Office down at Kew should be your best bet,' he decided.

'Just a moment, sir, I'll have a look.' The curator in the main entrance hall of the Imperial War Museum in Lambeth put down the telephone, swung the visitors' book towards him and ran a thumbnail down the list of the day's visitors. Then he picked up the phone once more. 'Yes, sir. Here we are. Came in just as we opened the doors.'

'Would you know if he saw anyone special? Anyone in particular?'

'Well now, we're not supposed to –'

'Please. It's very important.' The curator softened. It was part of Museum policy to be helpful, particularly to foreigners. And he recognized that accent a mile off.

'He went to see our Miss Fox, sir. Our senior numismatist.'

'How's that again?'

'Medals, sir. One moment. I'll put you through.'

A minute more and the American had forged another link in the chain. Gordon Hallam had left the Imperial War Museum at ten o'clock and was almost certainly now at the Air Historical Branch in Lacon House. The American thanked Miss Fox, rang off and glanced at his watch. It was now just after eleven.

He was catching up.

As Gordon walked along High Holborn towards the Underground station at Kingsway on his way to the Public Record Office at Kew, Lord Porterfield was a few miles east of Dorking on the A25 in Surrey heading towards Reigate. He was alone in the Bentley and glanced down briefly now at the map on the passenger seat beside him.

Ah, there was the sign. He decreased speed, turned the wheel gently and the heavy limousine swung off the main road down a quiet country lane edged with the bare bones of winter trees. A little further on and there was the uniformed policeman he had been told to watch for. He was standing in the middle of the lane, arms folded, a white police Range Rover blocking the lane behind him. Another police officer sat at the wheel. Lord Porterfield brought the Bentley to a halt. Surrey police wear no Divisional flashes on their epaulettes but the officer coming towards him now, hand raised, carried the letters CO on his shoulders. Special Patrol Group, noted Lord Porterfield approvingly: the outer ring.

'Afternoon, sir. Sorry about this. There's a burst water main a little further along.' He pointed. 'Take a while to fix, I'm afraid. If you'd like to turn round and –' He broke off as Lord Porterfield slipped a pale-blue identity card onto the sill of the driver's window.

'That's quite all right, officer,' said Lord Porterfield quietly. The man examined the card carefully, glanced inside the vehicle and then drew himself up a little straighter. 'Thank you, sir.' He bent closer to the window and pointed again: 'Second on the left. You'll be directed on from there.'

Lord Porterfield permitted himself a brief smile. 'Thank you, officer. I didn't imagine you would permit me to get lost at this stage.'

The man nodded. 'Be a bit hard from here, sir, I think you'll find.' He stepped back and saluted. The Range Rover slid across the lane and the Bentley moved forward. The policeman watched it disappear and then strolled back to his partner. Presently – 'Porterfield?' mused the man behind the wheel. 'New to the Cabinet, is he? Never heard of him.'

His mate tipped his cap to the back of his head. 'They're the ones you have to worry about, old son – the ones you never hear about.'

Lord Porterfield was stopped twice more before he turned in at the lodge gates of an imposing Georgian country mansion – once by another SPG team, once by a British Telecom maintenance crew with suspiciously short hair and an air of alert watchfulness. Once through the gates and onto private ground, however, the pretence of normality was abandoned altogether. As he drove up the beech-lined drive towards the main house, Lord Porterfield saw men with tracker dogs sweeping slowly across the lawns towards the woods. There was no one in the woods that he could see but that impression, he knew, was wholly deceptive. Eyes were watching his progress every inch of the way; mouths were speaking quietly into radios, fingers were adjusting binoculars. It all added up to security state Alpha, a rarefied condition light years away from Bikini Black, the normal security state for a mainland Britain under constant threat of attack from terrorists across the water.

An army Gazelle helicopter stood on the lawn, its rotor blades drooping tiredly to the ground. On the gravel in front of the main entrance five expensive, top-of-the-range limousines stood parked, each with a chauffeur who stood now in a group talking quietly as they waited upon the whim of their masters inside the house.

Lord Porterfield brought the Bentley to a halt and was met by an aide coming across the gravel towards him.

He was led up a flight of marble steps, across a wide vestibule and ushered through into a large drawing-room where a log fire blazed merrily in the hearth.

'Lord Porterfield, gentlemen,' announced the aide formally.

'Ah – and then we were six. Excellent. Come along in, Phillip,' greeted Ashley Parsons jovially as the others turned towards Lord Porterfield from around the fireplace, their cups raised. 'You're just in time for coffee.' Parsons moved a finger and a white-jacketed steward began to wheel a gleaming silver trolley across the carpet.

Discounting the steward there were five other men in the room. All were in their late fifties or early sixties; all wore that same indefinably solid air of command, carried in their lined, heavy faces the look that said they were familiar with the burden of high responsibility, the weight of other men's lives.

Lord Porterfield knew them well: Ashley Parsons, of course, Secretary of State; Sir Max Harrod, a leading government economist, strategist and, like him, long-time confidant of the Prime Minister. Beyond him, standing together by the window, were the two military men who made up this most secret inner cabal: Rear Admiral Percy Weeks, Commander-in-Chief Northwood and General Sir Frank Inkermann, C-in-C UK Land Forces. Lastly there was William Ottley, the American Deputy Director of the Central Intelligence Service looking vaguely ill at ease amid what he probably thought of as the last vestiges of the caste system of British regimental tradition.

Lord Porterfield mingled easily with his peers as they made practised, polished small-talk until the double doors opened quietly inwards at the far end of the drawing-room. 'If you would like to come through, gentlemen?'

They set down their cups and walked into an elegant dining-room whose polished oval table was set between a wide Adam fireplace and a deep bay window overlooking the lawns and gardens. Chairs were set around the top end of this table and a carafe of water, a glass, notepad and pencil lay next to each place. On the wall above the fireplace some long-dead ancestor of the mansion's owners gazed down sternly from another age.

They sat down in their appointed places, Lord Porterfield immediately to the right of the chair at the head of the table. Then a side door opened and the Prime Minister entered with a radiant, confident smile, golden head cocked to one side, impeccably dressed in blue two-piece and white silk blouse with a single rope of small pearls at the throat. The men stood as one.

'Good morning, gentlemen – Oh, please. Do sit down.' She took her place at the head of the table and sat down to a careful chorus of muted greetings, the service chiefs to her immediate left. The Prime Minister was at her most comfortable surrounded by senior officers from the services, a world she understood and in which she enjoyed widespread respect and a rare approbation. Now she turned to Ashley Parsons.

'Ashley, perhaps you would like to start?'

'Certainly, Prime Minister.' He cleared his throat. 'I should like first, if I may, to present Mr William Ottley.' He turned towards the American seated on his left. 'Mr Ottley left Washington as soon as your decision to bring Boadicea forward was communicated to the Pentagon. As from this moment he is our direct link between London and Langley, the Pentagon and the White House.'

The Prime Minister bowed her head gravely towards the American. 'Welcome indeed, Mr Ottley. Would you please convey my very warmest thanks to your Mr Bradley for such a rapid and open-handed response?'

'It will be my pleasure, Ma'am,' replied William Ottley with a little bow of his own. The Prime Minister turned back towards Ashley Parsons and nodded for him to continue.

'Thank you. You are all aware,' he went on, 'that in recent

months the planned deployment of American Cruise missiles at Greenham Common and Molesworth in the autumn of '83 has atttracted a veritable spotlight of adverse publicity, comment, even demonstration.' Heads nodded in sombre agreement. 'It further follows, of course, that any deployment from those bases under such circumstances, whether for practice or in times of national emergency, has long been recognized as tactically impossible.' Again they nodded, picturing the 'dual-key' technicians working at their posts in well-ordered silence while above their heads mothers chained themselves to the gates or tried to follow the missile launchers towards their bases of primary tactical deployment in the countryside nearby.

'You will also know that, in simple fairness to our American allies, it has become necessary to allay certain legitimate . . . concerns regarding our intentions.' Parsons deferred briefly towards William Ottley. 'Your countrymen look to us for proof that Britain is in deadly earnest regarding the deployment of Cruise in Britain – that it is not just a public relations exercise, something without substance to trade off against the Soviet S S20s at the negotiating table. The Prime Minister's decision to turn contingency planning into a fact of military life will, I know, provide Washington with the proof it requires.' Heads nodded as he paused to glance around the silent, listening table.

'For the last few weeks we have investigated the possibility of alternative sites for Cruise. Away from the demonstrators and television cameras,' he added softly, turning now towards General Inkermann. 'General?' he invited. 'Perhaps you would like to bring Boadicea up to date?'

'Yes indeed, Minister.' General Inkermann sat forward, bristling with enthusiasm and crisp, military efficiency. 'Prime Minister,' he began. 'Back in the early sixties, you will recall, Lord Beeching wielded his famous "axe" at the railway system of this country. As a result, thousands of miles of track were ripped up, stations were closed . . . and tunnels were sealed up, surplus to requirements.' He reached down to the side of his chair and lifted up a large sheet of perspex onto which had been mounted a large-scale map of south-west England. He tilted this slowly around the table.

A network of long-disused railway lines had been marked on

that map and every so often a tunnel or cutting had been ringed in red.

'My engineers believe we have found your sites of alternative deployment, Prime Minister, gentlemen,' said General Inkermann confidently.

It was less a suggestion, more a statement of fact.

# : II :

'Would you mind just signing in, please, sir?' Gordon Hallam took the proffered biro and wrote his name and address in the visitors' book in the foyer of Kew's Public Record Office behind Ruskin Avenue. A temporary pass was made out in his name, there was a cursory glance inside his briefcase and then he was permitted through into the main ground-floor reception area. After handing coat and briefcase in at the cloakroom ('– no pens allowed upstairs, if you don't mind, sir. Pencils only –') Gordon went up the stairs to the first floor where he collected a seat number and automatic page bleeper and then went through into the Reference section.

The open-plan working area exuded an air of quiet, professional efficiency as Gordon moved between the flickering computer terminals and the wide, chest-high cabinets of index cards and reference books towards the raised Inquiries counter. It was mid-week and the tables were occupied by a scattering of students and professional researchers with a shared interest in the past.

'May I help you?' asked a middle-aged woman with short grey hair and the air of an experienced archivist, whose spectacles hung down over her stout bosom on a length of gold chain.

'I . . . I hope so,' began Gordon uncertainly, feeling his way forward into uncharted waters. 'I want to find out about a particular wartime operation.'

'First or Second?'

'I beg your pardon?'

'World War: First or Second?'

'Second. I . . . er . . . I have a code-name, if that's any help. At least, I think it's a code-name: Apostle.'

The woman nodded. 'You'll find all the operational code-names over there.' She turned and pointed matter-of-factly towards a row of shelves against the far wall that were laden with bound volumes of government and ministry records. 'When you find the code-name you'll see a class and a piece number in the right-hand column of the same page. Make a note of those and then find a spare terminal. The rest is quite straightforward – instructions are printed on the display panel of each machine.' A brisk, business-like smile.

'Thanks very much.'

'You're most welcome.'

Gordon went over to the row of ledgers and began leafing through the index. He found four dark-blue volumes, each entitled 'Military Operations 39/45. Code-names'. Excited by the apparent ease with which he was cutting through forty years of historical undergrowth, Gordon lifted down the first volume and began running his finger down the 'A's': Operations Ambuscade ... Apocryphal ... Apple ... Aquaduct ... but no Apostle. Gordon checked again, ran right through the 'A's' from top to bottom. Nothing. Gordon replaced the blue volume on the shelf and went back to the inquiry desk and the same brisk, efficient archivist.

'I'm sorry, but I don't seem able to find it,' he began, feeling like one of his own pupils. 'Operation Apostle. I've checked the index but it's not listed.'

'Are you quite sure?'

'Positive.'

'You have a seat number? Pager?' Gordon nodded. 'I suggest, then, that you ask the computer,' she offered brightly. 'Feed in the information you have and see what it says.'

'Thank you.'

Back to the computer. Tap. Tap. Tap: in went Gordon's seat and the temporary ticket number he had been given downstairs. The computer digested all this and then waited, blinking steadily like some domestic reptile that was still hungry. Gordon re-read the instructions. Then he leant forward and tapped in slowly: OPERATION APOSTLE. INFORMATION PLEASE.

The computer threw out the word PLEASE for it was not programmed to respond to politeness. A green pulse appeared in the display panel's top left-hand corner and was followed by the order WAIT ... WAIT ... WAIT stripped in across the screen.

Gordon waited obediently. He was getting somewhere at last.

Or thought he was.

Two floors above his head the man who had been dragged away from his winter fireside on Boxing Day night by Stephen Rowley looked up suddenly from the report he was reading and stared for several seconds at the computer display terminal on the edge of his desk. It was flashing a red light and emitting a low-pitched, urgent buzzing. Kenneth Elton slapped his report closed and keyed in the manual override. The red light went out and the buzzing stopped. He hesitated for a moment and then long fingers rippled fluently over the keyboard as he queried the search alarm. Back came the reply: OPERATION APOSTLE REQUESTED TERMINAL 12 REFSEC. APOSTLE CLASSIFIED SECTION SEVEN RESTRICTED ACCESS. DECLASSIFIED JULY 2045. INVESTIGATE IMPERATIVE.

Kenneth Elton slipped on his jacket and went quietly out of the office.

Gordon Hallam was still sitting before the display unit, waiting for a reply to his query. He turned suddenly to find a thin, donnish man with spectacles standing at his shoulder looking down at the computer.

'Having a spot of trouble?' he asked pleasantly.

Gordon smiled, warming to the tone of the man's voice. 'Not sure, really. I punched in the information I wanted and was told to wait – see?' He gestured at the screen. 'Only it seems to be taking rather a long time.'

'Perhaps you'd like to tell me what it is you're after. I might be able to help.'

Gordon sat back, marshalling his thoughts. 'I'm trying to find out about something called Apostle – Operation Apostle,' he said. 'It was some kind of secret mission during the last war. As far as I can gather it was organized by something called – wait a second, I've got it here somewhere –' He slipped open his notebook and turned over several pages. 'Yes, here we are: Special Operations Executive.' He looked up.

'You know that for a fact, do you, Mr . . . er . . .?'

'Hallam. Gordon Hallam. No, no I don't – but everything points that way. I've been asking around, you see: Imperial War Museum, Air Historical Branch –'

'Is this for a book? An article you're writing?'

Gordon shook his head. 'No, no. It's a private thing. Personal. My father died recently, you see. When I was going through his things I found a medal he'd won during the war, something he'd never even mentioned when he was alive. Then I found – here, I'll show you.' Gordon rummaged in an inside pocket and took out the dog-eared picture of his father and the other paratroopers. Kenneth Elton picked it up and studied it without a word as Gordon breezed on: 'The plane there, see the letters – GXN? The Air Historical Branch told me it vanished on something called Apostle, a wartime mission out in the Middle East somewhere. Crashed on the way home, crew all killed. That chap there – the man in the middle – he's my father. I thought he spent the war as a clerk in London. Turns out he was with some sort of cloak and dagger outfit.'

'How very interesting,' murmured Kenneth Elton. 'And so now you want to see if you can find out about . . . what was it again? Apostle, did you say?'

Gordon nodded. 'That's right – Apostle. Only I've been through the list of code-names and it's not there.'

'Is it not?'

'No. Not a trace.'

'Well . . .' Elton hesitated. 'If you wouldn't mind waiting a few minutes, Mr Hallam, I'll see what I can find.'

'Oh. Well, if it isn't too much trouble . . . thanks. Thanks very much.'

'Not at all. Wait here. I shouldn't be more than a few minutes.'

Kenneth Elton returned to his office, closed the door quietly behind him and crossed to his desk, his face creased in a frown as he sat down and chewed absently at the end of a pencil. Hallam. Gordon Hallam. He wrote that down.

Then he consulted a small address book, lifted the telephone towards him and began dialling, his fingers drumming impatiently against the desk as he waited for his call to ring through. 'Er . . . extension 642, please.'

'642.'

'May I speak to Mr Stephen Rowley, please?'

'Speaking.'

'This is Kenneth Elton, Mr Rowley. Down at the Public Record Office. You may remember. We met on Boxing Day.'

'Yes, Mr Elton – I do indeed. What can I do for you?'

'Well . . .' began Elton cautiously. 'I won't mention any names – not on an open line, you understand – but you remember that business you came here about that evening? It had a certain . . . ah . . . what shall I say? . . . a certain ecclesiastical overtone to it?' Ecclesiastical overtone: that's rather good, thought Elton smugly; shows a flexible mind. At his desk in the Foreign Office Stephen Rowley stifled a groan of impatience. He had marked Elton down at the time as a man with an overrated sense of his own importance.

'Yes, Mr Elton. I remember.'

'Well . . . I just thought you might be interested to know someone's here now asking about that very same thing. He's looking for the same file . . .'

'What?' snapped Rowley, Elton's irritating personal mannerisms instantly forgotten. 'Who?'

'Thought you might like a name,' said Elton, glancing down at the pad on his desk. 'Fellow by the name of Hallam. Gordon Hallam.'

'Oh, *Christ* –'

'I beg your pardon? Hello? Mr Rowley?'

'Right – listen to me for a moment, will you? This is very important: just tell me everything he said, all right? Every single thing.'

'I . . . er . . . Let me think. Well, to begin with, the file was requested through the usual channels. That got nowhere, of course – not even a formal notification that it was S O E and thus, of course, still classified.' He paused. 'I have a little system of my own here whereby requests for documents of a certain category come through to my desk as well. So . . . when I saw the file had been requested, I decided to go down and have a few words; look at the lie of the land, as it were.'

'Go on.'

'Chap seemed remarkably open about it all, actually. Said, if I remember rightly, that his father had died recently and that he – this chap Gordon Hallam – had found a medal and a photograph that showed his father had been some sort of agent with S O E during the last war. Mentioned something about an aircraft crashing in the Middle East, I think he said, although I must confess I didn't follow all of it . . .'

'Right, I've got all that. Give me five minutes. I'll call you right back.'

'What –' But Kenneth Elton was talking to himself.

Stephen Rowley sat at his desk for a moment, thinking furiously. Then he got up, closed the door and dialled another number . . .

Lord Porterfield was in his Bentley driving back through the outskirts of south London – and he was a worried man. He was worried, not about Boadicea – that was progressing smoothly enough – but about Apostle. Five minutes earlier he had decided bleakly that it was not enough simply to remove those who had taken part in the original wartime operation, for the threat Apostle posed to Soviet internal stability would still exist, however deeply buried. No, no – it was the threat itself that must be physically removed, destroyed.

He had pondered upon that apparently intractable problem for most of the journey back to London – and then he had suddenly remembered the SAS team in the Afghan mountains. Now Lord Porterfield was going to the Signals' Wing of the Special Air Service headquarters off Chelsea's King's Road to arrange for the necessary signal to be encoded and transmitted.

The phone buzzed discreetly in its cradle beside the leather armrest. 'Porterfield.'

'Stephen Rowley, sir.'

'Yes, Stephen?'

'Something's come up, sir. Gordon Hallam is still digging around, I'm afraid. I don't know how far he's got but he's at the Public Record Office in Kew right now asking questions. And he's found some sort of photograph –'

'What? A photograph, you say?'

'Apparently yes, sir. The point is, he was asking about the operation. Quite specifically.'

Lord Porterfield's jaw tightened. 'I thought you told me . . .' he hissed angrily. Then he stopped and forced his temper back under control. 'All right. Never mind. He's still there, you say? At the Public Record Office?'

'Yes, sir. Our chap down there called not two minutes ago. He's waiting for me to call back.'

'Right. Tell him to keep Hallam there for at least one hour, understand? He is to tell him nothing, just stall him for one hour.'

'Might it not –'

'Just do it, man!' snarled Lord Porterfield. 'One hour. Longer if he can. Leave the rest to me.'

'Yes, sir,' replied Rowley, replacing the receiver slowly. Then he shivered suddenly in his warm office as Lord Porterfield's words echoed in his ears. But it wasn't just the words that had chilled him: the tone too had changed and become suddenly sinister, ominous, foreboding.

Like steel being drawn slowly from a scabbard.

Lord Porterfield pulled the car into the side of the road and thought for a moment. Two minutes more and he was speaking to William Ottley.

A little later and the American called Hastings was heading across London towards the Public Record Office. The journey would take him forty minutes but he would be there within the hour. Definitely.

When he got there he knew what to do. Ottley's orders had been quite specific.

Yuri Rashidov stumbled and almost fell, the rope sawing cruelly into the raw skin of his wrist as he lurched into a hidden gully and fought desperately to keep his balance. He tried to shake the sweat from his eyes and tasted its saltiness with dry, parched lips. Lungs threatening to burst, rupture to blown smithereens inside the tortured cavern of his chest, Yuri stumbled forward in a sweat-soaked haze of pain and suffering as exhausted, panting recruits in front and on either side raced towards the barracks that were impossibly far ahead, leaden legs threatening to collapse beneath their weight.

'YOU'RE STANDING STILL!' roared Sergeant Barak running lightly beside them, his feet dancing effortlessly over the frozen, rutted ground, a light sweat gleaming like oil on his broad, muscled chest.

Nikolai Samlar gritted his teeth and drove himself forward fuelled by pure, high-octane hate.

They were on the log race. For the third time this week.

Like all instruments of refined torture, the principle was simple enough: eight men lined up with toggle ropes, four on each side of a four-metre-long log, its length polished by the sweat and suffering of generations of army recruits. All they had to do was wrap their toggle ropes around the log, pick it up and run with it to the aptly-named 'Break-back Ridge' on the skyline, turn round and bring it back. And that was all there was to it – just so long as they did it within seventeen minutes.

'Left – Left – Left,' croaked the leader, a tall, raw-boned Latvian, as they swayed round a bend, crashed heedlessly through a thicket of gorse and hauled with superhuman effort towards the finishing line. 'Fifty! Fifty metres!' yelled the Latvian triumphantly, urging his team to even greater efforts. The NCO danced nimbly towards the line of gasping, panting soldiers and kicked viciously at the man struggling to keep pace behind Yuri. It was Nikolai Samlar.

'YOU'RE WALKING, YOU CRETIN!' bellowed the Sergeant. 'YOU'RE WALKING IT! PICK THOSE STUPID FEET UP!' He lashed out again with his boot and Nikolai fell sprawling sideways onto the frozen ground, dragging the rest of his team to a sudden, chaotic halt.

'No . . . no, oh . . . no,' groaned Yuri as the other teams streamed past with a triumphant shout as they sensed victory. Yuri's team struggled to their feet once more, grasped the rough, sweat-soaked lines of the hemp toggles and shambled into a run, their boots slipping and sliding on the iron-hard, frozen ground.

They came in last. They crossed the finishing line and dropped to their knees, utterly spent, the hated log still fastened to their wrists. Some retched weakly onto the ground and brought up a thin brown bile.

The Sergeant walked slowly towards them, breathing lightly, hands on slim hips.

'Disgusting.' His voice came from above, God-like. Not a man turned. Eight gleaming, sweat-streaked backs rose and fell as the recruits fought for breath, knowing with a dull and utter certainty what was coming next. What their reward would be. 'That was bloody awful, comrades,' continued the NCO. 'A load of old women on crutches could have moved faster than that – couldn't they, Samlar?' Nikolai didn't bother to look round. 'COULDN'T

THEY, SAMLAR?' Now Nikolai pushed himself to his knees and regarded the Sergeant with frank hatred. In the short life of the squad, the Sergeant's contempt for all recruits had focused upon him.

'We did the –'

'COULDN'T THEY, SAMLAR?' Nikolai stared back defiantly, chest heaving, shaking his head, trying to work saliva into a parched mouth as the Sergeant stepped closer and hunched down beside him, his mouth twisted into a sadistic little smile. 'Couldn't they – peasant?' he repeated, almost softly.

'I am a Tartar. I am not . . . not a peasant,' protested Nikolai quietly as those around him groaned at obstinacy that could only bring more pain to them all.

The Sergeant nodded. 'Couldn't they, Comrade-Tartar-peasant?'

Stubbornly, Nikolai refused to answer.

'Go on, Nikolai, tell him,' muttered Yuri under his breath. What did it matter? They'd all had it, anyway . . .

'Yes,' managed Nikolai finally.

'YES, WHAT?' roared the Sergeant, his face inches away, bad teeth framing a yawning hole.

'YES, COMRADE SERGEANT!' screamed Nikolai, dragging the energy up from his boots, from the bottom of his soul.

The Sergeant nodded. He looked almost pleased. 'My thoughts exactly, *salagi*.' He paused, relishing his moment of supreme power. He rose slowly to his feet and looked down without pity at the eight sweating, exhausted recruits. He waited until each one was looking towards him, waiting for the blow to fall like dumb oxen. 'So you will run again,' he announced softly. 'Just for the benefit of Comrade Samlar here.'

They ran again.

At last it was finished and they stood at ease in formation, chests heaving like bellows, the log discarded behind them, toggle-ropes slung over their left shoulders.

The Sergeant walked slowly along the front rank, looking into each panting, sweating face as he passed. 'You will be faster tomorrow,' he promised confidently, turning on his heel and walking back along the front rank. 'Now then –' He snapped his fingers and a junior Sergeant from the Quartermaster's office placed a sheet of paper smartly into his hands. 'There is to be an issue of greatcoats to all recruits. Dress for the Clothing Parade will be full winter working dress. At the Stores in exactly two minutes. I shall reserve something particularly unpleasant for the last man in line. Look up!' he barked sharply. 'Dismiss!'

The men turned to their right, paused and then broke away to race madly across the empty drill square towards their hut, fingers already fumbling with the fly-buttons on their baggy uniform trousers.

They crashed into the barrack hut and moved towards their narrow beds where their working dress uniforms waited for them, neatly folded, on their stools.

Nikolai Samlar and Yuri Rashidov found themselves shoulder to shoulder as they waited impatiently in the crush by the door as recruits squeezed past and hurried into the barracks. Seeing the mood of black, bitter anger that engulfed his friend, Yuri clapped a hand on his shoulder. 'Don't let him get you down, Nikolai. It's not worth it.'

Samlar swung round angrily. 'Him?' He jerked a contemptuous thumb towards the empty drill square. 'The man's a complete bastard. One day, I'm telling you, he'll push me too far. Then you'll see what sort of –'

'Yeah?' another recruit, a Russian called Yasnov from Kolomna, six foot three, all brawn and muscle, jabbed Samlar in the ribs as he pushed past. 'You keep that mouth of yours tight shut, Tartar, see?' A thick finger pointed under his nose. 'You've got the rest of us into enough trouble already.' There was a low murmur of agreement from others near by as Nikolai pushed angrily towards the bigger man, temper already rubbed raw.

'Yes? Listen, Yasnov, you Russian prick! Anytime you want to start –'

'Leave him, Niki. You'll be last again if you don't watch it,' warned Yuri as, all around them, men were bending over their equipment, stripping off sweat-stained trousers and working boots and struggling into working dress.

Yuri's remark about being late gave Yasnov, the Russian, an idea. He swept up the Tartar's carefully pressed uniform and held it aloft. 'Hey!' He was grinning now as the others looked up. 'Be a shame, eh, comrades, if Tartar-boy here was the last in line for his greatcoat – know what I mean?' Several faces split into a grin as Yasnov mashed Nikolai's uniform into a tight ball and threw it across the hut to another Russian crony. Then Yasnov picked up Nikolai's polished boots and tossed them, too, to other friends.

Nikolai swung round in alarm. 'Hey – cut that out! Give it here –'

The crumpled uniform, the two shiny black boots, moved around a sudden sea of smiling, hostile faces.

'Come and get it, Tartar!'

'This what you're after? Here, Stefan – catch!' – and the uniform moved on.

Yuri watched angrily, fists clenched at his side, noting how the squad divided as it always did – Russia versus the rest; Uzbekistan versus the rest of the world. Finally one of the Russians hurled the bundle towards Nikolai, turned on his heel and hurried after his mates towards the Quartermaster's stores.

Nikolai bent down, gathered up the clothes and began pulling off boots and trousers in feverish haste. Then he dressed and inspected the result in the long barracks mirror.

He had spent hours in the unit laundry room, working on the creases with damp cloth and brown paper, polishing away at those boots until he could see his own reflection in their glossy black toe-caps. Now the creases were gone, the boots were dull and lack-lustre, his buttons and shoulder-boards were askew. He looked like a sack of garbage.

Three minutes later Nikolai hurtled round the corner beyond the armouries and fifty-metre ranges and saw the rest of his squad drawn up in a neat, motionless line outside the Quartermaster's stores. The door to the stores was still closed, the greatcoat issue had not yet started and Sergeant Barak was nowhere in sight. Nikolai darted out into the open and ran forward. Just a few more paces and –

'THAT MAN – HALT!' The voice rang out and nailed Nikolai's boots to the ground. He froze instantly, sickeningly, the blood turning to cement in his veins. He stood at attention, palms pressed tight against the seams of his trousers, eyes staring straight ahead. He listened as metal boot-heels crunched across the gravel behind him. 'Name?' ordered the voice.

Nikolai swallowed. 'Samlar, Comrade Sergeant. Samlar, N., 95986455.' Was it his imagination, or could he actually *hear* the man smiling?

'Samlar? Again?' Incredulous.

'Yes, Comrade Sergeant.'

'You are the last man?' As though he couldn't believe his luck.

'Yes, Comrade Sergeant.'

'Why?'

'I –'

'STAND STILL!' screeched the Sergeant, stepping closer. 'Why?' More quietly this time.

'No excuse, Comrade Sergeant.' Nikolai had learned that much, anyway. There might be a reason, but never an excuse.

'Turn round.' Nikolai pivoted round until he was facing the Sergeant, his eyes fixed on a point an inch above the man's right eye. He felt the Sergeant's gaze sweep over his uniform and take in the creases, the scuffed boots, the twisted buttons. 'The order was full winter working dress,' said the NCO. Nikolai found himself wishing he would shout at him. He moistened his lips.

'Yes, Comrade Sergeant.'

'That means creases. Polished belt. Polished boots.' Sergeant Barak stepped forward, reached out almost tenderly and grasped a button that was hanging by a thread down the front of Nikolai's tunic. He pulled gently and the button came away in his hand. He held it up until it was level with Nikolai's mouth. 'Open,' he ordered curtly.

Nikolai opened his mouth and the Sergeant popped the button inside. 'Now swallow,' he commanded. Behind him, the line of waiting recruits outside the Quartermaster's stores was absolutely silent. 'You heard me – swallow it.' Nikolai tried but it wouldn't go down. He shifted the button to the side of his cheek like a metal gob-stopper.

'Can't, Comrade Sergeant,' he mumbled. 'It won't go down.'

'SWALLOW IT, SAMLAR!' With a huge effort the button disappeared and Nikolai's eyes swam with alarm. 'Open.' Nikolai did so and the Sergeant glanced inside. 'Good.' He made to move towards the waiting recruits. 'Wait here.'

Leaving Nikolai at rigid attention he marched over to the clothing parade and began rapping out orders. Standing there alone, isolated from his comrades, marked out for special punishment by their squad leader, Nikolai could only wait as, behind him, the stores were opened and the kit issue began. Presently the recruits began to stream past him on their way back to barracks, each man clutching a winter greatcoat.

Twenty minutes crawled by. Nikolai never moved. His eyes were locked on the edge of the armoury wall, his hands pressed tightly against his thighs. Finally he heard the door of the clothing store slam shut and heels crunch on the gravel. Sergeant Barak came round and stopped in front of him. He was holding a canvas field pack and an old greatcoat. He dropped the pack on the ground and held out the coat.

'Put it on.' Nikolai did so. The collar was too tight and the skirt of heavy, dark-brown serge fell almost to his shins. Nikolai fastened the belt and snapped back to attention. 'Right, then – follow me.' He turned and led the way along the gravel path past the gymnasium and officers' mess.

They turned off the gravel path presently, the Sergeant and the recruit, and entered the narrow belt of bare trees that ringed the Battalion's assault course. They kept walking, past the climbing walls and the seven-metre scramble net until the Sergeant halted in a clearing. Nikolai Samlar waited at attention behind him.

Now the Sergeant rummaged inside the grey field pack. He pulled out a standard issue respirator, the old-fashioned gas-mask with its filter-fox and face-mask with the two sinister cod-like eye pieces joined together by a length of serrated rubber hosing. Sergeant Barak threw the pack down at Nikolai's feet and pointed at a pile of stones. 'Fill it up.' Nikolai did so, going down on his hands and knees in the heavy flapping greatcoat as he crammed stones into the pack. He fastened the straps and stood up. 'Now put it on.' Again, Nikolai did so and stood there, waiting for punishment to begin. Barak walked around him slowly.

'I don't like you, Samlar,' he began almost conversationally. 'You and your kind – peasants from the other end of the earth. You're trouble-makers. You think you can change the system – do what you like. You can't. People like me will see to that.' He waved a hand towards the many obstacles that made up the assault course set up among the trees: the sheer walls that had to be scaled, the ditches and ramps that had to be leapt, the narrow buried tunnels half full of mud and stagnant water that had to be wriggled through, the scaffolding towers that had to be scaled and the ropes that had to be climbed. 'Now get moving.'

'Like this?' Nikolai gestured at the greatcoat. It would be like running the hundred metres in divers' boots.

Sergeant Barak tossed Nikolai the respirator. 'No – like this.' Nikolai stood there for a moment, not moving, the hatred he felt for the man welling up, reaching out for his throat. 'Well? What are you waiting for, Tartar? Put it on!' ordered the Sergeant – and still Nikolai did not move. Finally he ducked his face into the clammy rubber mask and jerked the head straps down angrily.

'How many times?' he demanded, the words muffled and distorted inside the ugly rubber mask.

The NCO sauntered away, sat down on a log, took out a packet of cigarettes and lit up. He inhaled deeply, blew out a long feather of smoke and waved the match lazily to and fro. 'Until I tell you to stop. Until I get tired. Get moving.'

Nikolai turned and broke into a shambling run. Gathering speed he ran up a smooth earthen ramp and leapt across the first ditch towards the thick hessian of the scramble net, fingers hooked into claws.

He might have been going for Sergeant Barak's eyes.

# : 12 :

In the central reading room of the Public Record Office at Kew, Gordon lowered his newspaper and glanced again at his watch with mounting impatience. It was 4.20 p.m., already dark outside – and one hour and fifteen minutes since that bloke had asked him to hang on and wait while he checked up on Apostle. Gordon glanced round – and as he did so he caught sight of Elton moving swiftly down the main stairs towards the exit. Gordon tossed the paper aside and hurried after him through the swing doors. 'Er . . . excuse me,' he called down the stairs.

Elton had a coat over his arm and a scarf and gloves in his hand. He was obviously about to go home. He turned, startled. 'Oh . . . er . . .'

'Haven't you forgotten something? You were going to look up Apostle for me, remember? I've been waiting ever since.'

'Er . . . yes. I'm sorry. I quite forgot.' Elton made no move to come back up the stairs.

'Well? Did you find out anything?'

'No. No. Nothing at all.' He turned away abruptly.

'What, nothing?' demanded Gordon peevishly down the stairs after him.

Elton twisted round. 'Nothing, no. You must have been misinformed.' He paused at the bottom of the stairs, glanced up at Gordon and hurried away.

'Thanks. Thanks a bundle,' muttered Gordon under his breath. He had just wasted one hour and fifteen minutes. Still, the place wouldn't close for another hour at least. Perhaps he could still salvage something from what was left of the afternoon . . .

He walked up to the Inquiries counter, picked on a fresh, pretty young girl of about nineteen and switched on his most charming smile. 'Hello.'

The girl glanced up and smiled back. 'Good afternoon. May I help you?'

Gordon nodded. 'Hope so, yes. If I wanted to find out about a particular Royal Air Force squadron during the last World War, where should I start?'

'What are you looking for – Squadron Diary? Operations Record Book, that sort of thing?'

'Yes,' decided Gordon instantly, 'that's right – the Operations Record Book. Is that kept here?'

The girl nodded. 'Should be, yes. What was the Squadron?'

'161. Based at Tempsford.'

Ten minutes later the red light on top of Gordon's pager winked a warning and Gordon went up to the counter to collect the Operations Record Book of 161 Squadron. It was a thick, cloth-bound volume with the Squadron's number and insignia – a broken shackle with the word 'Liberate' in a scroll beneath – painted painstakingly on the cover.

Gordon took the heavy volume over to his chair and began turning the old, ruled pages. Date after date, mission after mission as the Lysanders, the Hudsons and the Halifaxes of 161 Squadron had carried arms, agents and explosives into Nazi-occupied Europe, building a bridge of hope and defiance between wartime England and the dark mass of Europe in the days between the spring of 1942 and the end of March 1945 – each mission, each moment of heroism, danger and boredom reduced now by time to a hand-written, faded entry in a long-forgotten log book.

But there, near the end, he found what he was looking for:

And, in the margin, in red ink, someone had written in neat capitals: A/C MISSING CAT. E. CREW POSTED AS MISSING PRESUMED KILLED 23/3/45. OPERATION APOSTLE.

Gordon sat back, breathing deeply. Got you. Got you, you bastard.

Then he pulled his notebook towards him, jotted down the details, turned to a fresh page and sat back, pencil drumming against his teeth. Now he wrote firmly at the head of the page: 'Apostle existed' – and again he sat back, studying what he had written, conscious that something was still wrong. Finally, it came to him. The postcard. The postcard from Switzerland. The postcard from Switzerland and a phrase 'Mark' had used to his father. What had it been? Think. Yes, that was it: 'What price Apostle now?'

*Now.*

Gordon leant forward, crossed out the word 'existed' and wrote 'exists' in its place: Apostle exists.

He left the Public Record Office five minutes later without a backward thought about the strange behaviour of Kenneth Elton.

Or a glance over his shoulder.

The street lights had come on and it was very cold as Gordon jammed his hands into his coat pockets, turned up his collar and set off towards the Underground station at Kew Gardens, his thoughts focused upon his father and upon the things he had learned about him since discovering the medal on the night of the inquest. He walked briskly past neat suburban terraces, mingling now with a growing throng of commuters all making for the same place, their heels clipping urgently along the pavements as they hurried to get home out of the cold.

Which made following Gordon Hallam very, very easy.

He never looked round. Not once.

Rachel had been right, admitted Gordon to himself with a wry, private little smile as he hurried along: it *had* become a bit of an obsession. So – what did he know? What had he found out? He ran over the facts in his mind as he turned towards the bright neon sign of the station. Well, he knew that the mission had begun on 16 March; that it had gone from RAF Tempsford in a specially converted Lockheed Hudson of 161 Squadron which had crashed somewhere in Albania on the 21st. Gordon frowned suddenly: the 21st! That was five whole days later! Where the hell had the plane been between the 16th and the 21st? Greece? Somewhere in the Middle East?

'Single to Victoria, please.' He slid money onto the counter, took his ticket and edged out onto the crowded platform. It was now well into the rush hour and the platform was crammed. He moved towards the end of the platform, walked to the edge and glanced up and down the rails. Not a train in sight.

Then the rails began to tremble and sing. A train was coming. Herd-like, the press of commuters began to move closer to the platform's edge.

Hastings slipped through the crowd, unnoticed and unseen, his eyes locked on the back of Gordon's dark-blue duffle coat.

Gordon looked up suddenly as there came a sudden shout from the platform on the other side of the rails. Three skinheads were trying to cram together into a telephone kiosk, shouting and punching one another on the arms while a scattering of commuters buried their heads in the sand of their evening newspaper and tried to ignore them. It was while Gordon was watching them clowning around that the best idea of the day sneaked up and hit him between the eyes.

The telephone. The bloody telephone, of course! Mark, the man who'd written to his father from Switzerland – he was on the phone. So why didn't he ask *him* about Apostle? See what he remembered. Brilliant, Hallam, he said to himself as the train swung and rattled into view. Absolutely terrific. If he –

There was a sudden jolt in the small of his back and Gordon lurched forward. He overbalanced, lost his footing on the edge of the platform and fell over the edge. Dimly, through an agony of pain as he crashed down onto the rails, he heard a sudden scream of horror and the dry screech of brakes as the driver fought to halt the train even as it rushed down upon him and blotted out everything else with huge, dark menace.

Hastings turned and melted away into the crowd.

Kaleidoscopic images of terror: the black bulk of the train looming down on him; the yellow square of the driver's window framing the horrified grimace of the West Indian driver as he slammed on his brakes and tried to stop the train with his own desperate strength; the gleaming length of rail next to his own head being gobbled up as the train rushed forward out of darkness; the smell of dirt and soot and hot metal mingling with the certainty of approaching death as the screech of locked wheels grew to a roaring thunder in his ears.

Gordon had fallen across the outer rail. With a violent, convulsive jerk he now rolled his body inwards, tucked his hands under his stomach, hunched his head into his shoulders and tried to press himself into the permanent way as the train thundered over his head and all was noise and darkness and curdling, utter fear.

And then suddenly, miraculously, that long, drawn-out screeching had stopped and Gordon opened his eyes. For a long, precariously-balanced moment he wondered if this, in fact, was death. Then he became aware of the sharp stones under his hands and knees and that his shoulder felt as though someone was wriggling a red-hot poker through a hole in his shoulder-blade – and knew that he was still alive.

Sudden, random sounds: the hiss of hydraulics; shouted instructions; questions and answers from the platform somewhere in the darkness above his head. Gordon raised that head slowly and with infinite caution, a tortoise seeing if danger had passed. A trickle of hot water ran from some coupling onto his head and when he put up his hand he barked his knuckles on sharp, greasy metal.

Then there was the sudden crunch of someone jumping down onto the stone chippings and a torch was waving uncertainly towards him as Gordon heard the sudden rasp and pant of frightened breathing as a railwayman came looking for the pieces underneath the train. The torch beam slid over his face, passed on, slid back and settled. 'Oi! You all right?' The voice was compressed and flattened, dismembered by the dark closeness of the train. Gordon tried to speak but the words came out as a croak. He licked his lips. 'I . . . I think so.'

'S'truth. 'Ere – Mike, 'e's all right! 'E's down 'ere! 'E's still alive!' Another torch shone down from above.

'Listen, mate – stay there, all right? Don't move. Someone's gone to switch off the 'lectric, all right? Don't move.' Gordon nodded.

The first man crawled over the sleepers towards him, the torch waving in his hands. He wriggled alongside Gordon, played the torch-beam over his body, counted arms and legs and shook his head in wonder. 'Ain't you the lucky one . . .'

After no more than a decade the man on the platform above came back and told them it was safe to move. Gordon and the railwayman wriggled out from beneath the train and Gordon grunted in agony with a sudden, searing pain in his left shoulder as he tried to get up. He had to lean on the railwayman as they clambered slowly back up onto the platform and moved through the press of curious, silent commuters towards the ticket barrier. Then Gordon felt a blanket being draped over his shoulders and he was being helped towards an ambulance. It had backed up to the station entrance, its rear doors were open and its roof light was revolving blue across the sky.

'In you get, mate,' said the ambulanceman kindly. Gordon glanced round in a daze as strange, curious faces clustered near by.

'Look, it's all right – really. I'm fine.'

''Course you are, mate. Just had a bit of a shock, that's all. Come on now, in you get.' Protesting weakly, the blanket still draped across his shoulders, Gordon found himself sitting on the stretcher inside the ambulance as the doors were closed firmly behind him. Then the driver was pulling out of the station forecourt and his partner was reporting in to Control by radio. When he had finished he glanced round at their passenger and smiled reassuringly.

'Want to talk about it? It helps, sometimes. It's never as black as it looks, you know . . .'

'Pardon?'

'You know: the train. If you jumped because –'

'Jumped? I didn't jump –'

The ambulanceman shrugged. 'Look – chum: it doesn't matter to us one way or the other, see? But if it helps to talk about it, you know, get it off your chest . . .'

'I'm telling you: I didn't jump. I . . .' He paused. 'I slipped, that's all.'

'Yeah? All right, mate – you please yourself . . .'

Hastings watched the ambulance move out of the station forecourt and tapped on the window of a minicab parked near by. 'Follow that ambulance, will you? There's a friend of mine inside.'

Above the concourse at Heathrow airport's international Terminal 3 the flight indicator panel flickered as the display became instantly updated: Flight PA 602 from Washington had now landed.

Twenty minutes later passengers from Washington began to emerge into the hall below, customs and immigration formalities finally completed; businessmen and tourists, grandparents and small children, all moving now towards the cluster of people waiting for them beyond the barriers as they pushed their luggage ahead of them on unwieldy, overloaded metal trolleys.

Men waiting for other, less attractive women spared a quick, envious glance at the dark-haired woman in her mid-thirties who seemed to be travelling alone. She was an American, they thought: had to be. No other nation on earth groomed its women in such a manner, gave them such unassailable outer confidence. They glanced covetously at her legs, at the shape of her breasts and the tight cheeks of her bottom and then turned reluctantly away to watch for their own arrivals, the woman in chocolate-brown jacket and calf-length, cream coloured skirt brushed to the back of their minds, soon to be forgotten.

Had they either the time or the perception to watch her longer they might perhaps have considered it unusual for an attractive woman starting a long journey on her own to finish it without striking a casual, transitory friendship with some male passenger who would now offer to help with her luggage, share a taxi into town, perhaps even attempt to pursue the friendship further. But now, as she pushed her trolley towards one of the Change kiosks at the back of the terminal building, she was quite alone.

There *had* been an approach on the flight across the Atlantic as the man seated on her left had attempted to break the monotony of yet another transatlantic crossing by casual, harmless flirtation. Good-looking, smooth, successful now as an executive with Burmah Oil, he had nevertheless turned away after several minutes, recoiled from a sudden glimpse of inner coldness that had crept unbidden into those beautiful blue eyes even as they were talking; a look that had been in chilling contrast to the direct sexuality of the woman seated in seat G6.

The man – a former Marine Corps veteran – had sat back and puzzled over that look for some time as their 747 planed down across southern Ireland towards England, for the look disturbed him, jarred at his sense of well-being like an act of senseless cruelty.

The eyes had been dead, he decided finally – quite dead; they had seen things that had scarred the soul within. He had seen that look many times before in the Mekong Delta when he had been a junior officer. Then it had been in the eyes of his soldiers, in the faces of men familiar with the trade of killing. They had come to call it the 'thousand year stare' and it had been as much a part of his life then as the sound of artillery support or the stench of rotting flesh. Oh yes – he had seen that look before.

But never in the eyes of a woman.

Toni Johnson changed her dollars into sterling and was turning away from the Change kiosk when a quiet voice stopped her in her tracks. 'Hi, Toni.' She turned towards the voice at her shoulder and smiled a beautiful smile. It almost touched her eyes.

'Bill! My, my – the boss himself!' She kissed William Ottley on the cheek.

'Have a good flight?' She nodded as he took her arm, lifted her suitcase down from the trolley and guided her towards the automatic doors. 'Car's waiting right outside.'

'What have you got for me?' she asked when Ottley had handed her case to the driver and they were sitting together in the back of a hired Mercedes. Ottley reached down to a briefcase beside him, snapped open the locks and reached up to turn on the car's interior light.

'A target,' he said simply. 'One, possibly two.' The car pulled away from the parking bay and cruised slowly towards Terminal I, the Terminal for domestic flights within the UK. William Ottley opened his briefcase and handed the woman an envelope together with a photograph of a man frozen in mid-stride crossing the road. He was in his mid-sixties, grey-haired, running to fat. Toni Johnson studied the photograph for several moments and then tore open the envelope and extracted a thin slip of paper. It read simply: 'Peter Tillet. 17, Banner Crescent, North Shields, Newcastle.'

Toni Johnson looked up, her eyes alive for the first time. 'Termination?'

Ottley nodded. 'Uh-huh. As discreetly as possible. An accident.' He handed her a fat envelope which also was sealed.

'Money. Hotel accommodation. Car hire papers. It's all there.'
Finally he added an airline ticket, leant forward and pointed
towards the entrance to the Terminal buildings. 'Plane leaves in
twenty-five minutes. Have a good trip.'

The duty doctor in the hospital's casualty department turned
away from the X-ray clipped to the light screen and slipped a
pencil back into his breast pocket. 'Well, Mr . . . er . . . Hallam.
You'll be relieved to hear that nothing appears to be broken.
You've torn a shoulder muscle, that's all. Oh, and severe bruis-
ing, of course.'

'Of course,' murmured Gordon, gritting his teeth and wincing
with pain as he buttoned the cuff of his shirt.

The doctor turned to him again with a puzzled frown. 'How
did you say it happened?'

'I slipped,' lied Gordon. 'Slipped off the platform at Kew
station.' He'd been telling that story so often in the last hour and
a half that he had begun almost to believe it himself.

'You . . . slipped.'

Gordon eased into his jacket. 'That's what I keep telling
people. I'm not the jump-in-front-of-a-train type.'

'No . . . er . . . quite.' The doctor handed him a plastic jar of
tablets. 'Take a couple of these last thing at night. They'll help
you sleep.'

Gordon nodded and stuffed the pills into his pocket. 'That's
it? I'm free to go?'

The doctor looked up from his clip-board and nodded
agreeably. 'Yes, quite free. Only I'd take things easy with that
shoulder for a day or two if I were you.' Gordon slid the injured
arm gingerly down the sleeve of his duffle coat, thanked the
doctor and walked out of the casualty cubicle towards the reception desk. He felt almost light-headed with the pain in his shoulder, yet he was anxious above all else to get clear of the sterile,
antiseptic smell of illness, the over-heated claustrophobia of the
hospital.

Concentrating thus upon his own injuries, Gordon had no
eyes for the other patients in casualty. And none at all for the
man sitting in the waiting room reading a dog-eared magazine
who glanced up casually as he walked past.

Hastings watched Gordon push through the rubber-skirted doors and step out gratefully into the cold night air. Then he tossed the magazine aside and rose quietly to his feet.

He followed Gordon to Victoria station and was just behind him in the queue outside the ticket office.

They even caught the same train down to Lewes.

For Gordon, that journey south was a nightmare in itself. For most of the journey the train was crowded and he had to stand and protect his shoulder as best he could from the swaying of the train and the thoughtless jostling of other passengers. Between the ambulance and his hospital discharge, Gordon had been swamped, overtaken by events. Now, for the first time, there was a chance to think beyond the pain in his shoulder – and time too for reaction to set in as he relived again that moment of horror as he was flung forward into the path of the train.

Gordon raised a shaking hand to his face and discovered he was sweating. He smiled weakly at the look of motherly concern on the face of an elderly woman and took two of the pills the doctor had given him.

He had not slipped – he had been pushed. He knew that. Knew it from the force of the blow in his back as he had stood there on the edge of the platform. The question was: had it been an accident? Because if it hadn't been an accident . . . Gordon swallowed. He wanted very much to believe it had been an accident, a freak chance of misfortune. Yet no one had apologized. No one had rushed to his side afterwards to say how sorry they were. There had been nothing.

Suddenly, into Gordon's mind popped the picture of that man at the Public Record Office, looking up at him from the stairwell with a coat over his arm and an expression of . . . what had it been? Inner knowledge? Yes! That was what it had been as he tried to slide away towards the exit – inner knowledge.

And the only thing he could think of that tied that look to a shove under a moving train was a wartime mission called Apostle. And the fact that he, Gordon Hallam, had been digging into the past.

It struck Gordon then, like another blow in the back, that whoever had tried to kill him at the station would know that he had failed. And would therefore try again. Gordon sank gratefully into an empty seat.

The Gordon Hallam who got into the train at Victoria had had a lucky escape from the sort of random accident that could have happened to anyone. The Gordon Hallam who got out of that same train at Lewes was a different animal altogether. An animal who knew he was hunted.

Gordon left the train, crossed over to the newsagent's, swung round and then watched closely as the passengers streamed off the train and poured through the ticket barrier. Not until the platform was quite empty did Gordon go across to the line of waiting mini-cabs and climb gratefully into the rear. 'Sidcott, please,' he told the driver, sagging back with relief. At least he hadn't been followed. The taxi pulled out of the station.

Hastings stepped out of a doorway and watched it disappear up the road. Then he glanced at his watch, turned and walked up the road towards the town centre. He knew where Hallam was going, for he had been there before – on Boxing Day.

Besides, there was no hurry. He had all night.

Gordon paid off the taxi a hundred yards up the darkened lane and approached his father's house cautiously on foot. The place waited for him. With Rachel back home now in Stowcombe the house was dark and brooding and menacing and there was not a light to be seen. He pressed back against the hedge and stood there in the shadows, watching for the glimmer of a torch, listening for the slightest sound. But the only noise was the gentle rattle of the wind in the bare branches and the rasp of his own breathing to tell him how scared he was.

He eased open the garden gate, pressed back into the shadows and skirted round the front to the garden shed. He slipped off the padlock, groped around in the dark and emerged a moment later clutching a garden fork. Not much, perhaps, but better than nothing. He would have preferred a pistol. Or a belt-fed machine-gun.

Down the garden path towards the back door, the fork held down at his side. A pause while he searched his pockets for the key and then he was holding his breath as the lock went back with an audible click.

Now he was inside the kitchen with the back door closed and locked behind him. Darkness all around, the only sound the measured tick of the clock in the hallway and the hiss of tap water against a leaking washer. Gordon moved silently to the kitchen sink and tightened the tap, the fork still gripped in his hand.

Tick – tock – tick – and then Bong! as the clock struck out the hour and Gordon's heart crashed through the roof of his skull.

He'd had enough darkness. Gordon switched on the kitchen light, sagged back against the kitchen wall and blew out his cheeks in a long sigh of relief as he waited for his legs to stop shaking. Presently he eased out of his duffle coat with great care, made himself a sandwich and poured himself a stiff scotch. Then he turned off the kitchen light, went into the sitting-room with his drink and sandwich and eased down carefully onto the sofa. He sat there for five, then ten minutes, gazing vacantly into the fireplace, munching his sandwich as the scotch lined his stomach and soothed his ragged nerves.

Rousing himself at last, Gordon took his father's address book out of his jacket pocket, opened it at the page containing the telephone number of 'Mark. Apostle' in Zug and lifted the telephone towards him.

Then, almost as an afterthought, Gordon rose carefully to his feet, turned off the light in the hall and in the sitting-room and felt his way back to the sofa with the house now in total darkness.

And the garden fork still in the kitchen.

He lowered himself onto the carpet and sat back against the arm of the sofa, the pain in his shoulder now reduced to a dull aching throb. Then he lifted the telephone down onto his lap and dialled the international operator.

'I'd like a number in Switzerland, please: Zug 854399,' he said quietly. Yet to ears tuned to the silence of the house, to the slightest creak of a floorboard, his voice sounded loud as shouting in the dark, watching house.

'And what is your number, please?' He told her. 'One moment.' He waited. A ringing tone in a far-off, distant land followed almost immediately. If he had tried to dial Rachel in Devon it would have taken twice as long.

'*Ja?*' A foreign voice with, in the background, the clatter of dishes and the buzz of many voices. A kitchen somewhere; a restaurant perhaps.

'Hello? Zug 854399?'

'*Bitte?*'

'Oh. Er . . . *Ist das Zug* . . . er . . . *acht* . . . *funf* . . . *vier* . . . *drei* . . . *neun* . . . *neun?*'

'*Bitte?*'

'Ah . . .' muttered Gordon, struggling with the memories of a language he had not spoken since schooldays. 'Ah . . . *sprechen Sie English, bitte?*'

'*Ja,* I speak English a little. Can I help you, please?'

'Who am I calling, please?'

'This is Restaurant Oppel. My name is Tyschen – Bruno Tyschen. I am the owner.'

'I am calling you from England –'

'Yes, yes: I can hear you. I know that. What do you want, please?' Impatient now; the impatience of a man with customers to serve –

'My name is Hallam, Mr Tyschen – Gordon Hallam. Walter Hallam was my father. I wonder – did you . . . did you know him? During the war? Walter Hallam?'

'Walter? But of course! Of course I know Walter! You are his son, you say?'

Jackpot! thought Gordon as the tiredness dropped away. Hole in one. 'That is correct, yes! I am his son. I'm sorry to have to tell you that –'

'How is Walter? It is some years now since we –' The rest of the sentence was lost in a crash of crockery followed by a sudden gale of background laughter.

'My father is dead, Mr Tyschen – Walter is dead,' explained Gordon slowly, carefully. 'He was knocked down by a car and killed. That is why I am calling you.'

'Walter? Dead? It is not . . . not possible! When . . . when was this?'

'December 26th. Boxing Day.'

'I am sorry, Mr Hallam – truly sorry. Your father was a good friend. How do you British say – one of the best? A good friend and comrade during difficult times – during dangerous times, eh? You understand?' That gave Gordon the way in.

'I . . . I would like to ask you something that may sound a little strange, Mr Tyschen. Don't be offended if –'

'Offended? I am impossible to offend, Mr Hallam – impossible! Ask anyone! But please: quickly, eh? The customers, you understand? And speak loudly, yes? The noise here, she is very great. Not that I should complain, God knows, but –'

'Did Walter know you as "Mark", Mr Tyschen? During the war?'

'Yes! Yes, that is right! I was "Mark" and he was "Luke"! He told you about our little adventure, did he?'

'No. No, he didn't, Mr Tyschen: that's just the point,' explained Gordon hurriedly. 'What about Apostle – does that mean anything to you? Operation Apostle?'

There was a sudden bark of laughter down the line from Switzerland. 'Apostle? Of course! Your father and I –'

'That was a code-name, right?'

'That was *our* code-name, Mr Hallam – ours! Your father's, mine –'

'Was Dad an agent? For S O E? Is that what you're saying?'

Tyschen sighed impatiently. 'We were *all* agents, Mr Hallam – every one of us!'

'You mean there were –' The words snapped off suddenly and there was silence.

'Hello? Mr Hallam? Are you there?'

Gordon broke the connection with the tip of his finger and replaced the phone very, very gently.

He had just heard the faintest scratching sound. At the lock on the front door.

There it was again.

Gordon lowered the phone to the carpet as though it was fused. Then he rose slowly to his feet and crept behind the sitting-room door, his heart smashing against his ribs like a trip-hammer.

There was the faintest, faintest creak as the front door opened. Gordon pressed back against the wall, his scalp literally crawling with fear as he heard the soft, measured stealth of approaching feet. The feet stopped outside the sitting-room door, just inches away from Gordon as he held his breath, not daring to breathe. The door swung back, there was a long moment of stretching, pendulous silence – and then the steps receded.

For a second or two Gordon just closed his eyes, let out his breath and gave way to numb, paralysing terror as he imagined he heard the steps moving away and up the steps towards the first floor. Then, with a superhuman effort, he forced himself to move away from the wall. Because once the man had checked upstairs and found those rooms were empty he would come downstairs again. To wait. Perhaps here, in the sitting-room.

Gordon remembered the garden fork. Propped up beside the sink. In the kitchen.

It took every ounce of will to move away from behind that door and walk quiet as a shadow down the passage and into the kitchen.

He was three steps from the garden fork when two hands locked suddenly around his neck.

The shock of that first contact was utter, catatonic. Gordon let out a strangled scream and jerked convulsively to one side. The suddenness of his move, the strength Gordon found through fear, was enough to fractionally loosen the man's grip, to throw him off balance. Gordon broke free and lunged away, the breath sobbing in his throat as he fetched up against the kitchen units, the man clawing after him in the darkness without a word, without a sound. Gordon swept up the garden fork, whirled round and lunged blindly upwards. There was a moment's brief resistance and then the prongs slid forward. There was a stifled grunt. Gordon let go of the fork and blundered across the kitchen. Then there was a sudden rattle of breathing and a sliding, slithering thud.

And then, most unnerving of all, there was silence.

Gordon's legs gave way and he slid down to the floor, his back pressed against the kitchen units. He was sitting there still, hands pressed against the floor for support, when he felt something wet and sticky between his fingers.

It might almost have been water.

Gordon scrambled to his feet, groped his way to the light switch and snapped it on.

The adult human body contains, on average, ten pints of blood. Spread out across the kitchen floor, it looks like a great deal more.

A man lay crumpled on his side, the garden fork on the floor still attached to his body by two of the five ten-inch prongs that had pierced his throat.

Gordon gagged, stumbled to the kitchen basin and threw up.

What Gordon forced himself to do in the next two and a half hours would haunt him for as long as he lived.

To begin with, of course, he did nothing beyond surrender to the sickness, the disgust and the aching, rolling nausea that is the true concomitant to killing as he stifled the urge to dash out into the street and yell for help from anyone who would listen. But that, Gordon had the wit to realize, would inevitably lead to the police, place him within reach of whoever was able to arrange near-fatal accidents at Underground stations and enlist the help of dry little civil servants at the Public Record Office. So, no police.

Which meant there had to be no body.

Gordon turned off the kitchen light and went out into the garden where, in a corner of his father's vegetable patch safe from prying eyes, panting in the silence, sweating with fear, exertion and the lancing pain in his shoulder, he dug a shallow grave.

And then came the worst part of all.

Gordon forced himself to go back into the dark kitchen where, without pausing to think, he wrenched the fork from the dead man's neck, gritted his teeth and hoisted the stiffening corpse into a fireman's lift over his sound shoulder. Then he staggered out into the garden with his grisly burden, the man's head lolling companionably against the small of his back. Gordon closed his mind to that, staggered on down the garden and tipped the body into the grave with a horrible slithering thud that he would never forget.

Gordon had to stop then, hurry back indoors and pour himself another stiff drink from a bottle that rattled against the lip of the glass.

As he turned away from the dresser mirror he caught sight of his own appearance. He was caked and smeared with earth, his jacket and shirt were sticky with blood and his hair was sticking up in wet, sweaty spikes. Draping blankets over the back door and kitchen window in case he was overlooked, Gordon turned on the light and spent the next hour using his father's best towels to mop up the blood on the kitchen floor. Then he wiped the fork clean, washed, changed, crammed his own clothes and the blood-soaked towels into an old pillow-case, replaced the fork in the garden shed and went on down the path to fill in the grave.

He stopped suddenly, the hair rising on the nape of his neck.

Because where there should have been silence, there was sound. A tiny, scarcely audible electronic bleeping.

Hypnotized by terror, Gordon edged slowly closer and peered down into the dark grave.

The man had carried an electronic pager clipped to his belt. Now that pager was being activated as someone, somewhere, tried to contact him.

Gordon threw the pillow-case down into the grave and began shovelling soil onto the body with manic haste. Gradually the weep-weep-weep of the bleeper faded and the only sound was the sob of Gordon's breathing and the thud of falling earth.

# : 13 :

In their cave hide-out in the snow-capped mountains of Uzbekistan, the SAS Captain reached over and shook Ratbag by the shoulder. Around him, the other two members of his team began packing away their equipment and eradicating every last trace of their stay with a thoroughness born of meticulous training and a determination to survive that ignored the freezing cold and biting, knife-edged wind.

Ratbag had been curled up in his sleeping bag, his rifle at arm's reach. Now two eyes sprang open in the filthy, bearded face. 'We're moving, Ratbag,' said the officer quietly, tearing off the top sheet of the one-time code pad and holding it briefly over a hexamine fuel tablet where it flared into instant flame. He had spent the last hour decyphering a long signal from London. It included the fruits of Lord Porterfield's deliberations about Apostle.

'We're moving back?' asked Ratbag, pulling his sleeping bag apart and rising smoothly to his feet.

The officer shook his head. 'We're going north, over the border.' He glanced round at the others. 'Looks like we should have brought our buckets and spades. London want us to do a bit of digging.'

The barracks of the 117th Motor Rifle Battalion of the Soviet Army were dark and silent. It was a few hours before dawn and the only light came from a single bulb in the laundry room.

Nikolai Samlar had been there for hours.

Sergeant Barak had kept him on the assault course for ninety minutes, during which time Nikolai had never once stopped running. His glossy parade-ground boots had been turned into sodden, shapeless lumps and his greatcoat had more than doubled its own weight in mud and water – but he had not stopped as Sergeant Barak sat smoking on his log, watching closely as Nikolai floundered over the obstacles, his world reduced to pain and exhaustion through the misted-over eye-pieces in the hated, stifling respirator. Both heels rubbed bloody-raw in wet boots, soaked with sweat and dizzy with exhaustion, Nikolai had struggled on, refusing to give in.

At last Sergeant Barak had brought the torture to an end, stamping out his cigarette and sending Nikolai floundering off to rejoin the rest of his squad with a careless flick of the wrist.

But there Nikolai discovered his problems had not ended. He collected Demerits from the Regimental Zampolit officer for missing the period of political study; he collected Demerits for missing mess call and – most serious of all – he collected Demerits for being absent from weapon training without authorization. For the last of these offences – more physical punishment: press-ups, push-ups and a twenty-minute hobbling run up and down the edge of the parade ground, an assault rifle held high above his head. But this time, no respirator. No fucking respirator. Nikolai had almost enjoyed it.

For the other two offences: clothing parade at 0400. In full winter parade uniform: greatcoat, fur hat, polished brown belt with brass buckle, black boots.

And so, while his comrades slept between rough blankets in the crowded barracks at the end of the corridor, Nikolai worked in the laundry room, racing against that 4 a.m. deadline to restore the greatcoat and boots he had worn on the assault course to parade-ground condition.

He scrubbed his greatcoat with the little wooden nailbrush he had purchased from the commissary, scrubbed at the stains of mud and green bark until the tips of his fingers were white and bleeding, slung the sodden greatcoat over his shoulders and hobbled over to the cookhouse, teeth chattering with cold. There he used the last of his precious hoard of cigarettes to bribe a cook to put his boots next to the oven doors and permit him to lean back against the side of the oven and sleep for one whole hour while the greatcoat dried around his shoulders.

The hour skipped by and Nikolai awoke with a start. Someone was shaking him urgently by the shoulder.

'Whaa—?' Nikolai sagged back against the warm oven doors. 'What the hell are you doing here?'

Yuri Rashidov grinned down at his friend. 'Thought you could do with a bit of support – Here.' He thrust out a newspaper package.

Nikolai took it suspiciously. 'What is it?'

'See for yourself. Go on – open it.'

Nikolai tore open the package. Inside was a strip of sausage-meat sandwiched between two thick slices of coarse brown bread.

'Sorry I couldn't manage more. That bastard Yasnov was watching me like a hawk.'

Nikolai nodded. 'Thanks.' He stuffed the sandwich into his mouth and chewed busily, wolfing down the food, the energy. Through a mouthful of sandwich, cheeks bulging – 'What time is it?'

'Two. Just gone.' Nikolai scrambled to his feet and then stumbled, groaning. 'What's wrong?' asked Yuri. Grimacing, Nikolai pointed downwards. 'Take a look.' For the first time Yuri noticed Nikolai's feet. The toes were gummed together by dried blood.

Leaning on Yuri's shoulder, Nikolai gathered up his boots, tucked them under his arm and began hobbling towards the door. As he passed the swarthy cook in sweat-stained vest and apron, the man thrust a steaming tin mug into his hands. 'Here – take it.' Nikolai took the mug and slurped down the hot soup, burning his lips on the side of the mug in his haste.

'Thank you, comrade,' he managed.

The man made an off-hand gesture of dismissal. 'Forget it. I hate the bastards too,' he growled, wiping his hands on his dirty white apron.

Yuri shoved Nikolai towards the door. 'Let's go.'

Sixty-five minutes later.

'There. How's that?'

Nikolai leant all his weight onto the iron and there was a hiss of steam as he pressed in one of the final creases and looked up. Yuri was holding up one of his boots. It gleamed and shone beneath the single light bulb. Nikolai managed a quick grin and nodded his approval, the lines of exhaustion etched plain on his face.

'How much longer?' He had been asking the same question every ten minutes.

'That'll have to do.'

Nikolai stripped off his working trousers, rummaged around in his towel roll for his razor and shaved with slow, maddening care in cold water. Then he began dressing: best shirt and tie, brown uniform trousers; jacket and jackboots. He grimaced with pain as he stamped tender, bleeding toes into the same boots he had worn on the assault course.

Yuri held up the immaculate greatcoat and Nikolai slipped his arms into the sharply-pressed sleeves.

Nikolai picked up the brown waist-belt and fastened it carefully over his great-coat. Yuri bent down with a handkerchief and polished suddenly at a tiny blemish in the gleaming leather. The fur cap was placed at exactly the right angle and Nikolai was ready. He had beaten the clock. Beaten Sergeant Barak.

But he wasn't clear yet.

One last look in the mirror, then Nikolai brought his heels together with a smart click and threw Yuri his very best parade-ground salute.

Yuri grinned and tossed the shoe brushes into the box. 'You'll do, Comrade Tartar – at a pinch. If the Guard Commander's pissed out of his skull.'

Nikolai turned towards the door, then: 'I won't forget, Yuri. That's a promise,' he pledged seriously. Yuri turned away, embarrassed. 'Good luck, peasant.'

Nikolai made an obscene gesture, turned on his heel and went down the steps to the parade ground. He straightened his shoulders and began marching towards the guardroom: left-right-left-right – up the steps with the clock showing 0359: left-right-left-right . . . halt! Crash-bang, one-two.

'Samlar, N., 95986455 reporting to the Comrade Guard Commander for disciplinary inspection as ordered by Comrade Sergeant Barak, number six Platoon!' barked out Nikolai, his eyes nailed to the far wall.

The duty Sergeant yawned, swung round in his chair and reached for a clip-board hanging behind him. He consulted this, glanced up at Nikolai standing motionless before him, opened a drawer in his desk and took out a pair of spotless white cotton gloves. He rose to his feet and Nikolai's heart sank. This man was a Russian too, he remembered.

Hands clasped behind his back, the Russian Sergeant strolled forward and treated Nikolai to a careful, raking inspection. He glanced down at the clip-board once more. 'Ah, yes – Comrade Samlar. We've been hearing about you. You were on the assault course earlier today – correct?'

'Yes, Comrade Sergeant,' snapped Nikolai, eyes never moving.

A gloved hand swam into vision and stroked a gentle line down the row of gleaming, polished buttons. The Sergeant then inspected his fingertip, looking for dirt, for marks, for dust – anything. But the fingertip was clean. 'Well, well, Samlar,' he murmured, 'you have been a busy little blackass.' Nikolai never moved.

The Sergeant spent a further three minutes inspecting Nikolai from head to toe. He checked everything from the red-pointed star on Nikolai's cap to the back of his belt buckle; from the stitching of his red shoulderboards to the number of metal studs on the soles of his nailed boots. And he found – nothing.

Finally, it was over. 'You are dismissed, Comrade Samlar. I will mark your appearance as satisfactory.'

'Thank you, Comrade Sergeant!' Nikolai turned on his heel, went down the guardroom steps and marched away across the gravel.

'Pricks!' he muttered under his breath as a fierce, savage exultation took hold and brought with it the realization that he had beaten them: Barak, Yasnov, the guardroom – the whole stinking Russian Army, the people who had taken away his homeland, tried to take away his pride, his heritage, his tradition. And failed. 'Russian pricks!'

As Nikolai marched back to the barracks he began to sing softly under his breath. The men in the mountains of home would have recognized the ballad instantly.

It was shortly after nine in the morning as Gordon climbed stiffly down from the cab of a tall furniture lorry in a lay-by outside Ashford in Kent, slammed the cab door and raised a weary hand in thanks to the driver who had given him a lift.

Outside the cosy warmth of the cab it was raw and overcast and Gordon shivered in the sudden cold as he picked up his bag and set off towards the cheerful, steamy warmth of the transport cafe at the edge of the lorry park beyond a sea of churned mud and gleaming puddles. Perhaps someone over there would be able to give him a lift to Dover.

Gordon was going to Switzerland. To see Bruno Tyschen and ask him about Apostle. Face to face.

'. . . Well, then, what *are* you going to say to him?' persisted Bunny Vickers, holding up her husband's overcoat and watching his reflection in the hallway mirror as he grasped the sleeves of his jacket and slipped into his overcoat.

He shrugged helplessly. 'I . . . I don't know. I haven't decided yet. Dammit, Bunny,' he fumed,' I just want to know what the man's up to, that's all! It's about time somebody started asking a few questions.'

'So you're just going to march up to his house and bang on his front door, is that it?'

George Vickers sighed in exasperation. 'All I know is that if he *is* still involved, if he is still pulling strings, then it's time the Department knew about it. We're the ones whose heads start to roll when things come unstuck, not some . . . some chap who's supposed to have retired four years ago and who – what's the matter?'

'I just think you're over-reacting somewhat, that's all, darling. Just because of that business with the Press Office. There's probably some perfectly innocent explanation that –'

'There's more to it than just that, Bunny,' said Vickers with quiet obstinacy. 'There's the principle. Of accountability.' He turned to the oak chest and picked up his wife's car keys. 'I'll take the Mini, I think. Easier to park.'

Bunny nodded absently. 'George –' He turned, a hand on the door. 'You will be . . . careful, won't you, dear?'

He smiled. 'The man's only human, you know . . .'

She nodded and rested a slim hand lightly on his arm. 'Discreet, then.' She hesitated, brushing at the shoulders of his coat with her fingers. 'If he is still ... you know ... active, well-connected, he could make things awkward for you if you rubbed him up the wrong way. So be careful. Watch what you say, will you? For me?'

Vickers' eyes softened as he saw the concern in his wife's eyes. He patted her hand gently. 'I will, I promise.'

He crossed the mews courtyard to the row of locked garages, slipped behind the wheel of his wife's Mini and drove the short distance to Eaton Terrace, his face grave and thoughtful as he grappled with troubled thoughts that centred around a somewhat old-fashioned desire to restore a proper accountability to the workings of the Foreign and Commonwealth Office.

He parked in Eaton Terrace, glanced up at the tall, imposing buildings and walked briskly up the wide steps to Lord Porterfield's porch.

The front door was thick and soundproofed so that he had no impression of approaching footsteps until the door opened suddenly and he found himself the subject of silent scrutiny by a stout, elderly housekeeper. 'Good morning, sir,' she said with the merest hint of a Scottish accent.

'Er ... good morning. Is Lord Porterfield at home, please?'

'Are you expected, sir?'

'No. No, I'm not expected.'

Scottish lips compressed into a tight little line. 'And the name, sir?'

'Vickers. George Vickers. From the Foreign Office.'

The door was opened wide at last. 'If you wouldn't mind waiting in the hallway, sir, I'll see if his Lordship will receive you.' Vickers stepped inside and the door was closed firmly behind him. 'George ... Vickers. From the Foreign Office.' He watched, amused, as she mouthed the words carefully to herself, wrote his name on a slip of paper and placed it in the centre of a polished silver salver. Then, with a little satisfied nod, she walked slowly down the hall with the salver held out in front of her like some papal offering.

Vickers glanced around at his surroundings: massive grandfather clock ticking solemnly beside an old-fashioned coat stand; hunting scenes in heavy wooden frames galloping away towards a length of rich crimson carpet punctuated by polished brass stair-rods that disappeared up into the darkness of the first floor. Wealth, inheritance and solid Victorian tradition, thought Vickers: there probably isn't a plastic spoon in the house.

'Mr Vickers? If you would come this way? Lord Porterfield will see you now.' George Vickers went through into the drawing-room and the door closed softly behind him.

Lord Porterfield sat behind his desk, the morning's papers scattered around him, a coffee cup at his side. 'Good morning, George! Come along in – what a pleasant surprise,' greeted Lord Porterfield genially. Was there just a trace of wariness in the greeting? wondered Vickers, stepping forward to shake hands.

'Take a seat, take a seat,' offered Lord Porterfield, waving Vickers to an armchair opposite a desk still littered with a chaos of papers. 'Coffee?'

'Thank you – no,' declined Vickers firmly. Lord Porterfield must have sensed something in his tone for he glanced up, his cup poised.

'"This ... er ... this has to do with the Department, I take it?'

Vickers nodded. 'It has, yes.'

Lord Porterfield sat back, linked his hands together and regarded his visitor over the ridge of his knuckles. 'Please: I am at your disposal.'

'I ... er ... I confess I find this more than a ... a little awkward,' began Vickers. 'As you know, some days ago now you asked me to withhold certain ... ah ... information from our Press Department.'

Lord Porterfield nodded. 'I remember. And you were most co-operative.'

'– Information relating to the ... er ... stability inside the Soviet Union.'

Lord Porterfield stirred impatiently. 'Yes. What about it?'

'You asked me,' continued Vickers doggedly, 'to hold back all such reports from whatever source as a ... personal favour. Reluctantly, I agreed.'

'– For which I am most grateful, George. But you will forgive me if I don't quite see what –'

'"The point I am getting at, Lord Porterfield, is this: in the last few days there has been a significant increase in the volume of such reports, both from our embassies and from other more . . . clandestine sources. If this –' He broke off as there came a soft knock on the door. It opened and Lord Porterfield's housekeeper entered bearing the salver.

'Excuse me, my Lord – another gentleman caller.' She proffered the salver to Lord Porterfield who took the note and unfolded it.

'Thank you, Alice.' He read the note, crumpled it abruptly in his fist and glanced up at George Vickers. 'Excuse me one moment, George,' he said, rising heavily to his feet and following Alice out into the hallway. The door closed firmly behind him.

William Ottley was waiting by the coat stand. He nodded grimly as he saw Lord Porterfield coming down the hall towards him and held up a cassette of tape. 'Something here I think maybe you oughta hear.'

Lord Porterfield took Ottley's arm and guided him further down the corridor away from the drawing-room door. 'Would you mind waiting in the next room for just one moment, Mr Ottley?' He gestured towards the drawing-room. 'Someone in there I'd rather you didn't see – at least, I should prefer it if *he* did not see *you*. It might raise unnecessary complications.'

William Ottley shrugged. 'Sure. Whatever you say.'

But it did not work out that way. George Vickers had risen to his feet and crossed to the bay window overlooking Eaton Terrace itself. The porch was to his left and the centrepiece of its roofwork – an ornate brass hexagonal lamp dating from the turn of the century – was above and directly in line with the fanlight at the top of the front door. From where he was standing, George Vickers could see the reflection of Lord Porterfield's visitor in the glass of the lamp. He recognized instantly who it was.

George Vickers turned back into the drawing-room, his thoughts in a whirl. He began to walk back to his chair – and then stopped in front of Lord Porterfield's desk, his eyes caught by the words 'SECRET' and 'CONFIDENTIAL' stamped on one, two, three government papers. Frowning, George Vickers bent forward, pushed some more papers gently aside and found himself looking at a photograph of a man in his late twenties or early thirties clipped to a report entitled 'Gordon Hallam – An Evaluation'. This was followed by the man's age, address and occupation. Printed across these details in neat black capitals were the words 'EXECUTIVE ACTION'.

Vickers glanced around the desk, appalled: more papers, more reports, more secret government evaluations. Then his eye was caught by a black leather briefcase resting on the carpet propped against the edge of the desk. The clasps were unfastened.

Another glance at the door, another listen for approaching footsteps. Silence. He bent down, lifted back the top flap and reached inside. His fingers felt a thin file. He slid it out into the lamplight, glanced down – and everything seemed to freeze into stone around him.

For the first time in a long career as loyal servant to the Crown, George Vickers found himself looking at a document bearing the very highest security classification of all – 'COSMIC'. The file was called simply 'Boadicea'.

He paused, his breath catching in his throat as he began to feel the first stirrings of fear, of being out of his depth. Lord Porterfield had access to 'COSMIC'. As far as George Vickers knew, only a handful of inner Cabinet members had access to information of that category.

Which made Lord Porterfield one of two things: either very powerful. Or very dangerous.

He leafed rapidly through the file: an impression of neat, sparse paragraphs with, at the back, a detailed map of south-west England with a thin black line marking the course of some railway with, every so often, a cutting or tunnel ringed in red.

Vickers looked up fearfully, closed the report, replaced file and briefcase exactly where he had found them and slipped back to his seat. He was only just in time. No sooner had he composed his features into a mask of polite resignation than –

'Sorry about that, George,' murmured Lord Porterfield blandly as he came back into the room and closed the door firmly behind him. 'Now then – where were we? I'm afraid I cut you off in mid-stride . . .'

As George Vickers pushed his discoveries to the back of his mind and told Lord Porterfield lamely that he would require written ministerial instructions before he could agree to suppress further stories about dissent inside the Soviet Union, Gordon

Hallam was hurrying through the plate-glass doors of the Seaspeed Hovercraft Terminal beside Dover's Prince of Wales Pier.

He had made the cross-country journey in just under four hours, hopping lifts from Ashford along the twisting Kent lanes that link Lyminge Forest with the A2 between Canterbury and Dover. Now he presented his ticket at the barrier, dumped his bag on the scales, had a moment's fright as he waited for the heavy hand on the shoulder as he went through passport control past the uniformed police officer and joined the other passengers in the departure lounge.

So far so good. He'd made it. He was safe; out of danger. For the moment at least.

Presently he was gazing out at the angry sea with that thoughtful expression shared by all those forced to contemplate a Channel crossing in rough weather. Then his flight was called and Gordon walked out with the other passengers across a bleak, windswept expanse of concrete towards the waiting Hovercraft that stood huge and ungainly on dry land with the thick black skirts of its apron drooping forlornly at its sides.

Gordon was the last to board. Two minutes later the Hovercraft rose from the ground, skidded down the slipway and began buffeting and lurching sickeningly towards France.

In Eaton Terrace William Ottley reached slowly into an inside pocket, drew out a cheap, dog-eared diary for the year 1980 and handed it to Lord Porterfield without a word. Lord Porterfield flicked through the pages and stopped at the name scrawled in the fly-sheet: Peter Tillet.

'Very many thanks,' he said quietly. 'I am only sorry it was necessary to call upon your men for such an unpleasant task.'

Ottley shrugged. 'All part of the service, I guess. And . . . er . . . it was a woman, not a man. Just for the record.'

'Oh. I see.' Lord Porterfield paused. 'I don't suppose you've any news regarding the other fellow – Tyschen?'

In reply Ottley pressed the 'play' button on the small tape recorder on the table beside him. 'Listen to this,' he said cryptically.

'– I'd like a number in Switzerland, please: Zug 854399,' said Gordon Hallam's voice. Lord Porterfield made to interject but stopped as Ottley raised a hand. The tape ran on for several seconds, then – 'Who am I calling, please?'

'This is Restaurant Oppel. My name is Tyschen – Bruno Tyschen. I am the –'

Lord Porterfield slapped his hand against the table. 'You've found him! You've bloody well found him!' he exclaimed.

Ottley pressed the 'stop' button. 'That guy Hallam found him. All we did was set the tap, sit back and listen. This was recorded at 21.35 last night from a number in Sidcott, Sussex.' He glanced at a small notebook. 'Our records show that Bruno Tyschen was born Walter Wedzik in Kielce, Poland, 5 August 1915. Naturalized Swiss 1948. From that date until –'

'So *that's* why we couldn't find any trace of him in Britain!'

Ottley nodded. 'Guess so. You want to hear the rest of the conversation?'

'Please. Go on.'

The tape continued. Presently –

'– What about Apostle?' asked Gordon's voice. 'Does that mean anything to you? Operation Apostle?' In London, both men heard a sudden bark of laughter.

'Apostle? Of course! Your father and I –'

'That was a code-name, right?'

'That was *our* code-name, Mr Hallam – ours! Your father's, mine –'

'Was Dad an agent? For S O E? Is that what you're saying?'

'We were *all* agents, Mr Hallam – every one of us!'

'You mean there were –' At that point the tape ran on in silence and Lord Porterfield looked up inquiringly.

'He just stopped,' said Ottley with a noncommittal shrug. 'Just broke off in mid-sentence.'

'Why was that?'

'We don't know. We're checking on it. It could be anything, only . . .'

'Go on.'

'There's probably no connection but we've lost contact with our guy down in Sussex. He's not responding to the call-in signal.' Ottley tapped the tape recorder pensively. 'That call was made before ten. Couple of hours later he placed another call.' Again Ottley depressed the 'play' button.

There was the sound of dialling followed by the ringing tone that went on for several seconds. Then – 'Hello?' A woman's voice.

'It's me.'

'Gordon!'

'I'm . . . I'm sorry I haven't called earlier. I've . . . I've been busy.'

Lord Porterfield frowned and glanced across at Ottley. The American nodded and stopped the tape.

'Right. You hear that? Same voice – only it's changed. Gone sorta flat, dead. Like something's happened.'

The tape ran on – 'You all right, darling?'

'– You see?' interrupted Ottley. 'She notices it too.'

There were two or three minutes of question and answer, the questions coming from the woman, Gordon's replies becoming more and more monosyllabic. Then, as the stilted conversation neared its end – 'I've got to go and see Mark, Rachel. In Switzerland. Shouldn't . . . shouldn't be more than a day or two. Three at the most.'

'*Switzerland?* When?'

'Tomorrow.'

'Tomorrow? Gordon, love, we can't afford . . . what is it, darling? What's happened?'

'I . . . nothing's happened. It's . . . I can't tell you. Not now. I'll be in touch again soon.'

'You can't just disappear to Switzerland as if . . . anyway, what about your passport? Money?'

'My passport's here, in my wallet. I . . . I can change money at Dover. I love you. Remember that, Rachel. I love you.'

'Gordon – listen a minute; why don't I – Hello? Gordon?' There was a click.

Ottley stopped the tape and there was silence. Then Lord Porterfield sighed and looked up slowly. 'I wonder if I might ask one more favour,' he began.

Ottley nodded, the request already anticipated. 'Don't worry. It's already taken care of. Hallam won't be coming home.'

# : 14 :

George Vickers hurried into his office, dropped his coat across a chair, sat down and consciously forced himself to relax. Then he pressed the intercom on his desk. 'Laura – bring in the Courtesy file, will you? Right away, please.'

'Certainly, sir.'

The Courtesy file was a daily internal Foreign Office bulletin that listed as a matter of routine all the foreign nationals who had arrived in Britain and whose activities might be of interest to the Foreign Office. It listed the date of their arrival, the duration of their stay and any particular visa arrangements that might have been made on their behalf: if the Russians wanted to bring in another trade attaché for a two-day working trip, common international courtesy dictated that his name would appear on the Courtesy file. It would remain there until he left. Reciprocal arrangements exist in all major capitals of the world.

'Here you are, sir – the Courtesy file updated as from zero four hundred this morning. Is . . . is anything the matter?'

'No, no. Everything's fine, Laura, thank you.' She left and George Vickers turned hurriedly to the American section and began running a finger down a long list of names.

There was no William Ottley listed.

Take it easy, George, he told himself. Perhaps he has been replaced. Then there would be no need for his name to appear on the file. He reached for the phone and dialled an internal number.

'A7.'

'Michael? George here – George Vickers.'

'George! Nice to hear from you. How's that lovely wife of yours?'

'Er . . . fine. Fine. Michael – off the top of your head: you wouldn't happen to know current status on an American chap by the name of Ottley, would you? William Ottley? Used to be a fairly big wheel in The Company, if memory serves.'

'Hold on a second. I'll just ask Boris.'

'Thanks very much.' Boris was the computer. Vickers waited. Presently –

'Yes, here we are: William Francis Ottley. Current Status: Deputy Director Operations, Central Intelligence Agency. Ex-Saigon, ex-Belize, ex-Berlin. Present location: unknown. Born July –'

'Thank you, Michael. That's . . . that's fine.' George Vickers replaced the receiver slowly.

Midday. Paris time.

Gordon took a handful of coins from his coat pocket, elbowed his way through a throng of chattering Parisians and leant over the glass counter of the station buffet. *'Combien ça fait?'* he asked self-consciously, pointing at a length of crusty french bread and sausage. The stallholder dropped a shower of small change into the apron purse tied around her vast waist, flicked a twenty-franc note into a bulging wallet and swung towards her next customer.

*'Quatre francs, m'sieur,'* she intoned automatically as Gordon fumbled with unfamiliar coins.

*'Un, s'il vous plaît. Avec un café au lait,'* he added.

*'Eh, bien – sept francs vingt-cinq,'* totalled the Parisienne immediately. Which left Gordon floundering.

*'Ah . . . combien, Madame?'*

The woman regarded him scathingly. 'Seven franc twenty-five,' she translated. 'Here – I show you.' Huge sagging breasts lolling forward across the glass counter, she picked deftly through his loose change and four coins vanished into her purse in the twinkling of an eye. She slapped a few centimes onto the counter and turned to her next customer with a roll of the eyes and a Gallic shrug that spoke volumes.

Gordon squeezed away from the crowded counter with the uneasy feeling that he had been short-changed. Coffee and roll balanced precariously in his hands he edged along the crowded concourse towards the Departures and Arrivals display board where he dropped his bag between his feet and looked about him.

Paris. Gare de L'Est. He supposed he should have felt excited

– exhilarated, even – surrounded by a score of different platforms carrying thousands of passengers to the far-flung corners of Europe, but instead he felt dazed by the noise. Dazed and weary and grimy after a rough Channel crossing and a rail journey from Boulogne to Paris that had done nothing to ease the ache in his shoulder or lift the throbbing headache from over his eyes. Now he sipped his coffee carefully and watched the information change and flicker above his head. There it was: his train to Zurich would leave from Platform 7 at – Gordon lurched suddenly and stumbled forward as someone pushed into him from behind and sent the carton of hot coffee flying from his hand. It hit the concrete floor and splashed back over his shoes, his trousers, his bag.

Gordon swung round angrily, shaking hot coffee from his fingers and wiping ineffectually at his trousers with his handkerchief as the woman who had pushed into him clutched at his shoulder, looked aghast at what she had done and began a babble of apologies:

'I'm . . . I'm so sorry!' she exclaimed, slender painted fingernails up to her mouth. 'Some . . . some guy back there just pushed through and . . . what can I say? I really am terribly sorry . . .'

'That's O K, forget it,' muttered Gordon without looking up, head still bent as he wiped away at his trousers.

'Forget it? After what I just did? Look at them – they're wrecked! Gee, I don't know what to say . . . I guess –'

'Yeah. I get the message. You're sorry. I'm sorry too. But it's O K. Forget it.' If there was one thing Gordon disliked more than having hot coffee spilt down his trousers it was voluble Americans.

Americans.

'Please,' she insisted, 'I can't just . . . walk away and leave it like that – I've ruined your pants! Would you like another coffee? Let me get you another coffee – please.'

Gordon looked up. 'No,' he decided evenly. 'No, I think one coffee is probably sufficient. For these pants, as you call them, anyway. Only we call them trousers.' The woman smiled and despite his tiredness and irritation, Gordon found himself smiling too. She really was very attractive.

179 :

'You're English, right?' Gordon nodded and the woman gave a theatrical sigh. 'Thank God for that. Can you imagine if I had to try apologizing to – I don't know – some Greek? A Turk maybe?' She shuddered.

'Don't worry about it.'

'You're not mad? Not even a teeny bit?' She held up a pinch of fingers. 'I'd be screaming the place down by now if it was me, I guess.' She groaned again with exasperation. 'Would you believe it? I was just checking the time of my train here through to Zug when this . . . this ox of a man comes barging –'

'Zug? Did you say Zug?' demanded Gordon suddenly.

She nodded. 'Yeah – that's right. In Switzerland.'

'It's at one. One twenty-six,' said Gordon quietly. 'Platform 7. Over there.' He pointed.

The woman turned and studied him curiously. 'Now how did you know that?' she marvelled. 'You weren't even looking at the board.'

'You have to change at Zurich,' continued Gordon, enjoying his advantage. He paused. 'I'm going there too.'

'To Zug? You're kidding!'

He shook his head. 'No. True, I'm afraid.'

'Really? Well, how about that!' she exclaimed as Gordon held out his hand.

'Gordon. Gordon Hallam.' They shook hands.

'Hi, Gordon. Glad to know you. I'm Toni. Toni Johnson.' She smiled.


Five men were seated around the metal conference table in the heart of an underground bunker on the outskirts of west London. Known only as the 'Fairview Complex', its name had been chosen to conceal the reality of a steel and concrete command and control centre beneath the fostered allusion to quiet, leafy suburbia.

Of those who had met in that private country house outside Dorking, only William Ottley and the Prime Minister were missing. The Britons had been called together by General Inkermann to review the latest developments relating to Boadicea and the clandestine deployment of Cruise in the west country. There was an armed sentry on the far side of the blast-proof door and a large map of Britain and north-west Europe projected onto a screen let down from the ceiling.

Sir Max Harrod struck a match, puffed away strongly at his pipe and blew a long plume of smoke towards the shaft of light thrown by the projector. Then he hunched forward. 'Yes, yes,' he repeated, waving out his match impatiently and turning towards General Inkermann. 'I understand all that – but I am still not entirely satisfied about this question of *range*.'

'It is not a question of range,' interrupted Lord Porterfield acidly. 'It is a question of trust; of faith. Cruise has become a symbol of commitment to mutual defence at a time, gentlemen, when the Alliance is sorely in need of such symbols.' He paused and looked slowly around the table. 'You have all seen the reports, read the surveys, monitored the escalating demonstrations at Greenham Common and elsewhere. In recent months, while we have been losing faith in America, they have been losing patience with us. This government's willingness to deploy Cruise without the usual ... ah ... democratic safeguards of parliamentary approval shows our allies that Britain will indeed honour those obligations inherent in the North Atlantic Charter and which –'

'Excuse me,' interrupted General Inkermann quietly as a buzzer sounded at his elbow. He leant forward to the microphone. 'General Inkermann.'

'Northwood messenger waiting outside, General.'

'Thank you.' He pressed a button and the steel door slid back with a low whine. A man in his trim mid-thirties entered the room, moved to the General's side and lifted a black dispatch bag onto the table. It was chained to his wrist. The messenger took a key from his pocket, unlocked the case and handed General Inkermann a thin yellow file. He waited while the General signed the official form of acceptance and release and then withdrew as discreetly as he had arrived. General Inkermann looked up. 'Excuse me one moment, gentlemen.' He then read the file, closed it slowly and bent to the microphone once more. 'Next map, if you please – southern Ireland and south-west England.'

He sat back, drumming his fingers gently against the cover of the file as the map was changed to show Ireland, St George's Channel, the Bristol Channel and the south-west of England.

Then he rose to his feet, picked up his metal-tipped pointer and moved to a position beside the screen.

'At 0735 this morning the MV *Galveston Roads*, outbound from Mobile, Alabama, offloaded a cargo of containers at Dungarvan habour – here.' He tapped the map between Cork and Waterford in the Republic of Ireland. 'Eighteen of those containers held much-needed industrial spare parts for Ireland's ailing electrical industries; six contained medical supplies for onward routing to British ports and as such were immune to close examination by Irish customs.' He smiled dryly. 'Which was perhaps just as well. That particular convoy should reach Bristol and the south-west some time before dawn tomorrow morning.' He paused. 'This, as you all know, is the first consignment, the 'dry-run', as it were. If all goes well, then the other missiles will begin to arrive in approximately ten days' time.' He turned towards Lord Porterfield. 'I assume you will be available for a site inspection?'

Lord Porterfield nodded. 'By all means, General.'

'And the Prime Minister?' queried Sir Max Harrod testily, still nettled by that earlier snub. 'I trust *she* will be informed?'

Lord Porterfield nodded calmly. 'She has already been told, Max. There was a private meeting at Downing Street shortly before breakfast this morning.'

'Private meeting?' scowled Sir Max Harrod. 'I wasn't told.'

'No,' agreed Lord Porterfield equably. 'No, you weren't.'


George Vickers was sitting at his desk giving only half his attention to the papers that lay before him while he worried about Lord Porterfield. It was a mark of that inner preoccupation that when the phone rang beside him a little later he almost snatched up the receiver. 'Yes?'

'Peter Wilson here, George. Sorry it's taken a while to get back to you.'

'Not at all. What did you find out?'

'About that chap Porterfield, you mean? Nothing. Nothing at all.'

'What?'

'Chap's as clean as a whistle. Retired four years or so ago. Plenty of activity before then, of course, but after that – nothing.

Dropped right out of sight apart from the usual luncheon meanderings and so forth.'

'Are you quite sure? I mean – what about MI5?'

'I've had a word with both '5' *and* '6'. When I mentioned his name and told them to give me the gentle nod if he was still . . . you know . . . involved in some way they both denied it most emphatically. Seemed to take it almost as a personal affront. Sorry, old man, but there it is.'

'I . . . I see. And what about that teacher chap down in Devon?'

'Hallam? Drew a blank there too, old love. No one in SIS had heard of him – and he certainly isn't under any kind of surveillance.' The voice had begun to sound mildly irritated. 'Look, George – is everything all right?'

'Yes . . . yes. Everything's fine. Thank you . . . thank you, Peter.'

'You're welcome, I'm sure. But George –'

'Yes?'

'I hope you won't take this amiss, old love, but d'you think you could firm up these theories of yours a bit next time before you get me digging around for you? I've got a reputation to protect too, you know? A small thing, as they say, but mine own.'

'I'm sorry, I –'

'No harm done, George, no harm done. But bear it in mind next time, hmm?'

George Vickers replaced the receiver and sat staring at his jotter for long moments. Because the man was right: reputations *were* at stake; something like this, wrongly handled, could finish him; bury him forever. Perhaps even jeopardize retirement benefits, pension and gratuity. Such things had happened in the past . . .

Yet Lord Porterfield was up to something, he knew he was: he hadn't imagined those papers and charts, that file with the COSMIC security classification.

As if to reassure himself that he was not going quietly mad, Vickers slid open the top drawer of his desk and took out a tourist map of the west country. He had bought it on the way into the office that morning after leaving Eaton Terrace and had spent ten minutes inking in – from memory – the railway line and tunnels he had seen on Lord Porterfield's map.

As he studied the map an idea came to him in the tradition of great British compromises: between the twin minefields of blurting out his madcap theories to the august head of British Intelligence and forgetting about Lord Porterfield altogether there lay what he saw now as the sane, safe middle-ground: it was Friday afternoon. The weekend stretched ahead. He could take Bunny down to the west country, have a little snoop around and no one need be any the wiser. If he stumbled across anything . . . untoward, he could pass it on to the head of '5' first thing Monday morning – and if he didn't, well, at least he would have checked, stopped himself making an even bigger fool of himself. And at the very least he and Bunny would have had a weekend away together. In the country. That clinched it. On impulse George Vickers lifted the receiver. 'Laura?'

'Sir?'

'Get me the names of a couple of good hotels in Devon, will you? Somewhere between Plymouth, say, and Okehampton.'

'Certainly, sir.'

The Paris–Zurich Express burst out of the tunnel into sudden blinding sunlight with a triumphant blast of its whistle. Gordon started violently and then forced an apologetic smile across the small table that divided his seat from that of Toni Johnson as the train swayed and rushed through the winter countryside. They had just left Troyes and Mulhouse was still one hundred and fifty miles to the east.

He looks haggard, thought Toni Johnson, studying her target shrewdly behind the friendly smile; his nerves are all strung out . . . 'So –' she continued quizzically. 'What makes a school-teacher from Devon –'

'*Ex*-schoolteacher,' corrected Gordon. 'I got the push just before Christmas. Services no longer required . . .'

'Gee, that's too bad.'

Gordon shrugged. 'They already had two history teachers. I was the last to arrive. Times got tough, someone somewhere decided it was time for a bit of belt-tightening and my name

came up. Along with a fairly limp golden handshake, of course.'
He kept the tone casual, deliberately flippant, hiding the deep, personal wound beneath.

Toni Johnson frowned. 'Golden handshake?'

'Compensation,' explained Gordon, the bitterness only just below the surface. 'I was paid off. Not a fortune, but enough for a few months. Enough for this.' He waved a hand around the compartment.

'But why Zug?'

'Why not? I might as well ask you the same question,' countered Gordon.

She had been ready for that. Toni Johnson sighed. 'Oh, I don't know – impulse, I guess. This job of mine, the one I was telling you about in London? In the hotel? It folds up in another month or so. A girlfriend kept going on about how wonderful it was, this place Zug, so I just thought I had to come and see for myself. It may be the last chance I get. When the job folds it's back home to the good old US of A – and when I say Kansas is flat, boy, I mean it's *flat*.'

'The grand tour, then.'

'Something like that, I guess,' agreed Toni Johnson. Then she levelled a finger. 'Hey, come on now – your turn! All you did was turn my question around!' Gordon shrugged, eased his shoulder, lifted the coffee pot and gestured with it towards Toni's cup. She shook her head. 'Why Zug?' she persisted playfully, as though the answer was of little importance, a pawn on the board of casual flirtation.

Gordon poured black coffee slowly into his own cup, added sugar and stirred. Then he looked up. 'It's an obsession,' he confided quietly.

Toni Johnson leaned forward. 'How's that?'

'An obsession,' repeated Gordon. 'That's what my wife calls it, anyway: an obsession – a timely distraction I'm hiding behind to put off finding another job – or finding that I can't find another job.'

Toni Johnson shrugged helplessly. 'You lost me.'

'Forget it,' said Gordon awkwardly, stirring his coffee again unnecessarily. 'You don't want to hear it. It's a long and boring story. Send you to sleep.'

'So? Tell me a long and boring story – I'm not going anyplace.'
She smiled and leaned forward encouragingly.

'You really want to hear it?'

'Sure I do!'

'OK – but just remember: you asked for it.' Gordon drew a
deep breath and settled back in his seat: 'It started on Boxing
Day, the day after Christmas. We were at a . . . a party, Rachel
and I, with some friends at the bottom of this lane where we
live . . .'

Toni Johnson began to listen very, very carefully.


They were on the grenade ranges. In fighting order and steel
helmets.

The recruits stood shivering in the icy wind, grouped with
varying degrees of interest and trepidation around a cluster of
shrapnel-scarred E-shaped throwing bays a three-kilometre run
from the barracks. They had done all the theory inside the lecture
rooms. Now, at last, it was time to turn theory into practice.

A slim, flat wooden crate of Soviet RDG-5 fragmentation
grenades lay open at the feet of Captain Odinstov, their Olympian
Company Training Officer. Usually, basic training was left in
the hands of the Platoon NCOs, men like Sergeant Barak, but
now they were about to handle live grenades – and that, according
to standing orders, required the presence of a suitably qualified
officer. Just in case, as Sergeant Barak had explained with a
wolfish grin, one of the fools under his care decided to blow
himself into little pieces.

Yuri glanced sideways along the line of helmets towards Nikolai who was watching the Captain with interest as he picked up
the first grenade and examined it carefully. He handled it with a
certain respect, Yuri noticed – and rightly so, for the grenade
had just been fused. They all had.

Captain Odinstov checked the pin was correctly positioned
and then passed the grenade to the nearest man who took it
gingerly. 'Go on – examine it. Get used to it,' ordered the officer.
'Then pass it along the line.' He did so and the grenade moved
on. Carefully.

It looked like a small, olive-green egg with a raised metal rim
half-way along its length and a flat, stainless steel lever that was

folded back along its length and held in place by a steel split-pin linked to a pull-ring.

Nikolai glanced at Yuri and grinned, then pointed a finger a little further along the line of waiting soldiers. Tinrass, the Uzbek conscript who had already earned a special place of contempt for himself after breaking down and weeping when Sergeant Barak shouted at him on the parade ground, was already pale and nervous. When the grenade reached him he passed it on hurriedly, eyes averted.

'Right – pay attention,' ordered Captain Odinstov quietly. It was a pleasure to listen to Captain Odinstov, they had decided. He hardly ever shouted. He left that to his N C Os. 'Sergeant Barak.'

'Sir!' Crash-stamp as Barak came to quivering attention, big hands pressed tightly against the seams of his baggy combat trousers.

'You will take half the squad' – Odinstov made a brief cutting gesture down the centre of the group – 'and use those bays over there.' He pointed. 'I will take these men here. One man at a time into the throwing bay, the rest back under cover – there.' He pointed behind them to a line of sandbagged staggered trenches. 'You will personally accompany each recruit into the bay, supervise each throw and report when completed. Any misfires are to be noted carefully and reported to me when the detail is completed – understood?'

'Sir!' That too was part of an officer's responsibilities: to crawl out onto the range and detonate by hand and plastic explosive any grenade that had failed to explode. It was not a popular pastime.

'Right then – carry on.'

Sergeant Barak wheeled about and faced his half of the squad. 'You heard the officer,' he bawled. 'Over here – follow me!' Yuri and Nikolai exchanged glances. They were both in Sergeant Barak's squad.

The N C O picked up another crate of grenades and carried it over to one of the throwing bays. He took out the tin of fuses and began arming each grenade with swift, deft movements. When he had finished he moved forward and began counting off the men:

'One – two. One – two. One –' He worked his way down the line, tapping on the chest of each man in turn. When he got to Nikolai he paused. 'No funny tricks, blackass. You clown around out here and I'll ram one of these up your arse and pull the pin myself, understand?' He moved on and Nikolai gazed after him with glittering hostility. 'One – two. One – two – What's the matter with you?' He had stopped in front of Tinrass, who was pale and sweating.

'I'm . . . I'm nervous, Comrade Sergeant.'

'I'm nervous, Comrade Sergeant,' mimicked Sergeant Barak. He swung round. 'Right then – all of you: back to those trenches and wait to be called. Even numbers here, odd numbers over there. MOVE!' They moved. Yuri, Nikolai and about ten others ran back and jumped down into the sandbagged slit-trenches.

'First man,' bawled Sergeant Barak from the throwing bays.

'I'll go,' volunteered Nikolai instantly. He hoisted himself out of the trench and doubled over to Sergeant Barak and stood stiffly at attention, chest heaving. Barak glared at him closely for a long moment but said nothing. Then he took one of the primed grenades from the crate and handed it deliberately to Nikolai: a hated jailer giving a lifer a loaded rifle.

'Come with me,' he ordered coldly, turning on his heel and leading Nikolai into the throwing bay past a series of staggered concrete walls. 'Get ready!' he ordered, watching critically as Nikolai stood back, legs braced apart, left shoulder pointing down-range. Nikolai waited, grenade clenched firmly in his right fist, both knuckles pressing together across the centre of his chest, pin gripped in left index finger.

'Pull!' ordered Sergeant Barak. Nikolai tugged out the pin, glanced down, paused a moment longer – 'Throw!' – released the lever which flicked away over his right shoulder with a loud click, drew back his arm, lobbed the grenade cleanly over the lip of the parapet and crouched down onto his knees, just as he had been taught, all in one smooth movement. Two . . . three . . . There was a sudden sharp crash as the grenade exploded, the ping! of flying metal fragments against the outside concrete walls of the throwing bay, a brief swirl of dust – and silence. Nikolai rose slowly to his feet. Despite himself he was grinning like a schoolboy. It worked! He'd done all right!

'Next!' shouted Sergeant Barak with a quick glance down-range as Nikolai waited for some comment, some recognition that he had performed satisfactorily. None came. Sergeant Barak turned, found Nikolai still standing there and regarded him coldly. 'Well? What are you waiting for?'

'Sergeant, I –'

'What is it?'

'Recruit Tinrass, Comrade Sergeant. He . . . he appears very nervous. I was wondering if perhaps –'

Barak was nodding slowly, suspicions confirmed. 'So – you're his nursemaid too now, are you? One grenade and you think you know it all, eh? You're some kind of expert. You? You make me puke –'

'He's a danger. He's so twitched he's likely to –'

'SILENCE!' roared Sergeant Barak. 'Rejoin the others! Now! Immediately!' he ordered, the blood rushing into his face. 'When I want the advice of a . . . a fucking blackass like you I'll ask for it. NEXT!'

Nikolai turned and doubled angrily away, the grenade ring dangling forgotten from his fingers as he dropped back into the trench. For a moment heads crowded round asking how it had gone, what it was like, then – 'I . . . I tried to tell him,' he panted to Yuri.

'And?'

'And? And nothing! Bastard didn't want to know. He wouldn't even listen.'

The training session got into its stride. Presently the range was echoing to the regular crack of explosions and the brief howl and hum of steel fragments; to the orderly whistle blast of Captain Odinstov and the hoarse shouts of Sergeant Barak. Finally, only two men were left who had yet to throw a grenade. One of them was recruit Tinrass.

'Recruit Tinrass!' bawled Sergeant Barak from the throwing bay. 'Over here – on the double!' I only made it worse, thought Nikolai dully as Tinrass looked around wildly for some means of escape: he's been waiting for him, just to spite me.

'No, I . . .' began Tinrass, shrinking away inside that huge steel helmet.

'Recruit Tinrass!' The voice was louder now, nearer. In

another moment a shadow loomed suddenly above their heads and Sergeant Barak was glowering down into the trench, legs apart, hands on hips, like some huge giant come to devour tiny humans. He crooked a finger, eyes dancing with sadistic enjoyment as he watched Tinrass cower away from that beckoning finger. 'Come,' he ordered simply.

Pushed from behind by some, jeered at for his weakness by others, Tinrass emerged from below ground and disappeared towards the throwing bays. 'Double!' ordered Barak, striding ahead to wait for his victim beside the crate of grenades. Tinrass broke into a shambling run and stopped at shivering attention in front of the NCO whom he regarded now with pathetic anxiety.

'Keep still – what's the matter with you?' demanded Sergeant Barak.

Private Tinrass swallowed. 'I . . .'

'STILL!' shouted the Sergeant, watching as Tinrass tried desperately to freeze into immobility. 'Better – that's better. Now then –' Barak reached down slowly, picked up a grenade and regarded it almost lovingly. 'Cut a man in half, this will,' he said conversationally. 'Splatter him all over the countryside like mincemeat: legs go one way, arms another . . .' He stepped forward and unfastened the top two buttons of Tinrass's tunic. The recruit shied away, eyes bulging with terror as Barak slipped the grenade carefully inside, fastened the two buttons and patted Tinrass gently on the chest. 'You heard what the Captain said,' he soothed gently. 'Examine it. Get used to it.'

Nikolai, Yuri and half a dozen others watched from the lip of the fire-trench with only their helmets above ground. 'Look at that *bastard*,' muttered Nikolai. 'Can you believe that?'

'Bet you twenty Tinrass faints from fucking fright,' offered someone.

'Cigarettes or roubles?' murmured another as he picked up the challenge, eyes on the tableau thirty metres away.

'Cigarettes of course, shithead. Who wants money out here?'

'You're on.'

'All right with me. That bloke couldn't puke into a bucket without help.'

They watched as Sergeant Barak pushed Tinrass into the throwing bay. Both men vanished from sight.

Sergeant Barak stopped in the centre of the throwing area and turned round. 'Get ready,' he ordered. There was a moment's pause and then Tinrass began fumbling inside his tunic for the grenade. Barak's face broke into a grin as Tinrass took out the grenade and stood there looking at it, his face frozen with terror.

'Stand by –' warned Sergeant Barak, stepping back. 'Pull!'

Nothing happened. The words hadn't penetrated.

'PULL – YOU STUPID IDIOT!' shouted the Sergeant. Tinrass pulled. The pin came out with a savage jerk, the lever spun away – and he hesitated.

'THROW!' screamed Barak, the smile gone. Private Tinrass threw.

The grenade left his hand, bounced short against the inside lip of the parapet and rolled back into the throwing bay. It landed on the sand with a soft, innocent little thud two feet away from Tinrass's left boot.

Time froze.

In many ways it was an exactly predictable situation, something Barak should have expected and had actually been trained to deal with, if not with Private Tinrass, then with somebody else. Confronted with live ammunition for the first time in their lives, it is not unknown for recruits to lapse into a sudden, uncomprehending trance that freezes reaction-time and transforms rational, normal young men into the accidental, very apologetic killers of themselves, their friends and their comrades. In every army in the world such a possibility is recognized and allowed for, the dangers reduced by emergency drills to a sequence of actions calculated to retrieve a potentially disastrous situation by a combination of fast action and cool thinking. The Soviet Army is no exception.

Sergeant Barak was faced with two clear options in the three seconds that remained before the grenade exploded: he could push Tinrass aside, sweep up the grenade, throw it outside the throwing bay and drop to the ground – or he could dive the *opposite* way behind the nearest blast wall and leave Tinrass and the grenade to get on with it together.

Sergeant Barak took a half step forward, hesitated – and dived behind the wall.

One second become two.

There was a deafening explosion, the sound enlarged and magnified, reflected back inside the throwing bay by the thick concrete walls on every side.

Nikolai and the men in the slit-trench thirty metres away fell suddenly silent. That one sounded different. That one sounded trouble.

'Shit –' began Nikolai, scrambling up out of the trench and running forward. A thin coil of black smoke was rising from inside the grenade bay as Nikolai raced on, the others scrambling after him and coming up fast on either side as, away to his right, he heard the shrill blast of Captain Odinstov's whistle.

Nikolai swung round the concrete blast wall and the first thing he saw was Sergeant Barak. He looked dazed, mesmerized, staring down at a large chunk of raw meat. Then, with a sudden curdle of horror, Nikolai realized he wasn't looking at a piece of raw meat, he was looking at Private Tinrass.

Quick impressions seared across the mind's retina: one leg had been blown off above the knee; a bright red smear high up on the wall with, below it on the ground, a boot stuffed full of what looked like wet red and white rags; the wail of a military ambulance somewhere in the distance; a helmet lying a few paces away, still spinning, its chin-strap snapped with the force of the explosion.

The thing on the ground moaned and moved, tried to crawl away from the pain that consumed it. Nikolai crouched down, fingers tearing feverishly at the stitching on the hem of his tunic where each soldier kept his individual field dressing. He glanced quickly at Tinrass's face. Mercifully he was unconscious. He turned back to the leg.

The blood was everywhere: pumping, spurting fully half a metre up into the air in a crimson femoral fountain. Gritting his teeth, Nikolai reached forward and pressed his bare hand over the stump in an effort to stop the bleeding, pulling at his dressing pack with his teeth as his right hand turned crimson under his eyes and disappeared into the pulp of that shattered leg. The dressing spilled open at last. 'Dressings,' he screamed. 'More dressings – quickly!' He took his hand away, pressed the lint bandage down onto the stump and watched with sick dismay as the blood soaked through immediately. Blotting paper, thought Nikolai inconsequentially, it's just like the blotting paper we had at school. 'More dressings – quickly!' he shouted, looking wildly over his shoulder.

'Here –' It was Yuri, tearing open his own field dressing and thrusting it forward. Nikolai grabbed it and looked up. 'Another – quickly,' he said urgently, taking his hand away from the stump and clapping another bandage on top of the first as, behind them, someone started throwing up noisily. 'Another – then a rope, belt, anything,' muttered Nikolai as those dressings too turned red. 'Tourniquet, agreed?' He glanced up.

Yuri nodded rapidly several times and began fumbling at his own waist-belt. Tinrass was now deathly pale, his mouth sagging open, the breath rasping in his throat. Yuri ripped the belt from his trousers and held it up. 'Here – here –' But Nikolai shook his head. 'Can't,' he said shortly. 'You'll have to do it – Go on, quickly,' he ordered, fingers busy with the long, bloody red tapes that came from each side of the lint pads. Yuri scrambled round to the other side of the body and slid the leather belt under and round the upper thigh, fumbled with the belt-catch that was slippery now with blood and then dragged it tight across the severed limb. 'Tight . . . tight as you can,' urged Nikolai. 'Use your . . . use your bayonet scabbard.' There were three of the dressings in place now, one on top of the other – and still the blood was seeping through.

Yuri unclipped his bayonet scabbard from his left hip and slipped it between his leather belt and the bloody tatters of Tinrass's uniform trousers. Then, at a nod from Nikolai, he began twisting the bayonet furiously, like a key, and the belt bit deep into the thigh, pinching closed the severed artery and stemming the blood flow. Only then did they become aware of Captain Odinstov, pushing through the cluster of recruits and crouching down beside them. He glanced briefly at the dressings, felt the tourniquet and looked up at the two recruits.

'Good,' he nodded approvingly, reaching forward to feel Tinrass's carotid pulse as two medical orderlies hurried round the nearest blast wall, a brown canvas stretcher carried between them. Dimly, Nikolai was aware that the siren had stopped wailing: the ambulance must have arrived. 'Right – over there with the others,' ordered Captain Odinstov. Nikolai and Yuri rose to their feet and joined the cluster of waiting recruits. 'Sergeant Barak?' There was no reply. 'Sergeant Barak?'

'Sir?' The voice sounded almost subdued.

'Fall the men in on the road in two ranks and wait for me there.' He rose to his feet as the two medical orderlies lifted Tinrass onto the stretcher, covered him with a blanket and carried him swiftly towards the ambulance.

'Right: fall in – on the road,' ordered Sergeant Barak. 'Go on – move! It's all over.'

They moved away from the throwing bays and joined the other recruits who had come with Captain Odinstov from further up the range. Captain Odinstov spoke briefly to the two medical orderlies and glanced inside the back of the ambulance. Then he climbed inside, watched by two ranks of silent, thoughtful recruits. A minute passed. Then he reappeared, the doors were slammed shut and the vehicle was moving slowly down the track towards barracks. Too slowly, realized Nikolai suddenly: as though there was now no reason to hurry, nothing to be gained. The siren was absent too.

Captain Odinstov watched the ambulance pull away and then turned back to face the waiting recruits drawn up in their two ranks, his fingers reaching automatically inside his top pocket for notebook and pencil. Sergeant Barak wheeled, brought the men to attention and saluted, waiting for further instructions. In the front rank Nikolai looked at that hard, brutish face and tried to read signs of guilt, remorse, even conscience. He read nothing. Captain Odinstov returned the salute tiredly. 'Stand the men at ease, Sergeant.'

'Sir!' He turned. 'Stand at – EASE!'

'Right – listen to me,' began Captain Odinstov. Then, turning to Sergeant Barak – 'What was that man's name?' Was, thought Nikolai, *was*.

'Private Tinrass, Comrade Captain. An Uzbek.' As if therefore it didn't matter, thought Nikolai savagely.

Captain Odinstov looked up and cleared his throat. 'It is my duty to inform you that Private Tinrass has died,' he announced with a slight shrug. 'Despite the tourniquet, the field dressings . . . the injuries were too severe.' He looked along the motionless line of faces and tapped his notebook gently up and down against the palm of his hand. 'There will, of course, be a formal, regimental investigation – questions. It might be as well, while events are still fresh in your minds, to start now.' He paused. 'Sergeant Barak?'

'Well . . . he . . . er . . . he panicked, didn't he? Pulled out the pin, released the lever, then he . . . he dropped it.'

'He *dropped* it?'

'That's right, Comrade Captain, sir. Fumbled a bit, then dropped it. There wasn't a thing I could do.'

Captain Odinstov made a few brief notes, shut his notebook and slipped it back into his breast pocket. Bastard, thought Nikolai savagely. He's going to get away with it.

'Right, Sergeant Barak: there seems little point in –'

'Permission to address the Comrade Captain, sir!' sang out a voice from the front rank of recruits. Captain Odinstov swung round. So too did Sergeant Barak.

'Permission granted,' replied the officer formally as Nikolai waited at stiff attention.

'Private Samlar, N., 95986455, sir!'

'Ah, yes,' said Captain Odinstov, taking in the bloodstained tunic and remembering the face crouched beside the dying soldier. 'The man with the bandages. You did well, comrade soldier. What is it?'

'With . . . with the greatest of respect, Comrade Captain – Sergeant Barak is . . . mistaken.'

Everything stopped. Captain Odinstov took a slow step forward. 'What was that?'

'I said – with the greatest possible respect, Comrade Captain, Sergeant Barak is mistaken. We all saw it. Well, some of us, anyway –'

'Saw what, exactly?'

Nikolai swallowed nervously. 'Private Tinrass was one of the last to go into the grenade bay. He . . . he was very nervous, for some reason. We had seen him shaking; sick with fear almost, he was, over there – in the slit-trenches.' He gestured behind him. 'I . . . I was the first to throw. When my grenade had gone off I . . . I told Sergeant Barak that in my opinion –'

'In *your* opinion, Private?'

'Yes, sir,' nodded Nikolai miserably. 'In my opinion – in all our opinions if it comes to that, Private Tinrass was a danger. A danger to himself. To us.'

The Captain turned to Sergeant Barak. 'Sergeant?'

'That is correct, Comrade Captain – yes.'

'Go on.'

'Yes, sir,' persisted Nikolai doggedly. 'When it came for Private Tinrass to ... to throw a grenade, Sergeant Barak had to come over to the trench and get him – that's how nervous he was. We – that is, I – saw Sergeant Barak pick up a live grenade, unfasten the top button of Private Tinrass's tunic and place the grenade inside. He then fastened the tunic. Sir.'

Slow, crunching footsteps as Captain Odinstov came slowly, incredulously forward. 'He did what?'

'He put a grenade down the front of his tunic, Comrade Captain. Then he patted it – his chest, I mean. Private Tinrass's chest.'

'Continue.'

Nikolai shrugged helplessly. 'That's all I saw, Comrade Captain. He pushed Private Tinrass towards the throwing bay and we ... we didn't see any more. Next thing we heard was the ... the grenade going off, Tinrass screaming and –'

'Enough.' Captain Odinstov studied Nikolai for a long moment, trying to decide whether or not he was to be believed. Perhaps the recruit's swift action inside the throwing bay helped tip the balance. He glanced beyond Nikolai's shoulder at the two ranks of waiting recruits beyond. 'Who else saw what this man here has just described?' Nikolai waited in the silence, offering up a prayer to anyone who might be listening. Without support, without corroboration, he was done for; finished. Still nothing happened, no one came to his defence – and then Nikolai heard the sudden, blessed sound of boots stamping to attention.

'I did, Comrade Captain.' Nikolai let out his breath in a soundless sigh as he recognized the voice as Yuri's. Good old Yuri. Now he could hear more boots coming to attention.

'I did too, Comrade Captain.' That sounded like Altunin, the Belorussian.

'Me too,' piped up someone else.

'I saw it.'

One by one the non-Russians stepped forward. To a man.

Captain Odinstov came back into view, his face grave with the implications of what he had been told. The fool of a Sergeant might very well have acted incorrectly, stupidly, even criminally – but he was still *his* Sergeant, his responsibility. And he, Captain Gladius Odinstov of the 117th Motor Rifle Battalion, career soldier with eight years exemplary service behind him and due for promotion in the next four years, would still have to answer to the Colonel . . . He stepped closer. 'If this is some kind of trick . . .' he warned slowly.

Nikolai shook his head vehemently. 'It is no trick, Comrade Captain, I swear it.'

Captain Odinstov considered for a moment, then – 'Sergeant, have the men fall out and wait over there,' he ordered, pointing towards the deserted throwing bays. 'I want a word with you. Alone.'

Two ranks of silent, frozen-faced recruits dissolved presently into little knots of young soldiers as Captain Odinstov strode briskly out of earshot with Sergeant Barak hurrying at his heels, his face impassive beneath the metal rim of his helmet.

The men clustered around Nikolai, one or two congratulating him on speaking out but most complaining and despondent, convinced that their lives were about to take a further downward spiral as Sergeant Barak extracted his revenge for such overt betrayal in the weeks that lay ahead. Inquiry or no inquiry, few recruits were naïve enough to believe Sergeant Barak would be replaced for a piece of sadistic, brutal stupidity that could easily be explained away by that catch-all phrase so beloved by the Soviet Army – 'combat realism'. In the past, whole platoons had drowned during river-crossing exercises; sticks of paratroopers had been dropped too low and exploded like ripe pumpkins, their parachutes unopened; nerve-gas exposure demonstrations had gone fatally wrong and been hushed up – such stories were common knowledge among the recruits of the 117th. Each man knew therefore just how exhaustive the 'inquiry' would be into the loss of a single, replaceable, simple-headed recruit during grenade practice.

Now Private Yasnov, the Russian, bulled his way to Nikolai's side and shoved a boney finger in his chest. 'You just can't stop sticking your bloody oar in, can you?' he snarled. 'That useless prick Tinrass special to you, was he? Your own little bum-boy, maybe, eh?'

Something seemed to snap inside Nikolai's head. Private Yasnov had expected an argument, an exchange of insults maybe, perhaps a bit of chest-shoving. He was totally unprepared, however, for what happened next. Nikolai glanced away as though bored by the whole business and then suddenly took a quick half-step forward and kneed Yasnov brutally in the groin. As Yasnov hunched forward, knees pressed together, both hands diving towards his crotch, mouth opening and shutting as he emitted a thin keening sound, eyes starting out of his head, Nikolai brought up his knee again, this time into his face. Yasnov went crashing back onto the ground with blood pouring from his mouth as Nikolai leapt on top of him, smashing with his fists, butting down with the rim of his helmet, raining blow after blow on the body of the enemy as all the tension, all the anger and frustration of the last few hours exploded into animal rage, into a feral urge to tear and destroy. Yasnov curled up beneath him, trying to shield himself with arms and elbows as others leapt forward and tried to pull them apart before Captain Odinstov saw what was happening. Yasnov's mates began chopping at Nikolai's back, going for the kidneys. Then someone got a hand around Nikolai's throat and the two men were pulled apart.

The fire seemed to go out of the Uzbek as quickly as it had been kindled. Nikolai sagged back, panting and exhausted, knuckles raw and bleeding, head ringing from the clashing of their two helmets as Yasnov staggered to his knees, retching weakly. Nikolai permitted Yuri to push him back towards the throwing bays.

'What the hell got into you?' demanded Yuri. 'You went bloody mad back there. I thought you were going to rip his throat out . . .'

'I'd had enough, that's all,' managed Nikolai tiredly. He banged Yuri on the arm. 'It's over, OK? Forget it.'

'Yes, but –'

'I said: it's over, OK? Finished,' insisted Nikolai roughly. Then, seeing the hurt in his friend's eyes he went on more calmly: 'You want to know what's the matter, Yuri? I'll tell you.' He paused, gathering his thoughts, catching his breath. 'He's a Russian, right? Him – Barak – Captain Odinstov – they're all Russian.

Fucking master-race, right? You, me, that poor little sod Tinrass, scared shitless from the first day he put on uniform – we don't count, right? We're from the sewers, the gutters – isn't that what we're told, day in, day out? Because we're Uzbeks, because we're Moslems, we're inferior – even to bastards like Barak? Ha!' He laughed bitterly. 'Well, I tell you, I've had about enough, understand? Up to here,' he chopped viciously at his own throat.

'Take it easy, Nikolai, take it easy, will you? You know how it works – we all do. It's always been like that. A few more weeks and –'

'A few more *weeks*?' interrupted Nikolai angrily. 'A few more weeks – who for? For you, me? What about that poor bastard Tinrass? Not for him there aren't! For him it's over, finished! That . . . that bastard killed him!'

'You don't know that he –'

'He killed him – course he did! Pushed him over the edge. Well, I'll tell you something: I'm not going to wait a few more weeks, let that sod Barak turn me into a piece of raw meat,' he announced venomously, eyes fastening suddenly on the crate of grenades left outside the throwing bays by Sergeant Barak and overlooked in the excitement of the accident. Nikolai pushed away from the wall, went over to the crate and glanced around casually. Captain Odinstov and Sergeant Barak were thirty metres away, conferring together over the officer's notebook. The other recruits were still clustered around Barov and nobody was looking his way.

Nikolai bent down, scooped up a grenade, tucked it under his arm and sauntered back towards Yuri. Grinning.

'You're mad!' protested Yuri, goggle-eyed. 'You can't just –'

'Yes, I can,' corrected Nikolai calmly, showing Yuri the grenade and then stowing it carefully in an empty ammunition pouch attached to his webbing. 'I already have, see?'

'You can't steal one of those things,' protested Yuri, thoroughly alarmed. 'What when they discover it's missing?'

'What's Barak going to say? Please, Comrade Captain, one of my grenades has been pinched? They'd lock him up! He wouldn't dare report it.'

'He'll guess you took it, Nikolai. There'll be all hell to pay.'

Nikolai nodded. 'That's right,' he agreed grimly. 'All hell to pay.'

# : 15 :

The public-address system boomed and echoed up into the high steel girders of Zurich's busy railway station as Toni Johnson stood over their luggage and watched as Gordon's back receded towards the hot food counter.

The local train to Zug would not leave for another thirty-five minutes and Gordon had gone off to buy coffee, fruit and chocolate for them both. As Toni watched he was swallowed up suddenly behind a party of noisy German holiday-makers, their sunburned faces happy and animated beneath cheerful, brightly-coloured ski caps.

When she was quite certain Gordon had reached the food counter she slipped beneath the transparent perspex cupola of a public telephone kiosk and took a handful of francs from her bag. With a glance over her shoulder she pressed money into the coin box and began dialling a number she had memorized in London. Her call was answered almost immediately.

'American Travel Bureau,' said an American voice in distant London.

'This is Toni Johnson in Switzerland,' she announced, her voice flat and hard with none of the warmth that had made her such an engaging travelling companion on the long train journey from Paris. 'I have to speak with Bill.'

'This is William Ottley.'

'Hi, Bill. It's Toni. I'm in Zurich. Between trains.'

'Go ahead, I'm listening. Did he show?'

'He showed. We travelled here together. He was . . . very open.'

'I understand. Can you talk?'

'Briefly. He'll be back any minute.' She paused. 'Any change?'

'Why?'

'Because if this thing is only half as important as you guys think it is, then you've got problems. There's only one way to stop Hallam digging around. Let me take him.'

There was a brief pause. 'I'll have to call you back on that,' said Ottley finally. 'I'd better talk with our British cousins, see if there's been any change. What's your number?' She told him. 'How long have I got?'

'Five, ten minutes, no more. He'll be here when you call back, so watch what you say.'

'Will do. Oh – and Toni?'

'Yeah?'

'We found Hastings.' There was silence for a moment. Then – 'What does that mean?' asked Toni Johnson quietly.

'It means he won't be coming home. So just you watch that bastard, OK? You hear what I'm telling you? He's dangerous – dangerous as hell.'

'I hear you. But he's still only an amateur, right? Just give me the word, Bill. That's all I need.'

'I'll call you right back.'

William Ottley replaced the receiver slowly and sat back in his chair. There was something about the woman's cold-blooded dedication to the business of killing that scared him down to the depths of his soul.

Perhaps that was because he was the man who had found her, fitted the round peg into the round hole with such terrible perfection. If he had been compelled to put a date to it, to the moment Toni Johnson had moved a little apart from the rest of the human race, he would have said it had begun during the Tet offensive in January 1968 when, as a very young cypher clerk, she had been forced to witness the mutilation of her Marine Corps fiancé by the Viet Cong in the grounds of the American embassy in Saigon and had then been brutally raped and left for dead by the wiry little men who had stripped her of everything she had ever wanted, all she had ever valued. William Ottley had been the Bureau Chief who had picked up the pieces and recruited her into The Company. He was one of the very few who had access to her personal file back at Langley. It did not make attractive reading, but it went at least some way towards answering disturbing questions about the beautiful American with the cold, dead eyes.

*

General Inkermann sat back against the cushioned interior of the ministry Daimler, drummed his fingers with impatience and gazed sternly towards the front door of Lord Porterfield's home in Eaton Terrace. The fellow was taking a long time – where the devil was he? The General shot back a cuff and looked again at his watch, conscious in his precise, military fashion of the convergence of several carefully synchronized schedules: of their drive down the motorway to the west country that would start as soon as Porterfield came down to the car, of the Special Air Service Regiment surveillance and protection teams moving down from Hereford – and of the most important element of all: the container lorry that had travelled over from Ireland by ferry and which should even now be somewhere near the Severn Bridge.

At last! Lord Porterfield's front door had opened and the Ministry driver was coming down the steps carrying a suitcase with Lord Porterfield following behind, a fawn overcoat slung comfortably over heavy shoulders. General Inkermann too was in civilian clothes, although thirty-five years as a soldier meant simply that he had exchanged the khaki of service dress for the civilian uniform of senior officer in mufti: soft flannel shirt and club tie, tweed suit and trilby, light brown overcoat with dark leather buttons.

They might have been off to a point-to-point in the home counties with hip flasks and shooting sticks, but they weren't. They were off to witness Boadicea change from a theoretical symbol of Anglo-American trust and mutual commitment to a practical, awesome reality; to watch the first American Cruise missile slide into its new home beneath the curved, damp granite arches of a disused railway tunnel somewhere in south-west England.

Now the General sat back and waited as their watchful bodyguard beside the driver's seat suddenly stiffened. A man in his mid-thirties had turned into Eaton Terrace. Upon seeing Lord Porterfield coming down the last of the marble steps towards the waiting limousine he had broken into a sudden run. A little thing in itself, to be sure, but the bodyguard had been painstakingly and expensively trained in the observance of such little things – the sudden dilation of an eyeball, the face that sweated in a cold room, the fractional movement of a curtain at an empty window. Now he placed one hand on the door catch and the other on the cocked 9mm pistol beneath a copy of the *Daily Telegraph* lying carelessly on his lap. If a car backfired ten paces away he wouldn't so much as flinch a muscle – but if the man running towards him now suddenly pulled a grenade from his overcoat pocket, that man would be dead before his index finger had even curled round the pin.

Stephen Rowley stopped running when he saw Lord Porterfield had seen him and broke into a brisk walk as Porterfield raised a hand in greeting. The bodyguard sat back and made no move to leave the car. But nor did his hand emerge from beneath the folded newspaper.

'Put those things in the back, will you? I'll be with you in just one moment.'

The driver nodded. 'Very good, my Lord.'

Porterfield turned as Stephen Rowley came to a stop at his side. 'Afternoon, Stephen – just in time. Couple more minutes and you'd have missed me.'

'Yes, sir – sorry about that –' Rowley struggled to bring his breathing under control. 'It's . . . it's about George Vickers, sir . . .'

'Vickers? What about him?'

'He's . . . er . . . he's been asking rather a lot of questions, I'm afraid, sir. About you.'

'What?'

'Yes, sir. And when I went into his office about forty minutes ago to talk about the weekend duty rota his secretary told me he'd already left. For the . . . for the west country.'

'You say he was asking questions about me: what sort of questions?' demanded Lord Porterfield.

'Well, sir, as near as I can gather –' Both men turned as General Inkermann hailed Lord Porterfield from the Daimler. He was holding out a telephone. 'Call for you, Phillip. It's William Ottley.' Lord Porterfield strode to the side of the car and took the receiver.

'This is Porterfield . . .'

★

Gordon Hallam grinned as he saw Toni Johnson waiting for him outside a line of telephone kiosks at Zurich station, their bags at her feet. He held out a carton of steaming coffee. Toni Johnson made to take it but Gordon pulled back slightly. 'Now then,' he mused, 'how would you like it? Over your shoes? Over your skirt? Or would you rather I just –'

'OK, OK – I'm sorry!' she laughed, hands raised to ward off the words. 'You're never going to let me forget that, are you? Every time I –'

The phone began to ring behind her.

'It'll be for me,' she announced instantly. 'I'd told the hotel I'd be checking in about lunchtime. I just wanted to confirm they'd keep my room over.' She spun round with a bright smile and lifted the receiver as Gordon watched her over the rim of his coffee. 'Hello? Yes, this is Toni Johnson,' she said, holding a hand to one ear to keep out background noise. 'What's that?'

'I've spoken to our British cousins,' said Ottley quietly.

'You have? But I booked – in writing!' she complained, evidently disappointed.

'No change. You have the sanction. Sanction is confirmed.'

'Well, I guess that's better than nothing. Is that a single or double?'

'Double. Hallam and Tyschen. Both to go together.'

Toni Johnson nodded. 'Fine . . . fine. That's understood. I really appreciate that. Good-bye now.' She replaced the receiver and stepped away from the phone. Towards Gordon.

'Any problems?' he asked, holding out the coffee.

Toni Johnson shook her head and smiled a wide, friendly smile. 'Not anymore. Everything's just fine.'

# : 16 :

It was shortly before eight that evening as George and Bunny Vickers followed the elderly porter up the wide, creaking wooden staircase of the Bradstone Manor Hotel on the outskirts of Inwardleigh in Devon as he carried their cases slowly upstairs.

The Bradstone was a listed building, a Tudor manor in the grand tradition set in a magnificent sweep of private lawns and gardens glimpsed only briefly in the cone of their headlights as they swept up the dark drive to stop with a crunch of gravel before the ornate stone fountain.

Before the Mercedes had drawn to a halt the heavily-studded front door had opened and a porter had hurried outside towards them through the thin drizzle, umbrella raised. That attention to detail, to the comfort of its guests, held the key to both the Bradstone's appeal and its survival at a time when small private hotels were closing down like third-rate cinemas. As Bunny whispered as they climbed the creaking stairs, it was like stepping back into a bygone age: the age of service, of stability and cherished values; the age of their youth, long gone.

'This way, if you'll just follow me? You'll find the Courtney suite a little further along on your right.' The porter led them down a wooden-floored corridor and stopped outside a stout oak door. 'Here you are, sir,' he said, fitting a brass key into the heavy lock. 'The Courtney suite. I trust you will both be most comfortable.'

'I'm sure we will, thank you,' replied Bunny, following him through into a charming bay-fronted bedroom with soft floral prints on chairs and bedspread, whose mullioned windows looked down onto the lawns below. The bed itself was a huge four-poster. George and Bunny both marvelled at this while the porter placed their bags in a neat line and withdrew on silent feet, closing the door gently behind him.

Impulsively, Bunny moved to her husband's side and squeezed

his arm. 'Darling – this is going to be wonderful, just wonderful, I know it is! Just what we've both been needing,' she enthused. 'However did you find it?'

He told her as he lifted their cases onto the bed and Bunny began unpacking. As she sorted through their things George strolled across to the windows where he parted the curtains and gazed down at the gardens hidden below. Bunny studied him for a moment, noting with a wife's concern the tired stoop to his shoulders. She realized just how long it was since they had had a time together like this. Some good food and clean country air without the telephone breaking into their every private moment would give them both the respite they so badly needed. And there were bound to be lots of country walks hereabouts, she thought, reaching for a map lying on top of her husband's dressing-gown and opening it out with a stiff crackle of pages: walks in the country together, hand in hand, with no mention, just for once, of that wretched man Porterfield. He had dominated the conversation for most of the drive down from London.

She studied the map for a moment and then frowned. 'George?'

The map was the ordinary tourist map of Devon and east Cornwall but something more had been added. Someone had inked in the line of the old railway that had once crossed this part of the south-west – and every so often a cutting or abandoned railway tunnel had been ringed in red ink. 'George?' she repeated. 'What are these?'

'What are what?' asked George Vickers idly, his back still to the bedroom as he thought about what he would do in the morning, how he would begin to put his theories to the test without alarming Bunny.

'George – I'm talking to you.' He turned then and the ready smile vanished as he saw the map open across the suitcase and Bunny's hand pointing at the marks he had made. He stalked to her side, almost tore the map from her hands and folded it angrily away.

'They're nothing, d'you understand?' George thrust the map into the suitcase and slammed down the lid.

'George? Don't be ridiculous,' scoffed Bunny uneasily. 'What *are* those marks and things on the map?'

She made to retrieve the map from the suitcase but George caught her roughly by the arm. 'I've told you – nothing! Nothing at all!'

She wrenched her arm away and rubbed uneasily at his finger-marks on her soft upper arm. When she looked up at him again it was with the eyes she usually reserved for strangers. 'That's why we're here, isn't it?' she managed in a quiet voice that was not quite steady as realization slowly dawned. 'Those . . . those marks and things on the map. That's why we're here, isn't it? That's why we've driven all this way – you haven't come down here for a break at all, have you? Have you?' she demanded, shaking his arm. 'It's that bloody man, Porterfield!'

And saw the truth in his eyes as he turned away.

Gordon unzipped his toilet bag, arranged his things on the narrow glass shelf in the bathroom, had a wash and went back into the bedroom. He had taken a single room with bath on the second floor of the Hotel Ochsen in the centre of Zug. Toni Johnson had a room on the floor above. Now Gordon glanced around the bedroom that was spotlessly clean and comfortably modern, pushed back the heavy curtains and looked down into the street below.

His room was at the front of the narrow, six-storey hotel that boasted an ornate, carved wooden balcony and a turreted window at each corner. These overlooked a narrow cobbled square that gave onto the main road running parallel to the edge of the lake and connected Oberwil to the south with Lorzen to the north and west.

Zug itself lies along the north-eastern edge of the Zuger See roughly half-way between Zurich and Luzern and is pinned be-tween the lake and the steep rolling forest and heathland beyond Schönegg. On a clear day the tip of the Eiger is just visible to the south-west flanked by the peaks of the Mönch and the Jungfrau.

From his bedroom window, Gordon could see the gleam of still water beyond a jumble of pleasing, steeply-gabled red-tiled roofs that ran down to the pleasure-boat jetty at the water's edge. He turned back into the room suddenly and glanced at his watch. It was almost eight o'clock, one hour behind British time. He had come to Switzerland to see Herr Tyschen, to talk to

'Mark' face to face. If he left it any later the restaurant would be crowded and Tyschen would be too busy to talk. So he would go over and chat to him briefly now, before the evening got into its stride.

Gordon twitched his coat off the bed, locked the bedroom door behind him and took the cramped little lift at the end of the corridor down to reception on the first floor, the slow, grinding pain in his shoulder as familiar now as toothache.

The girl on the front desk told him how to find the Restaurant Oppel and a moment later Gordon was stepping outside into the crisp mountain air. It was dark and the road was lit by a necklace of street lamps and glowing shop windows. He turned up his collar, jammed his hands deep into his pockets and sauntered past the gold-statued fountain across the cobbled square towards the cluster of shops, houses and cheerful, inexpensive little restaurants that hugged the water's edge.

From her room on the third floor, Toni Johnson watched Gordon cross the road. Then she picked up her telephone and spoke to reception: 'Room 217, please.'

'I am sorry, Herr Hallam has just gone out.'

'Oh. Did he say where he was going? How long he'd be gone?'

'I cannot be sure, but he asked the way to Restaurant Oppel.'

'Is that near here?'

'A few minutes' walk, that is all.'

'Thank you.'

Toni Johnson took the stairs to the floor below and stepped quietly into the carpeted corridor. It was lined with framed prints of Swiss mountain scenes and each one was illuminated by soft, hidden lighting. The sound of laughter came from behind one door as Toni Johnson walked the length of the corridor, counting off the door numbers. She had almost reached the end when she heard the rattle of keys behind her as a door closed quietly. She turned to see a white-uniformed laundry maid emerge from another bedroom pushing a trolley of clean linen. The woman was middle-aged, broad of beam and wore her hair in an unfashionable bun.

Toni Johnson switched on her smile. 'Excuse me?'

*'Bitte?'*

'Oh.' Toni smiled again, reached forward and held up the

master key hanging from the maid's broad waist on a length of chain. She made a turning gesture with the key and pointed at Gordon's door. The maid nodded dutifully. Guests were always locking their keys in their bedrooms. She followed the American on silent shoes and keyed open Gordon's door obligingly.

'*Danke.*' The maid nodded and walked away with a swish of starched linen apron. Toni Johnson slipped inside Gordon's room, closed the door behind her and crossed to the window. She pulled the curtains closed, returned to the door and switched on the lights. Then she looked slowly about her, fixing the room's geography in her mind, noting where Gordon had put his suitcase and few belongings.

She began a careful, methodical search.

Rule number one: if you are about to kill a man, ensure first that nothing he leaves behind can speak for him. If the American who had killed Walter Hallam on Boxing Day night had observed that simple rule, all that followed could have been avoided.

But he hadn't – and so Toni Johnson moved silently into Gordon's bathroom and began sorting through his toilet things with slender, expert fingers.

Gordon turned down a narrow cobbled street lined with shops and shuttered private houses whose first floors hung out over the pavement. A wooden sign gleamed beneath gold lamplight and Gordon trotted up a steep flight of wooden steps and pushed open a heavy wooden door. He stood in the threshold of the Restaurant Oppel for a long moment as the steamy warmth and friendliness of the place reached out to envelop him as he took in a sea of pine tables and chairs surrounded by narrow wooden stalls set back against the walls. The ceiling was low and of wood too, the far end of the restaurant dominated by a long stainless steel serving counter behind which stood busy young waitresses filling out early orders for a gaggle of students and young office workers who wanted hot food at reasonable prices and didn't mind the absence of starched tablecloths. It was the sort of place Gordon would have turned to back home and his spirits lifted: the man who ran a place like this had to be accessible, friendly – and talkative.

'Hello,' smiled a young waitress in white blouse and skin-tight jeans as Gordon hovered uncertainly in the doorway. She handed him a large printed menu.

'Er . . . *ein, bitte,*' he managed, pointing a finger at his own chest as he decided on impulse to eat here too. He'd had nothing but railway snacks all day and he was famished. The girl turned and he followed the tight cheeks of her bottom towards one of the narrow booths set back against the wall. He sat down and she rapidly cleared away the second place setting. Gordon hid for a moment behind the large menu, composing a sentence in his mind. He looked up.

'*Wo ist Herr Tyschen, bitte?*' he asked.

The girl looked surprised. '*Bruno? Ein Moment, bitte.*'

'*Danke,*' nodded Gordon as the girl hurried away. In that sudden moment of waiting Gordon began to feel nervous. What if the man wouldn't talk to him, didn't have anything to add? It was all forty years ago, a long time, for God's sake; a different world. If he –

'*Ja?*'

Gordon looked up. Large, bewhiskered, pot-bellied, his girth struggling to escape behind a white cotton apron, the man towered above him and waited, wiping his hands on a dishcloth. Gordon was suddenly glad he wasn't a customer complaining about the food.

'Mr Tyschen?' asked Gordon, in English.

He nodded. 'I am Tyschen.'

Gordon pushed back his chair and rose awkwardly to his feet. He stuck out a hand. 'Gordon Hallam, Mr Tyschen.'

Tyschen frowned. 'Do I know you?'

For one awful moment Gordon thought the man had forgotten completely, just brushed him from his mind. 'Gordon Hallam, Mr Tyschen – Walter Hallam's son. From the war. We spoke on the telephone, remember? I called you from England.'

The frown cleared. 'Ah, now I remember – Walter Hallam's son! Of course, of course!' He gestured vaguely behind him. 'You will forgive me, eh? So many faces coming and going . . .' He grasped Gordon's hand and pumped it up and down as though he was trying to make up for lost time, clenching his fingers so hard in a huge, ham-like fist that the bones ground together. Gordon winced.

'Thank God you remembered,' he said, greatly relieved. 'For a moment I thought you'd forgotten.'

Tyschen shook his head and ran a hand through thick silver hair. 'No, no – I remember very well. Please –' He gestured for Gordon to be seated and waved an owner's hand towards the bar. 'You will take a drink with me, yes? What will it be – beer? Wine? Cognac?' A waitress arrived at their table and hovered expectantly.

'A beer will be fine, thanks.'

Tyschen held up two thick fingers. 'Two beers,' he ordered and the girl hurried away. 'So – what brings you to Zug, eh?'

'I wanted to meet you. Ask you about my father,' said Gordon simply.

Tyschen shook his head sorrowfully. 'I am sorry about Walter, about your father. In the old days we were very close. You know –' He studied Gordon for a moment and then nodded. 'You even look like him: the same eyes – and the chin too, I think. So, tell me: what is the business that brings you to our little town, eh? Zug is not so large a place.'

Gordon shrugged. 'No business. I just wanted to meet you, ask you about the war. About my father.'

Their beers arrived and Tyschen shifted half of his at a single swallow. He set down his glass and wiped at a frothy moustache with the back of a huge hand. 'And for that you come all this way – just to see me?' he demanded incredulously.

Gordon began to feel uncomfortable. 'I wanted to ask you about Apostle,' he admitted doggedly. Tyschen shook his head pityingly, threw back those massive shoulders and let out a great booming laugh. Gordon smiled uneasily, as though suspecting a joke at his expense. 'What's so funny?'

Bruno Tyschen rocked back in his chair until it threatened to go over backwards. Then he tipped suddenly forward, piled his weight over the table and wiped a hand across his eyes. 'Forgive me, Mr Hallam, but I find it amusing, this . . . this quest of yours. You come all this way to see me when . . . when the answers you want are right under your nose in England – right under your nose!'

'What do you mean?'

'I mean the files, the papers, the records – all are in England! Apostle was a British operation, Mr Hallam!'

'British and American operation,' corrected Gordon evenly. 'It was a joint mission set up under American Special Operations and the British Special Operations Executive.'

Bruno Tyschen studied him for a moment over the rim of his beer glass and Gordon had the feeling he was being weighed. Then Tyschen nodded. 'Special Operations Executive,' he echoed quietly, the words coming down the years from another age, another world. 'Quite right, Mr Hallam – quite right. What do they say? You have done your homework, yes?'

Gordon nodded. 'As much as I can. But the files are closed – they're not open to the public. I only got your name because I found it in Dad's address book.'

'You have not spoken with the others?'

Gordon paused, glass half-way to his lips. 'What others?'

Tyschen sighed and glanced over his shoulder. He hunched forward. 'Your father was "Luke", yes? I was "Mark".' He ticked the names off on his fingers as Gordon nodded.

'You sent my father a postcard right after Christmas. That's how I knew you were still alive.'

Tyschen nodded impatiently. 'Yes, yes – I sent your father a postcard.' He moved his chair a little closer. 'You should read your Bible, Mr Hallam: if you did you would know there were four chief Apostles – four, not two!'

'John and Matthew? You mean they're still alive – in England?'

Bruno Tyschen shrugged. 'Who can say? Your father and I, we were special friends, you understand? That was why we kept in touch, even over all these years – but the others?' He shrugged again. 'Who knows? Perhaps. If they are, you will find them back there' – he jerked a thumb over his shoulder – 'in England.'

'Who were they? What were their names?' asked Gordon, fumbling in his pocket for notebook and pencil.

'One was . . . let me see now . . . yes! One was called Peter – Peter Tillet.'

'That was his real name?'

'That was his real name, yes.'

'I thought agents weren't supposed to know each other's real names – just code-names.'

Tyschen shrugged. 'That is what we were told in our training, of course. But some of us, we were together a long time, you understand? And when you trusted someone like that . . . sometimes you let things slip, yes?' He paused. 'Peter . . . Tillet,' he mused, frowning as he tried to remember something. 'He came from somewhere in the north, I remember.' He gestured vaguely towards the top of an imaginary map.

'Scotland?' hazarded Gordon.

Tyschen shook his head. 'No, not Scotland. This place had the name "north" in it, I remember –' 'Northampton? Northfleet? North –'

Tyschen suddenly snapped his fingers. 'North Shields! That was the place – yes, North Shields!' He looked up triumphantly. 'Not bad, eh? For an old man? Forty years ago I hear that name and I remember it – like that!' He snapped his fingers again and Gordon scribbled in his notebook. Then he reached inside his jacket for the creased black and white photograph he had found in his father's wallet all those days ago. He laid it carefully on the table, turned it round and pushed it slowly towards his father's friend. 'Remember when that was taken?' he asked quietly.

Bruno Tyschen picked up the photograph and examined it in silence for several moments. 'My God,' he breathed finally, tapping a finger slowly against the faces of the three men standing in front of the Lockheed Hudson with their arms around one another's shoulders. 'My God – you see? That is me! That one – there! That is me, that is Walter and that . . . yes . . . that is Peter; Peter Tillet.' He looked up. 'Tell me – where did you find this?'

'It was in my father's wallet the night he died.' Gordon hunched forward. Mr Tyschen – please: will you tell me about Apostle?' he urged.

Tyschen turned suddenly as a crash came from the kitchens. The restaurant was beginning to fill up and the level of noise and laughter was rising accordingly. Tyschen turned back impatiently and spread his hands. 'Tell me about Apostle, he says! As if I have all the time in the world and do not have a business to run, customers to look after!'

'Please, Herr Tyschen,' pleaded Gordon. 'It's very important to me. That's why I've come all this way. I want to know what my father was doing, what you were up to.'

Tyschen relented. He sighed. 'What is it you wish to know?'

Gordon leant forward eagerly. 'Everything – as much as you can remember! What Apostle was, where you were sent, what you did in Europe that – what's wrong?'

Bruno Tyschen was frowning. 'Europe? I said nothing about Europe.'

'Well, no . . . I just assumed that –'

'You would be wrong, Mr Hallam,' corrected Tyschen quietly, 'quite wrong. We went further than Europe – much further.' He leant forward over his hands as Gordon hung upon every word. 'We went into Russia – into the Soviet Union.' He sat back. 'There. Now you know.'

Gordon stared at him, amazed. 'Russia? During . . . during the war? But . . . but she was on our side; an ally!'

Tyschen moved his head from side to side as though assessing some fine theoretical distinction. 'Then she was, yes – that is true. Nevertheless, that is where we were sent: to Russia; to a country inside the Soviet Union – Uzbekistan.' He watched Gordon's face. 'Another one who has never heard of it, eh? Here, I show you.' He delved in his hip pocket and pulled out a creased diary. He folded it open at a tiny map of the world and a thick finger came down and covered most of eastern USSR.

Gordon looked at the map, his mind spinning. 'But I thought . . . the plane crashed in Albania!'

'On the way back,' agreed Tyschen, nodding. 'We heard about that, a long time later, when it was all over. They were a fine crew. They carried us all the way – from Tempsford down to Foggia in Italy, Foggia to Sicily, Sicily to Alexandria – all in the strictest secrecy. Then across to Tehran, Karachi and Peshawar with extra fuel tanks – can you imagine a flight like that, Mr Hallam – in a Lockheed Hudson with no heating? It was hell, I can tell you – hell!'

'What happened at Peshawar?'

'What happened? We rested – that is what happened! We were all exhausted, the crew too. The next night we flew on over the border into Afghanistan and up over the Hindu Kush in a plane so cold our breath froze on the inside of the windows and our piss turned to yellow ice in the bottom of the tin! But we went on, over the border into Uzbekistan and our Dropping Zone between those two towns: Bukhara to the west and Samarkand to the east.' He paused, remembering. 'When we reached the Dropping Zone we jumped. Down into the desert.'

'My . . . my father jumped too?' asked Gordon foolishly, his mind trying to adjust to this new image of a father he once thought he had known.

Bruno Tyschen nodded. 'Of course. We all did. All four – or perhaps I should say all five of us.' He paused, waiting for Gordon to pick up on what he had just said.

'All *five* of you?' repeated Gordon inevitably.

Tyschen tapped the photograph and his finger slid from the three smiling faces to the cigar-shaped container lying at their feet. 'We took a body too,' he admitted quietly.

'A body? You mean a dead person?'

Tyschen smiled at his incredulity. 'Once he had been alive, most certainly – but a long, long time ago.'

'How long ago?'

'The thirteenth century, I think they said.'

'The *thirteenth century*?' echoed Gordon, pushing a hand through his hair.

Tyschen nodded. 'That is correct. There is a legend, you see – a legend still believed to this day by the people who live inside the Soviet Union in lands that were once ruled by Genghis Khan.'

'Genghis Khan? You wouldn't be pulling my leg, by any chance?'

Tyschen frowned. 'Pulling your leg? Oh – joking: you ask if I am joking? No – what I am telling you is all true, I swear it! Why should I waste my time telling you things that are not true?' He broke off suddenly and turned as a chef in white overalls came to his side and began an animated conversation in German that sailed over Gordon's head. After a moment or two Tyschen nodded, clapped his chef on the shoulder and turned back to Gordon.

'The damned fryer. Always it breaks down, just when it is most needed. I must go in one second, I am sorry –' He gestured back towards the kitchens.

'Please – you must tell me: what legend?' demanded Gordon urgently, his beer forgotten.

Tyschen looked at his watch and leant forward impatiently across the table towards Gordon. 'When Genghis Khan died he was buried in a secret grave in the desert somewhere between those two towns – Bukhara and Samarkand. Perhaps you know that already from your schooldays, eh?'

Gordon shook his head. 'No, can't say I do.'

'Well, believe it, for they do; the people out there – his descendants. When Genghis Khan died his empire began to . . . to fall into pieces, you understand? A legend was born among all those peoples who once had been free but who, over many, many years, found themselves under first one ruler, then another. Some empires lasted for hundreds of years, others a very short time. The Soviet Union? Sixty years, that is all.'

'What legend?' urged Gordon as Bruno Tyschen made to get up. 'What was the legend?'

'The legend said that when the grave of Genghis Khan is found, that will be the sign that the time has come to rise against the Russian oppressor, to become a great people once more.' He shrugged. 'Perhaps they are right. Perhaps it is true, I don't know. Perhaps the time is coming.'

He pushed to his feet, bent forward and tapped a finger against the container lying at the feet of the three S O E agents in the photograph. 'In there we carried the body of a thirteenth-century warrior king found during an expedition to Persia in 1927. We buried that body with the sword we had been given out in the desert: that was *our* Genghis Khan, our time-bomb. It was believed at the time that one day the West would perhaps be in a position to benefit from the "discovery" of that body and the revolt that would follow among a proud, backward people who put great store upon legend, upon tradition.'

'And it's still there?' breathed Gordon. 'Where you buried it?'

Again that characteristic shrug. 'As far as I know, yes – it is still there.'

'That's what you meant in the postcard,' said Gordon slowly, so sure that it was not even a question.

'Postcard?'

'The postcard you sent my father. It arrived after he had died. You wrote: 'What price Apostle now?' That's what you meant, wasn't it? What price Apostle now – after the Soviets have invaded Afghanistan?'

Tyschen nodded. 'Something like that, yes. The Afghans, the Uzbeks, the Tadzhiks – they're all descendants of Genghis Khan, all still Mongols at heart.'

'But the . . . the body. How did you –?'

'If you do not believe me, Mr Hallam, go and ask at your British Museum, eh? Ask them what happened to the body of the warrior king found near Tabriz by Professor Endlemann in 1927 – ask them, if you do not believe me!' He drained off his beer and smacked the empty glass down on the pine table. 'Now I must sort out this damned fryer, *ja*? Come and see me again. When there is more time.'

'When? When can I see you?' Tyschen shrugged as his chef beckoned urgently from the kitchen. Gordon reached out and gripped him by the arm. 'You told me there were four Apostles, Herr Tyschen, right?'

Tyschen nodded impatiently. 'Yes, yes: four Apostles –'

'You were "Mark", Dad was "Luke" – who was Tillet? Peter Tillet?'

'Peter? He was John.'

'And Matthew?' demanded Gordon urgently. 'What happened to Matthew?'

'Matthew? Nothing happened to Matthew – he was there, God rot his soul.'

Gordon leant forward. 'Why do you say that?'

'Why? Why?' Tyschen made an expansive gesture. 'Because that son-of-a-bitch betrayed us, Mr Hallam – he nearly cost us our lives. We got into a little trouble, yes? We were seen, soon after we landed, you understand? There was a fight. And Matthew? Matthew ran away – he hid! All the planning, the preparation? He was terrific! But when the bullets started flying?' He shook his head. 'He put his . . . his head in the ground, his ass in . . . in the air – and he hid! We should have killed him when we found him. If it had been left to me, that is what we would have done, there and then: buried him with the skeleton and the sword and the rest of it.'

'But you didn't?' prompted Gordon.

Tyschen shook his head. 'No, we didn't. Your father – he was the one who persuaded the rest of us to let him live, eh? To forgive and forget.' Tyschen reached forward and tapped Gordon's photograph with an angry finger. 'He is there, Mr Hallam – in your picture.'

'Where? There're only three people in the photograph, for God's sake!'

Tyschen sighed. 'Do you think we all smile at nothing, Mr Hallam? Like idiots? He *took* the photograph, eh? You see?' Gordon groaned with exasperation as Tyschen added reflectively. 'And if I saw the bastard again he would not be smiling, I promise you.'

'Do you remember Matthew's real name, by any chance?'

'Not by chance, Mr Hallam,' smiled Tyschen grimly. 'I remember it most deliberately. Matthew was the last to join, yes? He did not have time to learn our true identities but afterwards, when it was all over, I took the trouble to find out his . . .'

'Please. I'd really like to know.'

'His name was Porterfield, Mr Hallam: Phillip Porterfield. He came from London, I think.'

At that very moment Lord Porterfield was sitting in the back of General Inkermann's Daimler, the car tucked out of sight behind some trees near an empty lay-by on a long, slow hill to the south of Okehampton, in Devon. The only sound beyond the murmur of their desultory conversation as they waited in the darkness was the wind gusting in the trees and the soft drumming of the rain on the roof of the car.

Lord Porterfield poured another small measure of brandy from a silver hip flask into each of the metal tumblers on the fold-down tray in front of him and handed one of the tumblers to General Inkermann. The General glanced at the luminous face of his wristwatch. 'Any minute now, if they're keeping to schedule,' he said quietly.

They sat back, sipped the brandy sparingly and waited.

Six, seven minutes went by. Then they saw the glow of lights and heard the sound of a heavy lorry as it changed down and came grinding up the hill towards them, headlights blazing across white needles of slanting rain. The container lorry was preceded by a motorcycle and followed by two private cars and a van, their windscreen wipers flogging busily, their engines straining away in third as they came slowly up the hill and past the hidden Daimler. When the last of the red tail lights had dwindled into the distance General Inkermann turned towards Lord Porterfield. 'Well, that's that,' he said with evident satisfaction. 'So far, so good. I suggest we find ourselves a spot of hot dinner somewhere, don't you? It's going to be a long, wet night.'

But Lord Porterfield was frowning, worried by the proximity of those other vehicles to the container lorry carrying that first precious Cruise missile. 'What about those other vehicles – they were pretty damn close, weren't they? How many of those were ours?'

General Inkermann smiled in the darkness. 'I wouldn't worry about that, Phillip. They all were.'

# : 17 :

Two were on watch. Two were digging. In the desert scrubland between Bukhara and Samarkand in Uzbekistan.

The SAS team had spent the entire day lying up. Hidden, motionless, they blended unseen into a broken, boulder-choked gully while their officer crawled forward to take the first of a long series of cross-bearings from the hills and valleys behind them and the cluster of tiny villages lost in the foothills to the south-east.

He worked with infinite patience, inching the prismatic compass to his eyeline in long, measured seconds as he shielded the glass prism from the reflective rays of the winter sun. Finally he had wormed his way back to the others. 'Three hundred metres to your front. At the base of that rock shaped like a blacksmith's anvil, see it?' They had seen it. And so now, cloaked in darkness, they began to dig. To carry out London's orders.

Ninety minutes later Ratbag's spade rang against a large flat stone lying about a metre below the surface. He tossed the spade aside, dropped to his knees and brushed away the loose soil with his fingers. Then he looked up. 'Boss,' he called softly, 'I think I've found something.'

The officer crouched down beside him and ran his hands over plates of smooth stone lying butted together in a neat row. 'OK, let's see what we've got,' he said quietly. Ratbag handed him a small hand torch.

Shielding its face in his cupped hands the officer turned on the torch and a dull red glow suffused the bottom of the trench. Now they could see that the stones had been fitted together by hand so that they locked firmly together, making a solid lid over whatever lay beneath. The officer enlarged their hole at one side and cleared away the earth from the lip of the stone lid until he and Ratbag were able to hook their fingers over one edge. The officer nodded and they both heaved upwards, grunting with the effort as the heavy stone slab lifted towards them.

Immediately they wrinkled their noses with disgust as the rank, sour smell of decay rose to meet them. It was the same smell that had disgusted Driver Houseman in the back of the army lorry outside the jeweller Markstein's house in the blitzed East End of London almost forty years earlier. Now both soldiers tied cloths across their mouths and noses. Then the officer hunched forward again and shone the torch down into the open grave.

He saw that they had prised off part of the lid of a makeshift stone coffin. There, beneath their feet, lay a withered human skeleton, the eye-sockets staring emptily towards the heavens, the teeth bared in a grimace of anger at this latest disturbance. The arms were folded across a rib cage still swathed with the ragged tatters of cloth, the bones of the hands still clasped around the hilt of a sword that glittered in the red glow of the torchlight. 'Sodding hell,' breathed Ratbag. 'Sodding bloody hell.'

'Yeah,' muttered the officer as he gazed down at the skeleton he had been sent to destroy. 'Yeah. I'll go along with you there.' He thought for a moment. 'Soon as I try and lift him, this feller's going to fall apart. Get a groundsheet down here, Ratbag. Then we can toss the bones –'

'Hold it, boss. We've got company,' hissed Ratbag, slithering down into the grave, rifle suddenly at his shoulder.

There was a loose rattle of stones and then Trooper Hiller was crouching down beside the edge of the grave, pistol in his hand. 'Boss? Lovat's found a snooper. He's holding him over by the rocks there.'

'How many?' demanded the officer, climbing swiftly from the trench.

'Just the one, boss. Claims he's a shepherd.'

The officer moved silently to the cluster of rocks. There he found a boy of about seventeen sitting on the ground, shivering with fright, his hands clasped on his head as Lovat stood over him with a levelled rifle. 'What happened?' demanded the officer shortly as Trooper Hiller moved past to watch their front.

Lovat shrugged. 'Thought I heard a movement about twenty minutes ago so I had a look around. Found this joker creeping around on the other side of the rocks there. No one else in sight.'

'What's his story?'

'Says he's a shepherd from one of the villages back there.' He jerked a thumb towards the south-east. 'He's on his own, any road. Claims he fell asleep and only woke when I came looking for him.' Lovat shook his head emphatically. 'I don't buy it, boss. I'm not that fucking noisy.'

The officer glanced round, sniffed the air. 'His sheep. I don't see any sheep. Can't smell 'em, either.' He turned back to the others. 'You see any sheep?' They shook their heads and the officer thought for a moment. 'So – you think he saw something?'

Lovat shrugged. 'The torch? It's possible, I suppose.'

'Searched him?'

Again Lovat nodded. 'Not a thing.'

The officer crouched down and shone his torch into the face of the frightened young boy. The shepherd screwed up his face and smiled nervously, uncertainly, trying to ingratiate himself with these strange, dangerous foreigners. Then the officer began firing questions at him. Each was greeted with a shrug of incomprehension and that flickering, nervous smile. Finally the officer turned to Lovat, a decision taken.

'Take him over there,' he ordered, jerking his head. The boy was hauled roughly to his feet and shoved over to the open trench. 'OK, hold him there.'

The boy looked from one face to another, nervously. Then he pressed two fingers up to his mouth and mimed a deep inhalation. 'Cigarette, plez?' he tried, that young face fixed with its frightened, sickly grin.

The officer nodded. 'Give him a smoke, Lovat,' he ordered.

Lovat looked at him as if he was mad. 'A fag, boss? The smell'll carry for miles –'

'You heard what I said: cigarette. Give it to him,' he snapped. Lovat did so and, as the boy bent forward towards the match cupped in Ratbag's hand, the officer stepped behind him, lifted his silenced automatic until it was less than an inch behind the boy's left ear and squeezed the trigger. There was a soft phut! and the boy jackknifed sideways, sprawled across the rough ground and lay still, the cigarette still gummed to his top lip, the back of his head blown away.

Ratbag blew out the match and gazed down. 'Poor sod,' he

muttered. The officer tucked the pistol back into the folds of his clothing and jumped down into the grave. 'The groundsheet, Ratbag – quick as you can.' As if nothing had happened.

Twenty minutes later Lovat and Hiller swung the body of the young shepherd into the empty grave, tossed the cigarette down onto the crumpled, lifeless body and began shovelling earth back into the grave with swift, economical movements as, near by, their officer tied the last knot in a shapeless bundle and rose to his feet. It was done.

The body they had been sent to exhume and then scatter in the mountains on the long journey back across the frontier had ceased to be a skeleton clasping an ancient sword. It had become instead a heap of dry, brittle bones tied in a British Army groundsheet, without shape, without dignity, without mystery of any kind.

Not the stuff of legends at all.

As they turned away they heard the faint, lost bleating of a sheep. Looking, perhaps, for its shepherd.

Gordon was having a bath in his hotel bedroom, the steaming hot water easing the dull, aching throb in his shoulder as he lay back in the water and ran over what he had learnt; what Bruno had told him: the mission into Uzbekistan; the burying of a skeleton taken from the British Museum at the end of the war; the image of his father, leaping into space on the end of a parachute and then coming home and keeping quiet about his adventure for forty years out of . . . out of what, mused Gordon, soaping an arm? Out of loyalty? To the British government? After forty years? Living out his days on a meagre pension when everyone else was selling their memoirs, leaking stories to the Sunday papers about Churchill, Ultra and every campaign under the sun from Dunkirk to the Battle of Berlin?

There came a sudden soft tapping on his door and Gordon started, the fear never far below the surface. Then he rose dripping from the bath, wrapped a towel around his waist and moved to the door. 'Who is it?' he called.

'Toni. Toni Johnson.' He sighed. That was all right, then. He slipped the chain off the door and unfastened the lock. 'Hi!' she smiled. 'Mind if I come in?'

223 :

'Er . . . no. No. Come along in,' invited Gordon, stepping back into the room. 'I was just having a bath.'

'No kidding?' smiled Toni, her eyes running down over his body in a manner that was overtly suggestive, sexual.

'I won't be a moment.' Gordon returned to the bathroom, closed the door and began towelling himself dry. As he combed his hair in the mirror the door to his left opened slowly. Toni Johnson stood silently in the doorway, watching him as he parted his hair. Then Gordon forgot all about his parting as, in the mirror, he watched those slim fingers move to the buttons of her blouse.

'Be kind of a waste for you to get all dressed up again now, don't you think?' smiled Toni Johnson quietly. Gordon just stood there, stupidly, the towel hitched around his waist as the buttons came slowly undone.

Toni Johnson slid the blouse off her shoulders, tossed it casually back into the bedroom and reached behind her for the clasp of her black bra, her eyes holding Gordon's as she smiled a private, secret smile. Often in the past she had chosen to seduce those she was tasked to liquidate, finding some deep, inner gratification in the knowledge that those men who writhed and pumped upon her body, helpless as she moaned and moved beneath them in calculated frenzy, would soon be turned stiff and cold and staring by the woman they sought to penetrate, to abuse.

And still Gordon just stood there, watching her in the mirror.

The bra came loose and she shrugged her shoulders slightly forward in an elegant, utterly feminine gesture that aroused Gordon instantly so that now, for the first time, he turned towards her. Toni Johnson let her bra fall off her arms onto the bathroom floor, straightened up and squared back those lovely shoulders, watching Gordon's eyes as they feasted greedily on taut, shimmering breasts, each capped with a rosy, outthrust nipple. Gordon took a step towards her as he felt his throat tighten and his erection stir like a sword beneath the towel.

'I . . .' he croaked, ludicrously.

Toni Johnson raised a cool finger and pressed it gently against his lips. 'I know: you're married, right?' she whispered softly.

'Well, I'm not. And so what, anyway? Who's going to tell? Not me, Gordon – are you?'

Gordon moved still closer, not trusting himself to speak. Toni Johnson grasped his wrist gently and placed his hand carefully, deliberately, on one full, firm breast. Then she covered his hand with hers, pressed it towards her and began to rub in a smooth, caressive motion. 'That's it,' she encouraged huskily, eyes glowing now as she allowed Gordon to push her back against the cool, damp tiles of the bathroom wall and drive forward between her parted thighs as he continued fondling her breast. 'That's it, baby. You like that, don't you, Gordon?' she breathed as she began working her skirt up her thighs. 'Don't you, baby? Don't you? Go on, Gordon – do it. Do it to me.'

She ripped the towel away from around his waist and the telephone began to ring.

The bloody telephone began to ring.

Gordon started violently.

'Leave it,' she moaned. 'Fuck me, Gordon.' But the telephone wouldn't stop ringing. Just went on and on.

Gordon twisted away suddenly, went through into the bedroom and sat down on the bed. Then he pushed a hand through his hair, took a deep breath and lifted the receiver. 'Hello?'

'Gordon? It's me.'

'Rachel?' His wife. Like a leap into arctic waters.

'It's me, yes!'

'God. How . . . how did you know I was here?' Open-book Hallam.

'I didn't,' replied Rachel simply. 'I just tried all the hotels in Zug I could find. Yours was the fifth, I think. How are you, darling?'

'Er . . . fine. I'm fine. What . . . what is it?'

'You don't sound very pleased to hear me,' said Rachel doubtfully. 'Did I interrupt anything?'

'No. No. Not at all,' lied Gordon hurriedly with a guilty glance over his shoulder towards the bathroom. 'I was . . . I was in the bath, that's all.'

'I just wanted to check you were all right, you know? You sounded . . . well, weird last night. When I called you at Dad's. I thought I was talking to some kind of zombie. You frightened me.'

Was it really only last night? thought Gordon. It felt like a lifetime away. 'I . . . I know I did. I'm sorry.'

'You still sound a bit odd now . . .'

'I'm just . . . just tired, that's all.' That much was true, anyway.

'When are you coming home, love?'

Gordon sighed with exasperation. 'I've only just got here, darling –'

'I know.' She sounded suddenly frail, defenceless. 'I just miss you when you're not with me, that's all. It's not the same.'

'I miss you too,' he lied with another glance towards the bathroom. Toni Johnson was standing in the doorway watching him. Listening.

'What?'

'I'm missing you,' he repeated quietly.

'Pardon?'

'I said: I'm missing you! What's the matter with your line?'

'Nothing's the matter with my line. I just like to hear you say it, that's all. Have you seen that man Bruno yet?'

'Left him about an hour ago. He told me an incredible story – you'll never guess what Dad was up to: not in a million years!' As Toni Johnson listened from the doorway Gordon told Rachel about the mission and about the skeleton. Then, as he neared the end, he remembered something. 'Listen, Rach, there's something you can do for me, OK? I want you to call the British Museum in London. Talk to their Archaeological Department and ask someone there what happened to Endlemann's warrior, OK? You got that? Professor Endlemann's warrior. It was found in the Persian desert outside somewhere called Tabriz in 1927 or thereabouts.'

'Professor Endlemann's warrior. Yes, I've got that. I'll give them a call first thing in the morning.' She hesitated. 'How . . . how long do you think you'll be?'

Gordon thought for a moment. 'Another day should do it. I must have another word with Tyschen, though. See what else he can tell me. The man's a bloody gold-mine. Names, facts, dates – he remembers everything!'

'Gordon?'

'Yes?'

'You will look after yourself, won't you, darling?'

Gordon frowned. 'What's that supposed to mean?'

'Oh, you know . . . take care, that's all.'

'Course I will!' promised Gordon, the words sounding false and hollow even as they were spoken.

'Will you call me tomorrow? Before you leave?'

'Sure. Talk to you then.'

'O.K. Bye for now, darling. I love you.'

'I love you too,' replied Gordon, meaning it. He put the phone down slowly and looked round, expecting to see Toni Johnson standing waiting for him in the doorway, wondering how he could explain that –

Toni Johnson had gone.

Toni Johnson hurried to her bedroom, opened her suitcase and took out a flat, brown leather handbag. Her face was cold and hard as she remembered what Hallam had said on the telephone. So Tyschen was talking, remembering. Hallam could only act upon what he was told, upon what Tyschen remembered, chose to pass on. It was Tyschen, therefore, who was the primary target, not Hallam. Hallam, anyway, was already emasculated, ready for her. She had seen the look in his eyes, felt his hardness thrusting against her. She could take him whenever she chose. But Tyschen? Tyschen was still a threat. Still dangerous.

She took her handbag into the bathroom and tugged on the light above the basin. Then she unscrewed the slender shaft of her cosmetic razor, removed the blade and turned the bag inside out. She felt along the handbag's base and drew the razor-blade slowly along one edge, slicing through the thin nylon lining. Then she felt inside and drew out a slender steel instrument that shone brightly in the overhead light.

It was a surgeon's scalpel.

Toni Johnson turned off the light, went back into the bedroom and sat down to gaze for several moments at the scalpel as it lay quietly across the palm of her hand, its precision blade sheathed in a transparent plastic sleeve. She slipped the scalpel into another handbag, the one she would carry with her, and snapped the lock shut. Then she sat for long moments beneath the single lamp, both hands resting motionless on the arms of the chair, her features composed in a calm, almost hypnotic trance.

There was always this moment of inner stillness, this lull before the storm of killing.

Presently Toni Johnson took the local telephone directory from the bedside table and searched briefly for a number. Lifting the handset, she asked for an outside line and dialled. Then – 'I wish to speak to Herr Bruno Tyschen, please,' she said in flawless German. 'On a personal matter. A very personal matter.'

Gordon was also on the telephone in his bedroom. He was speaking to the operator at International Directory Inquiries, asking for the London telephone number of a Mr Phillip Porterfield. If he was able to contact him now, from Switzerland, he might be able to call in and see him on his way home to the west country.

'Hello? Caller?'

'Yes?'

'The only record I have listed is for a Lord Porterfield. And that number is ex-directory. I'm sorry.'

'Oh. Oh, I see.'

'Thank you.'

'Wait! Er . . . before you go: could you please just look up a number in North Shields, England? A Mr Peter Tillet?'

'One moment.'

Gordon waited. A minute later he had both name and address. The temptation was irresistible. He dialled. Within moments, it seemed, he could hear his call ringing in an English home on the other side of Europe.

'Hello?' A woman's voice, dull and lack-lustre.

'May I speak to Mr Tillet, please – Mr Peter Tillet?'

There was a sudden gasp, followed by muffled sobbing.

Gordon frowned at the handset. 'Hello? I said: may I speak to Mr Peter Tillet, please?'

'No. No, you can't,' said the same tearful voice choked with sobbing. In the background Gordon heard a man's voice say gruffly, 'Here, chuck – let me deal with that.' Then, to Gordon – 'Hello?'

'Mr Tillet?'

'No, no. It's his brother here, Michael.'

'Oh. It's really Peter I –'

'Yes, I know that. I . . . I don't know how else to put this, like, so you'll forgive me, I'm sure, if what I say comes as a bit of a shock, like . . . Peter died yesterday afternoon.'

Gordon went very still.

'Died? I'm . . . I'm sorry. I didn't know. Had he . . . had he been ill for some time, may I ask?'

'Pete? Ill?' There was a sudden, bitter laugh. 'He never missed a day's work. Not in his whole life.'

'Then can I . . . I mean . . . how did he . . .?'

'He was knocked down, wasn't he? Bowled over. Knocked down and killed not fifty yards from his own front door. By one of those American tourists . . . Hello? Hello? . . . Caller?'

Slowly, slowly Gordon replaced the receiver and sat down on the edge of the bed to stare at nothing as the world went into slow motion around him.

Peter Tillet: knocked down and killed by an American tourist.

Walter Hallam: knocked down and killed by an American tourist.

Coincidence, right? Had to be . . .

American tourists.

A sudden thought popped unbidden into Gordon's mind: Toni Johnson. She was an American tourist.

Gordon found himself breathing deeply, his palms sticky and damp with sudden fear. Then he poured himself a glass of water with a hand that trembled slightly.

Think, Gordon! Work it out. Use your brain. O K, O K – maybe she was exactly what she said she was: an American taking a few days' break in Europe before returning to the United States. So check. Check up on her. That wouldn't be difficult: what was the name of that hotel she said she worked for, the one in Reading? Holiday Inn, right? Had to be. They were all over the place.

He lifted the receiver in feverish haste. Directory Inquiries. Another delay. Then he was dialling the number in Reading and waiting as the room closed in around him and he heard the rasp of his own nervous breathing in the receiver mouthpiece. Glancing up he saw suddenly that the chain was off the door, the bolt unlocked. Anyone could walk in, kill him without warning. He dropped the phone on the bed, leapt to his feet and locked the door with feverish haste. When he picked up the phone again someone was talking to him. 'Hello? . . . Hello? Holiday Inn.'

'Ah . . . good evening. May I speak to someone in your personnel department, please?'

'I'm afraid they've gone home now, sir. Can the manager help you?'

'Yes, yes. Let me speak to him, please.'

'One moment.'

'Richard Southgate, duty manager. Can I help you?'

'Er . . . I don't know. I hope so. Do you have a Miss Toni Johnson working for you? She's an American.'

'No. No we do not.'

'You're sure?'

'We have no Americans working here at the Holiday Inn, caller. It is our policy to recruit local people wherever possible. Here, that's no problem.'

'You're sure? Positive?'

'Quite sure.' The voice began to sound vexed. 'Who is this calling?'

'I . . . thank you.'

Gordon slammed down the phone as though it had suddenly become red hot. He pushed nervously to his feet. Bloody hell. Bloody sodding hell! Hands thrust deep into hip pockets, Gordon stalked restlessly the length of the room, forcing himself not to jump to conclusions but to think things through. Perhaps he had called the wrong hotel, made a simple mistake . . . But even as he thought of these things his mind darted back to their meeting in Paris: to the spilt coffee and effusive apologies that had thrown them together and to the way in which Toni Johnson had then attached herself to his side. At the time he had put it down to a combination of accident and his own natural charm, to a stroke of luck. But now? Now it looked contrived. It had all been too easy, too convenient.

Christ – he dragged a hand through his hair and felt his scalp begin to crawl – he had told her . . . everything! Every sodding thing! About Dad, about Apostle; shown her the photograph of Dad and Peter and Mark – Jesus . . .

Mark. Must warn Mark.

Gordon pounced on the phone, fingers drumming in a frenzy of impatience as he waited for his call to ring through.

'Restaurant Oppel,' said a voice. The clatter of dishes and the sound of many voices filled the background.

'Herr Tyschen, please. It's very urgent.'

'*Bitte?*'

'Herr Tyschen, *bitte*!' Gordon almost shouted.

'Herr Tyschen is not here now. I am sorry.'

'Where is he?'

'He goes away. A little time ago.'

'Alone?'

'Please?'

'Alone? Was anyone with him, for God's sake!'

'I think so. He goes with –'

'– A woman? An American woman?'

'Just so – yes.'

Jesus.

Gordon banged down the phone, lunged for his coat and was out of his room and running down the corridor past a startled chambermaid before the waitress in the Restaurant Oppel had replaced the receiver.

# : 18 :

Bruno Tyschen was still grumbling as he led Toni Johnson up the long flight of wooden stairs to his private rooms on the top floor above the restaurant. 'What is it about this business?' he complained, ushering Toni Johnson through ahead of him. 'For forty years nobody wants to know about Apostle – forty years! Then all of a sudden, first this Englishman comes to see me and now you –'

'It'll only take a moment,' promised Toni Johnson as she looked about her. 'Hey, it's really neat up here! You married, Mr Tyschen?' she asked, almost as an afterthought.

He turned, surprised. 'Bruno Tyschen – married? No, no – I live here alone. Down there' – he gestured through two floors to the restaurant below – 'there are always too many voices. Up here there is just me and Theodore.'

Toni Johnson spun round. 'Theodore?' Then she relaxed as Bruno Tyschen picked a ginger cat off the sofa and began stroking its coat with thick, soothing fingers. He held him up admiringly.

'This is Theodore. We have been together a long time.' He replaced him fondly on the sofa and glanced up. 'And we never argue.' Toni Johnson smiled. She hated cats.

The living area was spacious and airy with a wide bay window looking out across the lake towards the distant town of Cham on the western shore. Sofa and chairs were grouped around an open hearth and the pine floor was highly polished and littered with thick rugs. Tyschen glanced pointedly at the brass clock on the mantelpiece and the gesture was not lost on Toni Johnson. 'So – what do you have to tell me that is so important?' asked Tyschen shortly.

'Have you got an atlas, Mr Tyschen? A map of the area?' she asked. 'I can explain better then.'

'A map? Of Zug?'

She shook her head and smiled, a hand resting lightly on the clasp of her handbag. 'The area where you were dropped. On Apostle.'

Bruno Tyschen nodded reluctantly. 'Yes, I have an atlas. But I still do not see why –'

'Please. It will only take a moment,' she smiled. 'Then you can get back to all those noisy customers.'

Tyschen sighed, crossed to a laden bookshelf and took down a large, slender volume. He took this over to a heavy wooden desk, sat down in a swivel chair, opened the atlas at a detailed map of the USSR and glanced over his shoulder. 'Come here. I will show you.'

'Great,' smiled Toni Johnson, coming round to stand naturally at his side. 'OK, just show me where you dropped – would you do that?'

Bruno Tyschen bent forward.

One of the last things he ever heard was the tiny metallic snick! as Toni Johnson opened her handbag.

Gordon pushed the restaurant door closed behind him and grasped the arm of a hurrying waiter. The man's pile of cluttered trays swayed precariously. *'Herr Tyschen, bitte? Wo ist Herr Tyschen?'* demanded Gordon, glancing round the crowded, busy restaurant. The waiter shrugged and hurried away. There was a waitress taking an order from a near-by table and Gordon tapped her urgently on the shoulder. She turned, angered at the sudden distraction. 'Where is Mr Tyschen?' he demanded again, conscious of the need for haste, of the minutes ticking away.

The girl glanced round helplessly as a supervisor hurried forward sensing a trouble-maker. A question was fired at Gordon in rapid German. He shook his head obstinately. 'Herr Tyschen – Bruno Tyschen?' he repeated, ignoring the curious glances from the tables around him.

'You are English, yes? You came here before?'

'I did, yes. I'm looking for Herr Tyschen.'

'Bruno? You are a friend of his?'

'That's right,' agreed Gordon readily. 'A friend. He left here a few minutes ago with an American – an American woman. D'you know where he went?'

The man pointed a finger at the ceiling. 'Upstairs, I think.'

'Upstairs? You mean he has a flat up there? An apartment?'

The man nodded and pointed outside. 'You must go outside, yes? Around the building on the right you will find a glass door that . . .' But already he was talking to himself.

Gordon pushed back outside and ran around the side of the building. A short set of concrete steps led to a small foyer and an inner flight of steep wooden stairs. Gordon took these two at a time and arrived panting on the first-floor landing. He glanced up.

The door at the top of the next flight was ajar and a thin wedge of lamplight shone out onto the landing.

Gordon climbed up the staircase – and then he paused, suddenly frightened as he looked up at the door that was not quite closed. It seemed to be beckoning. Maybe . . . maybe he should go back downstairs, get help, call the police. He hesitated. Get help? Call the police? And tell them what?

He went on, more slowly now as the noise from the warm, safe restaurant below receded behind him and he was left with nothing but the pant of his own frightened breathing.

He reached the top of the stairs and paused. There was a tiny illuminated bell push set into the door jamb. It bore the one word 'Tyschen'. Gordon pressed it and heard the buzzer sound inside the apartment. But there was no reply, no sound of movement.

'Mr Tyschen?' called Gordon nervously, pushing the door gently with his fingertips. It swung open obediently and Gordon craned forward across the threshold.

From where he was standing he could see into the main living area: sofa, chairs, fireplace with drawn curtains beyond, soft lights throwing comfortable shadows across thick carpets, the edge of a heavy wooden desk . . . 'Herr Tyschen? It's me – Gordon Hallam.'

And still there was no sound.

Gordon took a deep breath and stepped into the room. 'Hello?' There was a sudden thud and Gordon nearly leapt out of his skin. Then there was a soft miaow and a ginger cat dropped onto the polished floor from the arm of the sofa and slunk away into a corner.

Four cautious steps into the room now – and there Gordon stopped, his heart hammering violently against his ribs.

Bruno Tyschen was sitting slumped at his desk, one arm sprawled forward across an opened atlas.

He might almost have been sleeping.

For long, dragging milli-seconds of time, Gordon froze. Then he started forward across the floor, grasped Tyschen's shoulder and pulled him back in his chair. As he did so Tyschen's head rolled grotesquely against his arm and Gordon felt thick, sour bile rise to the back of his throat.

Blood ran from Tyschen's chest to collect in a thick, dark puddle in his lap. Now, as Gordon pulled his chair away from the desk and Tyschen's legs splayed obscenely beneath him, that blood began to drip onto the floor where it formed a dark, widening puddle on the bright planks of polished pine.

Gordon swallowed, forcing down the urge to throw up. Then he made himself lift away the side of Tyschen's jacket and feel beneath for the site of the wound with shaking fingers. He found it almost at once: a neat, surgical incision just below the ribs on the left side of Tyschen's body. Gordon took his hand away and stared with horror at the blood staining his fingers. Then – incongruous action – he wiped his fingers urgently against Tyschen's shoulder. It wasn't the priority, of course; it wasn't even necessary, but he was past the point of reasoned action and had come perilously close to that moment when he would turn and scream for help. The death of the man in his father's kitchen and the waking nightmare that had followed that event had not hardened him, inured him to further horrors. He was a redundant Devon schoolmaster, not James Bond or a member of the Special Air Service. He was very close to panic.

'Stay . . . stay there,' he muttered uselessly as the head lolled and rolled towards him once more. 'Just . . . stay there.' Gordon darted to the sofa, swept up a cushion and lunged back before Tyschen fell out of the chair to stuff the cushion between his jacket and the wound. He pressed the cushion tightly against Tyschen's chest and looked desperately for help into a face that such a short time ago had been so animated, so full of life, but which now carried the pasty grey hallmark of approaching death. He was about to look away – and then he caught the merest beat of pulse at Tyschen's neck and, as if to corroborate this physical impossibility, an eyelid flickered open and a froth of red bubbles burst from his mouth as he surfaced briefly from that deep, beckoning sea of darkness to strain towards Gordon, his full, slack lips struggling to shape the words that never came.

Tyschen was trying suddenly to move, his eyes starting forward out of his head with this last supreme effort as his left hand dropped towards one of the drawers of his desk and his fingers began scratching weakly at the handle. He managed to tug the drawer open perhaps two inches before the effort exhausted him and he sank back again into unconsciousness. Gordon reached down, pulled open the drawer and saw Tyschen had been trying to reach the curved butt of a revolver lying in the bottom of the drawer. Tyschen moaned and Gordon found himself stroking that cold, clammy forehead as he cast around desperately for something that would save the life that was running through his fingers even as he nursed him in an agony of impotence. 'Don't . . . don't try to speak, O K?' he managed in a husky whisper. 'You'll . . . you'll be O K. Only you mustn't . . . mustn't try to speak.'

There was a sound behind him.

Gordon turned to see Toni Johnson standing in the doorway. She appeared to see Tyschen's body for the first time and her face mirrored a nice mixture of horror, surprise and concern. 'Gordon? They told me downstairs that . . . oh, my God –'

'He's been stabbed. Someone stabbed him.'

'What? You're . . . you're kidding!' said Toni Johnson, aghast, as she came towards him. With a hand held casually behind her back.

'How did you get here?' demanded Gordon sharply.

'I . . . I came up the stairs. Here, let me –'

'No! Stay there!' ordered Gordon.

Toni Johnson looked at him as if he was mad. 'What? You can't be serious! Let me help, Goddammit! I can –'

'I mean it! Stay there!' shouted Gordon, his voice raw and ragged in his ears with the sound of his own fear.

'Hey, now listen,' soothed Toni Johnson easily. 'It's all right, Gordon, you know? Really. I'm a friend, right?' And still she came closer, one hand held behind her back as she stepped towards him.

Gordon reached down suddenly, jerked open the desk drawer and straightened up clutching Tyschen's heavy revolver in both hands. It shook and wavered around as he pointed it towards her – an accurate barometer of his own emotions: he didn't know if she had tried to kill Tyschen, didn't even know if the revolver was loaded, didn't know anything. Except that Tyschen was dying beside him, two other members of the Apostle team had been killed by American tourists and an American tourist stood before him now. 'Stay there,' he repeated.

She didn't take any notice. 'What? Now look, Gordon –'

'I mean it! Don't come any closer.' He thumbed back the heavy hammer and the double click-click of the action locking back froze her footsteps. 'What's that in your hand?'

'Look, Gordon, you've had a shock, right? Let me help. That guy needs to be in –'

'I said: what's that in your hand?'

'Nothing. Nothing's in my hand. Look, will you just –'

'Show me.'

Toni Johnson managed an uneasy little laugh. 'What is this? There's a guy there who –'

A thought suddenly struck Gordon. 'You say you just came from downstairs, right?'

She nodded. 'That's right. I –'

'I didn't hear you. I didn't hear you come up the stairs –'

Toni shrugged. 'Maybe you –'

'You come into the room, you see me standing over him, yet you never – stop! One more step and I'll fire, Toni – I swear it.' He waved the revolver gently to one side, drawing Toni away into the middle of the room. He risked a quick glance down at Tyschen but he hadn't moved, hadn't stirred. He took one hand off the gun and felt Tyschen's neck for signs of a pulse. There was no beat, no movement. 'He's gone,' said Gordon quietly. 'He's dead.' Both hands went back on the butt of the revolver and, in some strange fashion, the knowledge that there was now nothing more he could do strengthened him so that the barrel settled more steadily on the woman standing ten paces away.

'I'm waiting,' said Gordon. 'I want to see what's behind your back; what you're holding.'

Toni Johnson sighed, stooped down and picked up the ginger

cat that had padded across the carpet and was rubbing itself gently against her legs.

'You see – nothing.' She opened one hand.

'Now the other one.'

Toni Johnson smiled a crooked little smile and took her right hand slowly from behind her back so that Gordon could see the scalpel. And the cuff of her delicate, feminine blouse, stained with the blood of the man she had murdered.

The shock of that discovery, that realization, hit Gordon so hard that for a moment he thought he was going to pass out, collapse helplessly at her feet.

'You killed him,' he breathed, so quietly that the words barely carried. 'You *killed* him! Why?'

Toni Johnson shrugged as though he had raised some matter of casual interest. 'I was told to.'

'But *why*?'

'Because of what he knew. Because of what he told you.'

'Because of what he told *me*? Who . . . who told you to . . . to kill him?'

She shrugged. 'My people? Your people? It really doesn't matter.'

'*Who*?'

But Toni Johnson just shook her head, a teacher explaining a simple, immutable fact to a backward child. 'It doesn't matter – not to you, Gordon. And you know why?' She took a step forward, scalpel delicately poised between her slim fingers.

'Tell me.'

'Because I'm going to have to kill you too,' she replied simply. 'That's orders too, OK? It's nothing personal.'

'Nothing personal? Jesus Christ! How can you –'

Toni Johnson shook her head pityingly. 'They told me you killed Harry, only I guess that must have been an accident, right? You don't –'

'Harry?'

'The guy who was tailing you.' She was moving closer now all the time, her words buying distance.

'I didn't have any choice. He was –'

'You ever killed a woman, Gordon? In cold blood? With one of those?' She gestured at the revolver, now less than ten feet away. 'Because that's what you're going to have to do, you know. Or I'm going to kill you.' She stroked the cat gently, encircled his neck with those slim fingers and then suddenly squeezed and twisted deftly. There was a brief mew of protest and then the cat collapsed limply in her hands. She laid it carefully aside on the sofa. 'You see?'

Gordon watched, mesmerized, as she came forward more confidently as the gun began to waver, drop away –

'You're a teacher, Gordon, right? You haven't got the stomach for something like that, have you now? You're weak. You know that and I know that, don't we? So why don't you just put that thing down and –'

'How . . . but how could you . . .?'

'Oh, yes, Gordon – I can, believe me,' she whispered huskily as a strange light of anticipation and almost sexual enjoyment dawned in those cold, still eyes. 'I really enjoy it, you know? Truly. Every time I do it I get this –'

The gun went off with a deafening, shattering roar.

For the rest of his life Gordon would ask himself if he actually meant to fire or whether the gun went off by accident. All he would remember later was that one moment Toni Johnson was edging closer and the next the gun had gone off. Then there was nothing but a numbing ache in his wrists as the gun kicked high, with savage recoil and Toni Johnson had smashed back across the room and that deadly, soothing voice had ceased. The scalpel flew from her fingers as the force of the shot knocked her off her feet and sent her sprawling untidily across the floor, a neat, dark hole beneath her left nostril and her brains strewn across the polished pine floor as the heavy, soft-nosed .38 tore away the back of her skull.

The pistol fell from Gordon's nerveless fingers and dropped onto the floor with a dull thud. Gordon stood there for many seconds as the cordite fumes eddied around him, his mind numb and frozen as he gazed at the woman he had killed lying on the floor with her legs wide apart and those beautiful eyes staring emptily towards eternity.

She reminded him of a doll he had once found being kicked aimlessly along a corridor by a couple of third-year vandals: discarded, forgotten, ungainly.

And not at all beautiful.

Gradually Gordon drifted back, returned from that inner refuge of his mind to the reality of Tyschen's apartment above the restaurant; to murder and sudden death in a quiet Swiss town. He steeled himself for the shout of voices, for the crash of boots pounding up the stairs as people below rushed to investigate that single, deafening shot. He went to the door and peered cautiously outside, but the stairs were empty and there was silence. It occurred to him then that if he could not hear the restaurant, then they probably couldn't hear him, either.

That gave him an idea, a way of buying a little time before he too was embroiled in a formal inquiry that would bury him in endless questions, perhaps put him behind bars.

He went back into the living area, picked up the pistol and wiped the butt and trigger self-consciously with his handkerchief, just like they did on TV. Then he lifted Tyschen's dead right hand, gritted his teeth and forced Tyschen's fingers around the butt and inside the trigger guard. It was horribly difficult, the thick fingers stiff and ungainly so that he imagined them snapping off in his hand. He managed it at last and then allowed the hand holding the pistol to drop naturally across Tyschen's lap.

At which point Gordon had to rush into the bathroom where he was copiously and violently sick. He wasted more time then, just leaning against the cool tiles of the bathroom as the waves of sickness and nausea receded and the shock left him weak and shaking. Then he washed in the basin, towelled the clammy sweat from his face and hairline and studied himself briefly in Tyschen's mirror. He looked terrible, he decided: pale, strained and frightened – but he simply couldn't afford to wait any longer. Any moment someone else might come upstairs, knock on the front door . . .

He tidied the bathroom, cleaned up the toilet and risked flushing it a second time before hurrying into the living-room where he spent precious seconds just looking slowly around. What had he touched? Tyschen's shoulder, the gun – what else? The front door! He crossed the room, wiped the door handle carefully with his handkerchief and closed the door quietly behind him. He hurried down the stairs and pushed gratefully into the crisp, cold air of evening. The alleyway was empty and it was quite dark, although there were lights in the row of shops across the street.

How long since he had left the restaurant? thought Gordon. Five minutes, ten? He crossed the narrow alley, went into a gift shop and approached the counter where he waited impatiently for his turn and then pointed at the first suitable gift he saw: a box of chocolate liqueurs. He paid for the chocolates without speaking, aware that the woman serving him was looking at him rather oddly as he took the chocolates, nodded his thanks and hurried round the corner. There he paused, took a grip on himself and opened the front door of the Restaurant Oppel.

Everything was normal. So normal, so noisy, that Gordon half expected to see Tyschen standing at the counter, massive, jovial and indestructible. But he wasn't.

The supervisor was there instead, standing over one of the cash tills. Gordon waited until he was busy with a customer's receipt and then hurried to his side and tapped him on the shoulder. The man swung, saw who it was and sighed. 'Yes, sir? What is it now?'

Gordon shrugged with careful nonchalance and placed the chocolates on top of the till. 'He must be out – can't get a reply. Would you give him these with my compliments, tell him they're from the Englishman who came to see him? I'll be in touch again later, tell him. Oh – and d'you have the right time, please?'

The supervisor glanced at his watch with thinly-disguised irritation. 'Now – please: I am very busy.'

Gordon turned and left the restaurant with a cluster of laughing teenage customers. Mission accomplished.

Once outside he broke into a run until he came within sight of the Hotel Ochsen. He went inside, nodded a cheery greeting at the receptionist as he picked up his key and then took the lift upstairs. He was alone in the narrow car and he leant back against the wall, closed his eyes and blew out his cheeks with relief. How long did he have? One hour, two? Perhaps until morning, if he was very lucky . . .

Down the corridor and into his room with the door closed and locked behind him to sprawl full length on the bed, twist over and stare wide-eyed up at the ceiling.

Fighting off the urge to curl up and sleep, escape into the

safety of a warm bed and soft blankets, Gordon forced himself to swing his feet to the floor and reach for the phone. He asked for an·outside line and then dialled Rachel's work number in England. He wasted precious minutes as he waited, waited for the switchboard to answer. Then, at last, he was through: through to Rachel's supervisor and finally, to Rachel herself, on night shift in the Plymouth studios.

'Rachel – thank God. It's me.'

'Gordon? What's the matter?' she demanded. 'What's happened?'

He took a deep, steadying breath. 'Don't ask, OK? Just do what I tell you –'

'What? Where are you –?'

'Please! Just . . . just listen, will you? And do what I say, OK? I'm at the hotel, same as before. Still got the number?'

'Yes, I –'

'Listen! In' – he looked at his watch and made a rapid calculation – 'in fifteen minutes I want you to call here and tell the operator – *tell the operator*, that's very important – that I have to come back to England right away, OK? Tell her . . . I don't know, tell her your mother's been taken ill, my sister's had a bad car crash . . . tell her anything you like but she *must* understand that you are calling *to get me home*, understand?'

'What is it, love? What's happened?'

'Just do it, please! Fifteen minutes, OK? I have to come home immediately – right away – you got that?'

'Yes. But Gordon I must know –'

'Good. See you soon. I hope.' He banged down the receiver, went through into the bathroom, washed and dried again more thoroughly and tried to rub some colour into his cheeks. Again he inspected himself dispassionately in the mirror. Not a lot of change: he still looked bloody awful; still scared, still white, still shaky. Well, it would just have to do. He'd run out of options. Time too.

He went downstairs again, stood around reception for a few minutes looking at his watch until he had been seen by half a dozen of the waiters and waitresses and then sauntered through into the residents' lounge where he ordered a scotch and a dry

Martini. Then he sat down with the air of a man who was waiting for a friend to join him – and that was the worst part of all. He gave it three minutes, finished his scotch and ordered another. Then he got up, looked at his watch again and went back to reception. He smiled his most charming smile. 'I was supposed to meet Miss Johnson in the residents' lounge for drinks fifteen minutes ago,' he lied. 'Would you mind trying her room? She's probably forgotten.'

The girl turned, glanced at one of the wooden pigeon-holes behind her and reached up for a slip of paper waiting there for one of their guests. She glanced at the note, replaced it and turned to Gordon with a smile. 'I don't think that she is in, Herr Hallam. There is still a note for her here, you see?'

Gordon nodded. And smiled again. 'Would you mind just trying anyway?'

'Certainly, sir.' He waited until the girl had turned her back and then leant across the counter and snatched the note soundlessly from Toni Johnson's pigeon-hole. He crumpled it into his pocket as the receptionist turned away from her switchboard and shook her head. 'I am sorry, Herr Hallam, but there is no reply.'

'Oh,' managed Gordon, suitably nonplussed.

'Will . . . er . . . will you be taking dinner in the hotel tonight, Herr Hallam?' asked the receptionist.

'Yes,' decided Gordon, the thought of cooked food suddenly abhorrent. 'Yes, I think I will. Could I have a table in about fifteen minutes' time? A table for two?' He forced a smile and the girl smiled warmly back, fancying she sensed romance, perhaps even infidelity in the air.

'A pleasure, sir.'

'Thank you.' Gordon turned and walked back into the residents' lounge feeling the receptionist's eyes burning into his back. He sat back and waited, stifling the urge to dash upstairs to his room, throw things into a suitcase and rush off to the airport, home and safety. Only a few more minutes, he told himself; only a few more minutes . . .

He picked up a magazine and flicked idly through the pages. Then he remembered the note for Toni Johnson he had palmed into his pocket. When he was sure no one was watching he took it out and glanced down. 'Confirm completion via Rowley: 01–276 8041.'

It was a London number, he could see that much. But Rowley? Who the hell was Rowley?

Gordon crumpled the note into a ball and flicked it into the fire, the number memorized. He returned to the magazine. He was still gazing at the same picture twelve minutes later when the receptionist hurried to his side, her pretty face a mixture of concern and pity.

'Herr . . . Herr Hallam? Could you please come to the telephone at once? It is your wife in England. There is some bad news, I am afraid . . .'

Five minutes later Gordon was packing as the receptionist made up his bill.

Fifteen minutes later he was on his way to the station in a taxi, the hotel's sincere condolences ringing in his ears. There was a flight from Zurich to London Heathrow leaving at ten minutes to midnight.


A pale, soft glow of eerie white light seeped from the walls of the tunnel hidden in the dark, dripping woods as General Inkermann sat back on his shooting stick and glanced across at Lord Porterfield muffled in a thick, sheepskin coat. William Ottley stood beside him, a stopwatch held in a gloved hand, his breath steaming up into the cold night air as they waited.

'All set?' asked General Inkermann. The others nodded. General Inkermann glanced at the young officer standing at his side. The soldier's face, like those of his men, was streaked with camouflage cream. He lifted a small radio handset and cupped his hand over the transmitter.

'Stand by,' he ordered. 'All pickets report condition, over.'

There was a brief pause. Then, one by one, each of the two-man picket posts hidden out in the hills and valleys guarding the approaches reported in. Finally their officer was satisfied. 'Condition Alpha, General. Safe to proceed.'

'Very well.' General Inkermann lifted a small handset of his own. 'Let's just run through it again, shall we?' He depressed the transmit button. 'Take post,' he ordered.

Instantly there was the slam of a cab door and the sudden cough of a diesel motor echoing off the curved, damp tunnel walls as the container lorry came grinding forward out of the tunnel. Thirty, forty yards it came and then stopped with a sudden angry hiss of hydraulics. Again the driver leapt to the ground and sprinted round to the back of the vehicle. Again there was that low whine as the entire container area began to tilt upwards, elevating to forty-five, fifty, then fifty-five degrees as the flat sides of the lorry slid away to reveal the Cruise missile poised on the sloping launch ramp.

'Forty seconds,' murmured William Ottley without looking up as the folded, swept-back wings snapped down into place. The missile was fourteen feet long, nine and a half feet wide and weighed less than 2,000 pounds. 'Forty-five seconds,' intoned Ottley as, at the rear of the camouflaged launcher, an American major in heavy, black-framed spectacles worked feverishly at a display console, punching payload, trajectory, flight and target data into the missile's inboard intertial terrain-comparison computer. 'Seventy-five seconds –'

'Set!' called out the major, a hand raised suddenly above his head as the tableau froze around him.

'Seventy-six seconds,' announced William Ottley, looking pleased.

General Inkermann nodded, apparently also satisfied. 'Check. Check. Check,' ordered General Inkermann into the radio. 'Stand down. I say again: stand down.' He stood up and jerked his shooting stick out of the muddy ground. 'Right then, gentlemen, I suggest we knock it on the head for tonight, get things back under cover and seal up the tunnel. We'll try and get that time down tomorrow night, all being well.'

In the east the sky was beginning to lighten. Dawn was not far off.

# : 19 :

It was after 1.40 a.m. before Gordon Hallam came through the Customs hall at London's Heathrow airport. He hurried through the green 'Nothing To Declare' zone with, for once, nothing to declare. Not even the Duty Free allowance of cigarettes and spirits.

They had been somewhere high over France when the truth had finally dawned upon him, so that for the rest of the flight back to Britain all other thoughts had been pushed roughly aside and he had sat there in his aisle seat, shifting restlessly and glancing at his watch every half minute. The truth? The truth was this: that if they had taken the trouble to track him across France to Zug, to put a killer on his tail and arrange that carefully contrived accidental meeting in Paris with Toni Johnson, then they would know about his home, too. Running back to Stow-combe to burrow deep into familiar surroundings like a child seeking the warmth of its mother's breast was no sort of answer, for they could find him there with ease. Whoever 'they' were.

But where else could he go? What else could he do? If Rachel –

Rachel. Jesus. Rachel was alone in the cottage.

Gordon pushed heedlessly through the milling crowds of the airport concourse and grabbed the first vacant telephone he saw. He went through to the operator, gave his home number and waited, seething with impatience, for the tone that would tell him the phone was ringing beside their bed in the cottage; that Rachel was turning over and . . . but there was no ringing tone.

Just a single, unbroken signal.

'I'm sorry, caller. That number is unobtainable,' said the operator.

'What? It can't be! I mean . . . are you sure? Will you check again, please? It's very important.'

'One moment.'

Again she dialled. Again that breathless pause – and again that same signal: number unobtainable.

Gordon tried to quell a rising tide of panic. 'What's wrong? Why can't you get through, for God's sake?'

'Do you wish me to report the fault?' asked the operator coolly.

'Yes, yes – report the bloody thing! No – wait! I mean . . . hang on a second, will you?' Gordon dragged a hand through his hair.

'I'm sorry, caller, but –'

'Just wait, dammit!' he shouted. Peter. Peter and Claire, their friends in the house at the end of the lane – 'Er . . . can you get me the number of a Mr Peter Salter, please. The address is –' He frowned suddenly, trying to remember their address – 'The address is . . . Beggars' Rest, Stowcombe, Devon.'

'One moment, caller.'

'Oh . . . operator?'

'Sir?' Distant, frosty, hostile.

'Sorry about that. I'm . . . I'm a little tense, that's all. Nothing personal.'

'Yes, sir,' she agreed dryly. The temperature rose half a degree between them.

Presently the phone was ringing and Gordon stood by the airport coin box, money poised. Come on, come on – answer the bloody thing! There *had* to be a phone beside the bed. There were phones all over the place . . .

'Yes?' The voice was drowsy, sleepy, disgruntled. Like yours would be at 1.45 in the morning. After going to bed at 11.

'Peter? Peter Salter?'

'Speaking.'

'It's Gordon – Gordon Hallam. From up the lane.'

'Gordon. *Gordon*?' He heard a faint click as a bedside light went on and then the rustle of sheets as Peter Salter sat up. 'I won't insult your intelligence by asking if you know what time it is, old son –'

'Yeah, yeah – I know. I'm sorry. Listen, Peter – are you awake? I mean, really awake?'

Peter Salter yawned sleepily. 'Hanging upon your every word. The brain, as they say, is like a finely-honed –'

'Good. Listen: I'm at Heathrow airport. You got that? I'm calling from Heathrow. I've tried to get Rachel at the cottage but the line's out of order.'

'You're at Heathrow,' repeated Salter dutifully. 'You've tried to contact Rachel but the line's out of order. Oh. I see. So in the morning, you'd like me to –'

'Listen, Peter! Just . . . just listen, will you? This is important: I want you to go up the lane to the cottage and get Rachel to come back and spend the rest of the night with you, OK? I know it sounds crazy but there's a reason, just trust me. Rachel may be in danger if she stays in the cottage. I want her to stay with you and Claire, just for tonight.' There was a pregnant silence. He could almost see Peter scratching his head, peering at him oddly down the phone.

'You're serious, aren't you?' he said at last.

'Yes, I'm serious. Wish to God I wasn't. You're the only person I can turn to, Peter; the only person I can trust.'

'Let me get this straight: you want me to go up the lane – now – drag Rachel out of her nice warm bed and bring her down here? To sleep?' he demanded incredulously.

Gordon began to feel desperate. It sounded absurd, even to him. 'That's it, yes. You've got it exactly. Tell her the sooner she gets in to work in the morning, the better. She must stay there, at the studio, until I come and pick her up sometime between twelve thirty and one o'clock, all right?'

'OK, I've got it.' He paused. 'You in some sort of trouble, old lad?'

'Yes. Yes, I am,' admitted Gordon shortly. 'I'll explain it all later – if I ever get the chance. Thanks. Thanks a lot, Peter.'

He rang off and pushed out of the phone booth, an enormous weight lifting momentarily from his shoulders. What else? What else could he do to keep them both alive, lengthen the odds a little in their favour? Gordon dropped his bag at his feet, sat down on a plastic bench and rubbed his fingers into eye sockets that prickled with exhaustion. It would help just a little if he knew who was hunting him, for only then could he begin to fight back . . .

'Can I squeeze through here?' Gordon started violently: fear by association as the American accent rasped across raw nerves.

He looked up warily and then sagged back with relief as a girl hitch-hiker edged past, a blue-framed rucksack on her back with the stars and stripes stitched across one pocket.

Somewhere in the dim, dark reaches of Gordon's tired brain, the beginnings of a good idea rolled over and sat up.

It was in that moment that Gordon Hallam began to fight back. To turn defence into attack.

Gordon felt in his pocket for a crumpled five pound note, pushed himself to his feet and set off after the American teenager. 'Er . . . excuse me, please?' He tapped her gently on the shoulder and the girl swung round: cornflower blue eyes, Snoopy sweatshirt, teenage acne.

'Yeah?'

'Er . . . I wonder. Would you like to earn this?' he held up a five pound note between his fingers. 'All you have to do is make one phone call, OK? I'll tell you what to say. Just one phone call.' He saw the girl hesitate, wonder if he was her first British lunatic, and summoned up a tired smile. 'It's OK, really. It doesn't even have to be obscene. It's to a friend, OK? A joke.' He waited.

The girl thought for a moment, nodded, then grinned. 'Sure. Why not?'

In Shepherd's Bush Stephen Rowley was hauled from his sleep by the insistent burring of the trimphone beside the wide double bed. His girlfriend lay asleep beside him, her face buried in the pillows, a fan of silken hair spread across the sheets.

Rowley stirred, fumbled for his watch and groaned when he saw the time. It was just after 2 a.m. He reached out for the receiver and fumbled it off the cradle. 'Yes? Who is it?' he asked sleepily. There was a brief pause while he heard the pay tone, then coins were forced into the machine and the pay tone ceased.

'Rowley?' A woman's voice. With an American accent.

He yawned. 'Yes. This is Stephen Rowley.'

'Toni Johnson. I was told to call your number.'

Rowley came awake fast. 'Oh. Yes. One moment. Wait a second will you? I'll just get a pencil –'

'No. You wait,' said the woman's voice. 'There's . . . there's been a problem, OK?'

Rowley frowned. 'A problem? What sort of problem?'

There was a brief delay. He heard muffled voices in the background, then – 'I have to talk to you. Now.'

'What? It's two o'clock in the morning! I can't –'

'Now, O K? Terminal 2, Heathrow airport. By the Change kiosk, first floor. One hour from now, O K? One hour exactly.'

'Now wait a second, I can't possibly –'

'Just be there.'

The line went dead.

Stephen Rowley frowned at the receiver as the woman stirred languidly in the bed beside him. 'Stevie? Come back to bed . . .'

Rowley sighed. 'I can't,' he decided, fully awake at last. 'I can't. Something's come up. I've got to go out.' He threw back the bedclothes and swung his feet to the floor.

In Devon, a bewildered Rachel Hallam was following Peter Salter down the dark path towards the garden gate, her arms full of clothes and her mind full of questions. Peter Salter opened the gate and stood back politely to let her through, a ludicrous figure in wellington boots with a raincoat pulled over bright yellow pyjamas and a fishing hat perched on top of his head. 'I'm sorry, Rachel,' he said wearily, 'but that's all he told me. I'm just passing on the message.' He yawned sleepily. 'Come on – Claire's making up the spare bed.'

'How . . . how did he sound?' asked Rachel anxiously as she hurried after him down the lane with a backward glance at their dark, deserted little cottage. 'Gordon, I mean: how did he sound?'

'Scared,' admitted Peter Salter after a thoughtful pause. 'Rather scared.'

Heathrow airport's Terminal 2 was at its quietest as Gordon went across to the book and magazine stall and bought a copy of the previous day's *Daily Telegraph*. Then he went to the toy counter where, after much hunting around, he purchased the most realistic toy pistol he could find. He took it out of its plastic box and gripped the butt experimentally. With the newspaper draped over his wrist and hand, the barrel protruded no more than half an inch and, to his inexperienced eye, looked decidedly business-like. Gordon then went back to the row of seats a little way along from the Change kiosk and sat down to wait, the toy gun jammed in his pocket.

He opened the newspaper and began scanning the columns, looking for a story about the discovery of the body of an American in a Sussex garden. He found nothing.

At twenty minutes to three he went into the toilets on the first floor, locked himself into a toilet stall and stayed there for ten minutes, killing time in the one place where he could not be spotted, identified. Then he found his way to the Public Address system announcer, spoke with her briefly and edged his way back towards the Change kiosk.

One of the airport cleaning staff – the inevitable Pakistani – was working nearby with an industrial vacuum cleaner. Beside him a woman of about fifty stood sorting through a handful of foreign currency – and beside her stood a man of his own age in a well-cut overcoat. As Gordon studied him from a safe distance, unobserved, the man glanced at his watch and then looked around. As though he was looking for someone. Gordon slid back out of sight and waited, a grim smile of satisfaction on his face. It was going to work.

Suddenly the chimes sounded above his head and a soft voice announced: 'Would Mr Rowley – Mr Rowley – please go to the Left Luggage lockers on the ground floor where his friend is waiting. Mr Rowley, please.'

Gordon slid around the column and watched as the man in the overcoat moved obediently away from the Change kiosk and took the escalator to the ground floor.

Thirty paces behind him, his face hidden by the newspaper, Gordon followed.

At the bottom of the escalator the man turned to his left and walked briskly towards the Left Luggage lockers. As Gordon had hoped, the area was almost deserted. Gordon glanced over his shoulder, took the toy automatic from his pocket and folded the newspaper carefully over gun and wrist. Then he moved up softly behind Stephen Rowley. As Rowley paused and began to look round – 'Mr Rowley?' asked Gordon politely.

Rowley swung round. 'I'm Rowley. I –'

'Look down,' snapped Gordon. 'Don't say another word. Just look down.'

Rowley looked down, saw the muzzle of the pistol pointing at his stomach and paled visibly: 'Look, I –'

'Shut up. Do you have a gun? Quickly – do you have a gun?'

Rowley shook his head several times. 'A gun? No, no – of course not. I –'

'Over here and sit down. Come on – move!' They edged over to a row of plastic chairs and sat down, Rowley's eyes wide with fear.

'Your hands,' ordered Gordon. 'Sit on them.'

Rowley hurried to comply, his eyes never moving from Gordon's face. 'Please, Mr Hallam, I –'

'Let me explain something to you. Are you listening?'

Stephen Rowley nodded vigorously. He was a civil servant, a manipulator of perceptions, of personal opportunity. Not a gunman.

'In the last two days I have been forced to kill two people, do you hear what I am saying? Two. One was a woman. If you do not tell me what I want to know I shall kill you too. Right here. I am very near the end of my tether, Mr Rowley. I don't care much one way or the other.' Untrue, screamed Gordon to himself as Rowley nodded.

'I . . . I understand.' He swallowed.

'Good. Tell me – how did you know my name?'

Rowley shook his head vigorously. 'I didn't. I –'

'You said my name. I heard you. Lie to me again and I'll blow your head off. One – two –'

'All right. I . . . I recognized your . . . your face, yes.'

'How?' snapped Gordon.

'From the . . . from the photograph.'

'Photograph? What photograph?'

'At the . . . at the house. In Sussex.'

Gordon leaned forward. 'At Sidcott? You were at Sidcott?'

Again that nervous swallow. 'On the day of your father's funeral. There was a . . . a photograph. Upstairs, in the bedroom.'

'You searched the house? You searched the fucking house? While we were at the funeral?' snarled Gordon.

Rowley wriggled nervously. 'You . . . you asked me how I knew who you were; how I recognized you. I've . . . I've told you . . .'

'Why?' ground Gordon through clenched teeth. If it had been

a real gun he would have fired. And enjoyed it. 'Why? What were you doing there? What were you looking for?'

'I was told to look for any reference to . . . to . . .'

'Apostle?' prompted Gordon.

Rowley nodded. 'That's right, yes. To Apostle.'

'You took that postcard, didn't you?' demanded Gordon suddenly.

'It –'

'Didn't you?' shouted Gordon, the words bouncing back off the metal lockers and exploding in Rowley's face.

He winced. 'Yes,' he admitted finally in a whisper.

'Who told you to search Dad's house? Who were you working for?' There was silence. 'Who?'

'I can't say,' muttered Rowley. 'I daren't.'

'Yes, you can,' encouraged Gordon. 'It's easy. You think of the name, you open your mouth and you tell me. Now. Otherwise I'll kill you. It's called choices. Come on – you decide: same old three seconds. One – two –'

'All right. All right. I'll tell you.'

'I'm waiting.'

Rowley took a deep, shuddering breath. 'Porterfield, all right? His name's Porterfield.'

Gordon sat back, punched between the eyes by Rowley's words. 'Porterfield? *Phillip* Porterfield?'

'Lord Phillip Porterfield, yes,' confirmed Rowley dully.

'Lord Phillip Porterfield,' echoed Gordon, trying the words out in his mouth. 'What did he tell you? About Apostle?'

Rowley shrugged. 'Nothing. Nothing at all. Only that –'

'Go on.'

'Only that I was to go down to Sussex and make sure no papers were left lying around that could lead to any . . . awkward questions.'

'And the Yanks?' demanded Gordon. 'Where do the Americans fit into all this?'

Rowley looked up. 'The Americans? What Americans?'

'Come on!' snapped Gordon angrily. 'The people who knocked off Bruno Tyschen, Peter Tillet, my father?'

Rowley looked at him helplessly. 'What? I don't know anything about any killings . . .'

'You're lying!'

'I'm not. I swear I'm not!'

'You're lying, Rowley! How the hell d'you think I knew to call your phone number? D'you think I stuck a pin in the bloody directory?'

'I . . . I don't know.'

'Well, think about it! I got it off the American woman your Lord Porterfield sent to kill me!'

Rowley shook his head. 'Look – Mr Hallam: all I know is I was told to act as a clearing house, that's all. Just to take the message and pass it on. I swear to you that's all I know . . .'

'Pass it on where?'

'To Lord Porterfield.'

'What's his address?'

'He lives in . . . in Eaton Terrace. Only he's not there. He's gone away. To . . . to the west country.'

Gordon's head snapped up. 'Where in the west country?'

'I don't know. Honestly. He didn't tell me. I was just to pass that message on to another number in London, that's all.'

Gordon rose to his feet and stood looking down at Stephen Rowley, the gun still held under the newspaper. He believed him, that was the trouble: believed every word of it. So what did he do now – beat him unconscious? Tie him up with his own underpants?

Stephen Rowley was wondering too. 'What . . . what are you going to do?' he asked fearfully. Gordon looked down implacably for a moment, his mind drained of questions. And answers. Then he sighed and dropped gun and newspaper into Rowley's startled hands.

'Fuck knows,' he said wearily.

Apart from get home. Just as fast as ever he could.


They had been marching steadily through the mountains for five hours.

Now the British S A S officer held up a hand and they sank to the ground taking up automatic all-round defensive positions. Dawn was not far off and the moon would soon be gone. Then it would be time to hide up again and rest until darkness.

But first there was one last thing their officer had to do before he could transmit the 'Mission Completed' prefix back to London. One last act to perform.

Resting his rifle on the ground he untied the fastenings around his groundsheet bundle, walked to the lip of the ravine and crouched down. All that now remained of the skeleton they had exhumed from that desert grave was the skull. The rest – bones, sword, shreds of ancient cloth – had been thrown piece by piece from a dozen lofty crags and mountain paths to rattle down into the silent valleys below.

The officer picked up the yellowed, ancient skull, studied it briefly and then tapped it affectionately on the cranium. 'So long, sunshine,' he said. 'Be good.'

He curled back his arm and flung the human skull in a high, curving arc across the valley. It glittered briefly in the pale moonlight and then vanished from sight as it fell away into the darkness of the valley at his feet. There was a long, dropping pause and then the faintest rattle of sound far, far below.

And then silence. The silence of forever. Of eternity.

In a stone-walled hut in a village two hundred and sixteen kilometres to the south, an old man shivered restlessly in front of the fire and gazed sightlessly into the flickering flames as the spirit of his ancestors, of Mongol legend, destiny and fearful tradition, moved around him on silent, fluttering wings.

'Soon?' whispered one of the dark, watching faces that crowded around the campfire. The voice belonged to a man who held one of the new Russian Kalashnikov assault rifles. They were beginning to acquire quite a few Kalashnikovs. 'Will it be soon?'

The pale, old eyes of Radij opened slowly. 'Yes,' nodded the soothsayer slowly. 'Yes, my brothers. It will be soon. Very soon.'

# : 20 :

They could hear the tanks nosing about in the pine forest ahead, smell the diesel of their engines on the wind as the drivers gunned up their motors and churned the ground into a sea of mud as they jockeyed for position on the start line beyond the trees.

Four hundred metres to their front a Russian officer lifted his binoculars to his eyes and studied the edge of the woods, waiting for the first shiver of bare branches as the camouflaged tanks shouldered the trees roughly aside as they began to advance. He lowered his glasses, looked at his watch and lifted a whistle to his lips. He blew sharply. 'Right – that's it!' he shouted. 'Stop digging!'

Fifty metres in front of where he stood the recruits of the 117th Motor Rifle Battalion looked up apprehensively over the lip of their slit-trenches and then dug out a couple more shovelfuls of earth for good measure. This time the training exercise was called 'armour familiarization' and the slit-trenches, if properly constructed – four feet long, two feet wide and six feet deep – would save their lives.

'NCOs – Dress forward!' shouted the officer as, behind him, a dozen senior NCOs ran forward to stand beside each slit-trench as the recruits scrambled out of their holes, slid their short-handled entrenching tools back into their webbing fighting order and came to attention. The officer picked up a megaphone. 'Face your front – listen to me,' he ordered as, in front of them, the first tank broke through the thin screen of trees and came slowly forward belching black smoke from its exhaust.

The officer turned away and shouted an order to a near-by signaller. The man raised a triangular flag over his head. The tank stopped, its turret hatch opened and a red flag was waved back in reply as first one and then another T-34/85 nosed out of the bare woods like some ancient reptile scenting food. The T-34/85 medium battle tank dates back to 1943 and is now used in the Soviet Army only for training or second line units. But it still weighs the same thirty-two tons with a top speed of 34 m.p.h. and to a young recruit lying directly in its path as the ground shakes beneath him, a British Chieftain, an American Abrams or a Soviet T-34/85 all look like the same huge, terrifying steel mountain on the move.

The three tanks halted in line abreast, each now showing a red triangular flag from its turret, each with the sound of its engine reduced to a dull coughing roar.

The officer looked down at the three lines of trenches stretching forward in untactical mathematical precision with a recruit and NCO to each trench and a stationary tank now facing each line of slit-trenches. Normally, of course, the trenches would be camouflaged from the ground and from the air, their spoil hidden beneath carefully removed topsoil. But not today. The drivers needed something to aim for, to aim at.

He nodded approvingly. 'Good. And remember – no matter what happens, you are to remain *absolutely stationary* until the NCO to your left gives you the word of release. Move too soon and you'll do it all over again, so you might as well get it right the first time. Any questions?'

The tanks killed their engines and there was silence. Each man knew precisely what lay ahead: the men inside the tanks, because it was something they were used to, something they had done many times before with generations of recruits, the recruits themselves because 'tank kissing', as it was known, was part of the tradition, part of the myth of basic training along with the gruelling runs, the graft, the stealing and the bad food. Anyway, it was simple enough in all conscience: all they had to do was lie on the ground with their heels together and their left arm stretching in front of their helmet and stay there, without moving, until the tank's nearest track was within touching distance. Then, on the release word from the NCO crouching safely in their slit-trench beside them – but not one moment before – roll *between* the tank's tracks and drop cleanly into the trench as thirty-two tons of tank thundered overhead. Simple, really, as long as you didn't think too much about it. And the sides of your slit-trench didn't cave in and the tank didn't come grinding in after you.

Yuri was thinking about it. Sergeant Barak was standing beside him, staring ahead impassively at the line of waiting tanks with a mean little smile on his face. Yuri wetted his lips and glanced to his right. He was in the centre of the three lines of trenches, third trench back. Nikolai was somewhere behind him. He waited nervously. They all did.

'NCOs – take position!' shouted the officer finally through his megaphone. Sergeant Barak dropped down into Yuri's trench and looked up at him with that hard little smile of hatred. Since the death of Private Tinrass on the grenade range, Yuri Rashidov and Nikolai Samlar had become the twin focus of the Russian's enmity. An inquiry into the incident that had cost one Uzbek his life and Nikolai's related allegations made before Captain Odinstov, the training officer, had been vaguely promised somewhere up the line in Battalion, but nothing had come of it. No one in the 117th had the least faith in such promises anyway – and proof of the correctness of such cynicism lay in the fact that Sergeant Barak had not been relieved of his duties, not for one moment. In that sense, at least, nothing had changed.

'Take positions!' shouted the officer as his signaller dropped the red flag and raised a black triangle in its place. The red flags on the tank turrets disappeared, the hatches were closed and the engines coughed into life with a sudden black cloud of exhaust. There was a rattle of equipment as the recruits dropped flat on their stomachs beside the right hand edge of their trenches and stretched out their arms.

The tanks advanced.

They came forward steadily in perfect formation, gradually picking up speed: three iron monsters grinding forward, gun barrels questing to right and left like antennae as they churned towards the waiting line of trenches.

'Still! Stay still!' shouted the officer through his megaphone, his words lost in the rising roar of the engines as the T-34/85s moved forward.

'What's that smell, Rashidov?' shouted Barak above the noise, sniffing the air crudely.' Not shitting yourself already, are you?' Yuri said nothing. From beneath his helmet he watched the three approaching tanks, focused on the one in the middle, the one that was coming straight for him.

One hundred metres.

'How d'you feel, Uzbek?' shouted Sergeant Barak, grinning fiercely from the lip of the trench as Yuri felt the ground begin to tremble beneath him. 'Arsehole twitching yet?' Yuri looked away and swallowed, his mouth suddenly dry.

Fifty metres.

Now the three tanks fanned out as their drivers lined up with each row of slit-trenches. There was the sudden whine of hydraulics as a turret traversed and a gun swung round to train on some distant target. A brief pause – and then a stupefying crash that made Yuri's ears ring as the tank opened fire with its 85 mm. Yuri glanced at Sergeant Barak and the Russian's grin vanished. 'Wait, you bastard – wait!' he screamed, crowding into the end of the trench to thwart Yuri's imagined roll to safety. 'You're not buggering off yet!'

'I've traced that smell, Comrade Sergeant!' shouted back Yuri recklessly, caught up in the madness of roaring tank engines, the crash and sing of the guns, the sudden bite of cordite and the patter of debris as the other tanks opened fire. 'Know what it is? I'll tell you: a fucking Russian!' Barak's face clouded with rage as Yuri tore his eyes back to the tank bearing down on him as, away to his left, the first recruit flipped neatly into his trench and the tank roared harmlessly overhead.

Sergeant Barak spat disgustedly. 'Too soon, too soon. We can do better than that, can't we, Uzbek?'

Yuri's tank roared closer.

Two trenches further down Yuri's line the first recruit slapped a hand against the metal track cowling and rolled immediately to his left. He dropped safely into the bottom of his trench and the tank lumbered overhead showering him with stones and earth.

Twenty metres. Another recruit, another slit-trench. Now it was Yuri's turn.

'Wait . . . wait!' shouted Barak as the tank thundered down towards them, earth and stones flying from its churning tracks. Yuri waited, arm outstretched, teeth clamped together. He could see the black leather of the driver's helmet through the crewman's visor, actually count the rivets on the armoured plating – and still Barak crowded the edge of the trench. 'Wait! Wait!' he chanted, laughing manically above the mind-numbing howl of the tank engine. Arm trembling outstretched before him, Yuri waited. For one moment and another. And one more. Then the tank was suddenly upon him. He slapped its metal skin with his hand, spun to his left – and found his escape blocked by Barak's pressing hands as the sky blacked out above him and all was roaring noise and terror and a terrible crushing agony of pain in his left arm . . .

Nikolai was the last man in the right-hand column of trenches. He and his NCO instructor watched the tanks rolling forward towards them as one by one the recruits slapped a hand against their sides and rolled across to drop safely into their holes. Suddenly there was a blowing of whistles and the officer was yelling, 'CHECK! CHECK! CHECK!' as his signaller leapt to his feet waving a yellow flag frantically above his head. The tanks screeched and lurched to a sudden halt, whip aerials bending wildly. Then the tank in the centre backed away furiously, the hatch flew open and the tank commander clambered out of his turret and dropped to the ground.

'Some poor bastard caught it,' muttered Nikolai's NCO as the officer with the megaphone ran past them towards the stationary tanks and began bawling for medical orderlies over his shoulder. Across the exercise area recruits and their supervisors climbed from their trenches and hurried towards the silent little tableau as the two stretcher bearers ran past Nikolai, their First Aid satchels jolting on their hips as they doubled forward.

By the time Nikolai arrived they had loaded the moaning, writhing casualty onto a stretcher, swathed him in blankets and wrapped the crushed, bloody mess of his arm in shell dressings. 'Who is it?' asked Nikolai curiously as they all crowded forward. 'Anybody know?'

There were a few shrugs – and then some nudged him on the arm. 'It's your mate, I think. That bloke Rashidov.'

Nikolai shouldered his way through the press of onlookers and craned over the stretcher. 'Yuri? Yuri – can you hear me?' he urged as he looked down at the white, waxy face, the closed eyes.

Then a rough hand was pulling at his shoulder. 'All right, all right – give a man room,' grumbled the medical orderly, holding a morphine syrette up to the light. He broke the seal and thrust home the needle.

Nikolai shook off the restraining arm and bent down. 'Yuri,' he whispered urgently. 'Yuri – what happened? It's me, Niki.'

'All right, lover boy – you heard what the man said – stand clear,' ordered Sergeant Barak. 'Let him –'

'Who was the NCO in charge of this trench?' broke in a new voice. It belonged to the officer controlling the exercise and was high-pitched, nervous.

'I was, Comrade Lieutenant,' stated Sergeant Barak flatly, coming to attention. Nikolai looked up slowly with the first dawnings of suspicion.

'What happened here?' demanded the officer.

Barak shrugged; he wouldn't have seen much from where he was standing. 'Didn't move fast enough, did he, sir? Froze up like a fucking rabbit in a car's headlights.' On the stretcher an eyelid flickered open and a hand reached out from beneath the brown blanket to grasp Nikolai's wrist with sudden, urgent strength.

'He . . . he's lying,' panted Yuri with great effort, the words barely reaching Nikolai as he bent down across his friend. 'That . . . that bastard Barak . . .' he managed, in a husky, pain-filled whisper, '. . . he . . . he stopped me. Stopped me . . . rolling.'

Then the morphia took effect and Yuri slipped mercifully into unconsciousness. The stretcher was lifted from the ground and carried away between two straining orderlies.

Nikolai stood for long moments watching the two men struggle up the hillside towards the track and the waiting ambulance, his face a mask of bitter thoughts and of a private, terrible resolve.

When the young officer began questioning the tank commander and his driver about what they had seen, Nikolai moved apart from the others. He was not interested in the findings of any inquiry, in any formal apportioning of blame for what had happened to another 'blackass', another conscript, another Uzbek – he had heard all he wanted to hear.

And he had his grenade.

It was mid-morning in Devon as George and Bunny Vickers drove back towards the Bradstone Manor Hotel, their morning coffee with friends outside Yelverton the subject of desultory conversation as they took the A386 past the town of Tavistock over the western edge of the moors. It had been good to see the Warricks again, a pleasant interlude – but something was still niggling away at her husband, Bunny was sure of it; something to do with that map propped in front of him on the dashboard . . .

'George? What's the matter?' she asked as they began to decelerate, the left indicator flashing.

George Vickers glanced across towards her. 'Nothing's the matter, darling. I . . . er . . . I just want to turn down here for a minute or two. Won't take a second.'

The Mercedes turned off the main road and followed a quiet country lane for one, perhaps two miles as the silence built between them. George was driving more slowly now with one eye on the road, the other on the map balanced on his knee, their progress traced by a finger. Bunny could see they were heading towards one of those tunnel things ringed in red.

'Almost there,' grunted George Vickers presently.

They turned down a slightly narrower lane and drove on slowly for another three hundred yards. Then they turned a gentle corner and came to a sudden halt. Bunny looked up apprehensively.

Yellow trestles had been pulled across the lane ahead. Beyond these Bunny could see a workman's shed and piles of gravel. A corrugated metal hut had been pushed in under some trees and as they waited a man in orange waterproofs emerged from this and hurried towards them.

George Vickers wound down the window. 'Morning,' he called. 'Can't I get through?'

The man sauntered forward with an easy smile: friendly, weathered, mid-forties. 'Sorry about this, sir. There's been a bit of a landslip further on. County engineers say it must have been this last drop of rain.'

'Landslip? Where?'

The man pointed vaguely ahead. 'Tunnel up there. Mind you, I'm not surprised. Those places have been run down proper over the years.'

'Since Beeching, you mean?'

'That's it, sir. Since Beeching.' He grinned. 'Now then – if you'd just like to drop back a bit . . . ' Vickers nodded, rolled up the window and backed away down the lane.

The man in the waterproofs watched him go and then went back into the metal shack. He pulled a length of sacking away from an old oil drum in the corner, reached inside and lifted out a powerful radio transmitter handset. He glanced outside as Vickers' car receded and pressed a switch.

'Sabre seven to Control. Message, over.'

'Control to Sabre seven. Send. Over.'

'OK. He's gone,' he said softly. 'False alarm. Just another tourist lost his way.'

'Roger. Listening out.'


Gordon's train pulled into Plymouth station thirty-five minutes later.

He took a taxi directly to the television studios and walked through the double glass doors of reception with a sense of coming home. The girls behind the front desk knew him well and their friendly greetings pushed back some of the fear and exhaustion that had haunted him since ... since when? Since Sussex? Since the gun went off in his hand in Zug? A million years ago, anyway. Then they saw how haggard he looked, how tired and bedraggled, and their smiles changed to genuine concern: 'You all right, love?'

Gordon nodded. 'Tired, that's all.'

'You look ... well, terrible. Shattered.'

He dragged up a smile. 'Thanks. Thanks a lot.' He leaned heavily across the desk. 'Is Rachel still here?'

'She's on now.'

He twisted round and there was his wife on the monitor talking to the viewers. She looked fresh and beautiful and alive. Thank Christ. Gordon sat down and for long moments just watched her, drinking her in, not trusting himself to speak or break the spell.

'Gordon . . .' He turned. 'You sure you're feeling all right?'

He nodded. 'Yeah, really. You should see the other guy.' Another tired grin. Cliché, he thought to himself, pure cliché. But reality, he had discovered, was riddled with them: reality and illusion duplicating one another down a long hall of mirrors as you played to the role expected, conformed to expectation. Faithful unto death.

Young secretaries hurrying off to an early lunch in their smart office clothes, nervous guests for the live lunchtime magazine programme, harassed journalists and film editors – all glanced curiously at Gordon as they went past and he began to feel uncomfortable, a tramp loitering in the foyer of the Lord Mayor's Ball. He pushed to his feet and went back to the girls behind the front desk. 'I'll . . . er . . . I'll be outside, by the car. Would you tell Rachel, please? When she's finished?'

'Of course . . . 'Bye for now, Gordon.' He nodded tiredly, picked up his bag and went out through the glass doors and across the car park. He found the Volkswagen parked over by the far side and then remembered he didn't have a duplicate key. He dropped his bag beside the boot and sat down on a low wall to wait. It started to rain then, of course, but Gordon hardly noticed.

He waited ten minutes, sunk in the stupor of his own thoughts.

'Gordon?' A small, uncertain voice. He looked up. 'Gordon!' It *was* him! Rachel broke into a run and flew across the car park towards him, hair streaming, bags swinging wildly from her shoulder. Gordon's tired, lined face broke into the first smile of a long, long day as Rachel twisted between a row of parked cars and hurried towards him. She rushed into his arms and he hugged her fiercely, crushed her to him as the rain soaked down unnoticed. After a long moment she pushed him gently away and studied his face anxiously. 'What's happened, love? You look –'

He nodded tiredly. 'I know, I know. I look terrible. Everyone keeps telling me that. I'm tired, that's all. Feel as though I haven't slept for a week. The train was full of sailors coming back off leave and chucking down McEwans Export.' But it wasn't that at all. It was the knowledge that he, Gordon Hallam, had killed – that was what preyed on his mind, left him feeling as though he had gone crawling through the sewers of men's souls and could never, never be clean again. 'You all right?' he asked anxiously, studying his wife as she moved round to the other side of the car.

'Me? Yes, I'm fine. What was all that last night? Peter Salter came –'

'You're sure?'

'Sure I'm sure.' She smiled a brief smile.

'Come on, kid – open the car, will you? Before we both get washed away.' She bent down and unlocked the driver's door. Gordon threw his bag in the back and climbed in beside her. He slammed the door and stretched back in the seat, the balls of his hands pressed up into his eyes as he groaned aloud. Rachel looked at him anxiously, fitted the key into the ignition and started the windscreen wipers. Then Gordon reached out, covered her hand with his and turned off the ignition. He swung suddenly towards her, face twisting into a grimace.

'Rach, I . . .' he began. 'I . . .' He got no further. Suddenly the tears were coursing down his cheeks and he was burying his head in her shoulder as the fear and the yawning, terrifying emptiness broke through. Rachel pressed him tightly to her as she would a small, frightened child:

'Gordon . . . Gordon, love . . . what is it?' she soothed. 'It's all right now, darling. You're home. It's all right . . .'

For long moments Gordon couldn't talk, couldn't bring himself to answer, just clutched her to him as he soaked in the feel of her, of warm, living woman, as his mind dragged back to that broken, doll-like figure sprawled across the floor of Tyschen's apartment; to the man lying in a widening sea of his own blood in his father's kitchen in Sussex . . .

'I . . . I killed them,' he whispered huskily, so quietly that Rachel thought at first she had misheard. 'I . . . I killed them, Rach.'

'You . . . you what? Killed them? Killed who?'

'A man . . . and a woman,' admitted Gordon in a whisper of guilt as he pushed himself away from Rachel's shoulder and looked into her face with the tears streaming unchecked down his cheeks. 'I . . . I *killed* them,' he repeated, more quietly this time, as though even now he did not really believe it. 'I didn't . . . didn't have any choice.'

Rachel swallowed. 'Just . . . just tell me about it,' she managed, forcing herself to stay calm. 'Tell me what happened. Right from the beginning.'

Slowly, hesitantly at first but then with a strange, growing fluency, the words began to tumble out as Gordon told Rachel about the train at Kew, about the phone call to Tyschen from Sussex and about the fight in the darkness of his father's kitchen. Rachel listened, horrified, as he described how he had dragged the corpse out into the garden and buried it. He told her then about his meeting with Toni Johnson in Paris and about their journey together to Zug. He told her about Bruno Tyschen and the realization that Walter Hallam had been murdered. And he told her, finally, about Toni Johnson's death and his confrontation with Stephen Rowley.

It took a long time.

Bunny Vickers turned to her husband and sighed. 'Now where are we off to?' They had just turned left at a signpost to a village called Stowcombe.

'Chap down here I want to pop in and see. Won't take a moment,' he replied.

'I've heard that before,' said Bunny dryly. Her husband grunted but said nothing. He wanted to call on Gordon Hallam, the schoolteacher whose name had appeared on the Executive Action report he had glanced at on Lord Porterfield's desk. Presently they stopped outside Stowcombe post office. George Vickers took his umbrella out of the back and went across to the shop on the corner. A moment's inquiry and he was sliding back behind the wheel.

'It's just up here.'

They drove up the lane and stopped outside another low, whitewashed cottage. There was no one to be seen, no car parked outside the cottage. George Vickers got out and rang the doorbell. There was no reply. He stood there for several moments, the rain gurgling in the gutters and mottling his jacket. Then he returned to the car.

'No one in,' he announced unnecessarily. 'Have to try again later.'

'Who?' demanded Bunny, her patience finally exhausted. 'Who will you have to try and see again later?'

'Just somebody, that's all.'

She tugged his sleeve fiercely. 'What sort of an answer is that? George – look at me.' He turned. 'What is this? What's going on? This is supposed to be a holiday – a few days away from London.

The two of us – together. What *is* all this . . . this driving down country lanes, looking at old railway tunnels?'

He shrugged miserably. 'I can't tell you,' he answered softly. 'I'd like to, darling. But I just can't.'

Gordon and Rachel had just passed the Dartmoor Inn at Lydford when Rachel glanced across at her husband. 'Oh – I almost forgot: I called the British Museum first thing this morning.'

'The British Museum?' frowned Gordon, his mind miles away.

'Endlemann,' reminded Rachel. 'Professor Endlemann and that discovery of his, remember?'

'Oh, yes. What did you find out?'

'Professor Endlemann's Expedition to Persia in 1927 came back with two of these fourteenth-century mummified corpses – they found them in a series of ancient tombs in the hills behind Tabriz. There was a lot of fuss at the time, apparently, about British boffins rifling the historic treasures of another country. Anyway, that blew over eventually and the skeletons were put on display at the British Museum. They were there for years, right the way through the war, in fact. Then suddenly one just . . . disappeared.'

'What d'you mean?'

Rachel shrugged helplessly. 'That's it: it just . . . disappeared. Vanished. One day it was there on display and the next no one seemed to know where it had got to.'

'When? When did it go, did they tell you that?' asked Gordon.

Rachel nodded. 'Yes, they told me.' She paused, drawing it out.

Gordon jumped at the bait. 'March, right? March, 1945!'

Rachel nodded. 'March the 16th, 1945, yes.'

They drove on. Presently Rachel turned the car off the main road and they began driving down the familiar back lanes towards Stowcombe. As they drew near the post office –

'Just pull in here a minute, will you?' said Gordon quietly.

'What?'

'Here. Just stop.'

Rachel pulled in and turned off the engine. Then she turned inquiringly towards Gordon. 'Now what?'

'I just want to check it's safe first,' said Gordon awkwardly, a hand on the door catch. 'You never know, someone may have been into the cottage while you've been away.'

Rachel's eyebrows shot up. 'What? You're not serious!'

'Of course I'm bloody serious!' snapped Gordon. 'After what happened at Dad's? After what happened in Switzerland? I've never been more serious in my life!'

'I'm sorry. All I meant was –'

Gordon held up a hand. 'I'm going up to the cottage through the woods – round where we saw that badger. If everything's fine I'll . . .' he racked his brains '. . . I'll hang a towel out of the bathroom window. You can see that from the mouth of the lane down there.' He pointed. 'Then you can drive on up to the cottage. But if there's no towel, or if you hear any noise that –'

'Noise? What sort of noise?' asked Rachel nervously.

Gordon paused. 'If you hear any . . . shots, anything like that, just get away from here, understand? Get back to Plymouth, back to the studios. Tell them what happened, OK?' He forced a smile. 'Then you can come back with the telly cameras.'

Rachel swallowed. 'How long do I wait? Here, I mean?'

Gordon studied his watch. Say three minutes to the cottage through the woods; two minutes to look around outside; another four minutes indoors –

'Fifteen. Fifteen minutes,' he announced. 'It's now coming up to 1.53 and –'

'Synchronize watches, Batman –' It was a small joke, a pathetic attempt to force a smile. It didn't work.

Gordon whirled round and grabbed her roughly by the shoulders. 'I'm serious, for fuck's sake!' he shouted shaking her violently towards him as suddenly he saw *her* beautiful face white and waxy and staring. 'You think this is just some . . . some sort of *game*?' he stormed. 'Do you? Do you?'

Rachel twisted free, her eyes wide as Gordon added his fear to her own. 'Stop it, Gordon! Stop it, you're hurting me!'

Gordon released her and sat back, panting. There was a short silence, then – 'I'm sorry,' he sighed deeply. 'I'm sorry.' He glanced across. 'You all right, kid?'

She nodded. 'Just about.'

Gordon turned to the door catch and then swung back, remembering something; something important. 'How did you leave the cottage? Last night?'

'I . . . what do you mean?'

'Did you lock it – the front door?'

Rachel hesitated. 'I think so . . . I mean . . . I can't honestly remember . . .'

'Think! It's important!'

'Yes . . . yes, I did! I remember now. I remember because Peter Salter was standing in the porch as I –'

'What about the back?'

'That's locked too.'

'You sure?'

Rachel nodded. 'Positive. I . . . I always keep that locked when you're away.'

Gordon nodded. 'Bolts as well?' There were heavy coach-bolts, top and bottom. Bolts he would not be able to reach if he smashed one of the small panes of glass in the back door and reached inside for the key.

Rachel paused, then shook her head. 'No, no bolts, I'm almost certain. I only turned the key in the lock.'

'And the key's still there? In the lock on the inside?'

'It should be, yes –'

'– If it hasn't been moved,' finished Gordon for her grimly, his fear a dull, squirming ache in his bowels as he kept feeling the need to swallow. If he didn't go now he never would – 'OK, kid: I'm off. Don't forget – fifteen minutes. No towel in the window – any sounds you don't like, any shots – you get the hell out of here. Promise?'

'But I can't just . . . just leave you!' protested Rachel. 'What if –'

'Promise! I'm not going until you do . . .'

Rachel sighed and then nodded reluctantly. 'I promise.' She reached across and hugged him fiercely. 'You be careful, you hear, Mr Hallam? Don't take any silly risks.'

Gordon kissed her quickly. 'I'm the guy in the white hat, remember? Good guys always win.'

'You're the best guy,' she said softly, eyes shining.

'You're not so bad yourself.'

Gordon got out of the car and closed the door quietly behind him.

He went down the road a few yards, climbed over a stone wall and dropped into the narrow ribbon of woodland between the rising ground to his right and the lane to his left. A quick wave and he was gone.

Rachel had never felt so lonely in her life.

Gordon moved quickly through the bare winter trees, his feet scuffing the dead leaves. The lane now was twenty yards to his left, the cottage somewhere up ahead. He paused often, listening for sounds, watching for movement. He stopped whenever branches or twigs snapped underfoot. Like gunshots in the watching silence.

He looked up and over to his left through the bare branches and saw the looped telephone line that ran to the cottage along the near side of the lane. Twenty yards more and he saw why he had been unable to get through from Heathrow: a heavy branch from an oak had come down – presumably during a gale when he had been away – and had taken the line down with it. Presumably.

By accident? Or design?

Gordon moved forward slowly, crouched down to his knees and crawled his way forward over the last few yards to the edge of the wood. Then he dropped flat on his stomach, parted the last few branches and peered out at his cottage.

Nothing.

No strange cars, no men waiting for them with guns – nothing. A picture of rural innocence. He made himself wait then, quarter the outside of the cottage inch by careful inch as he searched for signs of occupancy, of disturbance, as he fought down the urge to just get up and walk forward, to believe the evidence of his own eyes and stop being such a fool. Stop playing cops and robbers. O K – game over.

But he didn't get up and walk forward, not then. He lay there for another two minutes while he planned his next move, stage by careful stage.

Then he wormed back several yards, scrambled suddenly to his feet, climbed sloping ground still hidden by a screen of trees and worked his way round to the rear of the cottage.

Again he crawled forward on his stomach, parted the bushes with infinite care and studied the back of his home from this new vantage point: milk bottles outside the back door, tea towels blowing on the line, cloche frames where Rachel had stacked them by the vegetable garden, spade propped against the back door. Nothing out of place. Nothing to worry about.

Gordon bunched to his knees, crouched forward and ran out from the woods, down the slope and across open ground towards the back door, his skin cringing as he felt the Vee sight settle on his shoulders, his back, over his heart. Don't run in straight lines, he remembered suddenly, the breath sawing in his throat as he jinked away to spoil a gunman's aim – and the trees looked down and laughed at him. He pressed flat against the kitchen door, panting and fearful – and the rooks overhead cawed their derision.

One, two, three seconds he waited. A quick glance in at the kitchen. It was empty; no one there. He picked up the garden spade, rammed its blade against the bottom window and a pane of glass burst inwards with a sudden tinkle of glass. Gordon reached inside in feverish haste, careless of the shards of broken glass, and reached for the key on the inside of the lock. It wasn't there.

Swearing under his breath in sudden fright, Gordon grasped the door handle and twisted. The kitchen door opened. He whipped inside and slammed the door behind him, his breath suddenly loud in the strange, hostile kitchen that had heard so much of their laughter. Gordon risked a quick glance into the sitting-room and breathed a sigh of relief. That too was empty. Correction: appeared to be empty. Casting around for a weapon – any weapon – Gordon tugged open the cutlery drawer and picked up a steak knife. If he could just get to the cupboard under the stairs he could lay his hands on a real weapon. But that was still nine paces away. He listened, heart thumping away. Still no sound anywhere else in the cottage; no creaking floorboards.

The key to the back door was on the window sill. He swept it up, locked the kitchen door and jammed the key into his pocket.

He darted across the sitting-room. One step, two, three, four – and he was pulling open the under-stairs cupboard, groping on the shelf at the back for his shotgun, fingers trembling with haste, back crawling with anticipation as he turned away from the area of greatest danger. The shotgun was only .410 bore, only good for rabbits and pigeons, but it still had two barrels – and that made it a helluva lot better than an Asda steak knife on special offer. Got the gun. A box of cartridges was there too. He tore open the cardboard carton, rammed a cartridge into the mouth of each barrel, snapped the gun closed and whirled round.

He had the place to himself.

Gordon moved slowly forward, vastly braver now with the shotgun gripped tightly in both hands. Now at least he had a chance. Kitchen, sitting-room, downstairs toilet, under-stairs cupboard, broom cupboard – all were empty. Which only left upstairs.

Up he went, one step at a time, feet keeping to the edge of each step, cocked shotgun held out in front of him. He took the bedrooms one at a time. As a demonstration of top-floor house clearance it was amateur enough, but it was sufficient. Each bedroom door crashed back in turn with Gordon flattened back against an outside wall. A quick glance through the gap between door and wall to make sure no one was lying in wait for him, a sweeping look into cupboards, a savage prod with the twin barrels at each fall of curtain – and on to the next. One bedroom, two bedrooms, three. All were empty.

Which only left the bathroom.

Gordon paused outside the bathroom door, wiped each trembling hand down the front of his jacket, took a fresh grip on the shotgun and burst into the bathroom, finger crooked around both triggers.

There was a sudden movement to his right. Gordon whirled and fired, all in one smooth, coordinated movement – and gave his own reflection in the bathroom mirror both barrels. The mirror shattered into tiny fragments and Gordon jumped back, ears singing, heart fluttering with pure, undiluted panic. There was no one in the house. It was all right: there was no one in the house! They were safe! Gordon sagged back against the wall and began to laugh helplessly with relief. The mirror. The bloody mirror! They'd paid thirty-five quid for that in Debenhams!

Gordon pushed open the bathroom window and waved a towel madly to and fro as he heard the comforting, familiar sound of the Polo's engine as Rachel came bouncing up the track towards the cottage. He sat down on the window seat, emptied the shotgun and watched her coming towards him, shaking now with reaction. With relief.

Then he rushed downstairs, threw open the front door and stood in the porchway waiting for her, waving the shotgun madly above his head as she flashed her headlights back in reply. The car skidded to a halt and Rachel got out.

'The key!' shouted Gordon, grinning broadly. 'The bloody key, woman! You'd left it on the window sill!'

A hand leapt to her mouth. 'God! So I did – I'd forgotten. I put the milk bottles out, last thing.'

'The milk bottles? The bloody milk bottles? I thought there was someone inside!' he exploded, still not angry, just vastly, so vastly relieved that it was all over. And that they were both still alive. 'Here –' he gestured impatiently. 'Come here. I want to show you something. Quickly!'

'What?'

'Come on, you'll see!' He dragged Rachel after him into the sitting-room. As he led her up the wooden staircase – 'You know that mirror you liked so much? The one I wasn't that keen on?'

'The one in the bathroom? What about it?'

'I . . . come and look,' he said, choking with laughter. 'I . . . I thought someone was standing there.' He threw open the bathroom door. 'Da-da! Not bad shooting, eh?' He laughed aloud at the look on Rachel's face as she took in the jagged fragments of glass still screwed to the wall, the litter of tiny pieces scattered over the floor like quicksilver. 'I'm surprised you didn't hear the shots,' remarked Gordon presently.

'Oh. I did,' said Rachel quietly.

'What?'

'I did. I heard them both.'

'Then why didn't you –?'

'I just wanted to be with you, that's all,' she said simply.

Gordon would remember that moment. For as long as he lived.

'You fool! You stupid *bloody* fool!' snarled Lord Porterfield down the telephone. He glanced round suddenly as one of the hotel waiters moved past the telephone kiosk with a tray of drinks and a deadpan expression. 'Go on,' he ordered, more calmly now as he stifled his anger. 'What else does he know?'

'He . . . he knows you're involved, I'm afraid, sir.'

'You told him? You *told* him I was involved?' demanded Lord Porterfield incredulously. In his flat in Shepherd's Bush, Stephen Rowley gripped the phone a little tighter and decided it was time to do what he could to look after self-interest.

'No, sir. Of course not,' he lied righteously. 'But he knew. I don't know how he knew or who had told him, but he referred to you by name.'

'In what context?'

'Regarding the mission we discussed, sir. He seemed to know rather a lot about that.'

'I see.' Lord Porterfield paused. 'Where is he now?'

'On his way home, I should imagine, sir. Back to Plymouth. Is . . . er . . . is there anything more I can do for you from this end?'

'No. You've done quite enough already,' snapped Lord Porterfield. 'It's time I took care of Hallam myself. Personally.'

It was four hours later and beginning to get dark outside the cottage as Gordon slept upstairs. After a meal, a shave and a bath he had crawled exhausted under the duvet. Now Rachel was working downstairs and the cottage was locked and closed against approaching winter darkness, the shotgun resting against the wall at the bottom of the stairs with the box of cartridges on the floor beside it.

Suddenly a pair of headlights swung across the drawn curtains and there was the sound of a car coming up the lane towards the cottage. Rachel went to the window and lifted back a corner of curtain, all her earlier fears flooding back as the car braked to a halt, a door slammed and footsteps approached the front door.

Rachel turned and fled upstairs. She rushed into their bedroom and shook Gordon by the shoulder. 'Gordon, Gordon – wake up! There's someone outside!' Gordon sprang awake with a start and stared around him, momentarily disoriented as he surfaced sluggishly from deep sleep. 'There's someone outside!' repeated Rachel urgently. Then the doorbell rang.

Gordon swung his feet to the floor and pulled on jeans and a polo-neck sweater, the old fear churning his stomach. 'How many?' he asked, in a whisper.

Rachel shook her head. 'I don't know. One car, anyway.'

'You expecting anybody?' asked Gordon, cramming his feet into his shoes.

Again Rachel shook her head.

The doorbell rang again as Gordon went cautiously downstairs with Rachel hard on his heels. He swept up the shotgun, loaded it with shaking fingers and snapped the breech shut. Then he went through to the kitchen and checked that the back door was still locked, his mouth suddenly dry again with that copper taste of fear. He waved Rachel back against the wall and stepped cautiously towards the front door. 'Who is it?' he shouted. There was silence. 'Who's there?'

'My name is Vickers,' answered a voice.

Gordon and Rachel exchanged glances. 'Who?'

'Vickers. George Vickers.'

'We don't know anyone called Vickers.'

'I . . . I appreciate that. I'm looking for a Mr Gordon Hallam.' This was greeted by silence. 'If you could perhaps just open the door . . .'

'Are you alone?'

'Apart from my wife, yes,' replied the voice, puzzled now. 'She's waiting for me in the car.' Gordon moved to the window, lifted back a corner of curtain and glanced outside. He could see a car waiting on side lights with the dark shape of someone's head in the front passenger seat.

'Gordon, this is ridiculous,' hissed Rachel from the shadows. 'We can't spend the rest of our lives hiding from people! What if he's harmless?'

Reluctantly, Gordon agreed. 'When I nod, you open the door, OK?' he whispered. 'Pull it well in towards you, you got that? I'll be back here.' He took a step back into the sitting-room and turned off the light. Rachel tugged back the heavy bolts and they shot back with loud thuds. Then she slipped up the catch and looked at Gordon. He nodded. She pulled open the door.

George Vickers stood waiting nervously in the porchway.

'Come in,' ordered Gordon from the gloom of the sitting-room, the shotgun held across his waist. George Vickers saw the shotgun and swallowed as he ducked his head beneath the lintel.

'You . . . you won't need that, I assure you,' he said nervously as Rachel closed the door behind him. Vickers swung round as the door slammed and the ancient bolts shot home.

'I'm Hallam,' announced Gordon. 'Sit down. Over there.' The barrel of the shotgun moved fractionally and Vickers sat. 'What do you want, Mr Vickers? Who sent you?'

George Vickers twisted his hands together nervously. 'Nobody *sent* me, Mr Hallam. I . . . I came to see you of my own accord.' He paused, casting around for the way in. What he actually wanted was to see if he could establish some kind of link between the man whose name he had found on Lord Porterfield's desk in Eaton Terrace and Lord Porterfield himself. At the same time, however, he was acutely conscious of the precariousness of his own professional position, of the sensitivity of 'COSMIC' and its implications. A senior civil servant couldn't go round bleating about classified secrets to all and sundry; that sort of thing just wasn't done . . .

'I . . . er . . . this is all rather awkward, Mr Hallam,' he began, taking the map from his coat pocket and tapping it abstractedly against his knee. 'I work for a certain . . . ah . . . government department, shall we say. Can you tell me: does the name Porterfield mean anything to you? Phillip Porterfield . . .?'

Fifteen minutes later there was a sharp knock on the door of Lord Porterfield's bedroom. He and General Inkermann had elected to stay in a small, comfortable hotel three miles north of Okehampton. Now, while the General took afternoon tea in the residents' lounge downstairs, Lord Porterfield prepared to go out. Alone. He turned from adjusting the knot of his tie in the wardrobe mirror. 'Come in.'

The door opened and General Inkermann's liaison officer stood framed in the doorway, a set of car keys dangling from his fingers. Like the others, he too was dressed in civilian clothes. 'Your car's arrived, sir. Four-door grey BMW. You'll find it parked just outside.' He paused. 'You're . . . er . . . you're quite sure you wouldn't rather I sent someone along with you?'

Lord Porterfield shook his head. 'Quite sure, thank you, Peters. It shouldn't take very long. Will you please tell the General I shall go directly to the rendezvous and meet him there a little later in the evening?'

'Very well, sir.' The door closed and Lord Porterfield folded a scarf carefully around his throat and slid into his overcoat. Then he went over to his bags on the spare bed and took a small, flat, three-sided leather valise from the bottom of his suitcase. He unzipped two sides of the valise and took out a beautifully worked Walther PP automatic pistol in 7.65 mm calibre. He pressed the magazine catch above the trigger guard and the magazine slid back into the palm of his hand. He checked the magazine, replaced it with a soft click and slid the weapon into his coat pocket. Then he fastened his overcoat, picked up car keys and leather gloves and went quietly down the ancient wooden staircase to reception. The manageress was standing behind the counter and looked up with a bright smile as he approached. 'Yes, sir. Can I help you?'

'I wonder if you'd be good enough to direct me to the village of Stowcombe?' asked Lord Porterfield politely.

Gordon and Rachel stood in the porch watching the rear lights of Vickers' car recede down the lane. As soon as it had disappeared Gordon led Rachel back into the cottage, slammed the door and stood over the fire rubbing his hands together. 'He's out there,' he muttered, perhaps to himself. 'The bastard's out there!' He crossed to the bookcase, took down an ordnance survey map of the area and spread it out on the coffee table. He studied the map for several minutes and then tapped a place decisively with his finger. 'There,' he said. 'Around about there. Got to be.

There's one of those tunnels he was talking about. It's only . . .
what? Three, four miles from here?'

He folded away the map, crossed to the hooks by the door and
took down his anorak. Rachel came back from the kitchen then
and stopped in the doorway.

'Gordon? You're not going out?'

'Only for a little while, love,' said Gordon, head bent as he
fastened the zip on his anorak. And missed the look on her face.
'Why?'

He glanced up. 'Why? You heard what that bloke Vickers
said: Porterfield's up to something – now! Down here! On our
doorstep. You expect me just to ignore that, turn the other cheek?
He's the man who had Dad killed, remember? Nearly got me
killed, too. So what am I supposed to do – just forget about it?
Leave it all to old man Vickers? Wait till Porterfield and his
cronies decide to have another crack at me?'

'You could tell the police,' tried Rachel in a small voice.

'The police? Ha!' scoffed Gordon. 'Little men on push bikes
with pointed helmets. It's a different league, Rachel.'

'All right then – what about me?'

'What about you? You'll be all right here, won't you?'

'I can't stay here!' she replied indignantly. 'Not on my own!'

Gordon reached for gloves and torch. 'Why not? You'll be
perfectly safe –'

'Gordon! Because I'm scared, that's why – can't you see that?'

He turned to his wife and placed both hands gently on her
shoulders. 'Look – love,' he sighed: the expert confronting the
ignorant surrendering to groundless fears. Or so he thought.
'We got back here at what time?'

'Two. Shortly after,' conceded Rachel.

Gordon nodded patiently. 'And it's now seven, yes? Just gone.'
He looked slowly around the room. 'And what's happened? Have
we come under rocket attack? Has this Lord Porterfield climbed
through the kitchen window with a knife between his teeth?'
Despite herself Rachel let a small smile escape. 'That's better.
You see? Nothing's happened – and nothing is *going* to happen.
Besides, you said it yourself not half an hour ago: we can't hide
from the rest of the world for the remainder of our lives. There's
a chance now I can find this bastard. Confront him.'

'And then what? Then what will you do, if you do find him? You've no idea what you're walking into!'

'Look – love: for days now I've been chased and bloody terrified, right? I've been knocked from pillar to bloody post by this man – you think I'm going to let him slip through my fingers now that *I* have the advantage, a chance of evening the score?'

'O K,' tried Rachel desperately. 'O K – so you find him. Then what do you do?'

Gordon hesitated. He hadn't really thought about that. 'I don't know,' he admitted. 'I'll have to see. Play it by ear.'

'Oh, great,' said Rachel sarcastically. 'Terrific. You'll play it by ear.'

'Look – if you're really worried I'll leave you the shotgun, all right? Anyone comes knocking on the door you don't like the look of, you can just stick that up his nostrils!'

Rachel shook her head impatiently. He worried her when he got like this. 'I couldn't. You know I hate guns, anyway.' She paused. 'Sometimes I just don't understand you, Gordon,' she said quietly. 'Two hours ago you were as scared as I was. Now you're . . . I don't know . . . you've changed.'

He shrugged. 'I over-reacted, that's all. All that leaping around with the shotgun.' He tried to take her in his arms but Rachel twisted away.

'No, I mean it, love. Don't go out – it'll be pitch dark. Leave it until the morning, at least.'

Gordon turned and pointed. 'There's the gun, see? And there's the ammunition.' He broke open the shotgun, checked the load, snapped the gun shut and placed it on the floor behind the sofa. 'I'll only be an hour or so. Promise.'

'An hour or so?' challenged Rachel with a terrible cold feeling in the pit of her stomach.

'All right, then: two. Two at the most.' He smiled reassuringly. 'Don't *worry*, love: you're safe here. Safe as houses.'

Of course she was.

Six minutes later he was alone.


Gordon pulled in to the side of the road, turned off the lights and sat for a moment in darkness, staring out through the windscreen. Then he turned on the roof light, opened out the map across the steering wheel and leaned forward. He had turned right just . . . here, on the outskirts of Mary Tavy. Then he had driven down to where he was parked now, just before the bridge. If he crossed the road and walked down . . . there, to his right, over the wall, he could cross the field and drop down to the railway cutting beyond.

He folded away the map, got out of the car and set off. Five minutes later he slid down a steep earth bank and felt rough chippings beneath his feet: the track of the old railway, now disused. Gordon paused then and looked about him in the darkness, the high banks of earth looming over him on both sides. He looked up and saw that the sky was overcast with few stars. A light drizzle drifted into his upturned face and somewhere over to his left he heard the harsh dry bark of a dog fox.

But no lights, no sound: nothing. Thrusting his hands into his anorak pockets, Gordon set off along the bed of the disused railway, his shoes swishing through the long grass. If he found nothing here he would go back to the car. Try further up the valley.

Five minutes later Gordon came to a halt. The high ground of the cutting on either side had tapered away to nothing and he was out in open country with fields on either side of the old track. In the distance ahead he saw a sudden flash of headlights on the main road, but that was all. He turned and began to retrace his steps. He did not hurry. He still had plenty of time . . .

The garden gate opened. And then closed with a soft click.

Rachel's head shot up instantly. There was someone outside, by the gate. Coming up the path to the cottage. She rose to her feet and backed towards the sitting-room wall, a hand up to her mouth. Straining her ears she heard the slow, measured tread of feet on the path leading to the front door and then held her breath as she waited for the bell to ring.

The bell rang. Welcome as the rattle of the key in the condemned cell on execution morning.

Rachel edged slowly towards the door: 'Who . . . who is it?' she called tremulously.

'Sergeant Rose, Ma'am – Okehampton police. Got a message here for a Mr Gordon Hallam.'

Rachel sagged back with relief and began tugging back the bolts. 'He isn't here, I'm afraid, sergeant. He –' She pulled open the door and the smile of welcome froze on her face. The man outside was too old to be a policeman. He was not wearing a uniform, either. But he was holding a small automatic pistol.

'Not strictly true, I'm afraid, Mrs Hallam,' admitted Lord Porterfield.

Rachel began to push the door closed but already he was across the threshold and into the sitting-room. 'In that case I think I'd better wait, don't you? Please – do shut the door.' Rachel closed the door slowly as Lord Porterfield walked into the centre of the sitting-room and looked about with an air of quiet approval. 'Very nice,' he said. 'Quite the little love nest.'

'Who are you? What do you want?' demanded Rachel.

Lord Porterfield turned slowly, slipped the pistol into a coat pocket and sat down in an armchair. 'When will your husband be back, Mrs Hallam?' he asked quietly.

'I . . . I don't know.'

Lord Porterfield studied her in silence for a moment. 'You don't . . . know,' he mocked. 'And if you did you wouldn't tell me, hmm?' Rachel didn't nod, didn't speak. She just stood there looking at him, terrified by the unspoken menace that lurked behind every well-groomed syllable. 'Then perhaps you would care to tell me where he has gone?'

Rachel remained stubbornly silent.

'Well?' demanded Lord Porterfield at last, his patience exhausted.

'Out. To see a friend. Look – who *are* you? What do you want?'

'I would have thought that was patently obvious, Mrs Hallam. I want to talk to your husband.'

'You're going to kill him – that's why you've come here, isn't it? Isn't it?' demanded Rachel with dull, sick certainty.

Lord Porterfield made a small gesture of deprecation. 'Nothing so melodramatic, I assure you,' he lied. 'I merely want to talk to him about . . . certain matters. Concerning his father.'

'Then why do you need that . . . thing?' She gestured at his coat pocket and Lord Porterfield glanced down.

'Ah, I see. You mean the gun? Merely for self-protection, I assure you.'

Rachel groaned. 'You're lying. I know you are.'

Lord Porterfield shrugged. 'You are at liberty to think what you wish, Mrs Hallam.'

'Liberty? Liberty? You mean I can move around in my own home without getting shot if I start rattling the teacups? Thanks very much!' snapped Rachel, stung to anger.

Lord Porterfield nodded. 'But of course. And an excellent idea, Mrs Hallam, yes. Why don't you make some tea for the two of us? While we're waiting.' Rachel paused, then turned on her heel and went into the kitchen.

Presently she returned with two teacups. They rattled slightly in their saucers and she hated herself for advertising her fear, her weakness. She handed Lord Porterfield one of the cups and then seemed to stumble as she crossed back to the sofa. The saucer slipped from her hands and the cup broke on the carpet. She glanced across at Lord Porterfield. 'I . . . I'd better get a cloth.' He nodded and she returned to the kitchen as Lord Porterfield watched her carefully over the rim of his teacup.

Rachel dropped to her knees and began picking up the pieces of broken crockery. She moved behind the sofa still wiping with the cloth. Then she rose to her feet. She was holding Gordon's shotgun. She levelled it coolly at Lord Porterfield's head and thumbed back both triggers.

'I only have one husband,' she said quietly, 'and I happen to love him very much. I won't let you take him from me. Now – put it down,' she ordered, the weight of the shotgun making it shake in her hands. 'The teacup. Put it down.'

Cup and saucer were lowered slowly to a side table as Rachel rested the barrel of the shotgun against the top of the sofa, crouched down and sighted down both barrels at Lord Porterfield. He watched her with remarkable unconcern.

'My dear young woman: do you really imagine –'

'Stand up. Slowly . . . slowly . . . I don't want to shoot but I will if you make any sudden movement. Don't make me shoot.'

'All right. All right.' Lord Porterfield sighed and rose slowly to his feet.

For a moment Rachel thought about searching him, going

through his pockets, taking the pistol, but it all seemed too complicated, too fraught with danger. 'Walk towards the door. Go on. Now. Very slowly.' Lord Porterfield did exactly what he was told as Rachel slid round the sofa towards him. 'Stop. Now: open the door and stand back.' Again he did what he was told. The door opened and darkness beckoned beyond. 'Keep going,' she ordered. 'Don't look round. And don't come back.' Hands raised, Lord Porterfield walked slowly across the porch.

Rachel waited until he was about twelve feet away and then slammed the door violently behind him. She fumbled with the bolts in a frenzy of haste and then almost collapsed against the door as they shot home. She was shaking violently, muttering to herself in fear. She dragged a hand through her hair, glanced round wildly and, still clutching the shotgun, dashed back into the kitchen where she checked that the door was bolted as well as locked, pulled down the blind and turned off the light. Back into the sitting-room to stop and listen, heart pounding furiously. There was silence. Then, very faintly, she heard the slow measured tread of footsteps working their way round the outside of the cottage. She followed them with her eyes and her ears and flinched with terror as she heard the rattle of the back door. Then the footsteps moved slowly away.

Rachel hurried to the telephone, swept up the receiver – and listened to the broken signal that told her the telephone was useless, the line down. She crashed the phone back onto its cradle and the ting! of the bell dragged on into a brooding, watching silence more ominous than screaming.

She was still shaking violently. Now Rachel looked down at the gun in her hands, broke open the weapon with trembling fingers, extracted the cartridges, flung them away across the room and dropped the shotgun onto the sofa as though it was contaminated. Then she turned off the lights, pressed herself into a far corner and slid to the floor where she sat, hugging her knees, her eyes two dark pools of terror. 'Help me, someone,' she whispered, teeth biting on an ivory knuckle. 'Please – someone – help me.'

Gordon climbed swiftly through the woods, his torch throwing a shaft of white light from side to side across the cluttered winter debris of broken branches and fallen leaves that carpeted the hillside. He had left the car in a lay-by and walked the last few hundred yards along the dark empty lane. Then he had pushed through a narrow hedgerow and started to climb.

At first he made good progress for the ground rose gently in front of him and the trees were thinly spaced. Then it had begun to rise more steeply as the trees and undergrowth had pressed in around him so that he had to force his way through thickets of thorn and elder.

He had to admit it – Rachel had been right: it was a mug's game, this crashing through the woods at night looking for . . . looking for what? He didn't even know that; not for sure. And already he had tripped and fallen half a dozen times, his shoes slipping and sliding on the wet ground as he panted uphill. It was cold too – and not a little eerie, this tramping through the woods at dead of night.

Gordon found himself pausing often, turning round and glancing nervously behind him as unfamiliar shadows loomed and threatened in the darkness. But there were no lights, no sounds save the sigh of the wind and the low murmur of a river somewhere off to his right. Gordon started suddenly as there was a clatter of noise and a rook took wing nearby. You must be mad, thought Gordon to himself.

Another twenty yards or so and he would turn back, he decided suddenly. Just get to the top of this hill.

It was then that he heard the low murmur of voices.

At first Gordon thought it was the river somewhere below him. Then he clearly heard the soft thud of a vehicle door closing followed by a soft growl as a powerful engine was brought to life.

Tiredness forgotten, Gordon crouched down and moved forward as quietly as he could. The wooded slope was gradual and undulating. As he went down over the crest of the hill feeling for dead branches, Gordon slid down into a gentle hollow choked with dead leaves. He raised his head slowly over the lip of the depression and looked down.

Two, three hundred feet further down the hill, through the bare trees, Gordon could see the track of the old railway running into the mouth of a tunnel. There were arc lights down there, arc lights and people – and a large container lorry that was being driven slowly forward out of the tunnel towards a group of men, two of whom were sitting back on shooting sticks talking earnestly to a soldier with blackened face and disruptive pattern uniform. A submachine-gun was slung over his shoulder.

As Gordon watched, all three turned to look back down the track. A grey BMW saloon drove slowly towards them and stopped. Then a man in his early seventies got out and joined the others. After a brief conversation all four men now turned to watch the lorry.

An arm was raised and the lorry ground forward on side lights only, the sound of its engine thrown back as a dull echoing roar against the curved roof of the tunnel. Then the lorry stopped with a sudden sigh of hydraulic brakes and another soldier jumped down from the cab and ran round behind the lorry as the whole storage area behind the cab began to lift and tilt swiftly upwards with a low whine.

Gordon crouched down in his hollow, mesmerized by the scene unfolding before his eyes. As he watched the sides of the lorry began to slide down to reveal a lean, tapering snout that reminded him – There was a flicker of movement to Gordon's left. He had just begun to twist towards it, just begun to bring up his torch, when the world exploded into blinding pain as something hard and heavy crashed into the side of his head and sent him sprawling sideways, the torch flying from his fingers. Then someone was kneeling on his back, his head was being rammed down into the leaf-mould and his arms were being wrenched behind his back in a vicious arm-lock that made the sinews crackle. Gordon nearly passed out with the pain in his bruised shoulder.

'Don't move,' hissed a voice in his ear. 'Keep very, very still.' Too terrified to think, far less move, Gordon froze into immobility. Then the knee came out of his back and he was hauled roughly onto his side. Gordon gulped in air as two dark shapes towered over him. Both were clad in the same dark, closely-fitting camouflaged uniforms and wore dark hoods that almost covered their eyes. Their faces were streaked with camouflage cream. One of the men stepped back to cover Gordon as his mate searched expertly, quickly, up and down Gordon's body, patting up under his armpits and down over his crotch. Those same expert hands found his wallet, the map in his pocket and two cartridges for the shotgun, left there from the last time he had been out shooting. There was a brief pause while these were handed back to the second man with not a word passing between them. Then one of the men stepped closer. 'Where's the shotgun, squire?'

Gordon spat out a mouthful of woodland carpet and shook his head. 'I . . . I haven't got a gun.'

'The shotgun' – another crashing, jarring blow to the face. This time Gordon felt a tooth break loose – 'where is it?'

Gordon turned his head to one side and spat blood. 'It's . . . at home,' he managed, twisting away from the blow that would follow.

'O K, leave it, Sandy,' ordered the other man quietly, a black shape in the darkness, more sensed than seen.

Sandy nodded briefly, stepped back from Gordon's side and picked up a rifle with something large and bulky clipped over the breech. It was an image-intensifier, a nightsight. They had been following Gordon as a pale, translucent green figure all the way up the hill, although Gordon would never know that. There was the faintest metallic click.

'Golf Zulu to Delta Yankee. Message. Over.'

'Send.'

'We have intruder. One only. Over.'

'Wait. Out.'

Instantly the lights were extinguished below and there was silence except for the wind in the trees. Then –

'Bring him in.'

'Wilco. Out.'

Gordon was hauled roughly to his feet. A black sack was pulled down over his head. 'Move,' ordered a voice.

A sharp shove in the back and Gordon began stumbling down the slope towards the railway tunnel. Every time he tripped strong hands gripped his arms; every time he paused he was shoved roughly forward to crash blindly through saplings and rip hands and arms on thickets of brambles. Then the ground suddenly dropped away beneath his feet and Gordon slid down onto the railway track and fell forward, sobbing for breath, the rough stones cutting sharply into his knees. He was hauled to his feet and pushed forward. One of the men spoke quietly into a radio. He wasn't even panting.

'OK, Sandy. Hold him there. They'll come to us.'

Gordon stopped suddenly. If someone grabbed you by the neck and jerked that hard, you'd stop too.

They waited in silence. Gordon rocked the loose molar gently from side to side with the tip of his tongue. He would have to go to the dentist after all this was over, he thought with sudden, absurd irrelevance. He hated going to the dentist. 'If I could just explain what –'

'Quiet,' snapped a voice. They waited in silence for several minutes. Then two hand torches detached themselves from the group silhouetted against the mouth of the tunnel and began bobbing slowly down the track. Head still covered by that black bag, Gordon saw nothing. All he heard was the steady crunch of approaching feet as his captors went forward to report. There was a brief murmured consultation as Gordon's wallet and map were handed over and examined. Then the footsteps crunched closer.

'Right. Let's have a look at him,' ordered a new voice. The bag was ripped from his head and Gordon squinted into the beam of several powerful torches. After a brief silence there was another short conversation and Gordon's sense of foreboding increased: as though his future had just been discussed. And decided.

Presently the torches came towards him once more, the feet crunched to a halt and another torch was shining directly into his eyes.

'Well?' demanded a well-educated voice. 'How much did he see?'

'Enough,' replied one of the SAS troopers laconically. There was a brief silence.

'Yes. I was afraid that might prove to be the case.' Gordon swallowed and wetted his lips: this was him they were talking about –

'Look . . . what is all this?' he began: 'All I –'

'Be silent.' The voice was scathing. 'Don't waste your breath on fatuous remarks, Mr Hallam. You have already put us to quite enough inconvenience.' There was another silence. As though something was being planned, some option being considered.

'We can't risk him,' decided an American voice finally. 'That's all there is to it. You let this guy wander off and –'

'Thank you, Bill. I am quite aware of the nuances.' More silence, stretching on to breaking point this time as Gordon tried to see behind the torch beams to the shadowy figures beyond. Finally – 'I should like a few words with Mr Hallam here. Alone.'

'Alone? Jesus, Phillip, you can't –'

'Alone, if you please. You too, Bill.'

They moved away, the soldiers' boots crunching on the gravel as they retreated to leave Gordon and Lord Porterfield alone, Gordon still pinned to the end of Lord Porterfield's torchbeam, his face screwed up against the glare.

'Where did you get this?' asked Lord Porterfield quietly as soon as the others were out of earshot. The torch flicked down and rested briefly on the sepia photograph of Walter Hallam, Bruno Tyschen and Peter Tillet standing in front of the Lockheed Hudson at Tempsford in March 1945. Not: 'How did you find us?' or 'What are you doing here?' but: 'Where did you get this?' with a glance at a sepia wartime photograph – and in that moment Gordon knew who it was who stood behind the torchbeam.

'It was in my father's wallet. The night you had him killed, Lord Porterfield. Or would you prefer it if I called you Matthew? For old times' sake?' replied Gordon evenly, sensing his words strike home.

'My, my. You have been busy,' murmured Lord Porterfield after a brief pause.

'Busy?' exploded Gordon, anger suddenly swamping his fear. '*Busy*? You bastard! Thanks to you I've been chased, hunted, bloody nearly killed – and why? Because I wanted to find out what my father had done for his country during the war, that's why!'

'You have been meddling in affairs that do not concern you,' snapped Lord Porterfield. 'If you –'

'Just tell me why,' interrupted Gordon recklessly. 'Why, after nearly forty years, it was necessary to kill all those people – why?'

'What makes you think you are entitled to an explanation?'

'Because there has to be a *reason*!' stormed Gordon. 'And because one of those men was my father! You owe me –'

'Owe you? I owe you nothing, Mr Hallam.'

'All right, maybe not me. But you owe my father something, don't you? Or have you forgotten? When you bottled out in the desert, lost your nerve or whatever after the drop – who was it who stopped the others from killing you there and then, eh? It was my father, wasn't it? And in return for that act of . . . of kindness, what do you do? You –'

'Who . . . who told you about that?' demanded Lord Porterfield, the first crack appearing in that urbane mask of self-control.

'Tyschen. Before you had *him* knocked off. He said you panicked. Ran away.'

'That is not true,' snapped Lord Porterfield from the darkness. 'That is a gross distortion of the truth. I could never expect that . . . that fool to . . .' He pulled himself up short. 'Never mind. It was all a long time ago now, as you say. In the past.'

'But why?' insisted Gordon. 'There has to be a reason.'

Lord Porterfield sighed. 'Because they knew about Apostle. They could not be trusted to keep their mouths shut, Mr Hallam. They posed a threat. They might have begun to talk.'

'Talk? My father never even told *me*! I lived with that man for almost thirty years and he never opened his mouth,' ground out Gordon. 'Bruno told me about Apostle, about the skeleton in the desert, about what he called the "time-bomb", about the legend – not my father. And do you know what I think?'

'What do you think, Mr Hallam?' asked Lord Porterfield, the torch playing directly into his face once more. 'I should be fascinated to hear your opinion.'

'I think: so what?' shrugged Gordon helplessly. 'So bloody what? What does it matter if there *is* an uprising inside the Soviet Union – if the whole population marches on Moscow – how does that threaten us? That's good, isn't it?'

'Do you really think that would be good, Mr Hallam? Do you? Are you really that naïve? Moscow would never permit such a thing – they would go to war rather than risk the fragmentation of their empire.' He turned and pointed the torch briefly towards the railway tunnel. 'Do you know what that is, Mr Hallam?'

'Yes,' admitted Gordon: 'Yes, I know what it is.'

'Tell me.'

'It's a Cruise missile,' replied Gordon, amazed at how calm he sounded. There was a Cruise missile deployed in a tunnel not five miles from home and he was standing here chatting about it as though it was the most natural thing in the world. To his surprise he realized he didn't even feel particularly offended that it was there.

'Yes. It's a Cruise missile. The first, I hope, of many that will help ensure our security.' He paused. 'What are a few lives when weighed in the balance against that?'

'Bugger all, I guess. Unless one of them happens to be yours. Or your father's.'

Lord Porterfield sighed impatiently. 'Tell me, Mr Hallam – as an intelligent, educated man: how many people in this country do you think would permit us to place these missiles here if they knew of their existence?'

Gordon shrugged. 'No idea. Haven't a clue.'

'Precious few. And why? Because it would upset their preconception of the way things are done. It would be . . . undemocratic' – the word was spoken with the utmost scorn. 'The public talk about . . . accountability, about referral to the people.' He shook his head emphatically. 'They do not want to take decsions, to be made responsible for their own destiny. They do not want true choice, for they cannot handle it. It frightens them, Mr Hallam.'

'But Apostle wasn't –'

'Apostle too: people do not *want* to be educated, to be confronted with complex choices. In this case, we are talking about nuclear weapons: about expansion or disarmament. We either buy the new generation of nuclear weapons that will counter a Soviet threat or we dismantle those we have because we perceive that the Soviet Union has no territorial ambitions; that the very words "Soviet threat" have become outmoded; a paper tiger, do you understand?'

'I'm listening, if that's what you mean.'

'Good. Now – if revolt were to grow *inside* the Soviet Union and that revolt was reported widely by the West so that people began to hope, to believe the Soviet Union was about to collapse upon itself, what would happen?' It was not a question. 'I shall tell you: that naïve hope would become a bromide, a palliative that, in time, would destroy the shield of deterrence that has maintained peace in Europe for the last thirty-five years.'

'You really believe that, don't you?' said Gordon, appalled at the man's cynicism, his manipulation of the hopes and fears of ordinary people. 'You really think that's the way it works: the Gospel according to Matthew.'

'Don't be trite. Of course that's the way it works,' snapped Lord Porterfield. 'Democracy? A code-word, that's all. Just like Apostle.'

'But you've missed something,' said Gordon shortly, shaking his head. 'You've missed something, all those years ago. Take a look at that photograph again, Lord Porterfield. You'll see that you're not quite as clever as you thought . . .'

The torch flicked down. Gordon looked up. The soldiers were twenty-five yards away. Far enough? It would have to be. He might never get another chance.

Gordon burst forward. He slammed into Porterfield, punched the torch from his hand, knocked him sprawling backwards and raced across the loose chippings to hurtle down the far slope, gaining precious yards of darkness, of safety, as he crashed headlong through the woods. The brambles scratched and tore at his face as he plunged madly downhill.

'Go! After him!' shouted a voice. Already Gordon could hear the crash and snap of branches behind him as they gave chase. First one torch then another blazed out into the woodland, then – 'Night-sights! Only night-sights!' yelled a voice and the torches snapped off. Gordon swung to his right and raced on, slipping and sliding as he smashed into trees and spun round against branches, the breath sobbing in his throat, his lungs searing with effort as he ran.

Suddenly the ground fell away beneath him and he tumbled head over heels into a leaf-choked gully. He lay there for several seconds badly winded, listening to the sounds of pursuit closing in around him. If he got up now they would see him, for he was almost under their feet. He twisted round and wriggled in tight against the bank where he began burrowing into the dead leaves, throwing armfuls of them back over his legs and body as he tried to escape, to sink from sight. To hide.

'Where is the bastard? I don't see him.' The voice was little more than a murmur. But it came from directly above where Gordon lay hidden. One of the soldiers was standing on top of the same slope, his feet braced apart, rifle butt tucked in against his shoulder as he panned the night-sight gently from left to right.

'What's control want us to do, then? Sit here all fucking night?'

'We search down as far as the river,' came the whispered reply. 'Two-nine and Two-seven are going to his house. Bastard only lives a couple of miles away – they'll wait for him there.'

'There! What's that?'

'Where?'

'Your four o'clock.'

The night-sight swung round. A pause, then –

'Badger, ya daft sod. Come on . . .' The two soldiers skirted the hollow and moved on.

Gordon rolled over to lie back, staring up at the stars, panting. He could hear the soldiers moving away down the hill, pausing every so often to raise that bulky night-sight and gaze for long, motionless seconds at a green-hued landscape. Then their quiet, stealthy sounds receded and Gordon pushed himself slowly to his knees. He wriggled forward over the edge of the gully, those last words ringing on in his head: 'Bastard only lives a couple of miles away – they'll wait for him there.'

Rachel.

Gordon stopped moving for a moment, tried to plan, tried to remember the map he had studied in the sitting-room back at the cottage less than an hour ago. An hour? It seemed like eternity. The river – they'd mentioned a river. Yes, that was it! There was a river at the bottom of this hill. If he kept to its bank and moved to his . . . left, then sooner or later he would reach the bridge. And if he climbed back up the hill just there he should come back to the road – and his car, only a few hundred yards further on . . .

He tore up handfuls of moss and lichen and smeared it over

his face, rubbed it over the back of his hands and down his neck as camouflage. Then he began to wriggle down towards the river, pausing every few yards to listen, listen, listen . . .

Two minutes later he had reached the bank of the river. He heard the water first, sensed the dampness seeping up to meet him – and then suddenly there it was stretching out before him, a gleaming swirl of movement in the darkness.

Hardly pausing at the water's edge, Gordon slid into the river stomach first, gasping aloud with the sudden piercing cold as it struck up into his bones, pinching and flattening his lungs so that he took breath in shallow little nips as the water swirled around him. Grasping the edge of the bank, his whole body submerged so that only his head showed above water, Gordon pulled himself slowly upstream, a man-otter evading the hunt.

The water had a vicious, tensile strength that attacked his limbs in turn, gnawing away at his reserves, draining him of warmth, of the will to go on. When he wanted to stop, to drag himself from the icy water almost moaning with the dull, aching pain, biting his lips together to stop his teeth chattering with cold, he thought of Rachel waiting for him in the cottage and of the danger that loomed about her. And went on.

He was in the water for ten minutes, perhaps a quarter of an hour, although it seemed much longer. Then suddenly the bridge was looming up ahead of him, huge and dark and brooding as it spanned the river ahead, water dripping off its damp, granite arches to hit the river with a hollow, resonant plop.

Keeping in against the bank, Gordon slid soundlessly beneath one of the giant granite buttresses. He stayed there for long seconds, listening, the icy water swirling around his neck, the river-bed a slime of flat stones beneath his shoes.

Presently he pushed himself away from the bank and half swam, half waded across the river, hidden from sight within the deeper darkness cast by the granite bridge. Water streaming from his clothes, Gordon dragged himself out onto the bank almost sobbing with cold. He pushed himself painfully to his feet and tried to press the water out of his sleeves and trousers, his teeth chattering with cold as cramp began to bite into both hips. He looked around but there was no sound, no lights coming towards him. Ignoring the pain, Gordon turned and pushed through chest-high bushes towards the stone parapet of the bridge, his shoes squelching noisily as he struggled through the dark, clinging undergrowth. He reached the wall of the bridge and again he paused to listen.

And all the time he was conscious of the need to hurry, to get on. To help Rachel.

Gordon hoisted himself up over the wall and dropped heavily into the lane. He hesitated a moment, gathering his wits, and then set off down the dark lane in an awkward, stiff-legged run towards where he had parked the car. He felt in wet pockets as he ran, hoping to God he hadn't dropped the keys, lost them in the river. He hadn't. He grasped the keys triumphantly in his fist and ran around the last corner with a final burst of effort, a marathon runner heading for the tape. There was the lay-by and there was the call box.

But no car. It had gone.

Gordon's final burst petered out and he just stood there staring stupidly at the empty lay-by, a widening puddle of water at his feet. His car had gone. Just . . . disappeared.

But not the call box. The call box was still there.

Gordon began running again, a plan half forming in his mind. A quick, furtive glance over his shoulder and he was pushing into the phone booth. He ripped up the receiver and – minor miracle – heard the dialling tone. He dialled three nines and waited for long drawn-out seconds, back-lit perfectly in the narrow illuminated box. He felt vulnerable, hideously exposed.

'Which service do you require?'

'Er . . .' Gordon's mind went suddenly blank, the pant of his breathing filling the confined space.

'Hello? Caller? Which service do you require?'

Gordon opened his mouth to reply and then forgot all about the operator as one of the small panes of glass just above his head suddenly burst into a thousand tiny fragments, showering him with shards of glass. Then it dawned on him: they were shooting at him. Shooting at him with silenced rifles!

He dropped the receiver and pushed frantically out of the phone booth, the operator's 'Hello? Caller?' echoing in the booth as the phone dangled on the end of its cable. Gordon paused outside the call box, looked wildly about him and then set off down the lane, twisting and turning as he ran to spoil their aim. There was a sudden shower of sparks and a savage hum as a bullet ricocheted off a stone six inches from his feet. Gordon jinked to one side, raced around a slight bend in the lane and glanced over his shoulder. Then he scrambled over the wall and ran on, twisting into the woods for twenty, thirty yards before throwing himself face-down in the bracken, utterly spent.

In the cotttage Rachel shrank back against the stairs as again that heavy fist banged against the front door. 'Open the door, Mrs Hallam. We know you're in there. Be reasonable, Mrs Hallam. No one's going to harm you.'

'Go away!' she shouted. 'I don't believe you! Leave me alone!'

There was a sudden splintering crash behind her and she whirled round. It came from the kitchen. Someone was smashing at the back door with a sledge-hammer. Another massive blow rocked the door loose in its frame and panes of glass fell out and smashed on the kitchen floor. One more blow and the door sagged open tiredly. A man in some sort of tight-fitting dark uniform, his face streaked in weird disruptive camouflage patterns, pushed the door roughly aside and stepped through into the kitchen without a word, the sledge-hammer held like a toy in his hands.

'Get out! Get out!' Rachel began to scream.

She rushed for the shotgun then, swept it up and pointed it with shaking hands at the lean giant stalking through the kitchen towards her while another fist crashed against the front door. 'Come on, Mrs Hallam – be reasonable!'

'Go away!' she screamed. 'Please! Please! Just . . . go away!'

The man with the sledge-hammer didn't even hesitate. He pushed a chair aside, moved with sudden, catlike speed and tore the shotgun from Rachel's hands. He broke the gun expertly and glanced inside the chamber. Then he tossed the shotgun contemptuously onto the sofa. 'Bloody amateur,' he said.

The shotgun hadn't even been loaded.

# : 22 :

On the outskirts of the Ukrainian mining town of Sambor, Private Nikolai Samlar of the 117th Motor Rifle Battalion of the Soviet Army pushed aside his single blanket and lay back staring at the ceiling, his bare chest gleaming with sweat in the stifling closeness and stench of the crowded barrack block.

All around him was the snore and sigh of sleeping soldiers. Stealthily, Nikolai felt beneath his mattress for his bayonet and slid it inch by slow, careful inch from its scabbard. Then he reached beneath his pillow for the grenade he had stolen from the ranges and lay back, as he stared unblinking up at the rafters, his mind picturing again the words in the letter he had received from home that same morning. It was the first letter to reach him since he had been conscripted. As usual, much of what his mother had written had been heavily scored through by the army censors but all army recruits had long ago learned the trick of erasing the heavy, blue wax pencil marks with a little kerosene stolen from the kitchens. He had done that sitting on the toilet, in the only place of privacy in the entire Depot, and it was there that he had discovered what had happened to his favourite uncle and eldest cousin.

On the day of his induction into the glorious Soviet Army, his uncle Rabalas and cousin Elia had taken part in a march, a demonstration just behind the railway station. They had been demonstrating against the Russian invasion of Afghanistan, against the denial of Tartar rights to a homeland, against the clumsy suppression by the State of Moslem self-determination. The demonstration had been dispersed by Russian soldiers and uncle Rabalas had been kicked to death by a Russian officer. His cousin Elia? Nobody knew what had happened to her. She had simply disappeared.

Nikolai stirred restlessly, remembering Yuri's story of what he had seen that day when he went back to his father's lorry for the tickets to the parade. He turned onto his side, the bayonet tucked under his body as he waited for the others to join him.

The others: how many would come, help settle the score? How many felt as he did? Not just for uncle Rabalas and cousin Elia but for their own comrades too. Of those who had started out from the holding depot in distant Uzbekistan, two already were gone: Private Tinrass, killed by Sergeant Barak on the grenade range – and Yuri, Yuri Rashidov, his friend, last seen being carried away on a stretcher, his arm swathed in bloody bandages. Again, Sergeant Barak had been responsible. Barak the Russian.

Nikolai glanced towards Yuri's empty cot and his knuckles tightened on the hilt of his bayonet. Already the orderlies had removed Yuri's bedding, taken his equipment scale back into store. It was as though an Uzbek conscript called Yuri Rashidov had never existed.

It was time to redress the balance.

Vakar came first, a dark shape barely seen as he moved stealthily to Nikolai's side and crouched down beside his stool, eyes sweeping around the mounds of dark, sleeping bodies as he searched for the first hint of detection. Then came Dalin, his eyes shining round and white with a fear, with a tension they all shared. He crouched down too, Adam's apple bobbing nervously. They waited one minute, perhaps two, but no one else came. The snores rose and fell around them and they were alone.

'I've . . . I've been thinking,' whispered Dalin finally. 'It's . . . what I mean is: it's crazy; madness! You'll . . . you'll never get away with it, Samlar! They'll catch you; they'll catch us all! Put us up against a wall and –'

'Shut it!' hissed Nikolai savagely, the fear in the man's voice rasping at his own taut nerves. 'We agreed, didn't we? Or are you another one of those who'll just sit there and take it?'

'Samlar's right,' whispered Vakar. 'We can't just lie back, let that bastard pick us off one by one –'

Nikolai reached out suddenly and grasped Dalin's shoulder with strong, lean fingers, as though in this way some of his outrage, his anger and his courage might flow between them. 'For me it's a matter of honour,' he hissed savagely. 'That's all – honour! Either you're with us or you're not! If you haven't got the stomach for it – piss off back to bed. Now.'

Dalin hesitated miserably. 'I'll . . . I'll keep watch for you,' he offered at last.

Nikolai nodded curtly and glanced round. 'Come on.'

He slid out of bed and the three of them crept down the centre aisle between the long rows of sleeping soldiers towards the cubicle at the far end of the barracks. They paused outside the Sergeant's flimsy door and exchanged nervous glances. Nikolai pressed Dalin on the arm, indicating he should stay outside. Then he nodded, took a deep breath, turned the handle and stepped into Barak's room with Vakar tight on his heels.

Sergeant Barak was sleeping on his stomach, his blankets thrown back, that gleaming head turned aside, mouth gaping open to reveal a reef of broken teeth. The two recruits from Uzbekistan stood looking down at him for a moment without sound, without pity. Then Nikolai began to unwrap his bundle. He handed Vakar a wad of the foot-wrappings they used in place of socks inside their thick, steel-shod boots and held up a short length of rope. 'Ready?' he whispered. Vakar swallowed and crouched forward. 'Now!' hissed Nikolai.

Vakar rammed the foot-wrappings into the gaping mouth, clapped a hand across Barak's jaw and leapt onto him as Nikolai wrenched his arms high up behind his back and bound them with swift, savage efficiency.

Sergeant Barak came awake with a sudden, animal snarl, thrusting his powerful body this way and that, kicking out with his legs as Vakar rode his shoulders. Then Nikolai got another cloth around the Sergeant's mouth and Vakar tied that too. Nikolai sat down heavily across Barak's legs and they paused, listening for noises outside. The room was quiet except for the muted strainings of their prisoner and the pant of their own laboured breathing.

Barak began growling something deep in his throat and the tip of Nikolai's bayonet pricked against the side of his neck. 'Quiet!' he hissed, his mouth inches from the Russian's ear.

At a gesture from Nikolai, Vakar climbed down slowly from Barak's back. When he was clear Nikolai bent down so that Barak could see who it was. 'Remember me, Comrade Sergeant?' he whispered as Vakar watched. 'Your Uzbek peasant – remember?' Small, close-set eyes glared up with hatred. 'Remember Private Tinrass, Comrade Sergeant? And Private Rashidov this afternoon? We've brought you a little present.'

'A mark of respect, you might say,' added Vakar. 'Of esteem.'

Nikolai began slowly unwrapping whatever it was that still remained hidden in the folds of his towel. The Sergeant watched as Nikolai tossed the towel aside and crouched down beside him again.

For the first time those small, close-set eyes registered fear as Nikolai held up the grenade.

'Recognize this, do you, Comrade Sergeant? RDG-5 hand grenade with a fragmentation radius of – what did you teach us now – fourteen metres?' Nikolai pulled away Barak's pillow so that his head dropped forward against the hard, bare mattress. Then he lifted Barak's head, slipped the grenade underneath and lowered Barak's face almost gently so that his nose was pressing directly against the fly-away lever, the grenade's serrated iron casing less than an inch from those close-set eyes.

Nikolai squatted down beside the Russian for the last time.

'If you move, Comrade Sergeant,' he whispered conversationally, 'you will release the lever. If you roll, Comrade Sergeant, the grenade will roll with you. And if you *sweat*, Comrade Sergeant . . . well, I wouldn't sweat if I were you, because then the grenade will slip and you will have exactly four seconds to think about the future.' Nikolai hooked his finger into the grenade ring and the Sergeant's eyes bulged with terror. 'So – think about *that*, Comrade Sergeant. From Privates Tinrass, Rashidov and the rest of us poor persecuted bastards. We're forced into your fucking army and told the enemy is out *there*' – he jerked a thumb angrily towards the west, towards NATO. 'But you know what? That's just a load of shit! I don't hate any Americans – I've never even met one. But you, Comrade Sergeant – cunts like you? You're all over the place; everywhere we look there's a sodding Russian! *You're* the enemy, Comrade Sergeant! The whole fucking Russian nation.' He pulled angrily and the ring came away in his fingers.

The grenade was now armed.

Sergeant Barak began to sweat.

Nikolai was just rising to his feet when the door burst open and Private Dalin started babbling apologies from the threshold. 'I'm . . . I'm sorry, Samlar! They made me tell –'

'Shut up!' ordered Yasnov, the Russian conscript, as he and half a dozen of his cronies shouldered their way into Barak's tiny room. The light snapped on and for a moment Nikolai just stood there blinking in the sudden brightness. Then Vakar, who was nearest, went down with a sudden coughing grunt of agony as Yasnov bulled forward wielding an entrenching tool. Then he paused, edge of the blade raised at Nikolai as he saw Sergeant Barak lying bound and gagged on the bed.

And saw the grenade.

'Fucking hell –'

With help so close Barak tried to twist round. The grenade slipped and there was a sudden metallic ping! as the lever flipped away.

There was a moment's stunned, horrified silence and then a mad, panic-stricken scramble to escape the blast and scythe of jagged steel fragments that must now follow.

Nikolai didn't hesitate. He would never have made it as far as the door, anyway. One foot on the edge of Barak's cot, a sudden leap – and Nikolai had burst shoulder-first through the flimsy wooden-framed window above the Sergeant's bed. He dropped heavily onto the frozen ground outside and scrambled to his feet with nothing worse than a sudden jarring pain in his left shoulder. He brushed the glass from his chest, raced along the side of the hut for a few metres and then flattened back against the wall.

There was a sudden crash and roar as the grenade detonated. Then there was a gout of yellow flame and smoke followed by the lazy patter of debris as pieces of brickwork, wood, glass and human remains began to shower down around him in a thunderstorm of violence. As the last echoes of the explosion rolled away leaving Nikolai half deafened, people began shouting, screaming, moaning for help and the lights sprang on across the Regimental Depot as the first bark of orders split the night air.

Nikolai began to run. He raced away towards the darkness, towards the perimeter of the camp and the steel mesh fence he had to climb if he was to stand any chance at all of getting away. He risked a quick glance over his shoulder and saw that fire had taken hold and a column of smoke and angry sparks was now billowing above the barracks roof, lit by the beam of several powerful searchlights.

He raced on, suddenly aware he was shivering violently from the cold. Looking down he saw with a start of surprise that he was barefoot and, apart from his trousers, quite naked. Unless he—

'Hey – you! Stop!' Nikolai swerved violently, lashed out with his fists and ran on.

'There! There he goes – quick!' A figure was leaning out of a hut window, pointing, silhouetted against the flames. Again Nikolai jinked and swerved, racing away from the pointing fingers, the bright lights. Must get to the fence, he panted to himself, climb the fence – get away. Run! Faster! Bare feet flying over broken ground, Nikolai raced away into the healing, velvet shadows, his mind darting like quicksilver from one possible avenue of escape to another. One thing he did know: there could be no going back – not for him; not now. And unless he could get out of the Depot, escape away into the darkness of the rolling pine forests, he was trapped. He might hide away, lie low for a bit, but sooner or later they would find him. And then . . . and then . . .

He ran on, bare toes stubbed and bleeding as they flew over ground hard as brick as he hurtled towards the boundary fence, dimly aware that, behind him, lights were springing up in other barracks and that above the bell of the fire truck and the wail of the military ambulances the public address system was ordering recruits to stand fast, report to their NCOs.

Nikolai crashed suddenly against the steel mesh of the perimeter fence and spun to his left, the wire singing and trembling beside him. Further to his left, he knew, a clump of firs ran down to the edge of the fence and one or two of the thicker branches actually overhung the fence itself. If he could just reach the –

There was a sudden crash of blinding white light as the perimeter lights sprang on and he was caught, transfixed against the gleaming wire by his own shadow.

'Halt! Stay where you are!' Nikolai turned and ran blindly to his right, searching desperately for darkness like some hunted woodland creature. 'That man – halt! Halt or I fire!' warned the voice of authority through a bull-horn. Nikolai ran on heedlessly as the first burst of machine-gun fire ripped high over his head.

High. They're aiming high; keep going, panted Nikolai to himself, fooling himself as he stumbled and almost fell. Suddenly he was in shadow again and he looked round desperately for cover. The tanks! The tanks they had used that same afternoon for armour familiarization! They were still here, laagered together for the night two hundred metres from the barracks! Perhaps if he . . .

Nikolai darted behind a tall pile of fuel drums and leant back panting. He couldn't run much further, that was sure. He risked a quick look behind him through a chink in the wall of fuel drums. The camp was ablaze with lights now as the fire-fighting teams ran out their hoses and disappeared into hut 544. Another military ambulance paused at the main gate then raced forward, siren wailing, twisting through clusters of bewildered recruits waiting for officers and NCOs to give them orders. Nikolai pulled back into the shadows. The searchlight. The searchlight and the machine-gun: they'd gone away, left him alone! He looked round, a plan half-forming in his mind.

There were the tanks – three of them, the nearest no more than twenty-five metres away! He looked round, steeled himself for the sudden shout of discovery and lunged out into the open. Fifteen metres, ten, five –

'Halt!' He'd been seen. Nikolai broke step, paused, looked over his shoulder and ran on, caught once more in the blinding glare of the searchlight. He reached the far side of the nearest tank and pressed back against its rough steel sides, panting, as another burst of fire crashed belatedly overhead. They can't shoot to kill, thought Nikolai exultantly: they can't shoot to kill! They haven't got the authority!

With that sudden certainty to give him courage Nikolai scrambled up onto the pitted steel chassis of the tank, hauled himself up the side of the turret and pulled at the hatch-cover with desperate strength. If it was locked, if some key was needed to –

It wasn't locked. It lifted beneath his hand. Nikolai hauled mightily and the hatch swung back. He scrambled up and dropped into the commander's position, the hatch swinging down on top of him as he crouched down protected now by almost three inches of armoured plate. The inside of the tank smelt of oil, cordite and diesel as he groped above his head for some kind of locking device, something that would prevent the hatch being opened from outside. He felt a small knurled wheel and turned this violently. There was a sudden click above his head and when he tried to lift back the hatch it refused to move.

He sank back against the dark, unseen side of the turret and jabbed his back painfully against protruding metal. No matter. He was safe.

And trapped too, although he had yet to realize it.

The pant of his own breathing filled the alien, diesel-impregnated darkness pressing around him.

There was a sudden flicker of light at his shoulder. Twisting round, Nikolai found he was able to peer outside through the narrow slit of the commander's periscope. A searchlight had just caught against the lens and its glare had been reflected down inside the turret. Even as Nikolai squinted at the world waiting for him outside, other searchlights turned towards him, pinning the tank against the dark backdrop of pine forests.

Nikolai fought down the urge to panic, to climb out with hands raised and surrender. He made an effort to pull himself together. He was in a tank, wasn't he? Think! You can get yourself out of this. Fingers ran feverishly over the curved interior of the turret and found switches, buttons and circuits. He tried them all haphazardly, willing his steel shell to rumble into life, to carry him away to safety. One worked. A warm, dull red light filled the cramped confines of the commander's turret and, now that he could see, a little of his fear was banished. He pushed down a hinged seat and sank down thankfully to rest back against the steel cupola. Presently he roused himself and began looking around more intelligently, trying to identify methodically the function of the many dials, levers and controls in front of his eyes.

That was the gunner's seat – there, just to the left of the breech of the 84 mm gun. Nikolai reached impulsively for the breech lever and pulled it towards him. The breech slid down into the well of the tank with a solid clang of metal. Nikolai bent forward and groped at the opening with his fingers but found nothing: the chamber was empty. He twisted round feverishly to look at the ammunition racks set into the curve of the turret ring but they were empty too. Down there though – down there, that was where the driver sat! Perhaps he could start up, just drive away, crash through the fence and keep going! He began to wriggle down into the driver's compartment and then stopped. It was hopeless. There would be some sort of key, for sure. And anyway, he couldn't drive a car, let alone a tank that –

'Private Samlar. Do you hear there? Private Samlar.' The voice whined and echoed weirdly through the loudhailer. 'We know you are in that tank. Come out. Do you hear there? Surrender.'

Nikolai scrambled back to the periscope and peered through the eyepiece, panting with fright. There were soldiers coming towards him – lots of them, all in extended line, the searchlights casting long black shadows before each man as they advanced. Most of them carried rifles.

'Private Samlar. It is over, finished. Surrender now, this minute, and you will not be harmed.' Nikolai found himself laughing nervously, the sound manic, inhuman in such a confined space. Not be harmed? Him? After what he had just done?

'Private Samlar. You have exactly one minute in –'

'FUCK OFF!' he screamed. 'FUCK OFF!' All of his fear, all of his strength, his energy and his anger went into that simple, tortured scream of impotent, hopeless defiance.

It was met by a short silence. Then –

'Private Samlar' – the voice was trying sweet reason now, was almost wheedling – 'Private Samlar: listen carefully. This is Colonel Eremenko, your Battalion Commander. We know that you –' Nikolai clapped his hands over his ears and began humming tunelessly to himself, trying to blot out the words of calculated reason, the words that could weaken him, crumble his pitiful defences. He had stopped thinking ahead now and had no plan of action, no thought of escape. All he knew was that once they took him he would be finished. So – better to stay here. Better to end it here in the tank. Only quickly, please . . . please be quick . . .

He cast around for some distraction and his eyes settled on the command radio. It was almost identical to the field set they had trained with and that, at least, was something he had mastered.

Nikolai turned the switches, set the cursor and a little red light glowed obediently.

'– Very well. You have twenty seconds in which to surrender,' boomed the loudhailer. 'Twenty seconds. Nineteen. Eighteen . . .'

Nikolai hummed louder. Then he picked up the radio handset, pressed its rubber mouthpiece to his face and depressed the pressel switch.

'Hello? Hello? This is Private Nikolai Samlar of the 117th Motor Rifle Battalion of the glorious fucking Russian Army; Private Nikolai Samlar. Hello? Hello? This is Private Nikolai Samlar calling any station. Do you read me, over?' He switched to receive and listened – listened to nothing but the hiss and crackle of static and to the remorseless voice outside.

'Fifteen. Fourteen . . .'

Nikolai swung away from the radio and took another quick squint through the periscope. Then he sat back hurriedly and closed his eyes as a sudden, cold dread settled around him like a shroud.

Two soldiers had run across the square and had thrown themselves to the ground, their legs splayed to one side in the characteristic firing position adopted by soldiers about to fire the Soviet RPG-7V anti-tank weapon. The legs had to be twisted round that way to avoid the savage back-blast when the weapon was fired from the shoulder. Then the HEAT* round would come wobbling through the air to squash against the outside of the turret and implode so that its sudden heat formed a molten metal scab on the inside of the turret that would peel off and flay around . . .

With a sudden coughing roar the two tanks on Nikolai's right suddenly surged into life and lurched forward. Out of the line of fire.

Nikolai closed his eyes, leant back against the turret wall, depressed the microphone switch . . . and began to sing quietly, almost to himself, as his mind suddenly dumped its burden of insurmountable problems and drifted away to the warm, sunlit days of his boyhood, to the village in the foothills of Uzbekistan; to his mother, father and three sisters. He found himself singing

*HEAT: High Explosive Anti-Tank.

a ballad, a song sung by the men of every village for miles around whether Uzbek or Tartar, Kazaks or Kirghiz. It was a ballad of hope, of pride and faith in the distant past, in the traditions that had made them what they were long before anyone with a Party badge in his lapel told them they were Soviets; it was a ballad of promise and defiance that would be extinguished not by imposed ideology from The Centre nor by a single crouching Russian with an anti-tank weapon to his shoulder –

'Twelve. Eleven . . .'


In a long, low grey metal hut in the northern mountains of Turkey on the south-eastern edge of the Black Sea, Signaller First Class Eugene S. Connor from Jackson, Mississippi, now serving with the 15th Signals Division ('The Big Ear') of the American Army on NATO's southern flank, leant forward suddenly towards his bank of powerful radio receivers and made a minute, feather-light adjustment to a tuning dial.

Their task was to monitor Soviet radio traffic from the other side of the Black Sea; to listen to and record every phrase, cypher and indiscretion transmitted by any one of a thousand different military units.

Everything they listened to was taped anyway for later analysis and evaluation, but just to show the Lieutenant how sharp he was, Connor now pressed the duty notification key and pushed one of his earphones away from an ear. He twisted round in his swivel chair.

'Hey, Lieutenant, sir – you wanna catch a piece o'this? They're playin' your song agin.' He grinned widely.

The Duty Lieutenant was a Russian expert. He spoke not only Russian but German, French and half a dozen other languages as well, specializing in the languages of the Soviet minorities. Now he crossed the floor of the monitoring station and switched Connor's signal through to the amplifier above their heads. Other soldiers, listening in upon routine frequencies, sat back and listened too. Then they exchanged glances and grinned. Somebody somewhere was singing. Singing on a fucking Soviet tank net . . .

'That's right, Connor,' nodded the Lieutenant. 'They're playing my song again. Where's it coming from this time?'

Connor paused and leaned forward. 'Ukraine, near as I can reckon it, sir.' The Lieutenant thought for a moment. So now it was the Ukraine: another pin in another map. In recent years, in recent months, he had picked up that ballad in half a dozen different places: on board a Russian destroyer steaming down the Baltic; in a major infantry exercise near the East German border; at a military airfield outside Kiev.

And where that song went there too, it seemed, went trouble – trouble for the Soviet authorities: there had been a mutiny aboard a Soviet Navy frigate in the Baltic when forty Estonian seamen had seized the ship, locked up their Russian officers and made a dash for neutral Sweden. Their ship had been attacked and disabled by Russian MIG fighters twelve miles outside Swedish territorial waters. A Rifle Section of the First Guards Army had gone AWOL* to a man in the Pripet Marshes half-way through a major exercise. Only one deserter had been found, cornered in a wheatfield outside Korosten. He had preferred suicide to capture and when they reached him he had the barrel of his rifle in what was left of his mouth and a bare toe curled around the trigger. In Vinnitsa, east of Lvov, Russian soldiers in the garrison there were now forbidden to leave their bases without senior, armed NCOs after three of their number had been found with their throats cut and their Russian cap badges torn off and stuffed into their gaping mouths.

Five years ago, incidents like these had been few and far between. Now, to the Lieutenant's personal knowledge, there had been forty-one recorded incidents of dissent, unrest and rebellion in the last five months. The pace was growing.

It was almost, he thought, as if that tune, that ballad had become a battle ensign, a banner of rebellion that was becoming more and more unfurled with every passing month.

As though a fuse had been lit.

'Sir? What's he goin' on about?' asked Private Connor.

The Lieutenant listened a moment longer and then turned witheringly towards the soldier. 'He is singing, Private, about a legend; about someone called Genghis Khan.'

'Is that so?'

*AWOL: Absent Without Leave.

'That is so, yes,' nodded the Lieutenant patiently. 'And about what will happen when his grave is found in the desert . . .'

'Two . . . one.' The Colonel nodded curtly to his Major. Who gave the order.

Private Nikolai Samlar, Tartar conscript into the most powerful army the world has ever seen, was eighteen years, six months and four days old when he died.

# : 23 :

Gordon rose slowly to his feet.

Five minutes had gone by since he had heard the sound of two pairs of boots running by on the far side of the stone wall; five minutes in which he had lain pressed against the ground shivering with fear and cold as he regained his breath, planned his next move. His next move? That was a bloody joke – he was shattered, drained of strength, of courage. Well, think positive – wasn't that what they always said? Look on the bright side.

Item One. His mind went blank. Come on, everyone had an Item One! To start with, he knew where he was, more or less. And he knew where the cottage was – one mile, a mile and a half in that direction if he went across country.

Item Two. He'd managed to lose the opposition, for the moment at least.

Item Three. He knew they were waiting for him at the cottage. Gordon phrased that another way: *they* didn't know *he knew* they were waiting for him at the cottage.

That was all right, then: Gordon Hallam – 0; Rest Of The World – 257. He managed a wry smile, moved cautiously through the bracken, picked up a track heading in roughly the right direction and broke into a shambling run.

He ran for forty minutes. Up steep, endless hills and along dark, sinister fire-breaks between stands of closely-packed Forestry Commission firs. He tore his hands on barbed wire fences and twisted his ankle as he ran down a narrow, timber-choked valley and waded across another fast, twisting stream. Then at last he broke through onto open ground, crossed a series of interconnected fields and came at last to a tarmac road. He stopped then, holding his side, his clothes steaming in the bitter night air as he grinned suddenly. He knew where he was; knew where he was to the inch: four hundred yards away from the mouth of the lane, two hundred yards from the nearest telephone.

He ran to the telephone. A second miracle and he was dialling 999 once more.

'Which service, please?'

'Fire . . . Fire brigade,' he panted. 'There's . . . there's a fire at Hobs Cottage, Stowcombe, you got that? Hobs Cottage, Stowcombe. Someone's badly burnt. I think someone threw a . . . a petrol bomb,' gabbled Gordon, his mind racing ahead, gambling everything on those few words overheard as he hid in the hollow: 'they'll wait for him there.'

Fire, police, ambulance – he'd given the operator something for all three – 'Will you send someone, please? Right away?' Lots of people, prayed Gordon; lots and lots of decent, well-meaning blokes crawling all over the place. Do that for me, just this once, prayed Gordon, let me be in time to save her and I'll never walk past another charity tin in my life. Promise.

'What is your number, please?' Gordon glanced down at the telephone and rattled it off.

'And your name, caller?'

'You're wasting time!' shouted Gordon into the mouthpiece, unaware that his call was already being relayed to the emergency services. He banged down the receiver, pushed out of the telephone kiosk and sprinted back up the lane.

Two, three minutes more and he was lying flat on his stomach gazing down at the back of the cottage, searching desperately for the simple signs of normality. He did not find them.

The door. The back door had been forced open. Ah, Jesus, no – Gordon scrambled to his feet and raced down the slope towards his home. Towards everything he loved.

Three hundred yards away an army sniper settled the crosshairs of his sights on the stumbling, translucent green toy running down the slope towards the cottage and took up primary pressure on the trigger of his specially converted bolt-action rifle. It is always the first shot that counts with snipers. Rapid fire is not necessary.

'He's coming now,' murmured the sniper to his partner crouching beside him. 'Target acquired.'

'Target green,' intoned his partner into the radio, indicating a clean shot, a good kill. When they heard 'Target confirmed' they could shoot.

'Come on . . . come on,' muttered the sniper, 'I'm losing him.' He relaxed suddenly, one cheek dropping down onto the butt of his rifle as his finger came off the trigger. 'Gone. Target is inside the cottage.' He sighed and glanced round at his mate. 'What's wrong with those dozy bastards? Do they want him taken out or not?'

Gordon crashed through into the kitchen, his shoes skidding on broken glass and splintered woodwork. 'Rachel?' he yelled, his voice echoing into the empty cottage. 'Rachel? Where are you?'

There was silence. Gordon rushed into the sitting-room, turned on the lights, took the stairs two at a time and threw open each bedroom door in turn. Nothing. Back down the stairs. He saw the shotgun lying on the sofa, picked it up, glanced inside and threw it back on the sofa, uncaring. 'Rachel!' he yelled. 'Rachel!'

Gordon went to the window, pulled back the curtain and glanced outside.

From the high ground above the cottage the sniper picked him up instantly, framed against the yellow square of the sitting-room window.

'Target green,' reported his observer without waiting for the marksman to confirm the shot. The bloke down there was going to pieces, making it easy for them.

Fifty yards down the lane General Inkermann glanced inside the rear of the BMW. Lord Porterfield sat there with Rachel Hallam beside him, her hands tied behind her back. 'Whenever you like,' stated Inkermann simply. Rachel strained suddenly towards the door but Porterfield pushed her back almost gently. He shook his head. 'I think we'll wait until he's out in the open.'

Inkermann looked doubtful. 'He's not going to move from in there. He's holed up.'

'I think he will,' said Lord Porterfield grimly, reaching forward. 'Go on thirty yards, driver. Then pull across the lane and turn off your lights, understand?' The driver nodded and brought the engine to life. Lord Porterfield glanced at General Inkermann. 'He'll come,' he predicted simply.

Gordon heard the sudden sigh of a powerful engine and crossed once more to the window. A grey BMW saloon was driving towards him. As he watched the car slewed across the track, the lights went out and the engine was turned off. Then an interior light snapped on and Gordon started forward. Rachel was in the back seat beside Lord Porterfield.

'Target green.'

'Hold. Hold. Wait.'

Lord Porterfield got out of the BMW, rested both elbows upon the top of the roof and cupped his hands to his mouth. 'Mr Hallam? Can you hear me?'

'Don't listen to him, Gordon –' screamed Rachel. Porterfield ducked down into the car and glared at his prisoner. 'Unless you wish to be gagged you will remain silent, is that clear?'

Rachel shook her head, on the verge of tears. 'But you can't just –'

'Shut up!' snapped Porterfield. He slammed the car door and turned back towards the cottage. 'Mr Hallam, your wife's continuing good health depends upon two things: first, upon my patience; second, upon your doing exactly what I tell you – do I make myself clear?' There was a pause. 'Mr Hallam? Can you hear me?'

Gordon heard him all right. He was busy loading the shotgun.

'Yes, I hear you, you bastard!' he shouted, cramming shotgun cartridges into his wet pockets, his teeth chattering with cold. 'What do you want?'

'Come out here. Into the open where I can see you. We have to talk.'

'Yeah? What about?'

'About how we can end this ridiculous misunderstanding.'

'Misunderstanding? My father wouldn't have called it that. Nor would Bruno Tyschen. Nor Peter Tillet. You're a murderer, Porterfield – a fucking murderer!' There was silence. Gordon slipped two cartridges into the shotgun and snapped the gun closed.

'I am not giving you any discretion in this, Mr Hallam: I want you out here within the next thirty seconds. Disappoint me and I shall have to retaliate. You will leave me no alternative.' Gordon risked another quick glance out of the window.

'Target – no, no. He's gone.'

Rachel was still sitting in the car. He had tried to read her expression, but she was too far away.

'Twenty seconds . . . Fifteen –'

Gordon moved to the door and slid back the bolts.

'Ten –'

Gordon took a deep, shuddering breath and stepped out into the porch, the shotgun held casually in one hand. It was a gesture, that was all, he thought numbly – and a pretty empty gesture at that. They held all the cards. They'd always held all the cards. He began to walk forward down the garden path towards the BMW waiting in the lane. Towards Rachel. He could see her turn towards him now quite clearly, see her mouth opening and shutting as she tried to shout something that –

'Target green. Target green.' Sight holding rock-steady on the exact centre of Gordon's forehead, the sniper's index finger took up the pressure, began to squeeze down on the end of the exhale –

'Target con— Wait. No. Wait. Hold.' In that split second before giving the command to fire, General Inkermann had suddenly become aware of the sound of sirens, then of lights in the lane behind him.

His holding order came fractionally too late.

There was a single whipcrack of sound that rolled and echoed around the hills and Gordon spun round and collapsed onto the path, the shotgun flying from his hand. The sniper had the bolt open and closed over a fresh round almost before he realized his observer was pounding him on the shoulder.

'That was a hold, you cunt! A hold!'

The sniper twisted round. 'Bollocks. He confirmed, I heard him.' He squinted through the sight at the body lying crumpled on the garden path. He sniffed, wiped the tip of his nose with the edge of his cuff and shook his head in disappointment. 'Reckon I pulled off a bit, anyway.'

Below them the lane was suddenly choked with vehicles. The ambulance arrived first, blue light flashing across the sky. Then a moment later a police car and motorcyclist turned up the lane and were followed by a pump escape manned by retained firemen that had come racing out from Tavistock.

'Bloody hell,' muttered the observer, looking down at the scene below and zipping his binoculars hurriedly inside his smock. 'Someone down there dropped a bollock. Where did that lot spring from?'

'Fuck knows.' The sniper twisted his left arm out of the rifle sling and pulled the tip of his foresight back behind cover. The bug-out presented no particular problems: that too was part of their training.

The ambulance had pulled to a halt and two driver/attendants ran towards the body lying motionless on the ground, a stain of dark blood seeping across the flagstones.

Lord Porterfield looked round in sudden alarm, saw the headlights, saw the police, saw the ambulance and half a dozen firemen moving eagerly towards the cottage and ducked down inside the BMW where he began fumbling with the knots that bound Rachel's arms behind her. He was still trying to untie her when the police sergeant tapped him politely on the shoulder.

'Evening, sir. Perhaps you'd like to tell me what's going on?' invited the sergeant, reaching for his notebook in the top left breast pocket as the last knot slipped free.

'There you are, m'dear,' said Lord Porterfield solicitously. Rachel looked up venomously and then hit him in the face with a small, balled fist. All her strength went behind the blow.

'You . . . bastard,' she hissed, scrambling past him to run down the path towards Gordon's motionless body. She pushed past the crouching ambulancemen and bent down, her eyes an agony of concern.

'Gordon . . . Gordon, darling,' she whispered. He had taken the bullet high up in the left shoulder. Away from the heart. But there was much blood and the glint of shattered bone.

An eyelid cracked open in the pale, ashen face.

'See?' he managed, coughing suddenly and grimacing with pain. 'The . . . white hats always win in the end.'

In the parched, arid foothills between Bukhara and Samarkand, the Uzbek farmer wiped the sweat from his eyes, took his lean, bony hands off the plough and crouched down beside the hot, broken earth. There was something in the soil, something that gleamed at him in the sunlight from just below the surface of his newly-turned furrow. He scraped the crumbling soil away with his hands, slowly at first and then with mounting excitement as he unearthed the gold hilt of an ancient sword, heavily encrusted with precious stones. And there was something else too. It looked like a skeleton. A very old human skeleton.

The farmer's discovery was made ninety-three kilometres to the east of the spot where Ratbag and the other members of the British SAS team had exhumed the skeleton buried by the Apostle team in March 1945.

That would have surprised Lord Phillip Porterfield, shaken him to the core. But it would not greatly have surprised Radij, the soothsayer in the mountains.

Soothsayers are seldom wrong.

The following article appeared in the *Guardian* on 30 December 1982 (extract):

## SOVIET SOLDIERS 'GUIDED REBELS'

**Islamabad:** Soviet soldiers from the Muslim republic of Uzbekistan helped Muslim guerrillas attack important airfields in Afghanistan last week by showing the way through minefields, Western diplomats said yesterday.

They said extensive damage was done to parked aircraft and airport buildings during the raid on the Baghram airfield, north of Kabul.

Uzbek soldiers guarding the base reportedly guided the guerrillas through minefields around the airfield perimeter.

Afghan guerrilla groups have reported growing support in Soviet Muslim republics bordering Afghanistan.

Earlier this year, travellers returning from the Soviet–Afghan border said that guerrilla groups claimed to have distributed thousands of their membership cards inside the republics.

The attack appeared to have coincided with a raid on Jalalabad airport, near the Pakistan border, on December 21 . . . (*Reuter*)

## MORE ABOUT PENGUINS, PELICANS AND PUFFINS

For further information about books available from Penguins please write to Dept EP, Penguin Books Ltd, Harmondsworth, Middlesex UB7 0DA.

*In the U.S.A.*: For a complete list of books available from Penguins in the United States write to Dept DG, Penguin Books, 299 Murray Hill Parkway, East Rutherford, New Jersey 07073.

*In Canada*: For a complete list of books available from Penguins in Canada write to Penguin Books Canada Ltd, 2801 John Street, Markham, Ontario L3R 1B4.

*In Australia*: For a complete list of books available from Penguins in Australia write to the Marketing Department, Penguin Books Australia Ltd, P.O. Box 257, Ringwood, Victoria 3134.

*In New Zealand*: For a complete list of books available from Penguins in New Zealand write to the Marketing Department, Penguin Books (N.Z.) Ltd, Takapuna, Auckland 9.

*In India*: For a complete list of books available from Penguins in India write to Penguin Overseas Ltd, 706 Eros Apartments, 56 Nehru Place, New Delhi 110019.

## SKYSHROUD

### Tom Keene with Brian Haynes

The certainty of instant nuclear retaliation has helped preserve a fragile international stability. But now the Head of United States Air Force Intelligence is convinced that the concept of Mutual Assured Destruction – MAD – is finished.

General Clarke Freeman believes the Soviets are perilously close to perfecting a Charged Particle Beam Weapon, an infallible defence against nuclear missiles. Safe from retaliation, Soviet global control is only the press of a button away. Yet while General Freeman talks, no one is listening – and already the clocks on project Skyshroud are unwinding remorselessly . . .

## EARTHRACE

### Tom Keene

### THE WORLD IS HIT BY A RECESSION. AND A SMALL AFRICAN COUNTRY HOLDS A KEY TO ITS FUTURE . . .

Peter Garrick and Anne Leonard are relief workers in a land where dried milk saves lives. Now they are caught up in Earthcom's reign of terror and a new East/West scramble for Africa as satellites make prospecting easy – and espionage and sabotage essential.

## SPYSHIP

### Tom Keene with Brian Haynes

### *TAKE*

the pride of Hull's fishing fleet and load her with top secret electronic equipment and send her to sensitive Northern waters.

### *IMAGINE*

a Russian submarine, a Royal Navy ship and a panic back at headquarters.

### *WATCH*

a messy, inexplicable sinking and Martin Taylor, a bloody-minded journalist, determined to scythe through the lies – and you have the starting-point for a five-star thriller with an uncanny ring of truth – *Spyship*.

*Big Penguin Bestsellers*

# LACE

*Shirley Conran*

A million dollar bestseller and a publishing sensation – *Lace* is the novel that teaches men about women ... and women about themselves.

'Which one of you bitches is my mother?' This question sears through the thoughts of the four women summoned so mysteriously to a glamorous New York apartment, unlocking the past and a secret – a secret that has enmeshed their lives and dogged their success, and one that lies at the heart of this scorching, sensational novel.

The story of four women, Judy, Kate, Pagan and Maxine, who took life as they found it and dared to make it a success. Against an international backdrop of the rich, the famous and the depraved, these women – bound together by ties stronger than love itself – created legends.

# CELEBRITY

*Thomas Thompson*

In the easy innocence of the fifties, three buddies craved celebrity – and it came their way ...

Kleber shot to fame as Pulitzer Prizewinner and the network's toughest TV interviewer. Mack cruised into screen stardom and sexual ambivalence. And TJ, the Prince of Temptation, became hallowed as the sex-crazed saint of a religious sect.

But none of them could forget that rainy night in Texas when, christening themselves the Three Princes, they had tasted their first secret fruit of evil. And now, twenty-five years later, it will lay them bare.

'A novel of mesmerizing richness and power' – *Publishers Weekly*